"I would h[...] from you."

"I thought about it," he said. "But you've done enough helping with the babies."

"I thought perhaps that you and I were about more than the babies, but maybe I was wrong," she said, looking away.

His heart slamming against his rib cage, he cupped her chin and swiveled it toward him. "You were right. You know you were."

Her eyes darkened with emotion and she stepped closer. She moved against him and slid her arms upward around his neck. She pulled his face toward hers and he couldn't remember feeling this alive. Ever.

His body was on full tilt in the arousal zone. He took a quick breath and forced himself to draw back. "I'm not sure I can pull back after this," he said. "If you're going to say no, do it now."

"Yes," she whispered. "Yes."

Suddenly a Family

NEW YORK TIMES BESTSELLING AUTHOR

LEANNE BANKS

&

LOIS FAYE DYER

**Previously published as *The Doctor Takes a Princess*
and *Triple Trouble***

 HARLEQUIN®

ISBN-13: 978-1-335-41881-4

Suddenly a Family

Copyright © 2021 by Harlequin Books S.A.

The Doctor Takes a Princess
First published in 2011. This edition published in 2021.
Copyright © 2011 by Leanne Banks

Triple Trouble
First published in 2009. This edition published in 2021.
Copyright © 2009 by Harlequin Books S.A.

Special thanks and acknowledgment are given
to Lois Faye Dyer for her contribution to the
Fortunes of Texas: Return to Red Rock continuity.

Recycling programs for this product may not exist in your area.

For questions and comments about the quality of this book, please contact us at CustomerService@Harlequin.com.

Harlequin Enterprises ULC
22 Adelaide St. West, 40th Floor
Toronto, Ontario M5H 4E3, Canada
www.Harlequin.com

Printed in U.S.A.

CONTENTS

Leanne Banks is a *New York Times* and *USA TODAY* bestselling author with over sixty-eight books to her credit. Leanne loves her family, the beach and chocolate. You can reach her at leannebanks.com.

Books by Leanne Banks

Harlequin Special Edition

Visit the Author Profile page at Harlequin.com for more titles.

The Doctor
Takes a Princess

LEANNE BANKS

This book is dedicated to all those underestimated women with tender hearts and big fears who hide it all with a big smile. Thank you for being so much more than we give you credit for.

Prologue

Ryder McCall raced the double baby stroller into the elevator just as the doors started to close. The twin boys cackled with glee at the wild ride as he pressed the button for the eighth floor. He'd already rescheduled the appointment with his attorney three times and he would have done it again if he'd known the nanny was going to bail on him. Again.

In the back of his mind, he counted his pulse. His heart rate was higher now than when he'd run a half marathon last year. His life was far different now, he thought as he glanced at the boys and caught a swishing movement behind him. Stepping to the side, he saw a woman dressed in a pink cocktail gown that skimmed over her creamy shoulders and her curvy body. The dress ended just above her knees, revealing a tempting glimpse of her legs and high-heeled sandals. The medical expert in him knew the negative impact of high heels on the human body, but the man in him was trying to remember the last time he'd been out with a woman. He was having a tough time remembering.

The woman smiled at him and gestured toward the twins. "They're adorable. I bet they keep you busy."

He nodded. "More than you could—"

The elevator suddenly jolted and dropped several feet, then stopped.

Ryder glanced at the boys at the same time he heard the woman's intake of breath. "Everyone okay?"

The twins just looked at them with wide eyes.

"Are we stuck?" the woman asked, her brow furrowed with worry.

"Let me see," he said and pushed the button for another floor. The elevator didn't move. He pushed the button to open the doors and nothing happened. He pushed the alarm button and a piercing sound filled the elevator.

The woman covered her ears. "Oh, my—"

A voice came on an intercom. "This is building security. Do you have a problem?"

"We're stuck," Ryder yelled over the terrible pulsating alarm. He heard a sob from one of the boys. A half beat later, the other started, louder.

"So sorry, sir. We'll come and fix it soon."

"Soon," he echoed as the twins began to cry in earnest. "When is soon?"

"As soon as possible," the woman on the intercom said and there was a clicking noise. The alarm shut off, but the boys were in high gear.

"Oh, the poor things. They must be frightened," the

woman in the elevator said. She paused a moment, then shrugged. "Here, I'll hold one of them."

Ryder shot a skeptical glance at her. "They haven't had their baths and they're very messy eaters." Tyler was wearing a gross combination of yellow and orange on his blue shirt while Travis clearly had not enjoyed his strained peas. Green smudges decorated the light blue shirt that matched his brother's.

The woman made a tsking sound. "Well, we have to do something. We can't let them keep screaming." She set her purse on the floor and held out her hands. "Go ahead, give one of them to me," she insisted in a voice that sounded as if she were accustomed to having her orders followed.

As a medical doctor and acting chief adviser for the residents at Texas Medical Center, he, too, was accustomed to having his orders followed. This time, though, he decided to allow the woman to take Tyler because the baby was clearly beyond upset. As soon as he set the boy in her arms, she bobbed as if she'd handled a crying baby before. Ryder hauled Travis out of his stroller seat and also bobbed.

The woman made soothing sounds and Tyler gradually quieted between hiccups. As usual, Travis took a little longer. He was the louder boy of the two.

"That's better," she said. "Who am I holding?"

"Tyler," Ryder said. "This is Travis. I'm Ryder Mc-Call. Thank you for your help."

"You're quite welcome," she said in a voice that seemed to combine several accents, none of which originated from Texas. "I'm Bridget," she said and fanned herself with the shawl draped over her arm. "Whew, it's getting warm already."

"And it's only going to get hotter until they fix the elevator. Are you feeling faint?" he asked, aware that plenty of people would grow light-headed in this situation.

She shook her head. "No."

"I'd offer you some water, but I was in a hurry when I left the house, so all I've got are bottles for the boys."

"Well, at least you have that," she said and glanced at her watch. "I hope we're not stuck for long. Perhaps I should call my friends." She bent toward the floor and shook her head. "I'm sorry, Tyler. I'm going to have to put you down for a moment," she murmured and carefully placed the tot in his stroller seat. She picked up her phone and punched some numbers, then frowned.

"Let me guess," Ryder said. "No service."

She nodded.

"Figures. The steel doors can sustain most catastrophes known to man, so they're bound to make it difficult to get a cell connection."

She bit her lip and winced. "Oh, I wonder if someone will call my security."

"They're on their way," he said, wondering if she hadn't understood the conversation he'd had with the woman earlier. Maybe she hadn't heard correctly, he thought, between the alarm bleeping and the boys screaming. "At least, they better be on their way. I hope the boys don't—"

"Need a diaper change?" she asked, nodding in understanding. "Time for the—"

"Nanny," he said in complete agreement. "I just wish I could find one who would stay around longer than two weeks."

"That sounds difficult. Are you working with an agency?"

He nodded. "Part of the problem is I work long hours."

"Hmm, and your wife?"

"I don't have a wife," he said.

Her eyes widened. "Oh, that must make it very difficult."

Ryder sighed. "I'm actually the boys' godfather. My brother and his wife were killed in an automobile accident one month ago."

Bridget gasped. "That's terrible. Those poor boys, and you, oh my goodness. Do you have any help at all?"

"Not unless I hire them," he muttered. "Do you have any children?"

She shook her head quickly, the same way he would have before he'd learned he would be raising the boys. "Two baby nieces," she said.

"That's how you knew to bob up and down with Tyler," he said.

"Yes," Bridget said and glanced at her watch again, growing uneasy. She'd agreed to the charity appearance she would be attending as a favor to her sister's long-time friend, and her security was only a three-button code away if she should need them. If her sister's friend became uneasy, however, she might call Valentina. Valentina might call security to check on her and… She shuddered at the public scene that would cause. Bridget was here in Dallas to do the job her brother had asked of her and as soon as she was done, she was off to Italy.

It was so warm that she was getting past the glow stage. Right now, she probably looked like she'd just finished a spinning class, although she did those as rarely as possible. Getting sweaty wouldn't matter that much to her if she weren't being photographed. During the last year and a half, however, it had been drilled into her that her appearance in front of the camera was a reflection of her country. It was her duty to look immaculate and to avoid scandal at all cost.

Bridget had slipped a few times on both counts. She might be a princess, but she wasn't perfect. Nor was she particularly patient. She could tell that Ryder, the other adult in the elevator, wasn't patient either. He was glancing upward as if he were assessing the structure of the lift.

"You're not thinking of climbing out, are you?" she couldn't resist asking.

"If no one shows up, I may have to," he said.

"And what were you planning to do with the babies?" she demanded, panicked at the prospect of being left alone with the twins. Now that she thought of it, Ryder's presence had made her feel much more reassured.

He shot her a level look. "The purpose of getting out would be to ensure safety for all of us."

He looked like a no-nonsense kind of man, strong, perhaps intolerant of anyone weaker than himself. Which would include her. Okay, she was making assumptions. But what else could she bloody do? She was stuck in an elevator with the man. She couldn't deny the appeal of his strong jaw and lean but muscular body. She also couldn't deny her admiration that he had taken on his brother's orphaned twins.

An instant parent of twin boys? The mere thought made her sweat even more. Bridget would have forced herself to accept her responsibility in such a situation, but hopefully with sufficient support. Multiple children, multiple nannies.

She sighed, glancing at the emergency button. "We've heard nothing. Do you think we should call again?"

"It will make the boys cry again," he said, clearly torn.

"I'll take Tyler," she said and picked up the baby. He flashed her a smile that gave her a burst of pleasure despite their situation. "You're a little flirt, aren't you?" she said and tickled his chin.

Ryder stabbed the button and the shrieking alarm started. Tyler's smile immediately fell and his eyes filled with fear. He began to scream. His brother began to wail.

Seconds later, the alarm stopped and a voice came on the intercom, but Bridget couldn't make out the conversation with Ryder as she tried to comfort Tyler. The only thing she knew was that Ryder had spoken in a firm, commanding voice that rivaled that of her brother's, and anyone in their right mind had better obey.

The intercom voice went away, but the babies still cried. Bridget and Tyler bobbed. "What did they say?"

"They said they would take care of us in five minutes," he yelled over the cries of the boys.

"How did you do that?"

"I told them I was climbing out in three," he said.

"Effective. I wonder if I should try that sometime," she mused. "Is there anything else we can do to settle them down?" she asked loudly, still shielding Tyler's closest ear with her hand.

A long-suffering expression crossed his face. "Just one thing," he said. "Row, row, row your boat, gently down the stream."

Bridget stared in amazement at this man who reminded her of a modern-day warrior singing a children's song and something inside her shifted. The sensation made her feel light-headed. Alarm shot through her. Or perhaps, it was the heat. Pushing the odd feeling and any self-consciousness aside, she sang along.

Six minutes later, the elevator doors opened with a swarm of firemen, paramedics and Bridget's security guard standing outside.

"Your Highness," her security guard said, extending his hand to her.

"Just a second," she said, putting Tyler into his stroller seat.

"Your Highness?" Ryder echoed, studying her with a curious gaze. "Why didn't you—"

"It—it causes a fuss," she said. "Will you be okay? Will the children be okay?"

"We're fine," he said, and she felt foolish for questioning such a capable man.

"Well, thank you," she said and extended her hand to his, noting that his hands were smooth, but large and strong. She felt an odd little spark and immediately pulled back. "And good luck."

"Your Highness, a medical professional is waiting to examine you," her security said as she stepped off the lift.

"I don't need a medical professional," she murmured. "I need a cosmetic miracle."

Chapter 1

Sitting at the kitchen table of her brother-in-law's ranch, Bridget watched Zach Logan hug her sister Valentina as if he were leaving for a yearlong journey. Instead, she knew he would be gone for only a couple of nights. Bridget resisted the urge to roll her eyes. Zach and Valentina just seemed so gooey in love.

"Call me if you need anything," he told her, then swung his young daughter, Katiana, up into his arms. "Are you going to be good for your mommy?"

Katiana solemnly nodded.

"Give me a kiss," he said.

The toddler kissed his cheek and wrapped her little arms around his neck.

Despite her earlier reaction, the scene tugged at Bridget's heart. She knew Zach and Tina had gone through some tough times before they'd gotten married.

Zach shot Bridget a firm glance that instinctively made her sit up straighter. He was that kind of man, confident with a strong will. Although she was happy Tina had found happiness with him, Bridget knew she would want a totally different kind of man. Charming, average intelligence, playful and most likely Italian.

"You," he said, pointing his finger at Bridget. "Stay out of elevators."

She laughed. "I can only promise that for a few days. When I go back to Dallas, I'm sure I'll have to face more elevators if I'm going to complete Stefan's latest job for me. If I have anything to do with it, I'm going to take care of it as quickly as possible."

Tina shot her a sideways glance. "Are you saying you're already tired of us?"

Bridget shook her head and walked to give her sister a hug. "Of course I'm not tired of you. But you know I've had a dream of having a long-delayed gap year in Italy and studying art for years now. I want to make that dream come true while I'm still young."

Tina made a scoffing sound, but still returned the hug. "You're far from losing your youth, but I agree you deserve a break. You've taken on the bulk of public appearances since I left Chantaine and moved here. I don't understand why you didn't take a break before coming here. I'm sure Stefan would have let you."

Stefan, their brother, the crown prince, could be the most demanding person on the planet, but what Tina said was true. He not only would have allowed Bridget a break, he had also encouraged it. "I want a year. A whole year. And he believes Chantaine needs more doctors. I agree. Especially after what happened to Eve—"

Her voice broke, taking her by surprise. She'd thought she'd gotten her feelings under control.

Tina patted her back with sympathy. "You still feel guilty about that. I know Eve wishes you didn't."

Bridget took a careful breath, reining in her emotions. "She saved my life when the crowd was going to stampede me. Pushed me aside and threw herself in front of me. I'm just so glad she survived it and recovered. I don't know what I would do if she hadn't…" Her throat closed up again.

"Well, she survived and you did, too. That's what's important," Zach said and pulled Bridget into a brotherly hug. "And now that you're in my territory, I want you to think twice before getting on elevators."

Tina laughed. "So protective," she said. "It's a wonder he doesn't find some kind of testing device for you to use so you won't get stuck again."

Zach rubbed his chin thoughtfully. "Not a bad idea. Maybe—"

"Forget it," Bridget said, the knot in her chest easing at the love she felt from both her sister and her brother-in-law. "I'll be fine. Think about it. How many people do you know who have gotten stuck in elevators? Especially more than once?"

"You were a good soldier," Tina said in approval. "And you still showed up for your appearance at Keely's charity event."

"She probably wasn't expecting me in my sad state with droopy hair and a dress with baby-food stain on it."

"Oh, she said they loved you. Found you charming. Were delighted by your story about the elevator. Most important, the donations increased after your arrival."

"Well, I guess baby-food stains are good for something, then. I'll leave you two lovebirds to finish your goodbyes in private. Safe travels, Zach."

"You bet," he said.

Bridget scooped up her cup of hot tea and walked upstairs to the guest room where she was staying. Her sister had redecorated the room in soothing shades of green and blue. The ranch should have given Bridget a sense of serenity. After all, she was miles from Stefan and his to-do list for her. She was away from Chantaine where she was recognized and haunted by the paparazzi whenever she left the palace. But Bridget never seemed to be able to escape the restlessness inside her. That was why she'd decided to skip a short vacation and take care of this significant task Stefan had asked of her. After that, she could take her trip to Italy and find her peace again.

No one had ever accused Bridget of being deep. She voiced her distress and upset to her family at will, but presented the rest of the world with a cheery effervescent face. It was her job.

Some of the conditions she'd witnessed during the past year and a half, the sights and sounds of children sick in the hospital, Chantaine's citizens struggling with poverty, cut her to the quick and it had been difficult to keep her winsome attitude intact. It irritated her how much she now had to struggle to maintain a superficial air. Life had been so much easier when she hadn't faced others in need. Life had been easier when someone hadn't been willing to sacrifice her life for the sake of Bridget's safety.

Even though Eve had indeed survived and thrived since the accident, something inside Bridget had changed. And she wasn't sure she liked it. Eve and Stefan had fallen in love and married. Eve cared for Stefan's out-of-wedlock daughter as if she were her own. On the face of it, everything was wonderful.

Deep down, though, Bridget wondered if her life was really worth saving. What had she done that made her worthy of such an act?

She squeezed her eyes shut and swore under her breath. "Stop asking that question," she whispered harshly to herself.

Steeling herself against the ugly swarm of emotions, Bridget set her cup of tea on the table. She would complete the task Stefan asked of her. Then maybe she would have settled the score inside her, the score she couldn't quite explain even to herself. Afterward she would go to Italy and hopefully she would find the joy and lightness she'd lost.

After three days of being unable to meet with the head of residents at Texas Medical Center of Dallas, Bridget seethed with impatience. Dr. Gordon Walters was never available, and all her calls to his office went unanswered. Thank goodness for connections. Apparently Tina's friend Keely knew a doctor at University Hospital and there just happened to be a meet and greet for interns, doctors and important donors at a hotel near the hospital on Tuesday night.

Bridget checked into the hotel and her security took the room next to hers. One advantage of being at Zach's ranch meant security was superfluous. Not so in Dallas. She dressed carefully because she needed to impress and to be taken seriously. A black dress with heels. She resisted the urge to paint her lips red. The old Bridget wouldn't have batted an eye.

Frowning into the bathroom mirror in her suite, she wondered what that meant. Well, hell, if Madonna could wear red lipstick and be taken seriously, why couldn't she? She smoothed her fingers over her head and tucked one side of her hair behind her left ear. She'd colored her hair darker lately. It fit her mood.

She frowned again into the mirror. Maybe she would dye it blond when she moved to Italy.

She punched the code for her security on her cell phone. Raoul picked up immediately. "Yes, Your Highness."

"I'm ready. Please stay in the background," she said.

"Yes, ma'am. But I shall join you on the elevator."

A couple moments later, she rode said elevator to the floor which held the meeting rooms and ballrooms. A host stood outside the ballroom which housed the cocktail party she would attend. "Name?" he asked as she approached him.

She blinked, unaccustomed to being screened. Doors opened at the mention of her title. Not in Texas, she supposed. "Bridget Devereaux and escort," she said, because Raoul was beside her.

The man flipped through several pages and checked off her name. "Welcome," he said. "Please go in."

"The nerve of the man," Raoul said as they entered the ballroom full of people. "To question a member of the royal family," he fumed as he surveyed the room.

Bridget smiled. "Novel experience," she said. "I'm looking for Dr. Gordon Walters. If you see him, by all means, please do tell me."

Thirty minutes later, Bridget was ready to pull out

her hair. Every time she mentioned Dr. Walters's name, people clammed up. She couldn't squeeze even a bit of information about the man from anyone.

Frustrated, she accepted a glass of wine and decided to take another tack.

Dr. Ryder McCall checked his watch for the hundredth time in ten minutes. How much longer did he need to stay? The latest nanny he'd hired had seemed okay when he'd left tonight, but after his previous experiences, he couldn't be sure. He caught a glimpse of the back of a woman with dark brown wavy hair and paused. Something about her looked familiar.

The dress was classic and on a woman with a different body, it would have evoked images of that actress. What was her name? Audrey something. But this woman had curves which evoked entirely different thoughts. The sight of the woman's round derriere reminded Ryder of the fact that he hadn't been with a woman in a while. Too long, he thought and adjusted his tie.

Curious, he moved so that he could catch a side view of her. Oh yeah, he thought, his gaze sliding over her feminine form from her calves to her thighs to the thrust of her breasts. He could easily imagine her minus the dress. His body responded. Then he glanced upward to her face and recognition slammed into him.

The woman speaking so animatedly to one of his top residents, Timothy Bing, was the same woman he'd met in the elevator the other night. Princess whatever. Bridget, he recalled. And of course, his top resident was utterly enthralled. Why wouldn't he be? The poor resident was sleep-deprived, food-deprived and sex-deprived.

Ryder was suffering from the same deprivation albeit for different reasons. He wondered why she was here tonight. Might as well cure his curiosity, he thought, if he couldn't cure his other deprivations. He walked toward the two of them.

Timothy only had eyes for Her Highness. Ryder cleared his throat. Both Timothy and the woman turned to look at him.

Timothy stiffened as if he were a marine and he'd just glimpsed a superior. Ryder almost wondered if he would salute. "Dr. McCall," he said.

Bridget looked at him curiously. "Doctor?" she echoed. "I didn't know you were a doctor."

"We didn't have much time to discuss our occupations. Your Highness," he added.

Out of the corner of his vision, he saw Timothy's eyes bulge in surprise. "Highness," he said. "Are you a queen or something? I thought you said you were a representative of Chantaine."

Bridget shot Ryder a glare, then smiled sweetly at Timothy. "I am a representative of Chantaine. A royal representative, and I hope you'll consider the proposal I gave you about serving in Chantaine for a couple of years in exchange for a scholarship and all your living expenses."

Ryder stared at the woman in horrified silence. She was trying to seduce away one of his prized residents. Timothy was brilliant. His next step should be to one of the top neurological hospitals in the States.

Ryder laughed. "Not in a million years," he said.

Bridget furrowed her brow. "Why not? It's a generous offer. Dr. Bing would benefit, as would Chantaine."

"Because Dr. Bing is not going to make a gigantic misstep in his career by taking off for an island retreat when he could be one of the top neurological surgeons in America."

Bridget's furrow turned to a frown. "I find it insulting that you consider a temporary move to Chantaine a misstep. Our citizens suffer from neurological illnesses, too. Is it not the goal of a doctor to heal? Why should there be a prejudice against us just because we reside in a beautiful place? Does that mean we shouldn't have treatment?"

"I wasn't suggesting that your country doesn't deserve medical care. It's my job, however, to advise Dr. Bing to make the best decisions in advancing his career and knowledge."

Princess Bridget crossed her arms over her chest and looked down her nose at him. "I thought that was Dr. Gordon Walters's job, although the man is nowhere to be found."

Timothy made a choking sound. "Excuse me," he said. "I need to…" He walked quickly away without finishing his sentence.

"Well, now you've done it," she said. "I was having a perfectly lovely conversation with Dr. Bing and you ruined it."

"Me?"

"Yes, you. The whole tenor of our conversation changed when you appeared. Dr. Bing was actually open to considering my offer to come to Chantaine."

"Dr. Bing wanted to get into your pants," Ryder said and immediately regretted his blunt statement.

Bridget shot him a shocked glance. "You're the most insulting man I've ever met."

"You clearly haven't met many residents," he said wearily. "I apologize if I offended you, but Timothy Bing doesn't belong in Chantley or wherever you said you're from."

"Chantaine," she said between gritted teeth. "I will accept your apology if you can direct me to Dr. Gordon Walters. He is the man I must meet."

Ryder sighed. "I'm afraid I'm going to have to disappoint you. Dr. Gordon Walters is not here tonight. He hasn't been working in the position as chief resident adviser for some time. It's not likely he'll return."

She cocked her head to one side and frowned further. "Then who will take his place?"

"No one will take his place. Dr. Walters is rightfully loved and respected. I am serving as his temporary successor."

Realization crossed her face. "How wonderful," she said, when she clearly found the news anything but.

Bloody hell, Bridget thought, clenching her fingers together. Now she'd put herself in a mess. She took a deep breath and tried to calm herself. Yes, she and Dr. McCall had engaged in a spirited discussion, but surely he would come around once he heard more about Chantaine and the program she was offering.

"Well, I'm glad I've finally found the person who is currently in charge. Our first meeting in the elevator showed that you and I are both responsible, reasonable adults. I'm sure we'll be able to come to an understanding on this matter," she said, imbuing her words with every bit of positive energy she could muster.

Dr. McCall shot her a skeptical glance. "I'll agree with your first point, but I can't promise anything on the second. It's good to see you again, Your Highness." His gaze gave her a quick sweep from head to toe and back again. "Nice dress. Good evening," he said and turned to leave.

It took Bridget an extra second to recover from the understated compliment that inexplicably flustered before she went after him. "Wait, please," she said.

Dr. McCall stopped and turned, looking at her with a raised eyebrow. "Yes?"

"I really do need to discuss Chantaine's medical needs with you. I'm hoping we can come to some sort of agreement."

"I already told you I couldn't recommend that Timothy Bing spend two years in your country," he said.

"But you have other students," she said. "I'm sure you have students interested in many different areas of medical care. Coming to Chantaine would enable the physicians to get hands-on experience. Plus there's the matter of the financial assistance we would offer."

"I'm sorry, Your High—"

"Oh, please," she said, unable to contain her impatience. "Call me Bridget. We've sung together in an elevator, for bloody sake."

His lips twitched slightly. "True. Bridget, I'm not sure I can help you. Again, my number-one priority is guiding my students to make the best career decisions."

Her heart sank. "Well, the least you can do is give me an opportunity to discuss Chantaine's needs and what we have to offer."

He sighed and shrugged his shoulders in a discouraging way, then pulled a card from his pocket. "Okay.

Here's my card. My schedule is very busy, but call my assistant and she'll work you in."

Work her in. Bridget clenched her teeth slightly at the words, but forced a smile. "Thank you. You won't regret it."

"Hmm," he said in a noncommittal tone and walked away.

She barely resisted the urge to stick out her tongue at him.

Raoul appeared by her side. "Are you all right, Your Highness? You look upset."

"I do?" she asked, composing herself into what she hoped look like a serene expression. She was finding it more and more difficult to pull off instant serenity these days. "I'm fine," she said. "I've just encountered a slight obstacle to completing my assignment for Chantaine."

She watched Ryder McCall's broad shoulders and tall form as he wove through the crowd. Slight obstacle was putting it mildly, but she'd learned that a positive attitude could get a woman through a lot of tricky spots. "I need to know everything about Dr. Ryder McCall by morning, if not before," she muttered and glanced around the room. It was amazing what one could learn about a person in a social situation such as this. She might as well make the best of it.

Ryder walked into his house braced for chaos. His home life had become one big state of chaos bigger than the state of Texas since he'd inherited his brother's boys. Instead of pandemonium, his home was dark and quiet, except for the sound of a baseball game. Ryder spotted his longtime pal Marshall lounging on the leather couch with a box of half-eaten pizza on the coffee table and a beer in his hand.

"Your sitter called me," Marshall said, not rising. "As your official backup. She said one of her kids got sick, so she couldn't stay. Just curious, where am I on that backup list?"

Pretty far down, Ryder thought, but didn't admit it. There were two middle-aged neighbors, an aunt on the other side of town and his admin assistant before Marshall. Ryder suspected he'd called in favors too often if everyone had refused but Marshall. "Thanks for coming. How are the boys?"

Marshall cracked a wily grin. "Great. Gave them a few Cheerios, wore them out and tossed them into bed."

"Bath?" he asked.

"The sitter took care of that before I got here. That Travis is a pistol. Didn't want to go to sleep, so I gave him my best Garth Brooks."

Ryder gave a tired smile. "Must have worked. I'll give a quick check and be right back."

"Cold one's waiting," Marshall said.

Ryder trusted Marshall to a degree, but he didn't think leaving the kids with his buddy from high school on a regular basis was a good idea. He wouldn't put it past Marshall to slip the boys a sip from his beer if he was desperate enough. When pressured, Marshall could get a little too creative, like the time he hot-wired the car of one of the school's top wrestlers because his own car had died.

Marshall owned a chain of auto-mechanic shops across Texas. He wore his hair in a ponytail and tattoos were stamped over his arms and back. He hadn't attended college, but he'd made a success of himself.

Most people couldn't understand their friendship because they appeared to be total opposites, but a mutual appreciation for baseball, some shared holiday dinners which had always included hotdogs and hamburgers and the fact that they both tried to show up during the hard times had made them like family.

With his brother Cory gone, Marshall was the closest thing to family Ryder had. His gut twisted at the thought, but he shoved the feeling aside and gently opened the door to the nursery. He'd learned to walk with stealthlike quiet during the last month. The possibility of waking the boys made him break into a cold sweat.

Moving toward the closest crib, he glanced inside and even in the dark, he knew that this was Tyler, and he was in Travis's bed. Travis was in Tyler's bed. He wasn't going to complain. They were both lying on their backs in la-la land. Which was exactly where he would like to be.

Instead, he walked on quiet footsteps out of the room and gently closed the door behind him. Returning to the den, he saw Marshall still sprawled on his sofa with the same beer in his hand.

"They're asleep," Ryder said and sank into a leather chair next to the sofa. He raked his hand through his hair.

"I coulda told you that," Marshall said. "I made sure they would sleep well tonight."

He shot a quick glance at Marshall. "You didn't give them any booze, did you?"

Marshall looked offended. "Booze to babies? What kind of nut job do you think I am?"

"Well, you aren't around kids very much," Ryder said.

"Maybe not now, but I was an in-demand babysitter in junior high school. Some things you don't forget. And just in case you're worried, this is my second beer. I wouldn't go on a bender when I was taking care of your kids."

Chagrined, Ryder rubbed his chin. "You got me. Sorry, bud. Being in charge of two kids is making me a little crazy."

"A little?" Marshall said and shook his head. "You've turned into the nut job. You know what your problem is, you're no fun anymore. Those babies sense it and it gets them all uptight, too. It's like a virus. You spread it to the babysitters and it makes them crazy, so they quit. You need to get laid and go to a ball game."

"Thanks for the advice," Ryder said. "I'll take your advice in a decade or so."

"Lord help us if you wait that long," Marshall said. "Maybe I could set you up with somebody. Take the edge off."

Ryder slid him a sideways glance. "I'll pass. You and I may root for the Texas Rangers, but we don't share the same taste in women."

"Your loss," Marshall said, sitting upright. "I know some women who could wear you out and make you sleep like a baby."

"I've learned babies don't always sleep that well."

"It's your aura," Marshall said. "That's what Jenny, my ex, would say. Your aura is poisoning your environment."

"A dependable nanny is what I need," Ryder said.

"Well, if you can get a sitter, I've got tickets to the Rangers game on Thursday. Take care, buddy," he said, rising from the couch and patting Ryder on the shoulder. "Keep the faith, bud. And move me up on that backup list. I'm more dependable than your Aunt Joanie. I bet she's always busy."

Ryder smiled despite himself. "You got it. Thanks. If I can find a sitter, I'll go to that game with you."

"I'll believe it when I see it. 'Night," Marshall said and loped out of the house.

Ryder sank farther into his chair, kicked off his shoes and propped his shoes onto the coffee table. He considered reaching for that beer, but drinking anything would require too much energy. Hearing the roar of the crowd and the occasional crack of the bat hitting the ball from the game on his flat-screen TV with surround system, he closed his eyes.

Making sure the twins were safe, taking care of his patients and covering for Dr. Walters were the most important things in his life, but he knew he needed help, especially with the twins. He'd never dreamed how difficult it would be to find dependable caretakers for the boys. His head began to pound. He could feel his blood pressure rising. Pinching the bridge of his nose, for one moment, he deliberately chose *not* to think about the next nanny he would need to hire and the deteriorating mental health of his mentor, Dr. Walters.

Ryder thought back to his high school days when he'd been catcher and Marshall had pitched. They'd won the state championship senior year. That weekend had been full of celebration. He remembered a cheerleader who had paid attention to him for the first time. She'd given him a night full of memories. Blonde, curvy and wiggly, she'd kept him busy. He hadn't lasted long the first time, but he'd done better the second and the third.

His lips tilted upward at the memory. He remembered the thrill of winning. There had never been a happier moment in his life. He sighed, and the visual of a different woman filled his mind. She had dark shoulder-length hair with a wicked red mouth and cool blue eyes. She wore a black dress that handled her curves the same way a man would. She would be a seductive combination of soft and firm with full breasts and inviting hips. She would kiss him into insanity and make him want more. He would slide his hands into her feminine wetness and make her gasp, then make her gasp again when he thrust inside her....

Ryder blinked. He was brick-hard and his heart was racing as if he were having sex. He swore out loud.

He couldn't believe himself. Maybe Marshall was right. Maybe he just really needed to get laid. His only problem was that the woman in his daydream had been Problem Princess Bridget Devereaux. Yep, Marshall was right. Ryder was a nut job.

Bridget read Dr. Ryder McCall's dossier for the hundredth time in three days. He hadn't had the easiest upbringing in the world. His father had died when he was eight years old. His mother had died two years ago.

Ryder had played baseball in high school and won an academic scholarship. He'd graduated first in his college class, then first in his medical-school class.

His older brother, Cory, had played football and earned a college scholarship. Unfortunately, he was injured, so he dropped out, took a job as a department-store manager and married his high-school sweetheart. They'd waited to have children. Six months after the birth of twin boys, they'd attended an anniversary dinner but never made it home. A tractor trailer jackknifed in front of them on the freeway. They both died before they arrived at the emergency room.

An unbelievable tragedy. Even though Bridget had lost both her parents within years of each other, she had never been close to them. Ryder had clearly been close to his brother. Now, a man who had previously been unswervingly focused on his studies and career, was alone with those precious motherless babies.

Her heart broke every time she read his story. This was one of those times she wished she had a magic wand that would solve all of Ryder's problems and heal his pain. But she didn't. As much as she wished it were true, Bridget was all too certain of her humanity.

In the midst of all of this, she still had a job to do. She needed to bring doctors to Chantaine, and Dr. McCall's assistant hedged every time Bridget attempted to make an appointment. She would give the assistant two more tries, then Bridget would face Ryder in his own territory. If he thought an assistant would keep her at bay, he had no concept of her will. Surprise, surprise, especially to herself. She may have portrayed an airy, charming personality, but underneath it all, she was growing a backbone.

Chapter 2

Ryder left the hospital and picked up the boys after the latest sitter unexpectedly informed him that her child had a medical appointment she could not skip. He had an important meeting with several members of the hospital board this afternoon which *he* could not skip. He hated to press his admin assistant into baby service again, but it couldn't be helped.

After wrestling the boys in and out of car seats and the twin stroller, he felt like he'd run a 10K race as he pushed the stroller into his office suite. Instantly noting that his admin assistant was absent from her desk, he felt his stomach twist with dread. She'd left her desk tidy and organized as usual. She'd also left a note on his desk. He snatched it up and read it.

Miss Bridget Devereaux called 3x this a.m. I can't put her off forever. Gone to my anniversary

celebration as discussed. Thank you for letting me off.
—Maryann

Ryder swore out loud then remembered the boys were in the room with him. "Don't ever say that word," he told them. "Bad word."

He recalled Maryann asking for the afternoon off— it had to have been a week or so ago. He'd been busy when she asked and hadn't given it a second thought. Now, he had to juggle his boys and an important meeting. He shook his head. Women managed children and careers all the time. Why was it so difficult for him? He was a healthy, intelligent man. He'd run marathons, worked more than twenty-four hours straight, brought a man back to life in the E.R., but taking care of these boys made him feel like a train wreck.

Ryder sat down at his desk and flipped through his contact list on his computer for someone he could call to watch the boys during his meeting. He sent a few emails and made three calls. All he got were voice mails.

"Well, hello, Phantom Man," a feminine voice called from the doorway.

Ryder swallowed an oath. Just what he needed right now. He didn't even need to look to know it was *Princess Persistent*. But he did and couldn't deny that she was a sight for sore eyes. Wearing another black dress, although this one looked a slight bit more like business wear, she smiled at him with that wicked red mouth that reminded him of what he hadn't had in a long time.

Dismissing the thought, he lifted his hand. "I have no time to talk. Important meeting in less than—" He glanced at the clock. "Thirty minutes. Got to find someone one to watch the boys."

"Not having any luck?" she asked.

"No."

"You sound desperate," she said, sympathy lacking in her tone.

"Not desperate," he said. "Pressed."

"Oh, well as soon as you give me a time for our meeting, I'll get out of your way."

"I already told you I don't have time," he said in a voice that no one in their right mind would question.

She shrugged. "All I want is for you to pull up your calendar and ink me in," she said. "You already agreed."

"Not—"

She crossed her arms over her chest. "You have your job. I have mine."

Travis arched against the stroller restraints as if he wanted out. The baby wore an expression of displeasure, which would soon turn to defiance and fury, which would also include unpleasant sound effects. Ryder loosened the strap and pulled him into his arms.

Tyler looked up expectantly and began the same arching action against the stroller. Ryder withheld an oath.

"Want some help?" Bridget asked.

"Yes," he said. "If you could hold Tyler, I have one more person I can—" He stopped as he watched her settle the baby on her hip. An idea sprang to mind. "Can you keep them for an hour or so?"

Her eyes widened in alarm. "An hour?" she echoed. "Or so?"

"Just for this meeting," he said. "I'll leave as soon as possible."

She shot him a considering look. "In exchange for an opportunity to discuss Chantaine's medical proposition with you, and you having an *open mind*."

"I agree to the first half. The second is going to be tough."

"How tough would it be to take your twins to your important meeting?" she challenged.

The woman was playing dirty. "Okay," he said. "As long as you understand, my first priority is my residents' professional success."

"Done," she said. "Did you bring a blanket and some food?"

"Whatever the sitter keeps in the diaper bag," he said, relief flowing through him like a cool stream of water. "Thank you," he said, setting Travis in the stroller seat. "I'll see you after the meeting," he said and closed the office door behind him.

Bridget stared at the babies and they stared at her. Travis began to wiggle and make a frown face.

"Now, don't you start," she said, pointing her finger at him. "You haven't even given me a chance." She set Tyler in the other stroller seat and dove into the diaper bag and struck gold. "A blanket," she said. "You're going to love this," she said and spread it on the floor. Afterward, she set Travis on the blanket, followed by Tyler.

The boys looked at her expectantly.

"What?" she asked. "You're free from the bondage of the stroller. Enjoy yourselves." She narrowed her eyes. "Just don't start crawling or anything. Okay? Let's see what else is in the bag."

Unfortunately, not much. She used up the small container of Cheerios within the first fifteen minutes and fifteen minutes after that, both boys had lost interest in the small set of blocks. She pulled out a musical toy and helped them work that over for several minutes.

Peekaboo killed a few more minutes, but then Bridget started to feel a little panicky. She needed more snacks and toys if she was going to keep the little darlings entertained. Grabbing some blank paper from Ryder's desk, she gave each boy a sheet.

Travis immediately put it in his mouth.

"Let's try something else," she said and crumpled the paper.

He smiled as if he liked the idea. Great, she thought. More paper. She crumpled a few sheets into a ball and tossed it at them. They loved that. They threw paper all over the room.

After a few more minutes, Travis began to fuss, stuffing his fist in his mouth.

"Hungry?" It would help so much if they could tell her what they needed. Luckily two bottles were also stuffed in the bag. She pulled out one and began to feed Travis. Tyler's face crumpled and he began to cry.

"Great, great," she muttered and awkwardly situated both boys on her lap as she fed them both their bottles.

They drained them in no time. Travis burped on her dress.

Bridget grimaced. A second later, Tyler gave her the same favor.

At least they weren't crying, she thought, but then she sniffed, noticing an unpleasant odor. A quick check revealed Travis had left a deposit in his diaper.

Ryder opened the door to his office prepared for screaming, crying, accusations from Bridget. Instead the boys were sprawled across her lap while she sang a medical magazine to the tune of *Frère Jacques*. He had to admit it was pretty inventive. His office looked like a disaster zone with papers strewn everywhere and he smelled the familiar, distinct scent of dirty diapers. He must have wrinkled his nose.

She did the same. "I didn't think it would be considerate to toss the diapers into the hallway, so they're in the trash can. I bundled them up as best as I could."

The boys looked safe and content. That was what was important. "It looks like you had a good time."

"Not bad," she said with a smile. "Considering my resources. You're really not set up for babies here."

"I can't agree more," he said and snatched up a few wads of paper. "What were you doing?"

"Playing ball with paper. It worked until Travis was determined to eat it." She gingerly lifted one of the boys in Ryder's direction. "So, when do we have our discussion?"

He tucked Tyler into the stroller and followed with Travis. Ryder was tempted to name a time next year but knew that wouldn't be fair. Better to get it over with. "Tonight, at my house," he said. "Do you like Chinese?"

"I prefer Italian or Mediterranean," she said, frowning as she rose to her feet. "At your house?"

"It's the one and only time I can guarantee for the foreseeable future."

She sighed. "It's not what I hoped for. How am I going to have your undivided attention?"

"Maybe we'll get lucky and they'll go to sleep," he said.

* * *

Four hours later, Bridget could barely remember what she'd said or eaten for dinner. The boys had taken a nap in the car on the way home and woken up cranky. She suspected they hadn't gotten enough of an afternoon nap. Although she resented the fact that she wasn't getting Ryder's undivided attention during their discussion, she couldn't really blame him. In fact, despite the fact that he was clearly a strong man, she could tell that caring for the twins was wearing on him. He loved them and would protect them with his life, but the man needed consistent help.

It was close to eleven before the twins truly settled down.

"I'd offer you a ride to wherever you're staying, but I can't pull the boys out of bed again," he said, after he had made the trip up and down the stairs five times.

His eyes filled with weariness, he raked a hand through his hair. Her heart tugged at his quandary. The urge to help, to fix, was overwhelming. "My security is always close by. He can collect me. It's no problem."

"I keep forgetting you're a princess," he said.

"Maybe it's the baby formula on my dress," she said drily.

"Maybe," he said, meeting her gaze. The moment swelled between them.

Bridget felt her chest grow tight and took a breath to alleviate the sensation.

"I'm sure you're tired. You could stay here if you want," he offered. "I have a guest room and bath."

Bridget blinked. She *was* tired, but staying here? "I don't have a change of clothes."

He shrugged. "I can give you a shirt to sleep in."

The prospect of sleeping in Ryder's shirt was wickedly seductive. Plus, she *was* tired. "I'd like to get your nanny situation in order for you."

"That would be a dream come true," he said. "Everything I've done so far hasn't worked."

"There may be a fee for an agency," she said. "I'm not sure how it works here. I'll have to ask my sister."

"I took the first and second suggestions that were given to me and they didn't pan out. It's imperative that I have excellent care for the boys. "

"I can see that," she said. "But do you also realize that you will have to make some adjustments as time goes on? Later, there will be sports and school activities where parents are expected to attend." Bridget remembered that neither of her parents had attended her school activities. Occasionally a nanny had shown up, but never her parents. "Have you figured out how you'll address that?"

He frowned thoughtfully. "I haven't figured out much. I haven't had custody very long. It's still a shock to all of us. I know the boys miss their mother and father, but they can't express it. I hate the loss for them. And I'm not sure I'm such a great choice as a parent. I've been totally dedicated to my career since I entered med school. Add to that how I've been filling in for Dr. Walters and it's tough. I don't want to let down my residents or the twins."

Bridget studied Ryder for a long moment. "Are you sure you want to step in as their father? There are other options. There are people who would love to welcome the boys into their—"

"The boys are mine," he said, his jaw locking in resolution. "It may take me some time, but I'll figure it out. The boys are important to me. I held them minutes after they were born. I would do anything for them. We've just all been thrown a loop. We're all dealing with the loss of my brother and sister-in-law. I will be there for them. I will be."

She nodded slowly. "Okay. I'll try to help you with your nanny situation."

He paused and the electricity and emotion that flowed between them snapped and crackled. "Thank you."

She nodded. "It's late. I may need to borrow one of your shirts and I should talk to my security."

"No problem," he said, but the way he looked at her made her feel as if he'd much prefer she share his bed instead of taking the guest bed alone.

Bridget took a quick shower and brushed her teeth with the toothbrush Ryder supplied. Pushing her hands through the sleeves of the shirt he left in the guest bedroom for her, she drank in the fresh scent of the shirt. She climbed into bed, wondering what had possessed her to get involved in Ryder's situation and she remembered all the things she couldn't control or influence. Maybe, just maybe she could wave a magic wand in this one and help just a little.

It seemed only seconds after she fell asleep that she heard a knock at the door. She awakened, confused and disoriented. "Hello?"

"Bridget," a male voice said from the other side of the door. "It's me, Ryder."

The door opened a crack. "I just wanted you to know I'm leaving."

Her brain moved slowly. She was not at the hotel. She was at Ryder's townhome. "Um."

"The boys are still asleep."

She paused. "The boys?" She blinked. "Oh, the boys."

He came to the side of her bed. "Are you okay?"

"What time is it?"

"Five a.m."

"Is this when you usually leave for work?"

"Pretty much," he said.

"Okay," she said and tried to make her brain work. "What time do they usually get up?"

"Six or seven," he said. "I can try and call someone if—"

"No, I can do it," she said. "Just leave my door open so I can hear them."

"Are you sure?"

"Yes. Check in at lunchtime," she said.

"I can do that," he said and paused. "Did anyone ever tell you how beautiful you are when you're half-asleep?"

Unconsciously, her mouth lifted in a half smile. "I can't recall such a compliment."

"Nice to know I'm the first," he said, bending toward her and pressing his mouth against hers. Before she could say a word, he left.

Bridget wondered if she'd dreamed the kiss.

She fell back asleep for what must have been 30 seconds and she heard the sound of a baby's cry. It awakened her like cold water on her face. She sat upright, climbed out of bed and walked to the boys' room. She swung open the door to find Travis and Tyler sitting in their cribs and wailing.

"Hi, darlings," she said and went to Travis. "Good

morning. It's a wonderful day to be a baby, isn't it?" She saw a twisty thing on the side of the crib and cranked it around. The mobile turned and music played. "Well, look at that," she said and touched the mobile.

Travis gave a few more sobs, but as soon as he looked upward, he quieted as the mobile turned.

Bridget felt a sliver of relief. "Good boy," she said and went to Tyler's bed and cranked up the mobile. Tyler looked upward and gave up his halfhearted cry, staring at the mobile.

Diaper change, she thought and took care of Travis. Then she took care of Tyler and hoisted both boys on her hips and went downstairs. She fed them, changed them again and propped them on a blanket in the den while she called her sister's friend for a reference for the best nanny agency in Dallas. Three hours later, she interviewed four nannies in between feeding the twins and changing more diapers and putting them down for a nap. When they fussed at nap time, she played a CD more repetitious than her brother's top-adviser's speech on a royal's duty. She'd heard that lecture too many times to count. The huge advantage to the babies' CD was that it included singing. Bridget wondered if she might have been more receptive to the lecture if the adviser had sung it.

The second prospective nanny was her favorite. She received letters of reference on her cell phone within an hour and sent a generous offer that was immediately accepted. After she checked on the boys, she ordered a nanny/babycam. Next in line, she would hire a relief nanny, but right now she needed a little relief of her own.

Bridget sank onto the couch and wondered when her

day had felt so full. Even at this moment, she needed to use the bathroom, but she didn't have the energy to go. She glanced at herself, in her crumpled dress from yesterday with baby formula, baby food and liquid baby burp. That didn't include the drool.

Crazy, but the drool was sweet to her. How sick was that? But she knew the twins had drooled when they'd relaxed and trusted her.

She laughed quietly, a little hysterically. Anyone in their right mind would ask why she was working so hard to find a nanny for a doctor with two baby boys. Maybe a shrink could explain it, but these days, Bridget had a hard time turning down a cause of the heart. And Ryder and the boys had struck her straight in the heart with a deadly aim. She hoped, now, that she would feel some sort of relief.

Leaning back against the sofa with her bladder a little too full, she closed her eyes. Heaven help her, this baby stuff was exhausting.

Ryder left the office early, determined not to leave Bridget totally in the lurch with the boys. Stepping inside the front door, he found Bridget, mussed in the most alluring way, asleep on his couch.

She blinked, then her eyes widened. "Oh, excuse me. Just a second," she said, then raced down the hallway.

He listened carefully, automatically these days. A CD played over the baby monitor, but there were no other sounds. A double check never hurt, he thought, and strode upstairs to listen outside the nursery door. Nothing. He opened the doorknob in slow motion and pushed the door open. Carefully stepping inside, he peeked into the cribs. Both boys were totally zoned out. He almost wondered if they were snoring but refused to check.

Backing out of the room, he returned downstairs to the den. Bridget was sipping from a glass of water.

"Are they still asleep?" she asked.

He nodded.

She grimaced. "I hate to say this. You have no idea how much I hate to say this, but we need to wake them or they'll be up all night. And I'm not staying tonight."

"Yeah," he said, but he was in no rush.

"I hired a nanny. She can start Monday. I've also ordered a baby/nannycam for your peace of mind. The next step is hiring a relief nanny because the twins are especially demanding at this age. Well, maybe they will be demanding at every age, but we have to deal with the present and the immediate future."

Ryder stared at her in disbelief. "How did you do that?"

She smiled. "I'm a fairy princess. I waved my magic wand," she said. "Actually I got into the best nanny agency in Dallas, used my title, interviewed four highly qualified women in between changing diapers, selected one applicant, received references, blah, blah, blah and it's done." She lifted her shoulders. "And now I'm done."

"I'm sure you are. In any other circumstance, I would invite you out to dinner for the evening."

"Lovely thought," she said. "But I feel extremely grungy. The opposite of glamorous. I'm going to my sister's ranch for the weekend. You can call me next week about all the doctors you want to send to Chantaine."

His lips twitched. "You don't really think I'm going to sell out one of my residents for this, do you?"

"Sell out is such a harsh term," she said with a scowl.

"I believe it's more accurate that you're giving them an opportunity for hands-on experience in a beautiful environment with a compensation that allows them to concentrate on treatment rather than their debt."

He lifted an eyebrow. "Pretty good."

She shrugged. "It's the truth. My security is waiting to drive me to my sister's house. Can you take it from here?"

"Yes, I can. Do I have your number?" he asked. "For that dinner I promised."

She looked at him for a long, sexy moment that made him want to find a way to make her stay. "Some would say I'm more trouble than I'm worth," she said.

"They haven't seen you with twins," he said.

She smiled slightly and went to the kitchen. Out of curiosity, he followed and watched her scratch a number across the calendar tacked on the fridge. "Good enough?" she asked.

"Good enough," he said.

"Don't wait too long to call me, cowboy doctor," she said and walked toward the front door.

"I won't," he said, his gaze fixed on the sight of her amazing backside. "G'night, gorgeous."

She tossed a smile over her shoulder. "Same to you."

Bridget felt Valentina search her face. "Twin boys? Dr. Ryder? What does any of this have to do with you?"

It was Saturday morning. Noon, actually, as she sipped her tea and entered the world of the waking. "I didn't mean to get involved, but I didn't have a choice. I mean, the boys were orphaned. Ryder is grieving at the same time he's trying to take care of the babies. Trying to take on someone else's job because he's medically unable."

Tina stared at her in disbelief. "Are you sure you're okay? Maybe you need more rest."

Bridget laughed. "I'm sure I'll take another nap, but the story won't change tomorrow. It was something I had to do." She paused. "You understand that, don't you? When you have to fix it if you can?"

Tina's face softened and she covered Bridget's hand with hers. "Oh, sweetie, I'm so sorry," she said, shaking her head.

"For what?"

"The Devereaux fixing gene has kicked in," she said. "It's a gift and a plague."

"What do you mean?"

"I mean, you finally understand what it means to be a Devereaux Royal," she said, her expression solemn. "If you see a need, you try to fill it. If you see a pain, you try to heal it. It's your purpose. It's our purpose."

"So, I'm going to be doing stuff like this the rest of my life?" Bridget asked, appalled.

Tina nodded and Katiana banged on the tray of her high chair, clearly wanting more food.

"Oh, I hope not." Bridget didn't want to feel that much. She didn't want to get that emotionally involved. Surely, she could get this out of her system once and for all with Ryder and the babies and then get back to her true self in Italy.

Bridget sighed. "What I really want to do is wrap up this doctor thing as soon as possible. I'm concerned it may not happen as quickly as I like."

"Why not?" Tina asked as she gave Katiana slices of peaches.

"I don't understand it all, but the way Ryder talks about it, going to Chantaine would be death for a physician's career. Sounds a bit overdramatic to me, but I need to get further information. In the meantime, Stefan has asked me to make some more official appearances, so I'll be traveling and spending more time in Dallas."

Tina frowned. "I don't like that," she said. "I thought you were going to spend most of your time here with me."

"I'll still be coming to the ranch as often as possible, but you know how Stefan is. He likes to maximize our efforts."

"How well I remember," Tina said with a groan. She dampened a clean cloth and wiped off Katiana's face and hands.

Katiana shook her adorable head and lifted her hands. "Up," she said.

"Of course, Your Highness," Tina said and gave her daughter a kiss as she lifted her from the chair.

Katiana immediately pointed at the floor. "Down."

"Please," Tina said.

Katiana paused.

"Please," Tina repeated. "Can you say that?"

"Psss," the toddler said.

"Close enough," Tina said with a laugh.

Bridget stared at her sister in jeans and a T-shirt and sometimes had to shake her head at the sight of her. "I'm just not used to seeing you quite so domesticated."

"I've been living here for more than two years now."

"Do you mind it? The work?" she asked. "At the palace, you could have had several nannies at your beck and call."

"I have Hildie the housekeeper, who may as well be

Katiana's grandmother, and Zach. I like the simplicity of this life. Before I met Zach, I always felt like I was juggling a dozen priorities. Now between him and Katiana, the choice is easy."

"Must be nice," Bridget muttered as Hildie, Zach's longtime housekeeper, strode through the door carrying a bag of groceries.

"Well, hello, all Your Highlinesses. We've got a roomful of royalty today. Miss Tina, did you offer your sister some of that strawberry bread? Looks like you're having a late breakfast. Although that should come as no surprise considering when she got here last night," Hildie said, lifting her eyebrow.

Bridget wasn't quite certain how to take the stern-looking gray-haired woman. Tina insisted the woman had a heart of gold, but she seemed to rule the house with an iron hand. "Good morning, Miss—"

"Call me Hildie, and it's afternoon. Do you feel like some pancakes or a turkey sandwich? You looked pretty rough when you got in last night," Hildie said as she began to put away groceries.

"She was taking care of twin babies," Tina said, clearly still amazed.

Hildie's jaw dropped. "Twin babies," she said. "You?"

Bridget grimaced. "I know it's totally improbable. Hopefully I won't be put in that type of situation again."

"She was helping a doctor who had become a guardian to his brother's two babies because the brother and sister-in-law were killed in an accident."

Hildie shook her head, her brow furrowing in deep sympathy. "That's terrible, just terrible. You did the right thing," she said to Bridget. "Let me fix you a pie. I'll fix you any kind you want."

Surprised, Bridget felt a rush of discomfort mixed with pleasure. "Oh, I don't need a pie. You're delightful to suggest it, but—"

"I insist," Hildie said.

Tina lifted her shoulders helplessly. "You're going to get a pie whether you like it or not. You may as well pick what you like, and I guarantee it will be the best pie you've eaten."

"Well, if you must, I would like the most decadent chocolate pie you can bake."

Hildie cackled with laughter. "Chocolate. You can tell the two of you are sisters. And you may try to hide it, but you have that fix-it compulsion just like your sister."

"I don't have that compulsion," Bridget insisted. "It's temporary. Like a virus. As soon as I take my long break in Italy, I'll be cured."

Hildie laughed again and shot her a look of sympathy. "Don't worry, Your Highliness. It may take a while, but you'll figure it out."

Bridget frowned because it seemed that Hildie knew something she didn't. Hmm. The prospect didn't please her, but the chocolate would help.

Chapter 3

Three nights later, Ryder met Bridget at an exclusive Mediterranean restaurant in Dallas. He remembered she'd said she preferred Mediterranean and Italian food. With the Dallas skyline outside the window beside them, he couldn't look anywhere but at her. Her blue eyes sparkled with a combination of sensuality and warmth. Her black dress—yet another one—dipped into a V that cupped her beautiful breasts and her lips were, again, red.

"Thank you for joining me," he said after they'd placed their order.

"Thank you for inviting me. Who's watching the twins?" she asked.

"A neighbor and her daughter. I'm paying double. Amazing how easy it was for them to commit when I said that," he said.

She laughed. "They're adorable but exhausting. How was the new nanny?"

"Scary efficient. This was her first day and she's already whipping all of us into shape," he said, amazed at how good he felt just to be with Bridget.

"Good. Next step is to get a backup," she said and took a sip of wine. "In the meantime, about Chantaine's medical program…"

He stifled a groan. "Do we have to discuss business?"

"Briefly," she said and lifted an eyebrow. "Remember that we held our discussion while the twins were screaming *after* I had cared for them during your meeting and—"

"Okay, okay," he said. "Do you want me to be blunt?"

"I would love it," she said, leaning forward and propping her chin on her hands.

"The truth is, there's no true professional advantage for the residents to go to Chantaine after they graduate. There's no extra education, association with an expert, or certification."

"So money is not enough," she said.

"No," he said.

"Hmm." She tilted her head. "So the whole game would change if Chantaine could offer exposure to a noted expert in a particular field?"

He nodded.

She took another sip of her wine. "Thank you."

He could tell her brain was already racing. "You're plotting and planning," he said.

She smiled, her sexy red lips lifting upward, sending a sensual heat through his veins. "Yes, I am. I'll figure something out. It's the Devereaux way."

"I did an internet search on you," he admitted. "You've *mostly* stayed out of trouble. How did you manage that?"

"I'm flattered. Of course, I did research on you right after the cocktail party. How did I stay out of trouble?" she asked. "It's all relative. My sisters did me a huge favor. I wouldn't wish it on her, but Ericka went to rehab, and then after that, Tina got pregnant. What a scandal. So my little tumbles—"

"Like the time you got smashed at the nightclub in Chantaine and made a scene—"

"That was Stefan's fault. Eve was with me and he couldn't stand the fact that she wasn't with him." She waved her hand. "But I won't fault him too much. He'd just discovered he had a baby from an earlier affair and was trying to work out his relationship with Eve."

"I remember reading an article about some sort of incident. A gang. She was hurt."

He stopped when he saw her gaze darken with emotion.

"She saved my life and nearly lost her own," Bridget said quietly as she ran her finger around the top of her glass. "It all happened so fast. I wish I had responded differently. She was hurt. She almost died." She lifted her glass and took a quick sip. "It was wrong. Her life shouldn't have been put in jeopardy for my sake."

He was shocked at the stark guilt he saw on her face. "These things happen. Decisions are made in microseconds. She's a Texas girl. She acted on instinct."

She bit her lip. "Maybe I need to learn some of those Texas-girl instincts," she muttered.

"Your instincts are pretty damn good. You took care of the twins when we were in a jam," he said.

"That's different," she said.

"Not as far as I can see. I won't lie to you. I can't make any promises about sending doctors to Chantaine. On the other hand, I've thought about having you in my bed way too much. I wish I could say it's just because you've got a killer body and I've done without, but the truth is, there's something else about you that gets me going."

Her lips parted in startled disbelief. "I—" She broke off and shook her head. "I don't know what to say."

"You don't have to say anything. I just wanted you to know," he said.

She met his gaze and he could tell she was undecided. He saw want and hesitation, and he understood it, but he was driven to find a way to get her to meet him halfway.

After a delicious dinner, Ryder drove Bridget to her hotel and insisted on walking her to her room. "You know security is watching me," she said as they stood outside her door.

"Do you want to step inside your room?"

An illicit thrill raced through her. Her guard would report to Stefan and he would fuss. She would dodge his calls the same way she had after spending the night at Ryder's house. What a hassle. "For just a moment," she said and slid her key card into the lock.

Ryder pushed open the door. Seconds later, she felt her back against the door and his mouth on hers.

"Do you know what your red mouth does to me?" he muttered and plundered her lips. He slid his tongue into her mouth, tasting her, taking her.

Her heart slammed against her ribs. She couldn't resist the urge to lift her fingers to his hair and scalp.

He groaned in approval and rocked his hips against hers.

Bridget gasped, her breath locking somewhere between her lungs and throat. Somehow, someway, she craved his warmth and strength. His passion and need struck her at her core.

"I want you," he said. "You want me. Let me stay for a while."

A terrible wicked temptation rolled through her. If he stayed, he would fill her and take her away from her uncertainty and emptiness. She knew he could take care of her, if only for a little while.

He French-kissed her, sending her around the world at least a couple of times.

"You want me to stay?" he asked, sliding his mouth down over her ear.

She inhaled, grasping for sanity. Closing her eyes, she tried to concentrate. "Yesandno," she said, running the words together. She dipped her head so that her forehead rested against his chin. "This is a little fast."

He gave a heavy, unsatisfied sigh. "Yeah, it is. But it's strong."

She nodded. "Sorry," she whispered.

"It's okay," he said cradling the back of her head. "It wouldn't work out anyway."

"Why is that?" she asked, leaning back to look at him.

"I'm a doctor. You're a princess," he said.

"So?" she asked.

"The two don't mix," he said. "And never will. Sweet dreams, Your Highness."

He left and Bridget stared at the door, frowning. *Why couldn't they mix?* Not that she *wanted* them to mix. And the *sweet dreams* thing really grated on her. That was what Eve had often said. It had seemed so sweet when she'd said it. Not so with Ryder. Bridget snarled. He was gone. Good riddance.

Ryder heard a knocking sound and shook his head as he glanced up during the meeting he was in to discuss the performance of the residents.

Dr. Wayne Hutt, Ryder's nemesis, knocked on the table again. "Dr. McCall?" he said. "Anyone home?"

"Pardon me," Ryder said in a crisp voice. "I was studying my notes."

"Apology accepted," Hutt said. "Drs. Robinson and Graham are having attendance issues."

"Dr. Robinson is concerned about the welfare of his family in rural Virginia and Dr. Graham's wife has just gotten pregnant," Ryder said. "They just need a little time to refocus. It won't be a problem."

"How can you be sure?" Hutt challenged.

Ryder fought his antipathy for his associate. "I'm sure," he said. "Just as Dr. Gordon Walters would be sure," he said, pulling rank because everyone knew Dr. Walters trusted Ryder over anyone else.

Hutt gave an odd combination of a frown and grimace.

Dr. James Williams, chief of everything, nodded. "We'll give these two interns two weeks to make adjustments. Dr. McCall, you'll speak to them?"

"Yes, sir."

Seven minutes later, the meeting ended, thank God. He returned to his office and sent emails to Drs. Robinson and Graham to set up appointments. He answered another fifty emails and stood to make late rounds with his patients.

A knock sounded outside his door and Dr. Hutt walked inside. "Hey, Ryder. Late night. I'm surprised you can do this with the twins."

Ryder resisted the urge to grind his teeth. "I've hired a new nanny and am getting new backup. Thanks for your concern. I need to do late rounds."

"Just a minute," Hutt said. "How's Dr. Walters doing? No one's talking."

"He's working through his recovery. These things take time," Ryder hedged.

"That's pretty vague," Hutt said.

"You know I can't discuss the confidential status of patients," he said.

"But Walters isn't really your patient," Hutt continued.

"He's my mentor and friend, the closest thing I've had to a father since my own father died when I was a kid. I'm not discussing his condition," Ryder said.

"It must not be good," Hutt said. "You know if the twins are too much for you, I'll be glad to step in and help."

Ryder just bet Hutt would like to step in and *help*. What Hutt really wanted was a promotion. What Hutt really wanted was to snatch Walters's position away from Ryder. Although Ryder hated that Walters couldn't fulfill his duties any longer.

"Thanks for the offer," he said.

"Seriously, Ryder. I have a wife and a child. The wife is the critical element. She makes it easy for me to do my job. When you don't have a wife…"

"I have a good new nanny," he said.

"It's not the same as a wife," Hutt counseled.

"Hmm. See you. Good night," he said and headed out the door. What Hutt didn't understand was that Ryder had never had any intention of getting married and having children. He'd observed his parents' disastrous marriage, his father's death and his mother's subsequent descent into alcoholism and death.

After that, Ryder had resolved that he wanted to heal people. Bag the personal relationships, with the exception of his brother and his family. His family became his patients, and after he completed his residency, his family included the new residents. And always Dr. Walters. He would never take a wife. His mind wandered to a visual of Bridget the last time he'd seen her, her eyes catlike with sensuality, her mouth soft and sensual, taking him into her. His mouth into her. When he really wanted to give her a lot more.

Ryder swore under his breath. This was all libido. He'd taken care of this issue before with other women doctors as career-driven as he was. No-ties sex provided a release that allowed him to do his job. Maintaining his focus on his profession and the twins was the most important thing. Bridget was just a distraction.

Bridget wandered around the medical association meeting and was bummed that Ryder wasn't there. He was probably taking care of the twins. She felt a deep tug of sympathy and quickly tried to brush it aside. Ryder didn't want her sympathy. They would never work. Remember? She covered her irritation with a smile as she nodded at someone else she didn't know.

Halfway through the evening, the shrimp bowl was refilled and Bridget put a few on her plate.

"I always wait for the refill at these things," a distinguished older man said to her.

She nodded in agreement. "I agree. Fresh is better. Bridget Devereaux," she said, extending her free hand.

"Dr. James Williams, University Hospital," he said shaking her hand. "Are you a pharmaceutical sales rep?"

She opened her mouth and it took a moment to speak. She smiled. "Not exactly. I'm representing the country of Chantaine. Very small country in the Mediterranean. We're trying to recruit more doctors. We're offering complimentary living expenses and paying special scholarships in addition to salary for a two-year stay."

Dr. Williams lifted his white eyebrows. "Really? I'll have to speak to my physician in charge of residents about that. Perhaps a couple of them could benefit from that."

"I would appreciate that very much. I'm sure you're a very busy man. Would you mind if I touch base with you in a week or so?"

"Not at all," he said. "Some of our residents have money challenges. Don't we all in this economy?"

"So true," she said. "Are you the speaker tonight?"

He shook his head. "No, I'm lucky. Eat and leave."

She laughed. "Don't rub it in," she said.

He laughed in return. "Tell me your name again. I don't want to forget."

"Bridget Devereaux," she said, deliberately leaving out her title. "I represent Chantaine. I'm honored to meet you."

"My pleasure to meet you, Miss Devereaux," he said, and ate his shrimp cocktail.

Bridget worked the room the rest of the night and arranged a visit to the pediatric wing at Texas Medical Center to make a public service announcement for public health. She also met several doctors who wanted to pursue a more personal relationship, but she demurred at the same time that she gave them her card which contained a number for her assistant.

By the time the evening was done, her feet were also done. Her mind wandered to Ryder and the babies, but she tried to push her thoughts aside. With a glass of white wine in her hand, she kicked off her high heels and watched television in her suite at the hotel.

She closed her eyes. Soon enough she would be in Italy with a gorgeous Italian man keeping her company. She smiled at the image, but soon another image flashed in its place. Ryder, sans shirt, stood before her and dragged her into his arms and began to make love to her. He was so hot that smoke rose between them, but the sensation of his skin against hers made her dizzy. His kiss made her knees weak. He made her want in a way she never had....

She felt herself sinking into the couch, her body warm and pliable. And alone.

Bridget blinked and sat up against the couch. This was just wrong. He'd already said they wouldn't work because of who he was, because of who she was. A part of her rebelled against the notion one moment. The next, she didn't. She didn't have room for this drama in her life. She had goals. She had Italy in her future.

Bridget washed her face and brushed her teeth, determined to put Ryder from her mind. As she fell asleep, though, she dreamed of Ryder and the boys.

* * *

A few days later, Ryder followed up on a surgery patient midday. The young man had been admitted to the E.R. with appendicitis. Ryder had operated and needed to give his stamp of approval for the teen to be discharged. He was stopped because there was filming in the pediatric unit.

Slightly irritated, he checked his text messages on his cell and answered a few.

"She's a princess making a video," one nurse said to another.

He snapped his head up at the comment. "Princess?" he repeated.

"Yes," the nurse said. "But she's very nice. Not at all snooty. I got her coffee and she was very grateful. More than a lot of doctors."

"She wasn't trying to save lives," Ryder said.

The nurse shrugged. "Anyone can say please and thank you, and she did."

Minutes later, Bridget appeared, lighting up the room with her smile. The chief of Pediatrics accompanied her, clearly dazzled.

"Thank you," she said. "Thank you so much from Chantaine and me. You have been wonderful."

"Isn't she wonderful? Now *that* is a princess," the nurse said.

Ryder wanted to make a wry, cynical response, but he was too busy staring at Bridget. And the damned pediatric chief. She seemed to glow. He remembered how she'd felt in his arms, how that wicked red mouth had felt against his. He remembered how she'd made him smile. Not many people had managed to do that during the last few months.

She squeezed the pediatrics chief's arm, then glanced around the room and waved. Her gaze locked with his and he felt a surge of need all the way down to his feet. It was sexual, but more, and confused the hell out of him. She gave a quick little wave and returned her attention to the pediatric chief.

Ryder felt an inexplicable surge of jealousy. *Where the hell had that come from?* Pushing it aside, he continued to his patient's room for the final exam. Less than five minutes later, he headed down the hallway toward his office. Rounding a corner, he nearly plowed into Bridget and Dr. Ware, the pediatrics chief, who was chatting her up. His body language said he wanted to eat her with a spoon. His hand placed on the wall above her head, he leaned toward her. Ryder fought the crazy urge to push him away, but turned his head instead.

"Ryder. Dr. McCall," Bridget said.

He slowed his steps and turned around and nodded in her direction.

"How are you? The twins? The new nanny?" she asked, her gaze searching his.

Ware stepped beside her. "Whoa, she knows a lot about you, McCall. How did that happen?"

Ryder shrugged. "Just lucky, I guess. I'm good. The twins are good and the new nanny is fantastic. I could say I owe you my life, but I'd be afraid you'd take it."

She shot him a look of mock offense. "You know better than that. Besides, it's not your life that I want," she said with a laugh.

Ware looked from one of them to the other, clearly

curious. "What *does* she want? And why in the world wouldn't you give it to her?"

"She wants my residents," he said, meeting her gaze.

"After they've completed your program," she insisted. "Plus, I only want to *borrow* them for a couple of years, and they'll be well compensated."

"You could throw her one or—" Dr. Ware's pager sounded. "Please excuse me. I need to go. You have my card, Your Highness. Give me a call. Anytime," he said with a hopeful smile and rushed away.

Bridget sighed and turned to Ryder. "Are you going to do the civilized thing and ask me to join you for lunch?"

"If I haven't been civilized before, why should I start now?" Ryder retorted because Bridget made him feel anything but civilized.

"I suppose because you owe me your life," she said with a glint in her eyes.

He gave a muffled chuckle. "Okay, come along. I better warn you that lunch won't last longer than fifteen minutes."

"Ah, so you're into quickies. What a shame," she said and began to walk.

"I didn't say that," he said, but resisted the urge to pull at his collar which suddenly felt too tight.

"I can't say I'm surprised. All evidence points in that direction."

"How did we get on this subject?" he asked.

"You said you wouldn't last more than fifteen minutes," she said, meeting his gaze with eyes so wide and guileless that he wondered how she did it.

"I said *lunch* won't last—" He broke when he saw

her smile. "Okay, you got me on that one. I hope you don't mind cafeteria food."

"Not at all," she said as they walked into the cafeteria.

He noticed several people stared in their direction, but she seemed to ignore it. They each chose a couple dishes and he paid for both, then guided her to a less-occupied table at the back of the room. "How did your video go today?"

"Hopefully, well. I interviewed Dr. Ware about preventative health for children. I also need to do one for adults. But enough about that. How are the twins?" she asked, clearly eager for information.

"I think the new nanny is making a big difference for them. This is the most calm I've seen them since I took custody of them," he said. "The nanny also suggested that I do some extra activities with them, but I haven't worked that into the schedule yet."

"What kind of activities?" she asked, and took a bite of her chicken.

"Swimming," he said then lowered his voice. *"Baby yoga."*

"Oh. Do you take yoga?" she asked and sipped her hot tea.

"Never in my life," he said. "The nanny seems to think this would increase bonding between the three of us."

"That makes you uncomfortable," she said.

He shrugged. "I hadn't planned on having kids. I guess I'm still adjusting, too."

"You've been through a lot. Perhaps you should see a therapist," she said.

"We're doing okay now," he said defensively.

"I don't suggest it as an insult. The palace is always giving us head checks especially since my sister Ericka had her substance-abuse problem. I'm surprised it's not required in this situation."

"A social worker has visited a few times to check on things. She actually suggested the same thing," he said reluctantly. "She said I need to make sure I'm having fun with the boys instead of it being all work."

"There you go," she said. "I think it's a splendid idea. You just seem incredibly overburdened and miserable."

"Thank you for that diagnosis, Your Highness," he said drily and dug into his dry salmon filet. "Funny, a friend of mine said something similar recently."

"We all have to protect against burnout. I would say you're more in danger of it than most."

"Is there such a thing as princess burnout?" he asked.

"Definitely. That's what happened to my sister Valentina. She carried the load too long."

"And what are you doing to prevent burnout?"

"I have an extended break planned in my future. In the meantime, I try to make sure I get enough rest and solitude whenever possible. As soon as I wrap up the doctor assignment, I'll get a break. I'm hoping you'll toss me one or two of your residents as Dr. Ware suggested to get the ball rolling."

"It's going to be more difficult than that," he said.

"I don't see why it needs to be. It's not as if I'm seriously asking for your top neurosurgeons. We would love a general practitioner or family doctor. In fact, we would prefer it."

"You and the rest of the world. We actually have a shortage of family physicians, too."

"Again, I'm only asking to *borrow* them."

"What do you think of Dr. Ware?" he asked, changing the subject again.

"He's lovely. Unlike you, he's totally enchanted with my position and title."

"Part of my charm. Part of the reason you find me irresistible."

"You flatter yourself," she said.

"Do I?" he challenged. "You've missed me."

"Of course I haven't. You already said nothing would work between us. Of course, that was after you tried to shag me against the hotel door. I mean, you obviously have the attention span of a fruit fly when it comes to women and—"

He closed his hand over hers. "Will you shut up for a minute?"

Surprisingly, she did.

"I dream about you whenever I get the rare opportunity to sleep. I've dialed your number and hung up too many times to count. You can't want to get involved with me right now."

"It's not for you to tell me what I can and can't want. Lord knows, everyone else does that. Don't you start."

"Okay," he said wearily.

"So what are you going to do about it?" she challenged.

If he said what he *wanted* to do, he could be arrested. "I think I'll show instead of tell," he said and watched with satisfaction as her throat and face bloomed with color. He wondered if her blush extended to the rest of her body. It would be fun to find out.

Chapter 4

Two days later, Bridget's cell phone rang and her heart went pitter-patter at the number on the caller ID. "Hello," she said in a cool voice.

"Hello to you, Your Highness. How are you?" Ryder asked.

"I'm actually getting ready to make an appearance for a children's art program in Dallas," she said, smiling at the people who were waiting for her.

"Okay, I'll make this quick. Are you free tonight?"

She rolled her eyes. The man clearly had no idea how many demands were placed on her once people got word she was in the area. "I'm not often free but can sometimes make adjustments. What did you have in mind?"

"Swimming," he said.

"Excuse me?" she said.

"Swimming with the twins and pizza," he said.

"The pizza had better be fabulous. Ciao," she said and disconnected the call, but she felt a crazy surge of happiness zing through her as she followed the museum representatives inside the room where the children and press awaited.

Bridget gave a brief speech about the importance of art at all levels of society and dipped her hands and feet in purple paint. She stepped on a white sheet of paper, then pressed her handprints above and finished with her autograph.

The crowd applauded and she was technically done, but she stayed longer to talk to the children as they painted and worked on various projects. Their warmth and responsiveness made her feel less jaded, somehow less weary. Who would have thought it possible?

After extensive rearrangements of her schedule, Bridget put on her swimsuit and had second thoughts. What had possessed her to agree to join Ryder for a swim class when she was in a nearly naked state? She didn't have a perfectly slim body. In fact, if honest, she was curvy with pouches. Her bum was definitely larger than her top.

Her stomach clenched. Oh, bloody hell, she might as well be thirteen years old again. Forget it, she told herself. It wasn't as if anything could happen. She and Ryder would have two six-month-old chaperones.

Within forty-five minutes, she and Ryder stood in a pool with Tyler and Travis. Tyler stuck to her like glue, his eyes wide and fearful. "It's okay," she coaxed, bobbing gently in the water.

Ryder held Travis, who was screaming bloody murder.

"Are we having fun yet?" he asked, holding his godson securely.

"Should we sing?" she asked, trying not to be distracted by Ryder's broad shoulders and well-muscled arms and chest. For bloody's sake, when did the man have time to work out?

"They would throw us out," he said. "You look good in water."

She felt a rush of pleasure. "Thank you. Is Travis turning purple?"

"I think it's called rage," he said.

"Would you like to switch off for a moment?"

"Are you sure?" he asked doubtfully.

She nodded. "Let me give him a go," she said.

Tyler protested briefly at the exchange, then attached himself to Ryder. Travis continued to scream, so she lowered her mouth to his ear and began to quietly sing a lullaby from her childhood. Travis cried, but the sound grew less intense. She kept singing and he made sad little yelps, then finally quieted.

"Aren't you the magic one?" Ryder said.

"Luck," she said and cooed at the baby, swirling him around in the water. "Doesn't this feel good?" she murmured.

By the end of class, they'd switched off again and Travis was cackling and shrieking with joy as he splashed and kicked and Ryder whirled him around in the water.

As soon as they stepped from the pool, they wrapped the boys in snuggly towels. Ryder rubbed Travis's arms. She did the same with Tyler and he smiled at her. Her heart swelled at his sweetness. "You are such a good boy. Isn't he?" she said to Ryder.

"You bet," Ryder said and pressed his mouth against

Tyler's chubby cheek, making a buzzing sound. Tyler chortled with joy.

"That sound is magic," she said.

Ryder nodded as he continued to rub Travis. "Yeah, it is." His glance raked her from head to toe and he shook his head. "You look pretty damn good."

Bridget felt a warmth spread from her belly to her chest and face, down her legs, all the way to her toes. "It's just been a long time for you," she said and turned away to put some clothes on Tyler.

A second later, she felt Ryder's bare chest against her back. An immediate visceral response rocked through her and she was torn between jumping out of her skin and melting. "Yeah, it has," he said. "But that shouldn't make you so damn different from every other woman I've met."

Her stomach dipped. "Stop flattering me," she said. "Get your baby dressed. You don't want him chilled."

After pizza and a raucous bath time, Ryder and Bridget rocked the babies and put them to bed. Ryder would have preferred to usher Bridget into his bed and reacquaint himself with the curves he'd glimpsed in the pool, but he would have to bide his time. Hopefully not too long, he told himself as his gaze strayed to the way her hips moved in her cotton skirt. He'd thought he was so smart getting her out of most of her clothes by inviting her to the baby swimming class. Now he would live with those images all night long.

"Wine?" he asked, lifting a bottle from the kitchen before he joined her in the den.

She had sunk onto the sofa and leaned her head back against it, unintentionally giving him yet another seductive photo for his mental collection. One silky leg crossed over the other while the skirt hugged her hips. The V-neck of her black shirt gave him just a glimpse of creamy cleavage. For once, her lips were bare, but that didn't stop him from wanting to kiss her.

Her eyes opened to slight slits shrouded with the dark fan of her eyelashes. "One glass," she said. "I think everyone will sleep well tonight."

Speak for yourself, he thought wryly and poured her wine. He allowed himself one glass because he wasn't on call.

"It's amazing how much they can scream, isn't it?" she said as he sat beside her.

"They save up energy lying around all the time. It's not like they can play football or baseball yet."

"Have you thought about which sport you'll want them to pursue?" she asked.

"Whatever keeps them busy and tired. If they're busy and tired, they won't be as likely to get into trouble," he said.

"So that's the secret," she said with a slow smile. "Did that work for you?"

"Most of the time. I learned at a young age that I wanted a different life than the life my parents had."

"Hmm, at least you knew your parents," she said.

"Can't say knowing my father was one of my strong points."

"Well, you know what they say, if you can't be a good example, be a terrible warning."

He chuckled slightly and relaxed next to her. "I don't want to be the same kind of father he was. Drunk. Neglectful. Bordering on abusive."

"You couldn't be those things," she said.

"Why not? You've heard the saying, an apple doesn't fall too far from the tree."

"You've already fallen a long way from that so-called tree," she said. "Plus, you may be fighting some of your feelings, but you love those boys." She lifted her hand to his jaw. "You have a good heart. I liked that about you from the first time I met you."

"And I thought it was my singing voice," he said and lowered his mouth to hers, reveling in the anticipation he felt inside and saw in her eyes.

She tasted like a delicious combination of red wine, tiramisu and something forbidden that he wasn't going to resist. Ryder was certain he could resist her if he wanted. If there was one thing Ryder possessed, it was self-discipline. The quality had been necessary to get him through med school, residency and even more so now in his position at the hospital and with the twins.

For now, though, Ryder had decided he didn't want to resist Bridget. With her lush breasts pressing against his chest, discipline was the last thing on his mind. She was so voluptuously female from her deceptively airy attitude to her curvy body. He slid one of his hands through her hair as she wiggled against him.

A groan of pleasure and want rose from his throat as she deepened the kiss, drawing his tongue into her mouth. The move echoed what he wanted to be doing with the rest of his body and hers. He wrapped his hands around her waist. He slid one down to her hips and the other upward to just under her breast.

He was so hard that he almost couldn't breathe. She was so soft, so feminine, so hot. With every beat of his heart, he craved her. He wanted to consume her, to slide inside her....

Ryder slid his hand to her breast, cupping its fullness. Her nipple peaked against his palm. The fire inside him rising, he tugged a few buttons of her blouse loose and slipped his hand under her bra, touching her bare skin, which made him want to touch every inch of her. He couldn't remember wanting to inhale a woman before.

The next natural step would be to remove her clothes and his and after that, caress her with his hands and mouth. After that, he wanted to slide inside her…. She would be so hot, so wet….

All he wanted was to be as close to her as humanly possible.

From some peripheral area of his brain, he heard a knock and then another. Her body and soul called to him. He took her mouth in another deep kiss.

Another knock sounded, this time louder, but Ryder was determined to ignore it.

Suddenly his front door opened and Marshall burst into the room.

"Whoa," Marshall said. "Sorry to interrupt."

Ryder felt Bridget pull back and hastily arrange her shirt. "Who—" she said in a breathless voice.

"My best friend from high school, Marshall," Ryder said. "He has a key," he continued in a dark voice.

Marshall lifted his hands. "Hey, I called and you didn't answer. I started getting worried. You almost always answer at night. We've had a beer three times during the last week." His friend stared at Bridget and gave a low whistle. "And who do we have here?"

Irritated, Ryder scowled. "Show a little respect. Prin—" He stopped when Bridget pinched his arm. Staring at her in disbelief, he could see that she didn't want him to reveal her title. "Bridget Devereaux, this is Marshall Bailey."

His friend moved forward and extended his hand. Bridget stood and accepted the courtesy.

"Nice to meet you, Bridget," Marshall said. "It's a relief to see Ryder with a woman."

Embarrassment slammed through Ryder and he also stood. "Marshall," he said in a warning tone.

"I didn't mean that the way it sounded. The poor guy hasn't had much company except me and the twins." Marshall cleared his throat. "How did you two meet anyway?"

"Okay, enough, Mr. Busybody. As you can see, I'm fine, so you can leave."

"Oh no, that's not necessary," Bridget said and glanced at her watch. "I really should be leaving. I have an early flight tomorrow."

"Where?" Ryder asked.

"Chicago. They have a teaching hospital. I'll be meeting with the hospital chief to present the proposal for Chantaine's medical exchange."

"Oh," he said, surprised at the gut punch of disappointment he felt when he should feel relieved. "I guess this means you've given up on our residents."

"No, but you haven't been at all receptive. My brother Stefan has instructed me to explore other possibilities. Your program was our first choice due to the quality of your residents and also the fact that you have so many family doctors and prevention specialists. But because you're unwilling to help…"

"For Pete's sake, Ryder, help the woman out," Marshall said and moved forward. "Is there anything I can do?"

Marshall was really getting on Ryder's nerves. "Not

unless you have a medical degree and are licensed to practice," Ryder said.

"I believe my driver is here. Thank you for an action-packed evening," she said with a smile full of sexy amusement.

Ryder would have preferred a different kind of action. "I'll walk you to the car," he said, then shot a quick glance at Marshall. "I'll be back in a minute."

Ryder escorted Bridget to the limo waiting at the curb. A man stood ready to open the door for her. Ryder was disappointed as hell that she was headed out of town. Stupid. "So how long will you be gone?" he asked.

She lifted a dark eyebrow and her lips tilted in a teasing grin. "Are you going to miss me, Dr. McCall?"

His gut twisted. "That would be crazy. The only thing I've been missing for the last month is sleep," he lied.

"Oh, well, maybe you'll get lucky and get some extra sleep while I'm gone. Ta-ta," she said and turned toward the limo.

He caught her wrist and drew her back against him. The man at the car door took a step toward them, but she waved her hand. "Not necessary, Raoul."

"You must enjoy tormenting me," he said.

"Me?" she said, her blue eyes wide with innocence. "How could I possibly have the ability to torment you?"

"I don't know, but you sure as hell do," he muttered and kissed her, which only served to make him hotter. He turned her own words on her. "So, Your Highness, what are you going to do about it?"

She gave a sharp intake of breath and her eyes darkened as if her mind were working the same way as his.

She bit her lip. "I can call you when I return from Chicago."

"Do that," he said.

Ryder returned to his house to find Marshall lounging on the sofa and drinking a glass of red wine. "This isn't bad," he said.

"Glad you like it. In the future, give me a call before you drop in. Okay?"

Marshall looked injured. "I did call you. You just didn't answer." He shook his head and gave a low whistle. "And now I understand why. That's one hot babe, and she reeks money. A limo came to pick her up? You sure know how to pick 'em. How did you meet her?"

"In an elevator," Ryder said, not wanting to give away too many details. As much as he liked his old friend, Ryder knew Marshall could gossip worse than an old lady.

"Really?" Marshall said, dumbfounded. "An elevator. Was it just you and her? Did you do anything— adventurous?"

"Not the way you're thinking," Ryder said in a dry tone, although if it had been just him and Bridget in that elevator without the twins, his mind would have gone in the same direction.

"Well, I'm glad you're finally getting some action," Marshall said.

Ryder swore. "I'd say you pretty much nixed that tonight. Between you and the twins, who needs birth control?"

Marshall chuckled. "Sorry, bud, better luck next time. I thought I'd see if Suzanne was hanging around tonight. She stays late for you sometimes."

Realization struck Ryder. "You didn't come by to see

me. You came to see my nanny. I'm telling you now. Keep your hands off my nanny. She's not your type."

"Who says?"

"I say."

"Why isn't she my type? She's pretty. She's nice," he said.

"She's six years older than you are," Ryder said.

"So? She doesn't look it. She's got a fresh look about her and she's sweet. Got a real nice laugh," Marshall said.

"I'm not liking what I'm hearing," Ryder said, stepping between Marshall and the television. "So far, Suzanne is the perfect nanny. I don't want you messing with her. The boys and I need her."

"She's an adult. She can decide if she wants me to mess with her," he said with a shrug.

"Marshall," he said in a dead-serious voice. "She's not like your dime-a-dozen girls running fast and loose. She's not used to a guy like you who'll get her in the sack and leave her like yesterday's garbage."

Marshall winced. "No need to insult me. I've had a few long-term relationships."

"Name them," Ryder challenged.

"Well, there was that redhead, Wendy. She and I saw each other for at least a couple of years."

"She lived out of town, didn't she?" Ryder asked. "How many other women were you seeing at the same time?"

Marshall scowled. "Okay, what about Sharona? We lived together."

"For how long?"

"Seven weeks, but—"

"Enough said. Keep your paws off Suzanne."

Marshall slugged down the rest of the wine and stood. "You know, I'm not a rotten guy."

"Never said you were."

"I just haven't ever found the right girl," Marshall said.

"As long as you and I understand that Suzanne is not the right girl for you, everything will be fine."

Three days later, Bridget returned from her trip to Chicago. She hadn't snagged any doctors, but she'd persuaded one of the specialists she'd met to visit Chantaine and offer lectures and demonstrations. She was getting closer to her goal. She could feel it. Even though what she really wanted to do tonight was soak in a tub and watch television, she was committed to attend a charity event for Alzheimer's with the governor's son, who was actually quite a bit older than she was. Part of the job, she told herself as she got ready. She thought about calling Ryder, but every time she thought about him, she felt a jumpiness in her stomach. Bridget wasn't sure how far she wanted to go with him because she knew she would be leaving Dallas as soon as she accomplished her mission.

There was something about the combination of his strength and passion that did things to her. It was exciting. And perplexing.

Preferring to have her own chauffeur, Bridget met Robert Goodwin, the governor's son, in the lobby of her hotel. He was a distinguished-looking man in his mid-forties who reminded her of one of her uncles. She decided that was how she would treat him.

Her bodyguard Raoul, who occasionally played double duty in making introductions, stepped forward. "Your Highness, Robert Goodwin."

She nodded and extended her hand. "Lovely to meet you, Mr. Goodwin. Thank you for escorting me to an event that will raise awareness for such an important cause."

"My pleasure, Your Highness," he said, surprising her when he brought her hand to his mouth. "Please call me Robert. May I say that you look breathtaking?"

"Thank you very much, Robert. Shall we go?"

By the time they arrived at the historical hall, Bridget concluded that Mr. Goodwin's intentions were not at all uncle-like and she prepared herself for a sticky evening. Cameras flashed as they exited the limo and Mr. Goodwin appeared to want to linger for every possible photo as he bragged about her title to the reporters.

"Everyone is excited to have a real princess at the event tonight. People paid big bucks to sit at our table."

"I'm delighted I could help the cause." Sometimes it amazed her that a single spermatozoa had determined her status. And that spermatozoa had originated from a cheating jerk of a man who had never gotten her first name right. Her father.

"Would you join me in a dance?" Robert said, his gaze dipping to her cleavage.

"Thank you, but I need to powder my nose," she said. "Can you tell me where the ladies' room is?"

Robert blinked. "I believe it's down the hall to the left."

"Excuse me," she said and headed for the restroom, fully aware that Raoul was watching. She wondered if she could plead illness. After stalling for several moments, she left and slowly walked toward her table. Halfway there, Ryder stepped in front of her.

"Busy as ever," he said.

Her heart raced at the sight of him. "So true. I arrived back in town this afternoon and had to turn right around to get ready for this event."

"With the governor's son," Ryder said, clearly displeased.

"He could be my uncle," she said.

"Bet that's not what he's thinking," Ryder countered.

She grimaced and shrugged. "It's not the first time I've had to manage unwelcome interest, and if my appearance generates additional income for this good cause…"

"True," he said, his eyes holding a misery that grabbed at her.

"What brings you here?"

"Dr. Walters. He has had an impact on hundreds of doctors, but now he can't recognize himself in the mirror."

"I'm so sorry," she said, her heart hurting at the expression on his face. "Seeing you, hearing you, makes me glad I came. I'm ashamed to confess that I was tempted to cancel because I was so tired after returning from Chicago."

His gaze held hers for a long emotional moment. "I'm glad you didn't give in to your weariness this time."

"Even though I have to face Mr. Anything-but-Good Robert Goodwin," she said.

"Give me a sign and I'll have your back," he said.

She took a deep breath. "That's good to know. I can usually handle things. This isn't the first time."

His gaze swept over her from head to toe and back again. "That's no surprise."

Her stomach dipped and she cleared her throat. "I should get back to my table. I'm told people paid to sit with me. I'm sure it has nothing to do with my title."

His lips twitched. "Not if they really knew you," he said.

"You flatter me," she said.

"Not because you're a princess," he said.

"Call me tomorrow."

"I will," he said.

Bridget returned to her table and tried to be her most charming self and at the same time not encouraging Robert Goodwin. It was challenging, but she was determined.

After the meal had been served, he turned to her. "I'm determined to dance with you."

"I'm not that good of a dancer," she assured him.

He laughed, his gaze dipping over her cleavage again. "I'm a good leader," he said and rose, extending his hand to her. "Let me surprise you."

Or not, she thought wishing with all her heart that he wouldn't surprise her. She didn't want to embarrass the man. She lifted her lips in a careful smile. "One dance," she said and stood.

They danced to a waltz, but he somehow managed to rub against her. She tried to back away, but he wrapped his hands around her waist like a vise, drawing him against her. Suddenly, she saw Ryder behind Robert Goodwin, his hand on his shoulder. Robert appeared surprised.

"Can I cut in?" Ryder asked.

Robert frowned. "I'm not—"

"Yes," Bridget said. "It's only proper."

Robert reluctantly released her and Ryder swept her into his arms.

"Thank goodness," she murmured.

He wrapped his arms around her and it felt entirely different than it had with Robert. She stared into his eyes and felt a shockwave roll through her. "When did you learn to dance?"

"A generous woman taught me during medical school," he said, drawing her closer, yet not too close.

Bridget felt a spike of envy but forced it aside. "She did an excellent job."

He chuckled. "It was all preparation," he said. "Everything we do is preparation for what waits for us in the future."

"I would have to be quite arrogant to think your preparation was for me," she said, feeling light-headed.

"You look beautiful tonight," he said, clearly changing the subject. "I hate having to share you with anyone else."

Her stomach dipped. "It's part of who I was born to be. Duty calls," she said.

"But what does Bridget want?" he challenged. "Meet me in the foyer in fifteen minutes."

"How?" she asked.

"You'll figure it out," he said.

Chapter 5

She would figure it out, Bridget thought as she surreptitiously glanced at the diamond-encrusted watch that had belonged to her grandmother. Two minutes to go and she was supposed to be introduced to the crowd within the next moment.

"As we continue to introduce our honored guests, we'd like to present Her Highness, Princess Bridget Devereaux of the country of Chantaine."

Bridget stood and smiled and waved to the applauding crowd. She hadn't known she was a table head, but it wasn't unusual for event organizers to put her in the spotlight given the chance. Because of her title, she was a source of curiosity and interest.

Spotting Ryder leaning against the back wall as he pointed to his watch, she quickly squeezed her hand together and flashed her five fingers, indicating she needed more time. Then she sank into her seat.

Robert leaned toward her. "I was cheated out of my dance. We need to hit the floor again."

"I wish I could, but my ankle is hurting," she said.

Robert scowled. "Maybe because of the man who cut in on our dance."

She lifted her shoulders. "Perhaps it's the long day catching up with me."

"You're too generous. We could try a slow dance," he said in a low voice.

"Oh no, I couldn't hurt your feet that way," she said. "But I would like to freshen up. Please excuse me," she said and rose, wondering why she was going to such extremes to meet Ryder when she was supposed to be concentrating on making an appearance.

Her heart was slamming against her rib cage as she tried to take a sideways route through the tables along the perimeter of the room. With every step, part of her chanted *This is crazy—this is crazy.* But she kept on walking, so she must indeed be crazy. She stepped into the foyer and glanced around the area.

Something snagged her hand. She glanced over her shoulder and spotted Ryder as he pulled her with him down a hallway. "Where are we—"

"Trust me," he said and pulled her toward the first door they came upon. It was an empty dark room with a stack of chairs pushed against a wall.

"What are we doing?" she asked, breathlessly clinging to him.

"Hell if I know," he said, sliding his hands through her hair and tilting her head toward his. "I feel like a car with no brakes headed straight for you."

"So, we're both crazy," she said.

"Looks that way," he said and lowered his mouth to hers.

Her knees turned to water and she clung to him. His strength made her feel alive despite how tired she felt from her long day of travel. Shocked at his effect on her, she loved the sensation of his hard chest against her breasts. She wanted to feel his naked skin against hers. She growled, unable to get close enough.

He swore under his breath as his hands roamed over her waist and up to the sides of her breasts. "I can't get enough of you," he muttered and took her mouth in a deep kiss again.

She felt dizzy with a want and need she denied on a regular basis. It was as if she was suffering from a more delicious version of altitude sickness. His mouth against hers made her hotter with every stroke of his tongue. More than anything, she wanted to feel him against her.

"Ryder," she whispered, tugging at his tie and dropping her mouth to his neck.

He gave a groan of arousal. "Come home with me. Now," he said, squeezing her derriere with one hand and clasping her breast with the other.

Too tempted for words, she felt the tug and pull of duty and courtesy over her own needs. Bloody hell, why couldn't she just this once be selfish, irresponsible and rude? A sound of complete frustration bubbled from her throat. Because she just couldn't. She was in the States on official business from Chantaine and she'd been assigned to represent a cause important to her and her people.

"I can't," she finally managed. "It would just be wrong and rude and it's not just about me. I'm sorry," she whispered.

"I don't know what it is about you, but you make me want to be more reckless than I've ever been in my life. More reckless than flying down Deadman's Hill on my bicycle with no hands when I was ten."

Bridget felt the same way, but she was holding on by the barest thread of self-restraint. Suddenly the door whooshed open and closed, sending her heart into her throat. Her head cleared enough to realize this situation could provide the press with an opportunity to paint her family in a bad light.

She held her breath, waiting for a voice, but none sounded.

"It's okay," he said as if he understood without her saying a word. "Whoever opened the door must have glanced inside and not spotted us. I'll leave first, then you wait a minute or two before you leave. I'll warn you if it looks like there's a crowd waiting for you."

She paused, then nodded slowly.

Ryder gave her shoulders a reassuring squeeze and kissed her quickly, then walked toward the door. Bridget stood frozen to the floor for several breaths and gave herself a quick shake. She moved to the door and listened, but the door was too thick. She couldn't hear anything. Counting to a hundred, she cracked open the door and peeked outside. No crowd. No photogs. Relief coursed through her and she stepped outside.

"Your Highness, I was worried about you," Robert said from behind her.

Her stomach muscles tightened and she quickly turned. "Robert, how kind of you."

"What were you doing in there?" he asked.

"My sense of direction is dismal," she said. "I went

right when I should have turned left. Thank you for coming to my rescue. Now I can return to our table."

He slid his hand behind her waist and she automatically stiffened, but he seemed to ignore her response. "We can leave, if you like. I could take you to my condo…."

"Again, you're being kind, but we're here for an important cause."

"Afterward—"

"It's been a full day for me flying from Chicago. I appreciate your understanding that I'll be desperate to finally retire," she said. One of her advisers had instructed her that one should speak to another person as if they possessed good qualities…even if they didn't.

"Another time, then," Robert said, clearly disappointed.

Bridget gave a noncommittal smile, careful not to offer any false hope.

When Bridget didn't hear from Ryder for three days, she began to get peeved. Actually, she was peeved after day one. He'd behaved like he was starving for her and couldn't wait another moment, then didn't call. She considered calling him at least a dozen times, but her busy schedule aided her in her restraint.

On Tuesday, however, she was scheduled to meet with a preventative adult health specialist in preparation for a video she would be filming with the doctor as a public service announcement for Chantaine.

Afterward, she meandered down the hall past his office. She noticed Ryder wasn't there, but his assistant was. Bridget gave in to temptation and stepped into the office. "Hello. I was wondering if Dr. McCall is in today."

The assistant sighed. "Dr. McCall is making rounds and seeing interns, but he may need to leave early for family reasons. May I take a message?"

"Not necessary," she demurred, but wondered what those family reasons were. "Are the twins okay?" she couldn't help asking.

The assistant nodded. "I think so. It's the nanny—" The phone rang. "Excuse me."

The nanny! The nanny she'd selected for Ryder and the boys had been as perfect as humanly possible. Perhaps more perfect. What could have possibly happened? Resisting the urge to grill the assistant about her, she forced herself to walk away. Her fingers itched to call him, but she didn't. It would be rude to interrupt his appointments with patients or the residents.

Bothered, bothered, bothered, she stalked through the hallway. The pediatric department head saw her and stopped in front of her, smiling. "Your Highness, what a pleasure to see you."

"Thank you, Doctor. How are you?" she said more than asked.

"Great. Would you like to get together for dinner?" he asked.

"I would, but I must confess my immediate schedule is quite demanding. Perhaps some other time," she said.

"I'll keep asking," he said and gave her a charming smile that didn't move her one iota.

Brooding, she walked down the hall and out of the hospital to the limo that awaited her. A text would be less intrusive, she decided, and sent a message. Two minutes later, she received a response. *Nanny had emergency appendectomy. Juggling with backup.*

WHY DIDN'T YOU CALL ME? she texted in return.

Her phone rang one moment later and she answered. "Hello."

"It's been crazy. I've even had to ask Marshall for help."

"Why didn't you ask me?" she demanded.

"You told me your schedule was picking up. I figured you wouldn't have time," he said.

True, she thought, but she was still bothered. "You still should have called me."

"You're a busy princess. What could you have done?" he asked.

Good question. She closed her eyes. "I could have rearranged my schedule so I could help you."

Silence followed. "You would do that?"

She bit her lip. "Yes."

"I didn't think of that."

"Clearly," she said.

He chuckled. "In that case, can you come over tomorrow afternoon? My part-time nanny needs a break."

"I'll confirm by five o'clock tonight," she said. "I have to make a few calls."

"Impressive," he said. "I bet your reschedules are going to be disappointed. Too bad," he said without a trace of sympathy.

She laughed. "I'll call you later," she said and they hung up and her heart felt ten times lighter.

The following afternoon, Bridget relieved the backup nanny while the twins were sleeping. From previous experience, she knew her moments of silence were numbered. She used the time to prepare bottles and snacks for the boys.

Sure enough, the first cry sounded. She raced upstairs and opened the door. Travis was sitting up in his crib wearing a frowny face.

"Hello, sweet boy," she whispered.

He paused mid-wail and stared at her wide-eyed.

"Hi," she whispered and smiled.

Travis smiled and lifted his fingers to his mouth.

Bridget changed his diaper. Seconds later, Tyler awakened and began to babble. Tyler was the happier baby. He was a bit more fearful, but when he woke up, he didn't start crying immediately.

Bridget wound Travis's mobile and turned her attention to Tyler. She took each baby downstairs ready to put them in their high chairs. Snacks, bottles, books, Baby Einstein and finally Ryder arrived carrying a bottle of wine.

"How's everybody?" he asked, his gaze skimming over her and the boys, then back to her. "Did they wear you out?"

"Not too much yet," she said. "It helps to have a plan."

He nodded. "With alternatives. I ordered Italian, not pizza. It should be delivered soon."

"Thank you," she said.

"I'm hoping to lure you into staying the night," he said.

"Ha, ha," she said. "The trouble with luring me after an afternoon with the twins is that I'll be comatose by nine o'clock at the latest. I talked to your part-time sitter and she told me Suzanne will be out for a few more days. Is that true?"

He nodded. "She had laparoscopic surgery, so her recovery should be much easier than if she'd had an open appendectomy."

"Then I think the next step is to get a list of your backup sitters and inform them of the situation and make a schedule for the children's care. So if you don't mind giving me your names and contact information, I can try to get it straight tomorrow."

He blinked at her in amazement. "You're deceptively incredible," he said. "You give this impression of being lighthearted and maybe a little superficial. Then you turn around and volunteer to take care of my boys, recruit doctors for your country and make countless appearances."

"Oooh, I like that. Deceptively incredible," she said, a bit embarrassed by his flattery. "Many of us are underestimated. It can be a hindrance and a benefit. I try to find the benefit."

Ryder leaned toward her, studying her face. "Have you always been underestimated?"

She considered his question for a moment, then nodded. "I think so. I'm number four out of six and female, so I think I got lost in the mix. I'm not sure my father ever really knew my name, and my mother was beginning to realize that her marriage to my father was not going to be a fairy tale."

"Why not?"

"You must swear to never repeat this," she said.

"I swear, although I'm not sure anyone I know would be interested," he said.

"True enough," she said. "My father was a total philanderer. Heaven knows, my mother tried. I mean, six children? She was a true soldier, though, and gave him two sons. Bless her."

"So what do you want for yourself?" he asked. "You don't want the kind of marriage your parents had."

"Who would?" she said and took a deep breath. "I haven't thought a lot about it. Whenever Stefan has brought up the idea of my marrying someone, I just start laughing and don't stop. Infuriates the blazes out of him," she said, and smiled.

"You didn't answer my question," he said.

His eyes felt as if they bored a hole through her brain, and Bridget realized one of the reasons she was drawn to Ryder was because she couldn't fool him. It was both a source of frustration and relief.

"I'm still figuring it out. For a long time, I've enjoyed the notion of being the eccentric princess who lives in Italy most of the year and always has an Italian boyfriend as her escort."

"Italian boyfriend," he echoed, clearly not pleased.

"You have to agree, it's the antithesis of my current life."

"And I suspect this life wouldn't include children," he continued with a frown.

Feeling defensive, she bit her lip. "Admit it. The life you'd planned didn't include children...at least for a long while, did it?"

He hesitated.

"Be honest. I was," she said.

"No," he finally admitted. "But not because I was in Italy with an Italian girlfriend."

"No, you were planning to do something more important. A career in medicine. Perfectly noble and worthy, but it would be hard to make a child a priority when you have the kind of passion you do for your career. A child would be...inconvenient."

He took a deep breath. "We choose our careers for many reasons. I wanted to feel like I had the power to help, to cure, to make a difference. It was more important for me to feel as if I were accomplishing those goals than building a family life." He shrugged. "My family life sucked."

"There you go," she said in complete agreement. "My family life sucked, too. In fact, I wanted to get so far away from it that I wanted to move to a different country."

He chuckled. "So how is it that Princess Bridget is changing diapers and taking care of my twins?"

Bridget resisted the urge to squirm. "I won't lie. I once thought children were a lot of trouble and not for me, but then I got a couple of adorable nieces. I still thought I wouldn't want to deal with them for more than a couple hours at most with the nanny at hand to change diapers, of course." She bit her lip. "But it's just so different when they're looking at you with those big eyes, helpless and needing you…. And it would just feel so terribly wrong not to take care of them."

"And how do I fit into it?" he asked, dipping his head toward her.

"You are just an annoying distraction," she said in a mockingly dismissive whisper.

"Well, at least I'm distracting," he said and lowered his mouth to hers.

Bridget felt herself melt into the leather upholstery. She inhaled his masculine scent and went dizzy with want. He was the one thing she'd never had but always wanted and couldn't get enough of. How could that be? She'd been exposed to everything and every kind of person, hadn't she?

But Ryder was different.

She drew his tongue deeper into her mouth and slid her arms around his neck. Unable to stop herself, she wiggled against him and moaned. He groaned in approval, which jacked her up even more.

From some corner of her mind, she heard a sound. "Eh."

Pushing it aside, she continued to kiss Ryder.

"Eh."

Bridget frowned, wondering....

"Wahhhhhhh."

She reluctantly tore her mouth from Ryder's. "The babies," she murmured breathlessly, glancing down at Travis as he tuned up. The baby had fallen on his side and he couldn't get back up.

"Yeah, I know," Ryder said. "I'm starting to understand the concept of unrequited l—"

"Longing," she finished for him because she couldn't deal with Ryder saying the four-letter L word. It wasn't possible.

"Bet there's a dirty diaper involved," Ryder muttered as he tilted Travis upright.

"Could be," she said and couldn't bring herself to offer to change it. She covered her laugh by clearing her throat. "I wouldn't want to deprive you of your fatherly duty."

He gave her a slow, sexy grin. "I'll just bet you wouldn't."

"It's an important bonding activity," she said, trying to remain serious, but a giggle escaped.

"Can't hold it against you too much," he said. "You've been here all afternoon."

Bridget rose to try to collect herself. Her emotions were all over the place. Walking to the downstairs powder room, she closed the door behind her and splashed water against her cheeks and throat. Sanity, she desperately needed sanity.

The doorbell rang and she returned as Ryder tossed the diaper into the trash before he answered the door. He paid the delivery man and turned around, and Bridget felt her heart dip once, twice, three times.... Adrenaline rushed through her, and she tried to remember a charming, gorgeous Italian man who had affected her this way. When had any man affected her this way?

Oh, heavens, she needed to get away from him. She felt like that superhero. What was his name? Superman. And Ryder was that substance guaranteed to weaken him. What was it? Started with a K...

"Smells good. Hope you like lasagna," Ryder said.

"I can't stay," she said.

"What?" he asked, his brow furrowing.

"I can't stay. I have work to do," she said.

"What work?" he asked.

"Rescheduling my meetings and appearances. I also need to take care of the childcare arrangements for the twins."

He walked slowly toward her, his gaze holding hers. She felt her stomach tumble with each of his steps. "You're not leaving because you have work to do, are you?"

She lifted her chin. "I'm a royal. I always have work to do."

He cupped her chin with his hand. "But the reason you're leaving is not because of work, is it?"

Her breath hitched in her throat.

"You're a chicken, aren't you?" he said. "Princess Cluck Cluck."

"That was rude," she said.

"Cluck, cluck," he said and pressed his mouth against hers.

After making the schedule for the twins' care, Bridget paid her sister an overdue visit. Valentina had threatened to personally drag her away from Dallas if Bridget didn't come to the ranch. Her sister burst down the steps to the porch as Bridget's limo pulled into the drive.

"Thank goodness you're finally here," Tina said.

Bridget laughed as she embraced her sister. "You act like I've been gone for years."

"I thought you would be spending far more time here, but you've been appearing at events, traveling to Chicago. And what's this about you helping that physician with his twin babies? Haven't you helped him enough?"

"It's complicated," Bridget said. "He's had some childcare issues. I think they're mostly resolved now."

"Well, good. I think you've helped him quite enough. Now you can spend some time with me," Tina said as she led Bridget into the house. "I have wonderful plans for us. Two aestheticians are coming to the ranch tomorrow to give massages and facials then we spend the afternoon at the lake."

"Lake?" Bridget echoed. All she'd seen was dry land.

"It's wonderful," Tina reassured her. "The summer heat and humidity can get unbearable here. We have a pond with a swing, but we're going to the lake because Zach got a new boat. Zach and one of his friends will be joining us tomorrow afternoon. Then we'll have baby back ribs for dinner."

Bridget's antennae went up at the mention of Zach's friend. "You're not trying to set me up, are you?"

"Of course not. I just thought you'd enjoy some no-pressure male companionship. Troy is just a nice guy. He also happens to be good-looking and eligible. And if you two should hit it off, then you could live close to me and—" Tina paused and a guilty expression crossed her face. "Okay, it's a little bit of a setup. But not too much," she said quickly. "Troy and Zach are business associates, so we'll have to drag them away from talk about the economy."

Bridget's mind automatically turned to Ryder. There was no reason for her to feel even vaguely committed to him. Her stomach tightened. What did that mean? she wondered. "I'm not really looking right now," Bridget said.

"I know," Tina said. "As soon as you take care of the doctor project, you're off to Italy and part of that will include flirtations with any Italian man who grabs your fancy. But if someone here grabs your fancy…"

"Tina," Bridget said in a warning voice.

"I hear you," Tina said. "Let's focus on your amazing niece."

"Sounds good to me. I've missed the little sweetheart," Bridget said as they walked into the kitchen.

"Missed her, but not me!" Tina said.

Bridget laughed. "I adore you. Why are you giving me such a hard time?"

Tina lifted her hand to Bridget's face and looked deep into her gaze. "I don't know. I worry about you. I wonder what's going on inside you. You smile, you laugh, but there's a darkness in your eyes."

Bridget's heart dipped at her sister's sensitivity, then she deadpanned. "Maybe it's my new eyeliner."

Tina rolled her eyes. "You're insufferable. I always said that about Stefan, but you're the same, just in a different way."

"I believe I've just been insulted," Bridget said.

"You'll get over it. Hildie made margaritas for us and she always makes doubles."

Chapter 6

Bridget's morning massage coupled with one of Hildie's margaritas had turned her bones to butter. By the time she joined Tina, Zach and Troy on the boat, she was so relaxed that she could have gone to sleep for a good two hours. For politeness' sake, she tried to stay awake, although she kept her dark sunglasses firmly in place to hide her drooping eyelids.

Troy Palmer was a lovely Texas gentleman, a bit bulkier than Ryder. Of course Ryder was so busy he rarely took time to eat. A server offered shrimp and lobster while they lounged on the boat.

"Nice ride," Troy said to Zach.

Zach smiled as Tina leaned against his chest. "My wife thought I was crazy. She said I would be too busy."

"Time will tell," Tina said. "But if this makes you take a few more breaks, then I'm happy."

"You're not neglecting my sister, are you?" Bridget asked as she sipped a bottle of icy cold water.

Zach lifted a dark eyebrow. "There's a fine line between being the companion and keeper of a princess."

"I believe that's what you Americans call baloney. You work because you must. It's the kind of man you are. I love you for it," Tina said. "But I also love the time we have together."

Zach's face softened. "I love you, too, sweetheart."

Bridget cleared her throat. "We're delighted that you love each other," Bridget said. "But I'm going to have to dive overboard if we don't change the subject."

Tina giggled. "As you wish. Troy, tell us about your latest trip to Italy."

"Italy?" Bridget echoed.

"I thought that might perk you up," Tina said.

Troy shrugged his shoulders. "I go three or four times a year. Business, but I usually try to work in a trip to Florence."

"Oh, Florence," Bridget said longingly. "One of my favorite places in the world."

Troy nodded. "Yeah, I also like to slip down to Capri every now and then…"

Bridget's cell phone vibrated in the pocket of her cover-up draped over the side of her chair. She tried to ignore it, but wondered if Ryder was calling her. Dividing her attention between Troy's discussion about Italy and thoughts of Ryder, she nodded even though she wasn't hanging onto his every word. Her phone vibrated again and she was finding it difficult to concentrate.

She grabbed her cover-up and stood. "Please excuse me. I need to powder my nose."

"To the right and downstairs," Zach said. "And it's small," he warned.

"No problem," she said cheerfully and walked around the corner. She lifted her phone to listen to her messages. As she listened, her heart sank. Tomorrow's sitter was canceling. She was calling Bridget because Ryder was in surgery and unreachable.

Pacing at the other end of the boat, she tried the other backup sitters and came up empty. Reluctantly, she called Marshall who answered immediately.

"Marshall," he said. "'Sup?"

"Hello, Marshall," she said. "This is Bridget Devereaux."

"The princess," he said. Ryder had told her that Marshall had performed a web search and learned who she was. "Princess calling me. That's cool."

"Yes," she said, moving toward the other end of the boat. "There's some difficulty with sitting arrangements for Ryder's boys tomorrow morning. I was hoping you could help me with a solution."

"Tomorrow morning," he said. "Whoa, that's a busy day for me."

"Yes, I'm so sorry. I would normally try to fill in, but I'm out of town at the moment," she said.

"I might have a friend—"

"No," she said. "As you know, Ryder is very particular about his backup sitters. He won't leave the twins with just anyone."

"True," Marshall said. "Although I'm last on the list." Silence followed.

"I'm last on the list, aren't I?" Marshall asked.

"Well, you're an entrepreneur," she managed. "Ryder

knows you're a busy man with many demands on your time."

"Yeah," Marshall said. "How much time does he need?"

"Five hours," she said, wincing as she said it.

Marshall whistled. "That's gonna be tough."

"Let me see what I can do," she said. "I'll make some more calls."

"If you can have someone cover things in the early morning, I could probably come in around ten."

"Thank you so much. I'll do my very best," she said.

"Bridget," Tina said from behind her.

"Bloody hell," she muttered.

Marshall chuckled.

"To whom are you speaking?" Tina demanded.

"A friend," Bridget said. "Forgive me, Marshall. My sister is after me."

"Good luck. Keep me posted," he said.

"Yes, I will," she said and clicked off the phone. She turned to face her sister with a smile. "I'm just working out the timing of an appearance."

"Which appearance is that?" Tina asked.

"In Dallas," Bridget said. "I must say I do love Zach's new toy. I think it will be a fabulous way for the two of you to relax."

"Exactly which appearance in Dallas?" Tina said, studying her with narrowed eyes.

"Stop being so nosy," Bridget said.

Tina narrowed her eyes further. "This is about that doctor with the twins, isn't it?"

"His sitter for tomorrow has cancelled so we have to find another."

"We?"

Bridget sighed. "If you met him, you'd understand. He performs surgery, advises residents and he's an instant father."

"Perhaps he should take some time off to be with his new children," Tina muttered.

"It's not that easy. His mentor has Alzheimer's and he's trying to fill his position unofficially."

Tina studied her. "You're not falling for him, are you?"

Bridget gave a hearty laugh at the same time she fought the terror in her soul. "Of course not. You know I prefer Italian men."

Tina paused, then nodded. "True, and although you love your nieces, you've always said you couldn't imagine having children before you were thirty."

"Exactly," she said, though she felt a strange twinge.

"Hmm," Tina said, still studying her. "Is this doctor good-looking?"

Bridget shrugged. Yes, Ryder was very good-looking, but that wasn't why she found him so compelling. Giving herself a mental eye roll, she knew Tina wouldn't understand. "He's fine," she said. "But he's not Italian."

Tina giggled and put her arm around Bridget. "Now that's our Bridget. That's the kind of answer I would expect from you. Come back and relax with us."

Bridget smiled, but part of her felt uncomfortable. She knew what Tina was saying, that Bridget wasn't a particularly deep person. The truth was she'd never wanted to be deep. If she thought too deeply, she suspected she could become depressed. After all, she'd been a fairly average child, not at all spectacular. She hadn't flunked out in school, but she hadn't excelled at anything either. Except at being cheerful. Or pretending to be cheerful.

"I'll be there in just a moment. I need to make a few calls first."

"Very well, but don't take too long. Troy may not be Italian, but he's very good-looking and spends a fair amount of time in Italy."

"Excellent point," Bridget said, although she felt not the faintest flicker of interest in the man. "I'll be there shortly."

Several moments later, Bridget used all her charm to get the part-time sitter to fill in for the morning. Relieved, she called Marshall to inform him of the change.

"Hey, did you hear from Ryder?" he asked before she could get a word in edgewise.

"No. Should I have?" she asked, confused. "I thought he was in surgery."

"He's apparently out. He just called to tell me Dr. Walters passed away this morning," Marshall said.

Bridget's heart sank. "Oh no."

"Yeah. He's taking it hard. He hadn't seen Dr. Walters in a while and he'd been planning to try to visit him later this week." Marshall sighed. "Dr. Walters was the closest thing to a father Ryder had."

Bridget felt so helpless. "Is there something I can do?"

"Not really," Marshall said. "The twins will keep him busy tonight and that's for the best. The next few days are gonna be tough, though."

She saw her sister walking toward her and felt conflicted. "Thank you for telling me."

"No problem. Thanks for taking care of the childcare for tomorrow morning. Bye for now."

"Goodbye," she said, but he had already disconnected.

"You look upset," Tina said.

"I am."

After 9:30 p.m., Ryder prowled his den with a heavy heart. His mentor was gone. Although Dr. Walters had been mentally gone for a while now, the finality of the man's physical death hit Ryder harder than he'd expected. Maybe it was because he'd lost his brother so recently, too.

Ryder felt completely and totally alone. Sure, he had the twins and his profession, but two of the most important people in the world to him were gone and never coming back. He wondered what it meant that aside from his longtime friend Marshall, he had no other meaningful relationships. Was he such a workaholic that he'd totally isolated himself?

A knock sounded on his door, surprising him. Probably Marshall, he thought and opened the door. To Bridget. His heart turned over.

"Hi," she said, her gaze searching his. She bit her lip. "I know it's late and I don't want to impose—"

He snagged her arm and pulled her inside. "How did you know?"

"Marshall," she said, then shot him a chiding glance. "I would have preferred to hear it from you."

"I thought about it," he said, raking his hand through his hair. "But you've done enough helping with the babies."

"I thought perhaps that you and I were about more than the babies, but maybe I was wrong," she said, looking away.

His heart slamming against his rib cage, he cupped her chin and swiveled it toward him. "You were right. You know you were."

"Is it just sex? Are you just totally deprived?" she asked in an earnest voice.

He swallowed a chuckle. "I wish."

Her eyes darkened with emotion and she stepped closer. She moved against him and slid her arms upward around the back of his neck. She pulled his face toward hers and he couldn't remember feeling this alive. Ever.

His lips brushed hers and he tried to hold on to his self-control, but it was tough. She slid her moist lips from side to side and he couldn't stand it any longer. He devoured her with his mouth, tasting her, taking her. Seconds later, he realized he might not ever get enough, but damn, he would give it his best shot.

He slid his fingers through her hair and slid his tongue deeper into her mouth. She suckled it and wriggled against him. Her response made him so hard that he wasn't sure he could stand it. His body was on full tilt in the arousal zone.

He took a quick breath and forced himself to draw back. "I'm not sure I can pull back after this," he said, sliding his hands down over her waist and hips. "If you're going to say no, do it now."

Silence hung between them for heart-stopping seconds.

He sucked in another breath. "Bridget—"

"Yes," she whispered. "Yes."

Everything in front of him turned black and white at the same time. He drew her against him and ran his hands up to her breasts and her hair, then back down again. He wanted to touch every inch of her.

She felt like oxygen to him, like life after he'd been in a tomb. He couldn't get enough of her. He savored the taste and feel of her. Tugging at her blouse, he pushed it aside and slid his hands over her shoulders and lower to the tops of her breasts.

She gave a soft gasp that twisted his gut.

"Okay?" he asked, dipping his thumbs over her nipples.

She gasped again. "Yesssss."

He unfastened her bra and filled his hands with her breasts.

Ryder groaned. Bridget moaned.

"So sexy," he muttered.

She pulled at his shirt and seconds later, her breasts brushed his chest. Ryder groaned again.

The fire inside him exploded and he pushed aside the rest of her clothes and his. He tasted her breasts and slid his mouth lower to her belly and lower still, drawing more gasps and moans from her delicious mouth. Then he thought about contraception. Swearing under his breath, he pulled back for a second. "Give me a few seconds," he said. "You'll thank me later."

He raced upstairs to grab condoms and returned downstairs.

"What?" she asked.

"Trust me," he said and took her mouth again. He slid his hand between her legs and found her wet and wanting.

Unable to hold back one moment longer, he pushed her legs apart and sank inside her. Bridget clung to him as he pumped inside her. She arched against him, drawing him deep.

He tried to hold out, but she felt so good. Plunging

inside her one last time, he felt his climax roar through him. Alive, he felt more alive than he'd felt for as long as he could remember.... "Bridget," he muttered.

Her breath mingled with his and he could sense that she hadn't gone over the top. He was determined to take her there. Sliding his hand between them, he found her sweet spot and began to stroke.

Her breath hitched. The sound was gratifying and arousing. A couple moments later, she stiffened beneath him. He began to thrust again and she came in fits and starts, sending him over the edge.

He couldn't believe his response to her. Twice in such a short time? He wasn't an eighteen-year-old. "Come to bed with me."

"Yes," she said. "If I can make my legs move enough to walk upstairs."

He chuckled and knew the sound was rough. Everything about him felt sated, yet aroused and rough. "I'll help."

"Thank goodness," she said.

He helped her to her feet, but when they arrived at the bottom of the steps, he swept her into his arms and carried her up the stairs.

"Oh, help," she said. "I hope I don't give you a hernia."

"If you do, it'll be worth it," he said.

She swatted at him. "You're supposed to say I'm as light as a feather even though I may weigh half a ton."

"You took the words out of my mouth. You're light as a feather," he said.

She met his gaze and her eyes lit with a glow that both warmed and frightened him. "Excellent response," she said and took his mouth in a sensual kiss that made him dizzy.

"Whoa," he said and stumbled the rest of the way to his room. He set her on the mattress and followed her down. "You smell amazing," he said inhaling her scent. "You taste incredible," he said and dragged his tongue over her throat. "I want to be inside you all night long."

Her breath hitched again and she swung her legs around his hips. Sliding her fingers into his hair, she pulled his mouth to hers. "Do your best," she whispered and he thrust inside her.

Later that night, Bridget awakened, finding herself curled around Ryder. She was clinging to him. Her body said she wanted all of him, as much as he could give, as much as she could receive. But it wasn't just her body that craved him; some part deep inside her felt as if she belonged exactly where she was.

Her breath abandoned her. How was she supposed to manage this, this physical, yet highly emotional relationship with a man like Ryder? It wasn't even a man like Ryder. It was Ryder himself.

Ryder slid his thigh between hers, sending her sensual awareness of him into high mode. "You're awake," he said, sliding his arms around her. "You weren't planning on going anywhere, were you?"

"No. Just thinking."

"I'll put a stop to that," he said and distracted her again with his lovemaking. Afterward, she fell asleep.

The sound of a baby crying awakened her minutes later.... *Had it really been hours?* she wondered as she glanced at the alarm clock. Looking beside her, she saw that Ryder had already left the bed. The second baby started crying and she rose from the bed and pulled on one of Ryder's shirts. Thank goodness it covered her nearly to her knees because she'd left her own clothes downstairs.

She met Ryder in the hallway as he carried a baby in each arm. "Sorry our good-morning song woke you," he said with a wry, sleepy grin. His hair was sleep-mussed and a whisker shadow darkened his chin. Shirtless, he wore a pair of pajama pants that dipped below his belly button. She couldn't remember when he'd looked more sexy.

Reining in her thoughts, she extended her hands to take one of the twins. "I can help."

Tyler immediately fell toward her and she caught him in her arms.

"He made that decision pretty quickly. Can't fault his judgment," he said with a chuckle. "I already changed their diapers."

"Really?" she said, astonished.

"Don't look so surprised," he said as he led the way down the stairs. "My baby-care skills are improving."

"Congratulations," she said and put Tyler into one of the high chairs while Ryder slid Travis into the other high chair. She immediately put a few Cheerios on the trays while she prepared the bottles.

Ryder prepared the oatmeal. "You're getting faster at this baby stuff, too."

"I watched Suzanne one morning and took notes. She's so efficient."

"I'll be glad when she can come back," he said.

"Oh, speaking of that," she said. "The part-time sitter should be here any—"

A knock sounded at the door and Bridget felt a sliver

of panic as she glanced at her bare legs and thought of her clothing strewn across the den. "Oh, bloody— Stefan will have my head. I'll be back in a couple moments," she said and grabbed her clothes and scrambled upstairs to get dressed. She glanced in the mirror and tried to tame her hair before she returned to the stairs.

Ryder met her halfway with an inscrutable expression in his eyes. "Embarrassed to be caught with an American doctor?"

"Not embarrassed so much as I wouldn't want my brother Stefan to find out. He really prefers we maintain a squeaky-clean image. And unfortunately we never know when someone may leak something to the press. That can turn into a huge mess."

"So you keep all your lovers hidden?" he asked.

"There haven't been that many," she said. "Do you really want paparazzi standing outside your door assaulting you with questions about me?"

"Good point," he said. "I'm going up to my study for a while. Dr. Walters's wife has asked me to write a eulogy for his memorial service."

Bridget's heart twisted at the grief Ryder was clearly trying to conceal. "I'm so sorry. Are you sure I can't do anything for you?"

His lips twitched. "You did a damn good job distracting me last night."

She felt her cheeks heat. "I was thinking of a cup of tea."

He shook his head. "I drink coffee. Breakfast would be nice, though."

She blinked. "Food. You want me to prepare food?" she echoed, at a loss. She'd taken one cooking class in her younger years and couldn't remember anything from it except how to put out a fire on a stove top.

He chuckled. "Sorry. I forgot your position, Your Highness."

She immediately felt challenged by his tone. "Well, it's not as if I can't prepare a meal. I just don't do it on a regular basis."

"When was the last time?" he asked.

She lifted her chin. "I prepared lunch for the twins just last week."

He laughed again, this time louder. "Bottles and jars of fruits and vegetables."

"They seemed to like it," she said. "Okay, what would you like for breakfast?"

"I'm guessing eggs Benedict would be too much to ask," he said.

She glowered at him.

"Okay. I'll go easy. Scrambled eggs, toast and coffee."

"I'll be right back with it," she said, muttering to herself as she continued down the rest of the stairs. This was ridiculous. Why should she care if Ryder considered her unskilled in the kitchen? He obviously respected her other talents such as organizing his childcare.

After a brief consultation with the sitter, however, Bridget burned everything, even the coffee. She cleaned up her mess and started over, this time cooking everything on low. It seemed to take forever, but she finally got the job done and took the tray to Ryder's upstairs study.

He opened the door, wearing a distracted expression. "Thanks," he said, took the tray and closed the door.

She frowned, but took a breath. He was performing a difficult task. He needed understanding and patience.

Bridget went to his bedroom and arranged for a cleaning service. In her opinion, the house needed regular servicing. The sitters shouldn't be expected to clean in addition to keeping the twins. The twins were already a handful. An hour later, the cleaners arrived and she decided to take more coffee to Ryder.

She knocked on his door with the cup outstretched.

"Thanks," he said, still distracted as he accepted the cup. He closed the door again. She hesitated to interrupt, but thought it best to remove the dirty dishes, so she knocked again.

He opened the door, his eyebrows furrowed. "What?" he asked, almost in a curt voice.

"I thought I would take your dishes from breakfast," she said.

"Breakfast?" he said, his brow furrowing more.

"Yes, the eggs and toast you requested," she said.

"Oh," he said and went into his office. Seconds later, he returned with his uneaten eggs and toast.

"You didn't touch them," she said.

"Yeah, sorry. I'm really hung up over this eulogy."

Her frustration spiked. "I fixed these eggs and you didn't take a bite."

"I apologize. Really," he said, his face grief-stricken. In another instance, she would have screamed. But she knew Ryder was suffering.

"Fine," she managed in a tight voice. "What would you like for lunch?"

"Oh, anything. A ham sandwich. Thanks, *B*," he said and closed his door again. *B?* She'd never been called *B* in her life.

She helped the sitter with the boys, then took another trip to Ryder's study with a ham sandwich.

"Thanks," he said and accepted the sandwich.

"Are you okay?" she asked before he could close the door in her face.

He shook his head. "I'm not there yet." He leaned forward and pressed a quick kiss against her mouth.

After that brief meeting, Bridget left because she sensed Ryder needed his space and she was determined to respect it.

Ryder finally finished writing the eulogy. He had no idea what time it was until he glanced at the clock. 4:30 p.m. Whoa. Later than he intended. Good thing he'd cancelled all his appointments and that this wasn't a surgery day. Stretching his neck, he glanced around the room and noticed the sad-looking ham sandwich on the table on the other side of the room.

His heart swelled at the thought of Bridget bringing him food, reaching out to him. Taking the plate, he walked downstairs expecting to see the fresh, sexy face of Bridget Devereaux.

Instead he was greeted by Marshall.

"Hey, dude," he said. "How's it going?"

"Okay," he said. "The twins?"

"Down for a nap," Marshall said.

"Bridget?"

Marshall lifted a brow and smoothed back his hair with his hand. "She was here?"

"Yeah. She fixed me breakfast and a sandwich for lunch," Ryder said, frowning.

"Breakfast," Marshall repeated.

Reluctant to reveal details about his relationship with

Bridget, he shrugged. "She showed up early. You should know. You told her about Dr. Walters. I was working on his eulogy."

Marshall winced. "Sorry, bro. I'm guessing she left a while ago. The sitter didn't say anything about her."

Ryder's gut tightened. "Okay, I guess she had other things to do."

"Well, she *is* a princess," Marshall said.

"Yeah," Ryder said.

"You're starting to fall for her, aren't you?" Marshall asked.

"Hell no."

Chapter 7

"Dr. Walters was more than a brilliant doctor. He was a father figure to many of us who'd never known a father. He was an advocate at the same time that he demanded the best of every resident who crossed his path. He was the best man I've ever known," Ryder said and glanced at the large group who had gathered to remember Dr. Walters.

His gaze skimmed the crowd and stumbled over a classy young woman wearing a black hat and black dress. *Bridget.* Her presence gave him a potent shot of strength.

He continued with the rest of his eulogy, then made his way toward Bridget. The seat beside her was empty. Her eyes widened as he stepped in from the aisle.

"Thanks," he whispered, sitting down and clasping her hand between them.

"There was no other choice than to be here for you," she whispered.

His heart swelled at her words and he squeezed her hand, trying to remember the last time someone had been there for him like this. No expectation, just support and some kind of emotion close to love. Yet it couldn't be love, he told himself.

Her hand, however, sure felt great inside his.

A couple hours later, Ryder and Bridget joined Mrs. Walters for an afternoon meal. Dr. Walters's widow seemed to have aged a decade within the last year.

"You were his favorite," she said to Ryder, her eyes full of pain as she smiled. "He wasn't supposed to have a favorite, but he did."

Ryder's heart squeezed tight. "He was the father I never had. He challenged me and empathized with me. He made me want to be my best."

Mrs. Walters nodded. "He was an inspiring man."

"I'm lucky that he was my mentor," Ryder said.

Mrs. Walters nodded and frowned. "He was a wonderful, wonderful man. But we never had children. Our family life was always dependent on his schedule." She paused. "If there was one thing he might have changed before he...went away..." She swallowed over her grief. "I think he may have spent more time with his family. Me. His brothers and sister. Until he began to fade, he didn't realize how important relationships were." She closed her eyes for a moment, then shrugged. "I'm rambling." She patted Ryder's hand. "Never forget that you are more than that hospital. Never," she said.

Shaken by her fervent expression, he took a quick breath. "I won't," he said.

Within a half hour, he escorted Bridget to his car. "Come back to my house," he said.

She paused a half beat, then nodded. "Yes."

Moments later, they walked into his house. The sitter sat on the couch reading a book. "Hi," she said. "Everything go okay? The twins are sleeping and they've been no trouble."

"Good to hear it," he said. "I'm gonna change my clothes. Will you be here for a while?"

The sitter nodded. "I'm scheduled to be here till six. Then I have a class."

"Thanks," he said and turned to Bridget. "There's a place I want to take you."

"If it involves hiking or swimming, I'll need to change clothes," she warned him.

"You'll be okay."

Seven minutes later, he pulled in front of a waterfall fountain. Man-made but spectacular.

"It's beautiful," she said as they walked close to the fall and lifted her face to the spray. "Have you been here often?"

"Yes," he said, squeezing her hand.

"I can see why," she concluded and closed her eyes. "Whenever I have a few minutes near water, it reminds me of Chantaine. For all my complaining about being chained there the last year, I can't deny the effect water has on me. Makes me wonder if I have a gill somewhere. What about you?" she asked. "You've been landlocked most of your life, haven't you?"

"Yes, but I find that spending some time near water, and I mean more than a shower or swimming pool, balances me out. Especially if something is bothering me."

"It's natural that Dr. Walters's passing would upset you," she said.

"It's more than that," he said. "Now that he is really gone, his position with the residents will need to be filled."

"You want it very much, don't you?" she asked.

Ryder felt torn in two completely opposing directions. "I feel a huge responsibility. The other doctor who would want the job comes off as callous. He doesn't care about helping residents with problems. His first instinct would be to cut them from the program. Dr. Walters probed deeper before making that kind of decision and he made himself available to residents for conference. The goal at our hospital is to approach the physician as a complete person so that he or she, in turn, treats the patient as a complete person."

"The doctors in your program are very fortunate to receive that kind of benefit, but based on what Dr. Walters's wife said, it must be difficult for the adviser to strike the balance as a complete person." She sighed. "In a different way, serving our country as royals can be an all-consuming proposition. Makes you wonder if there's such a thing as balance outside of a yoga class."

Her yoga reference made him smile. "How is it you can make me feel better on such a dark day?"

"One of my many delightful skills." She glanced again at the fountain. "Have you ever wanted to jump in one of these and get completely wet?"

"Yes," he said. "Where I was raised we had a small fountain in the town in front of a bank. When I was a little boy, I jumped in it and stomped around. Got a paddling that kept me from sitting down for a week."

"Was it worth it?" she asked.

"Before and during, yes. Afterward no."

"I almost took the plunge once in Italy, but I knew I would be arrested and there would be a big fuss."

"So you restrained yourself," he said.

She frowned. "Yes, but one day. Maybe soon after I'm able to bring back some doctors to Chantaine and I take my long vacation in Italy…"

"Is that why you're in such a rush to import doctors?"

"Trust me, I've earned this break. Even Stefan agrees, but he and I both know Chantaine needs doctors. After my sister-in-law was injured so horribly while saving my life, it became even more clear. I still—"

The darkness in his eyes surprised him. "You don't still hold yourself responsible, do you?"

She paused a half beat too long. "Of course not. The gang stampeded her. Even security was taken by surprise," she said as if by rote.

"But you still feel responsible," he said.

"She wouldn't have been there if I hadn't begged her to join me," she said. "For someone to put her life on the line for me, and it wasn't as if she had taken an oath to protect me. She just did it because of who she is."

"And because of who you are," he said.

"Now that's a stretch," she said. "I spend a lot of time at charity events and school and business openings. It's not as if I'm in a research laboratory finding cures for dreadful diseases."

"No, but you're helping raise money for those research scientists, and someone needs to do it. Don't underestimate your importance. You inspire people to give more than they usually would."

"Perhaps," she said, but clearly wasn't convinced. "Now I just need to find a way to inspire doctors to come to Chantaine. At least I've already got one specialist willing to hold seminars," she said, then shook her head. "But today isn't about me or Chantaine. It's about you, Ryder. How else can I help you with your grief?" she asked in a solemn tone.

His mind raced in a totally different direction down a path filled with hot kisses and hot bodies pressed against each other. He couldn't help but remember the sight of her naked body in his bed. He couldn't help but want her again.

Her eyes widened as if she could read his mind. "You're not serious," she said. "Men. Sex is the solution for everything."

"There are worse ways to deal with grief," he said.

"True, but with the sitter at your house, it would be difficult to indulge that particular solution," she said.

"You're right," he said. "I should get back to the hospital. I canceled my schedule for the rest of the day, but making up for a lost day is hell."

"Absolutely not," she said, then bit her lip. "I suppose we could go to my suite."

His gut twisted at the prospect of holding her again. He didn't understand his draw to Bridget. All he knew was that his life had seemed full of darkness and when he was with her, he felt lighter. With his demanding schedule, he felt as if he needed to snatch whatever stolen moments he could with her. "That's an invitation I can't imagine turning down," he said, sliding his fingers over a silky strand of her hair.

Her breath hitched and he found the response gratifying and reassuring. He was damn glad to know he wasn't the only one feeling this crazy attraction.

* * *

After an afternoon spent drowning his devils in Bridget's bed, a cell-phone alarm sounded.

"Time to go," Bridget said, then rubbed her mouth against his cheek and pulled away.

He caught her just before she rose from the bed. "What's the rush?"

"It's five-thirty. The sitter will be leaving at six," she said with a soft smile and pulled on a robe.

"Damn, it's that late?" He glanced at the alarm clock beside the bed to confirm her announcement and shook his head. He raked his hand through his hair. "Hey, come back to the house with me. We can get something delivered."

"I'm sorry, I can't. I have a previous commitment this evening. I'm attending a forum to promote the prevention of gang violence. As I'm sure you can imagine, this is a cause near and dear to my heart. The Dallas district attorney will escort me," she said.

Ryder's gut gave a vicious twist. He'd heard the current D.A. was quite the lady's man. "I'm guessing Corbin made those arrangements," he said, unable to keep his disapproval from his tone.

"I believe he did. I'm only using a part-time assistant while I'm in Texas, but the arrangements went through her. She left me a dossier on him, but I've been too busy to scan it."

"I can tell you what you need to know," he said rising from the bed. "Aiden Corbin was elected two years ago and is a hound dog when it comes to women."

"What exactly is a hound dog?" she asked.

Ryder scowled. "It's a man who will do just about anything to get women into his bed."

"Is that so?" she said and shot a sideways glance at him. "It seems to me I've met several *hound dogs* here in Dallas."

"Hey, I'm no hound dog. I'm a hardworking doctor trying to take care of my brother's twin babies."

"It's really hard for me to buy your defense with you standing naked in front of me," she said, her glance falling over him in a hot wave that made it hard for him to resist pulling her right back into bed.

"I'm not used to being with a woman who has to fight off my competitors with a stick," he said.

She blinked. "Competitors," she echoed. "That would suggest I view these men on the same level as you, which I don't."

"What level is that?"

She paused then frowned. "Different. Besides, I don't have to beat the men off with a stick. And you must remember their primary attraction to me is due to my title and perhaps the erroneous view that I'm loaded."

"You underestimate your appeal."

"Hmm," she said. "Minus my title, I'm extremely average."

"You're wrong," he retorted. "You're beautiful and talented. You're…magic," he said, surprising himself with his words. Even though they were all true, they weren't the kinds of things he would usually say.

Bridget paused. Her eyes shimmering with emotion, she threw herself against him and wrapped her arms around him. "That's the nicest thing anyone has ever said to me. I'm not sure I agree, but it's quite wonderful that you would actually think those things about me.

Thank you, Ryder. I will cherish your words forever," she said, then pulled away.

Something about her thank-you reminded him that his relationship with Bridget was temporary. That was fine with him. Lord knew, with everything on his plate, he didn't have time for a real relationship with a woman. For that matter, he'd never taken time to have a *real* relationship with a woman. He'd always been too busy with his career. So this relationship was no different, he told himself, but something about that didn't settle right with him.

That night, after he'd tucked the twins into their cribs and watched the rest of the ball game, he half glanced at the local news. Just as he was about to switch the channel, a video of Bridget and the D.A. appeared.

"Her Royal Highness, Bridget Devereaux of Chantaine, accompanied Dallas's district attorney, Aiden Corbin, to a special discussion at the Dallas Forum tonight. Reporter Charles Pine reports."

"Your Highness, welcome to Dallas. I'm curious, how can a small, idyllic island like Chantaine have a gang problem?"

"My country is quite idyllic, and we're quite fortunate that we have only occasionally had problems with gangs. Still, there have been incidents, and we are always exploring ways to prevent such problems in the future. Mr. Corbin has generously offered to present his experiences and knowledge by visiting our country in the future."

"Sounds like a rough gig, Mr. Corbin," the reporter joked.

Corbin gave a wide smile that looked lecherous to

Ryder. "The princess is being very generous with her public and charitable appearances while she visits our city. The least I can do is to share my expertise in return."

Ryder bet the D.A. wanted to share more than his expertise. His stomach burned from the pizza he'd eaten earlier. His cell phone rang and he saw the caller ID belonged to Marshall.

Ryder answered the call, but Marshall started talking before he could open his mouth.

"Hey, what's your babe doing with our slimeball D.A.?"

"It's just business," he said, grinding his teeth at the same time.

"Business with the horn dog of the century?" Marshall asked. "If she was my woman, I wouldn't let her anywhere near Corbin."

Ryder bit his tongue. He'd had the same strange primitive reaction, but he had to contain himself.

"Whoa," Marshall said after the short silence. "You didn't say anything. Does that mean she's fair game? Because I gotta tell you that's one sweet piece of—"

"Don't even think about it," Ryder said. "With a sharp knife, I could disembowel you in less than sixty seconds."

Marshall gave a dirty chuckle. "Gotcha. I was just kidding. I'm focused on someone else. I could tell something was cooking between the two of you. The way you act about her. The way she acts about you."

"What do you mean the way she acts about me?"

"Well, she's busted her royal ass trying to make sure your boys have got good care," Marshall said. "Speaking of good care, I took a bucket of chicken to your nanny the other day. Seemed the charitable thing to do."

"You took food to Suzanne?" Ryder said. "I told you to leave her alone."

"It was just chicken. She's been recovering, for God's sake. Give the poor girl a break," Marshall said.

Ryder narrowed his eyes. "You don't deliver chicken unless you're hoping for something for yourself."

"I'm insulted," Marshall said. "I can be a nice guy. Listen, I don't have time for this. I'll just tell you that you might want to keep an eye on your little princess because Aiden Corbin is known for poaching. G'night, Mr. M.D."

Ryder opened his mouth to reply, but he knew Marshall had clicked off the call. Marshall had always called him Mr. M.D. when he thought Ryder was getting too big for his britches. Trouble was, what Marshall had said about Corbin was right. The other trouble was Ryder had no real claim on Bridget, so the only thing left for him to do was stew. No way, he told himself. There was no good reason to stew over a temporary woman. He'd never done it before, and he wasn't going to start now.

Bridget left two messages on Ryder's cell during the next two days, but he hadn't answered. She worried that something may have happened. What if there'd been a problem with the nanny? Had his workload tripled as a result of Dr. Walters's death? She already knew he'd been reluctant to touch base with her when things weren't going well, so she decided to make a quick trip to his office at the hospital.

He was in a meeting with a resident, but just as she

started to leave a message with his assistant, the resident exited his office.

"I'll let him know you're here," his assistant said.

Another moment later, Ryder opened his door. "Come in," he said.

Wondering at his abrupt tone, she entered his office and watched as he closed the door behind her. "I was concerned when I didn't hear back from you. Is everything okay with you and the twins?"

"No problem," he said. "Suzanne returned to work and the boys seem to be fine."

She frowned at how remote he seemed. "Are you sure you're okay? You seem—"

"Busy," he said in a firm voice.

"Well, I didn't mean to bother you," she said.

"I have another two or three minutes," he said.

Her jaw dropped of its own volition. "Excuse me?"

"I said I have another two or three minutes. Then I need to go to a meeting."

"Why are you acting this way?" she demanded.

"What way?"

"As if we're strangers," she said. "As if we've never shared a bed."

His eyes suddenly darkened with turmoil. "We don't have a committed relationship."

Bridget's heart twisted. She felt as if he'd slapped her. "Does that mean you have to act rude and uncaring?"

He paused. "No, but we both know this isn't a long-term relationship. You have your reasons. I have mine. There's no need to pretend anything different."

If she felt he'd slapped her before, she now felt he'd stabbed her. "I wasn't pretending. I was just caring," she said. "Clearly a mistake," she said and turned toward the door.

He grabbed her arm just before she reached the doorknob.

She turned, feeling more confused than she could remember in her life. "Why are you acting this way?"

"Our relationship isn't normal," he said.

"Well, you're not normal and neither am I, so why should it be?"

"I have no right to comment on what men you spend time with," he said

Realization swept over her. "Oh, for bloody sakes, is this about the D.A.?"

"Saw you on the news," he said. "He was trying hard."

"And got nowhere," she said. "Do you really think I would hop into bed with him after I'd just been with you? Do you really think I would hop into bed with anyone? You must think I'm the most promiscuous woman ever born."

"You get a lot of offers," he said and she could see he was torn. He was accustomed to being in control and now he wasn't.

"I get offers because I'm a princess, not because I'm me," she said.

"Not—"

She shook her head. "Okay, we'll have to agree to disagree. Again. The point is I haven't engaged in a meaningless affair, well, ever," she said. "It's just not my nature. And my affair, I'm not sure I like that word. My relationship with you isn't meaningless. I don't exactly know what it means because you and I seem to be headed in different directions. But I'm incredibly drawn to you. I can't explain it and I don't particularly like it. It's bloody well inconvenient, but damn it, you're important to me."

He stared at her for a long moment, then gave a short, humorless laugh. "Ditto."

"What does that mean?"

"Exactly what you said. I'm willing to ride this horse to the end of this race if you are."

Bridget had to digest his words. She wasn't accustomed to such references.

"I mean we'll take it till the end and then kiss each other good-bye," he said.

The word good-bye bothered her, but she didn't feel as if she had any other choice.

"Deal?" he asked, extending his hand.

She slowly placed her hand in his. "Deal."

He pulled her against him. "Come over tonight," he said.

Her heart slammed against her rib cage. "I'd like to, but I have a previous engagement."

"Damn," he said. "Just tell me it's not with Aiden Corbin."

She shook her head. "It's with the head of Pediatrics."

Ryder swore. "That's better?"

"You told me if I bring medical experts to Chantaine to do temporary training, then I'll have a better chance of attracting doctors."

"Why can't you choose old, married experts?" he grumbled.

She smiled. "Introduce me."

He lowered his head and gave her a long kiss that made her head spin.

When he pulled back, they were both breathing hard. "What about tomorrow night?"

"I have an engagement," she said. "But I'll rearrange it."

"Okay. Tomorrow night is another water class for the twins. I'll order takeout for us." He gave her a quick firm kiss. "You'd have more fun with me than the Pediatrics department head tonight."

Ryder arrived home a few minutes late that night to find Marshall's truck parked in front of his house. He opened his front door to find Marshall bouncing Tyler on his knee while Suzanne was changing Travis's diaper.

Tyler squealed. Marshall grinned. "Looks like somebody's glad to see you," he said and immediately handed the baby to Ryder.

Ryder's heart lifted at the baby's obvious joy and he kissed him on his soft cheek. Travis also gave an earsplitting shriek.

Suzanne glanced up at him. "I've already fed them, but they're a little worked up. That may be due to Marshall," she said with a faintly accusing expression.

"Hey, I was just entertaining them until you got home," Marshall said and picked up Travis. "I thought I'd try to give Suzanne a break from the heavy lifting."

Uh-huh, Ryder thought. "It's okay. I'm glad they're in a good mood. Can you give me a quick minute to talk to Marshall?"

"Of course," Suzanne said. "There's no rush. And if you want to change clothes, I can wait for that, too."

"Thanks," he said and gave a sharp jerk of his head to go outside to Marshall.

Ryder carried Tyler in his arms and Marshall carried Travis. "What the hell do you think you're doing?" Ryder demanded.

"Hey, I'm just helping out your nanny. You don't want another one to quit because of these wild boys, do you?"

"Suzanne had no intention of quitting. She's just recovering from her appendectomy," Ryder said.

"All the more reason for me to stop by and help her. These boys are getting bigger every day."

"She doesn't need your help."

"Says who?" Marshall challenged.

"Says me," Ryder retorted. "You just want to get into her pants."

Marshall shot him a quelling glare that would have worked with any other man.

Not Ryder. "Stay away from my nanny."

"You're just edgy because you're not getting any," Marshall said.

"That's none of your damn business," Ryder said.

"It is if it makes you act like a jerk," Marshall said, then sucked in a quick breath. "Listen, I like Suzanne. I think she likes me. I wanna give this a try."

"She's not your kind of woman," Ryder said.

"Well, maybe I've been going after the wrong kind of woman."

Ryder groaned. "If you wreck my nanny, I'll kill you."

"Give me a chance," Marshall said. "She is."

Ryder swore under his breath. "Okay, but if you mess up her mind…"

"Yeah, yeah, yeah," Marshall said. "When are you

supposed to see your princess again? For the sake of all of us, I hope it's soon."

Filled with misgivings, Ryder watched his nanny drive off in Marshall's wake to a restaurant. Maybe he was just jealous, a voice inside him said, and he brushed it aside. The boys were rowdy and demanding and absorbed every ounce of his energy by the time they fell asleep.

When he awakened the following morning to the sound of Travis screaming at the top of his lungs, he could have sworn it was the middle of the night. Instead, it was 6:30 a.m.

Stumbling into the twins' bedroom, he picked up the baby and held him against him. "Hey, bud, what's up? You're okay."

Travis's cry melted to a whimper, and Ryder sensed the baby was missing his real father and mother. The thought twisted his gut. Poor kid would never know his real dad and mom. He was stuck with Ryder, and Ryder knew he would never be the father his brother would have been.

Chapter 8

Later that morning, Ryder joined the chief of staff with Dr. Hutt in a meeting to discuss the future of the adviser program.

"There's been some debate over how we should continue this program in the future now that Dr. Walters is no longer with us," the chief of staff said.

"It's one of the things about our program that makes it distinctive and appealing to residents," Ryder said. "I can't imagine changing it."

"I agree that the program should continue," the chief said. "But Dr. Walters was one of a kind and we may need to make changes."

"Not if those changes will negatively impact the residents," Ryder countered.

"The residents needed to be toughened," Hutt said. "They've chosen the medical profession. It's a demanding field, so they need to be ready to take on their jobs. Long hours and dedication to excelling in their fields are critical."

"They also need to deal with their patients as individuals. We enforce that teaching by treating them as individuals," Ryder said, feeling his back get up, ready for a fight.

"You're too soft on them," Hutt said.

"You treat them like a machine because that's how you treat your patients," Ryder said.

"Gentlemen," the chief of staff intervened. "There's no need for insults."

Ryder resisted the urge to glare at him and took a quick breath. "Forgive me," he said. "But Dr. Walters was very important to me. It would be an insult to him if I didn't present his point of view in this discussion."

"And you think I'm not," Hutt said. "Dr. Walters was my adviser, too. I worshipped the ground he walked on. What he taught me was the importance of discipline."

Ryder couldn't disagree. Discipline was critical to a doctor's success. "I've never disagreed with the importance of discipline, but Dr. Walters also emphasized to me to remember the human element."

"You're both right," the chief said. "And you've both clearly demonstrated your superior ability as medical doctors. The difficulty is that Dr. Walters spent an unbelievable amount of time counseling residents at the same time he managed his patient load. There was rarely a time he wasn't here at the hospital. Neither of you can make that kind of time commitment."

"I have a very understanding wife."

"I have a perfect nanny."

"Therefore," the chief of staff said. "I am going to assign both of you as intern advisers."

That sounded like a horrible idea to Ryder. "I can't imagine that Dr. Walters would approve."

"Unfortunately, Dr. Walters isn't here to give his advice. I agree that the advisership is one of the unique features of our program, but I can't in good conscience assign the total advisership to you, Dr. McCall, given your new family obligations."

"The two of you will have to work together or I will find new advisers," the chief continued. "The three of us will meet in two weeks."

Ryder led the way out the door, barely resisting the urge to slam it shut behind him. "This is a joke," he muttered.

"Hey, I don't want to work with you either. Just because you were Gordon's favorite doesn't mean the rest of us didn't see how great he was. And don't try to deny it. How did you get the financial relief you needed when your mother was dying?" he challenged.

Ryder's fingers itched to punch Hutt in his face. "He pointed me in the direction of several teaching opportunities. One of them worked out. It was that or wait tables. How did *you* get through med school?"

"You know how I got through. My parents paid for me. I started partying a little too much once I graduated and he told me I had to toe the line or go somewhere else. Rode my butt every time I walked into the hospital. I learned the hard way the importance of discipline."

"I did, too. I just learned it about ten years earlier than you did because I had to," he said and turned away.

Hutt caught his arm. "Just curious, what would it

take for you to give up the advisership and let me take it over?"

"A miracle," Ryder said.

"Too vague. I can't shoot for that," he said.

His colleague's response took him by surprise. "You gotta understand the guys who don't have parents who can pay their way. You gotta understand the guys who don't get into school because their daddy knows somebody. I'm not sure you can get there. Ever."

"You're an ass," Hutt said.

"So are you," Ryder said.

"Maybe that's why the chief is making us work together."

"Unless he's hoping we'll kill each other," Ryder muttered and went to his office.

That night, although Ryder physically did everything the teachers instructed them to do with the babies, Bridget could tell his mind was somewhere else. She tried not to focus on it as she watched Tyler put his face in the water and blow bubbles.

"Good boy," she said, praising the baby. "Good for you. Such a brave, brilliant boy."

Travis must have taken a competitive cue because he plunged his face in the water and lifted it, choking. Frightened, he began to cry.

"Oh no, that water went down the wrong way," she said, passing Tyler to Ryder and holding out her hands for Travis. "Poor thing. No need to go diving," she gently chastised him. "Watch," she said and lowered her mouth to the water and blew bubbles.

Ryder followed her lead and blew bubbles, making a sound with his deeper voice.

Travis quickly dried up and stared.

"Do it again," she said.

Ryder repeated and Travis let out a belly laugh.

Bridget couldn't resist laughing, too. "What a brilliant sound," she said. "Do it again."

Ryder dipped his head and shot her a dark, mocking look. "Yes, Your Majesty." He blew bubbles and this time, both Travis and Tyler laughed.

"Well done," she said. "Just a couple more times."

"Want to give it another go?" she asked Travis. "We can do it together." She lowered her mouth to the water to blow bubbles. "Come on."

Holding him securely, she dipped his chin in the water. He made a motorboat sound with his lips. Slowly, she lowered his mouth and he made the same sound. Just before he breathed in water, she pulled up his chin, and again he let out a belly laugh.

"Good boy," she said. "Brilliant."

"You never say that to me," Ryder muttered.

"Perhaps you need to try harder," she retorted.

He groaned and she felt his gaze sweep over her body with a flash of instant need before he hid it. 'You could drive a man insane, Your Majesty," he said.

"Your Majesty is incorrect. If you're going to address me correctly, you should say Your Highness. Or if you want to irritate me, you could use the term my brother-in-law's housekeeper uses. Your Highliness."

"I like that," he said. "Has a nice ring to it. Your Highliness."

She scowled. "So what put you in a bad mood at work? Did one of your patients develop a secondary infection?"

"Hell no," he said frowning. "How did you know something happened at work?"

She rolled her eyes. "Because you're here and not here at the same time. You do everything the teachers say, but you're not really here. Some women would be insulted."

"It's probably best if I'm not completely here because looking at you in that bathing suit could make things embarrassing for me when I step out of the pool. But because you asked, there are some complications with the resident advisory position. I have to deal with the equivalent of the M.D. devil."

She winced. "That can't be enjoyable. Then again, would he be easier to deal with than you?"

He shot her a deadly look. "If you don't mind dealing with someone who will lie to your face."

She frowned. "Bloody hell for both of us," she muttered under her breath.

The teacher ended the class and Bridget and Ryder climbed out of the pool with the boys. Bridget changed Travis's drenched diaper while Ryder changed Tyler's. "You and your brother are the most brilliant, fabulous boys in the world. Never doubt it," she said and rubbed her nose against Travis's.

The baby laughed and grabbed at her. Her heart twisted in her chest. "So sweet."

"You're good with them," Ryder said.

"Shocking, isn't it?" she said.

"I think both of them have a crush on you," he said, leaning toward her. "Or maybe all three of us."

She smiled, feeling a surprising flood of warmth flow inside her. "You think they really like me? I've never thought of myself as good with babies."

Travis pressed a wet, open-mouth kiss against her cheek.

"Yeah, they clearly hate you," Ryder said.

She sighed. "I never thought I could adore babies this much."

"Me either," he said, drawing Tyler against him. The baby snuggled against him. "Not sure about this fatherhood thing. I didn't have the best example."

"Neither did I," she said. "He couldn't ever remember my name."

"You're joking," he said, disturbed by the complacent expression on her face.

She shrugged. "My mother's job was to reproduce. There were a bonus of girls. She stopped after the second son which was after Phillipa and me."

"You weren't close to your mom either, were you?" he guessed.

"Hers wasn't a happy marriage. My mother had high hopes when she married my father, but she ended up terribly disappointed. So yes, I'm ill-prepared to be a loving mother. The only part of my background that gives me hope is my siblings. Stefan and Tina were more like parents to me."

"I guess that's another thing we have in common. We didn't have the best parents in the world. We were just on opposite ends of the spectrum. Yours were royal. Mine were dirt-poor," he said. "How did I get lucky enough to have a princess half-naked in a pool with me?"

"And your twin boys," she added, laughing. "I'm glad they like me. It's amazing how they get under your skin."

"Yeah," he said, looking down at Tyler. "I just hope

I can figure out how to keep them safe, happy and feeling like they can conquer the world."

"I think you will," she said. "If anyone can, you can."

"The great thing about the swimming class is that it totally wears out the boys and they sleep like babies should," Ryder said, sitting on the couch beside Bridget with his hand wrapped around hers. "The bad thing is that it wears me out, too."

She gave a low, throaty chuckle that grabbed at his gut. "Times ten," she said.

"If you're as tired as I am, then you better stay the night," he said.

She slid him a sideways glance. "My driver could take me home. It would be no problem."

"Maybe not for him, but it would be for me," he said, drawing her head toward his and taking her mouth in a long kiss.

When he pulled away, Bridget sighed. The sound was magic to him. He couldn't get enough of her and he hated himself for it, yet he couldn't avoid it.

"Does that mean you'll stay the night?" he asked. "I can promise I'll wake you up in the middle of the night."

She lifted her hand to the back of his head and drew his lips to hers. "Just do your best," she said and he vowed he would.

The next morning, Bridget awakened to the sound of babies crying and the sight of an empty bed. She'd stayed the night with Ryder, and he had apparently left early this morning. Pulling one of his shirts around her and buttoning it, she walked toward the nursery.

Walking inside, she nearly bumped into Suzanne.

"Oh, please excuse me," Bridget said, covering a yawn.

Suzanne yawned in response. "No problem," she said. "I arrived a little late and Dr. McCall left right out the door."

"He has a lot on his mind," Bridget said.

Suzanne nodded. "I can tell. You can go back to bed. I can handle the boys."

"No, I'll carry him downstairs," Bridget said, changing Travis, then picking him up and holding him against her. "No need to cry. You're probably still tired from all that swimming."

"They can steal your heart pretty quickly, can't they?" Suzanne asked, smiling at Bridget as she cuddled the baby.

"Yes, I never dreamed I could feel this much affection for two little semi-humans who spit peas at you, scream bloody murder and can get downright stinky. Whenever anyone asked me how I felt about babies, I always thought they were fine if they belonged to someone else."

"I was just the opposite," Suzanne said. "I wanted to have children, but I couldn't. My husband felt the same way. That's a big part of the reason he left."

Saddened by Suzanne's confession, Bridget frowned as she followed the nanny downstairs. "But there are other ways, adoption, surrogacy…."

"He wanted children the natural way," Suzanne said.

"I'm sorry. It was clearly his loss. I have to believe there's a better man in your future," Bridget said.

Suzanne's cheeks turned pink. "Maybe, but I'll never marry again. The ending was just too painful. What about you? Is marriage in your future?" she asked as if she wanted the attention diverted away from her.

Bridget blinked, uncomfortable with the question, so she gave her automatic response as she put Travis into a high chair. "No time soon. Italy is calling me first, and then we'll see."

"What about Dr. McCall?"

"Oh, he's not interested in marriage. He has his hands full with the boys and his practice and the residents at the hospital. I'm certain it's not in his plans to marry anytime soon."

"Plans can change in an instant," Suzanne said. "I bet he didn't plan to be a daddy to twins either."

"So true," Bridget agreed, growing more uncomfortable with the conversation with each passing second. "It's definitely been a shock. That's enough of an adjustment without adding a wife into the mix."

"Hmm," Suzanne said as if she didn't quite agree but wouldn't say more.

Bridget felt a rush of relief. "Can you handle the feeding? I'd like to take a shower."

"No problem. Take your time," Suzanne said.

As Bridget stepped under the warm spray of water in Ryder's shower, she smelled the scent of his soap and felt surrounded by him again. She wondered if she and Ryder were making a mistake by becoming involved. She preferred the notion that her attraction to him was strong but temporary; however, between her surprising, growing feelings for the babies and her assignment to set up a program for doctors to Chantaine, their relationship was complicated at best.

Bridget dressed and allowed her hair to air-dry with the plan to perform her daily makeover at her hotel suite. She lingered at Ryder's house, playing with the twins until her phone rang and it was Stefan.

Her stomach sank with dread at the prospect of talking to her brother. So far, she'd successfully avoided speaking to him directly by keeping him apprised via email. Stefan was a wonderful, good-intentioned but interfering brother, and because he was crown prince, he could get more than a bit bossy. His new wife, Eve, had helped to rein him in, but the man had been born to rule. Some traits could never be eradicated.

"Hello, Stefan. My, you're up late. How are you?" she asked, moving away from the twins so he wouldn't hear them in the background.

"I'm fine. I need to discuss the progress with the doctor program—"

Tyler let out a loud scream as Bridget left his sight. Bridget winced, walking quickly toward one of the downstairs bathrooms and closing the door.

"What was that? It sounded like a wild animal," he said.

Close enough, she thought ruefully. "It was a baby. I guess it's naptime. Now, regarding the doctor program, I've hit a snag with—"

"Baby," he echoed. "What are you doing with a baby? You don't like children."

"I don't dislike children," she said. "I've just never spent much time with them. That was a twin infant I met by chance. I've gotten to know the family because they've had a bit of a crisis. Everything is headed in the right direction now, though. About the doctors for Chantaine—"

"This wouldn't be one of Dr. Ryder McCall's twin nephews, would it? Valentina told me you've been spending quite a bit of time with Dr. McCall and his children."

Valentina had snitched on her. She would have to be more careful what she said to her sister. "It turns out Dr. McCall is the resident adviser for the Texas Medical Center. I've been trying to persuade him to participate in our program, but he says that working on Chantaine isn't prestigious enough because we don't already have any specialized programs or research in place."

"Chantaine, not prestigious enough," he said, his tone dripping with fury.

Bridget had indicated that she'd not made as much progress as she wanted because the head adviser was ill and the hospital was undergoing transition, which was partly true. She'd hoped she wouldn't have to tell Stefan the full truth because she'd known he would be offended. "I reacted the same way. Told him he was the most insulting man I'd ever met. Now to accomplish my task, I'm stuck trying to get him to compromise," she said with sigh.

Silence followed. "Bridget, you're not trying to use seduction as a way of convincing the man, are you?"

Bridget laughed, partly from hilarity, partly from hysteria. If Stefan only knew. Heaven help her if he did. Then again, Raoul would talk if pressed. "If only it were that easy," she said. "The man is almost as stubborn as you are," she said.

Another silence passed, and Bridget could feel her brother's tension through the phone line. "That doesn't bode well for our plan. You've begun to approach other hospitals."

"Yes, I have, but I'm getting similar, though more politely worded, responses. Because of that, I've begun to invite various high-level doctors to Chantaine to conduct training and seminars. So far, three doctors have committed."

"Excellent," he said. "We may need to expand our search."

"I know. I'm hopeful that if I can recruit some additional specialists that we'll be able to overcome the objections of our top choices for hospitals," she said.

"Bridget," he said. "I know that part of the reason you feel strongly about this is because of what happened to Eve," he said.

"Of course I do. Thank goodness she received the care she needed in time."

"I feel the same way. Just keep your meetings businesslike," he said.

Bridget frowned. "What do you mean?"

"I mean, you can be charming and you're young and attractive. These men could become enamored with the idea of seducing a princess. I wouldn't want your reputation to suffer as a result of any misplaced determination."

"Now, I believe I'm insulted. Do you really believe I'm so easily swayed? And do you think this is the first time I haven't had to put up with unwanted advances?"

"There's no reason for you to be insulted. I'm just looking out for you. What do you mean, unwanted advances?" he demanded. "Raoul is supposed to stay on top of that."

"Unless you have something further to say that could be construed as helpful, I believe we've spoken long enough. I have things to do as I'm sure you do, too."

"Bridget, do not hang up on me. I'm not finished," her brother commanded.

She was tempted to push the button to disconnect. So tempted that her finger itched. "I'm waiting," she finally said.

"Phillipa is coming to Texas for a visit," he announced. "She's been acting depressed for the last few weeks and she's had a terrible time working on her dissertation. Eve thinks getting away from Chantaine and taking a break from her studies will help her."

Her stomach twisted in concern. "You don't think she's ill, do you?"

"No, she's been checked out by the royal doctors, but after Ericka's drug problems, I can't take any chances."

Alarm shot through Bridget. Her sister Ericka had become dependent on drugs and spent more than one stint in rehab. Thank goodness, she'd left her problems behind and she was now happily married to her French film-director husband. "I can't believe our Pippa would get involved with drugs. Not after how much all of us suffered when Ericka was having her problems."

"I don't think she is, but she's lost weight and seems miserable and distracted. A change of pace will refresh her."

"Between Valentina and me, we'll do our best," she promised.

"The initial plan is for her to spend most of her time at the ranch, but I'm sure she'll come into Dallas for a visit," he said.

"Yes," she said. "Thank you for letting me know. And how are Eve and Stephenia?"

"Eve is wonderful. Stephenia is a terror, but I swear I think she's already learning to read. Still quite demanding that I read to her every night if at all possible," he said, his tone a mixture of exasperation and tenderness.

"You're a lucky man, Stefan, to have a wife and daughter who love you," she said, then couldn't resist adding, "along with your loyal, subservient siblings."

He gave a short laugh. "Yes to both, although my siblings will never be subservient."

"It's not in our genes," she said. "Give my love to Eve and Stephenia."

"I will. And Bridget," he said, "if you can't work things out with this Dr. McCall soon, we'll move past him and onto someone more cooperative."

Bridget's stomach twisted at the thought. "I hear what you're saying."

"Good," he said. "All for now. We'll talk soon."

Bridget took a deep breath as the call was disconnected. Her mind raced with thoughts about Phillipa, Ryder and the twins, and her assignment to recruit new doctors to Chantaine. She grew dizzy under the opposing priorities and returned to the den with the idea of heading outside to clear her head.

On her way, however, Travis screeched at her.

"His version of hello?" she said to Suzanne.

"I think so," Suzanne said. "It's time for their morning nap and Tyler is almost there. Travis is next."

"I'll take him," Bridget said and went to the blanket on the floor to pick up the baby. "How are you doing, mister?"

He made an unintelligible sound and plastered his open mouth against her in a wet baby kiss.

Her heart turned over. "You're such a flirt," she accused in a voice she knew was far too affectionate.

He put an open-mouth kiss against her cheek again.

"Too much," she said and cuddled him.

Travis snuggled against her and sank his head against

her throat. He sighed and seconds later, his breathing became more regular. Another half minute and she felt drool sliding down her neck.

It was the sweetest moment of her week. Or month. Or longer.

"You have a calming effect on him," Suzanne whispered. "He looks like he could sleep right there against you forever."

Travis sighed against her skin and she felt the terrible urge to tear up. Heaven help her, she needed to get her emotions under control.

Travis wiggled again and clung to her as if she were the most important person in the world. Her heart dipped at the way the baby made her feel. He was so vulnerable. She wanted to take care of him, make him feel safe.... Yet, he wasn't her baby.

Bridget savored his baby scent and the sensation of his healthy, chubby baby body in her arms. What an addictive combination. She wanted to hold him until nighttime...or later... Is this what happened to parents? Perhaps this is why babies survived. They made you want to take care of them. Forever.

It took another few moments in the rocking chair, but Bridget finally decided Travis could hit the sack. She carried him upstairs to the nursery and gently placed him in his crib. Tyler was already asleep. Travis was the fussier baby. That should have made him less desirable, but Bridget considered it a challenge to comfort him and help him fall asleep.

"Very good for a princess," Suzanne said from the doorway. "Are you sure you don't have some magic you're hiding in your back pocket?"

Flattered, Bridget quietly stepped from the room and

pulled the door shut behind her. "You should know better. The only magic with babies is if they feel safe."

"They both feel safe with you," Suzanne said.

Bridget's heart twisted. What did all of this mean? "I should go. I have appointments and phone conferences."

"Princess things to do," Suzanne said with a gentle smile.

Bridget nodded. "But if you have a problem with the twins, call me."

Suzanne sighed. "You hired me to take care of the twins. Yet you feel you need to help. Why is that?"

Bridget's stomach clenched again. "I'm not any kind of expert. It's like you said earlier. They sneak up on you and grab your heart."

Chapter 9

After Bridget finally tore herself away from the babies, she threw herself into her task of soliciting visiting medical experts for Chantaine. It irritated her when the experts laughed off her proposal, but she persevered and won two maybes and one new definite yes for her efforts.

Between her schedule and Ryder's, they only managed text messages and a few phone calls. Although she was tired by bedtime, she was surprised at how much she missed Ryder and the boys. Just as she fell asleep, her cell phone rang. Her heart skipped at the caller ID.

"Hello," she said.

Before she could say another word, he said. "Dinner. Tomorrow night. 7:00 p.m. No excuses. It's been too long."

She laughed, crazy thrilled to hear his voice. "Oh my. Is it a doctor thing that you give orders like a royal?"

"Maybe," he said. "I can't talk. I've got to check on a patient," he said.

"This late?" she asked and heard the sound of voices in the background.

"He's diabetic and he's experiencing some complications from surgery. I'll stay another hour to make sure he's stable. Tomorrow night, I'm taking you out."

The next morning, soon after Bridget awakened, she received a call from her sister Tina. "We're coming to town for dinner tonight. You must join us."

"Oh no. I'm sorry, but I already have a commitment," Bridget said, immediately feeling edgy because she knew Tina had talked to Stefan.

"Is it business or pleasure? Because if it's pleasure, we can all go out together," Tina offered.

Bridget paused. Her dinner with Ryder promised pure pleasure, but if she discussed Chantaine's medical program, it could be construed as business.

"I can tell by your hesitation that it's pleasure," Tina said before Bridget could pull an excuse together. "We'll pick you up for a six-thirty dinner at the Longhorn Club."

"It'll have to be a 7:00 p.m. dinner," she automatically corrected. "Ryder has already set the time and I'm sure he'll be busy going from the hospital, home and back out again. In fact, this may not be such a good idea after all. He's extremely busy lately. I haven't seen him myself in three days."

"Three days," Tina repeated. "If that's such a long gap of time between your dates, then I would say the two of you are getting quite cozy. All the more reason for me to meet him."

Resenting her sister's interference, Bridget frowned.

"And which member of the royal family gave your husband Zachary the stamp of approval while the two of you were seeing each other?"

"None, but my pregnancy put a different spin on the situation—" Tina gasped. "You're not pregnant, are you?"

"Of course not," Bridget said.

"But the two of you must be serious for you to get all snippy with me," Tina continued. "The only way you can disprove it is if you and your doctor meet Zach and me for dinner tonight. Ciao, darling," she said and hung up.

Bridget swore at the phone and tossed it on her bed. She didn't want to share Ryder with her sister or anyone else at the moment. She was appalled to admit, only to herself, that she'd missed Ryder and the twins terribly during the last few days. It had taken every bit of her self-control not to dash over to his house to hold the babies or to visit Ryder at the hospital. She knew, however, that she was growing entirely too attached to all three males. And now Ryder would have to face an inquisition from both her sister and her brother-in-law. She wouldn't blame Ryder if he ran screaming.

Deciding to give him the easy way out, she sent him a text message. *Change of plans. My sister and her husband insist we join them for dinner. I'll understand if you can't join us.*

When he didn't immediately answer, she suspected he was trying to word his response and took a shower, feeling glum, bordering pouty. Amazing how one phone call from her nosy sister could send her mood into the pits. When she got out of the shower, her cell phone dinged to indicate a message.

I'm in. Where?

Her heart turned cartwheels and she gave him the name of the restaurant along with a warning that her sister's interrogation could rival the American's CIA. Although she much preferred sharing an evening with Ryder without the company of her sister, she couldn't deny she was excited to get to see him, period.

That night, Bridget fought a surprising spate of nerves on the way to the restaurant. "Tell us more about your doctor," Tina said.

"You'll meet him soon enough," she said. "He's very work-oriented, but he's making adjustments now that he's the guardian for his twin infant nephews." She deliberately changed the subject. "Stefan told me Phillipa will be coming for a visit soon. He sounded worried. Have you had a chance to talk with her?"

"I've called, but she hasn't returned my call, which has me concerned. What about you?"

"I just left a message telling her I was looking forward to seeing her. She may need to relax a little before she's ready to talk. I didn't want to put any more pressure on her. I wondered if it was related to her studies, but Phillipa has always thrived under academic pressure."

"I think a little quiet time at our ranch will help her and we can come into town for a little fun. Of course, you could spend more time at the ranch, too," Tina said in a pointed voice.

"I have a task to complete and I can't do it from the ranch," Bridget said, refusing to give in to her sister's dig. "Now I'm in the process of trying to lure medical specialists to come to Chantaine so we can attract more medical doctors to our program."

"And what about your Dr. McCall? How would he feel about visiting Chantaine?"

Bridget laughed at the thought, yet felt a twinge of sadness at the same time. "He's far too busy with his work at the hospital and with the twins. I can't imagine his even considering it."

"Oh, I don't know," Tina said. "Maybe because the two of you are so close—"

"Not that close," Bridget said flatly.

"If you're looking for doctors who would like to combine a vacation with teaching in Chantaine, I might know a few," Zachary offered.

"Oh, that would be fabulous. Please do let me know of any of your connections," Bridget said.

"Zachary recruited an obstetrician to the small town close to the ranch, so he might be able to give you some tips," Tina said.

"Part of it is finding the right person. Not every doctor wants to practice in a big city hospital. You may have your heart set on Texas Medical Center, but the truth is some highly qualified doctor in a backwater town might like the idea of spending some time on an exotic island with easy access to Europe."

"Thank you," she said, her mind already exploring possibilities. "I hadn't thought of that."

Tina squeezed her husband's arm. "What an intelligent, resourceful man."

"Well, I got you, didn't I?" he said and Bridget felt a twinge of longing. How would it feel if Ryder acted the same way toward her? Biting her lip, she gave herself a hard mental shake. She had other plans. Italy beckoned.

She arrived at the exclusive restaurant and was seated with Tina and Zach. Ryder arrived fifteen minutes later, appearing distracted as he strode to the table. "Sorry," he said and leaned down to kiss her full on the mouth. "I've missed the hell out of you," he whispered.

He turned to Tina and Zach. "Your Highness," he said. "Your Highness's husband."

Both Tina and Zach chuckled. "Please call me Tina," she said.

"And I'm Zach," he said, rising to offer his hand.

"Excuse me if I'm checking my cell phone messages. I have a patient teetering on the edge tonight. He's diabetic and I would have preferred not to operate, but this wasn't an optional procedure."

"Is this the same patient you were watching last night?" Bridget asked.

"Yes," Ryder said. "He improved, but I'm concerned about circulation to his extremities."

Bridget automatically extended her hand toward his beneath the table. Ryder responding by clasping it against his knee. "If you need to leave," she began.

"I can stay for now. I just need to check my messages," he said.

"We're glad you could join us," Tina said. "You've certainly captured Bridget's attention and that's not easy to do."

Bridget fought a rise of heat to her cheeks. "Tina," she said.

"Really?" Ryder said. "That's encouraging news because wherever she goes the men are chasing after her."

"I told you that's just because of my title," Bridget said.

"Not true," he said.

"Exactly," Tina said, and Bridget felt her sister study her intently.

Bridget picked up the menu. "I wonder what the specials are tonight."

The waiter took their orders, Ryder frequently checked his phone messages and even excused himself once to make a call.

"Is this what you want for your future?" Tina asked. "He's been half-focused on his phone throughout the entire meal."

"He could have cancelled, but he came. If someone important to you was in the hospital, wouldn't you want to know his doctor was this conscientious?"

Tina frowned. "I suppose. I just can't see you being happy with someone so intent on his career."

Bridget leaned forward. "Ryder and I haven't made any mention of commitment," she whispered. "We're just enjoying each other's company."

"As long as he's not enjoying the company too much," Zach said.

"I'm not pregnant, if that's what you're asking," she said.

"Low blow," Tina said.

"You deserve it," Bridget said, feeling pushed to the edge. "Stefan told me you tattled about me seeing Ryder. I would have expected better from you."

"It's my duty to look after you," Tina said.

"Isn't that the same thing Stefan said to you?" Bridget challenged.

Tina gasped in offense. "Well—"

Ryder reappeared at the table, relief written on his face. "Good news. My patient's condition is improving."

"Excellent news," Bridget said as the waiter cleared the plates from the table.

"Excellent," Tina agreed, though she shot Bridget a sharp look. "Bridget tells me you've recently taken over the guardianship of twin baby boys. That must have been traumatic for all of you. My sympathies on the loss of your brother and sister-in-law."

"Thanks," Ryder said. "Bridget has actually helped smooth the waters with the twins. She found a nanny who has been a perfect fit. Until she stepped in, I was scrambling. I had several quit on me. With my profession, I need dependable childcare."

"Well done, Bridget," Tina said, appearing impressed and vaguely surprised.

"Your friend Keely helped. She gave me the name of the top nanny agency in Dallas," Bridget said.

"But Bridget interviewed the candidates and selected the final choice," he said.

"Bridget isn't known for her affinity for babies," Tina said.

Thanks for nothing, Bridget thought.

"Neither am I," Ryder said bluntly. "But she stepped right in. She's been a lifesaver. The boys adore her."

"And what about you?" Tina asked. "What are your intentions?"

"Tina," Bridget scolded.

"It's a good question," Zach said, backing up his wife.

Bridget balled her fists in her lap. "You do not have to answer that question, Ryder."

Ryder placed his hand over hers underneath the table. "I don't mind answering. Bridget and I have just met. Neither of us know what the future holds. Based on the demands our lives place on us, I know our relationship is temporary."

Bridget's heart fell to her feet. Even though she agreed with Ryder's assessment, hearing the words wounded her to the quick. *She was temporary.*

The interminable meal finally ended fifteen minutes later. Ryder shook hands with her sister and brother-in-law, then brushed a kiss against the corner of her mouth. "Miss you," he murmured just for her ears. "Call me."

A few moments later, she sat in the back of her brother-in-law's SUV, still feeling shell-shocked.

"I can see why you like him," Tina said. "He's his own man and clearly isn't after you because you're royalty. Plus, it doesn't appear that he intends to keep you from going to Italy," she added with a low laugh.

Bridget couldn't muster the careless response she should have been able to toss back to her sister. Silence stretched inside the car.

"Bridget, are you okay? Why are you so quiet?" Tina asked, turning around to look at her.

Bridget thanked heaven for the darkness. "I'm just tired," she said.

"Are you sure? You were always such a night owl."

"I'm sure," she said, trying not to resent her sister for pressing Ryder. It had been so much easier for her when her relationship with Ryder had remained undefined. Some part of her must have craved the sense of possibility with him. He was so different from any man she'd ever known. Ryder and the babies almost made her rethink Italy.

Blessedly, Zach pulled in front of her hotel. Relief rushed through her. If she could just get upstairs without another inquisition. "It was so wonderful seeing both of you. Thank you for dinner," she said and stepped outside the car when the valet opened her door.

Tina rushed outside her door. "Bridget," she said, studying her face. "I know something is wrong."

"Nothing is wrong," Bridget said, pushing a strand of her hair behind her ear. "I told you I'm just tired."

"I don't believe you," Tina said. "I can sense you're upset."

Bridget lost her patience. "Why should I be upset? You just grilled my boyfriend and me. I had a perfectly wonderful evening planned with him, but instead we went to dinner with you and might as well have been sent to walk across coals."

She watched her sister's face fall in desolation. "I'm so sorry," Tina said. "Zach and I just wanted to make sure this man wasn't going to take advantage of you."

"Would you have wanted Zach to receive the same kind of grilling you gave me?"

"I didn't know you felt the same way about Ryder that I felt about Zach," Tina said.

"It doesn't matter how you judge my feelings. It matters how I judge my feelings. I'm an adult. I don't need my sister, brother, brother-in-law and everyone else legislating or judging who I see." She lifted her chin. "Have a little faith in me for a change."

Tina's eyes turned shiny with tears. "Oh, I'm so sorry. I did the same thing to you that I didn't want done to me."

Bridget took a quick sharp breath. She hated to hurt her sister, but Bridget needed Tina to believe in her. Just a little. "Yes, you did. Do you really believe I'm so stupid that any man can get my attention?" she asked, then continued before her sister could continue. "I know I acted like a spoiled brat when I had to come back from Italy after two weeks to cover for you, but I still came back and I still covered. I'm not a total ditz."

"Oh, Bridget," Tina said, shaking her head and clasping Bridget's hands. "I never thought you were a ditz. I always knew you were underestimated. I owe you a huge debt for stepping in for me and also dealing with Stefan. I just don't want you to be hurt."

Bridget bit the inside of her lip. Too late for that, she thought. "I won't be," she reassured her sister and gave her a hug.

"Don't be mad at me," Tina whispered.

"I'm not," Bridget said.

"Promise?" Tina asked.

"Promise," Bridget said.

"You'll never bring another man around me, will you?" Tina asked.

"It'll be a while," Bridget said with a rough laugh. "I need to hit the sack. Long day tomorrow. I love you." She waved to Zach and gave her sister one more hug, then walked inside the hotel toward her suite. When she got inside, she collapsed on her bed and gave in to her tears.

Bridget soldiered through her appointments the next day. Just after four-thirty as she was headed back to her hotel to change for a dinner appearance, she received a call from Suzanne.

"Your Highness, I probably shouldn't call you, but I thought you should know," the nanny said in a tear-filled voice.

"What is it? What's wrong?" Bridget asked.

"It's Travis. His fever shot up to 105 degrees," she

said. "We had to take him to the hospital because it was too late for the pediatrician."

Bridget's heart sank to her feet. "Where is Ryder?"

"He's at the hospital," she said. "In the emergency room with a pediatric specialist." She gave a muffled sob. "I'm at Ryder's with Tyler."

She fought the urge to hyperventilate. Nothing could happen to that baby. Nothing. "I'm going to the hospital."

"Ryder didn't tell me to call you," Suzanne said.

"Well, he bloody well should have," Bridget said and told her driver to head for the hospital.

Ryder had never felt so helpless in his life as he watched his nephew, now his son, suffer the tests necessary to make him well. Travis screamed at the top of his lungs. "I'm sorry, Dr. McCall, but I think we're going to need to do a spinal tap."

Sweating everything but blood, Ryder nodded. "Do what you have to do to make him well." Ryder was well aware that Travis's condition was deteriorating. He couldn't remember feeling this kind of terror ever before.

After the spinal, Ryder heard a ruckus outside the examination room. A nurse entered. "I'm sorry, but there's a woman outside. She says she's a princess. She insists to be allowed inside with you and your son."

The nurse may as well have hit him with both fists. *She's a princess.* It was Bridget. A crazy sliver of relief slid through him. *Your son.* The words echoed inside his brain over and over. "Let her in," he said.

Seconds later, Bridget burst into the room wearing a hospital gown. She glanced from him to Travis, who was curled up exhausted on the table. Ryder would have preferred his cranky cries to his silence. He touched the baby's arm.

Bridget touched Ryder's.

Struggling with a terrible sense of desperation, he covered her hand with his.

"Can I hold him?" she asked.

"Not yet." They'd been instructed to wait to hold Travis, who was hooked up to an IV.

"He's going to be all right," she said softly as she held Ryder's hand. "He's a strong baby."

"He's always the one to cry the loudest and the longest," Ryder said, surprised at the strength of the fear he was fighting. Medically, he understood everything that was being done, but some part of him felt it wasn't enough. There had to be more. There had to be a way.

A few more moments passed. Bridget squeezed his hand and took a deep breath. "Can we hold him now?" she asked the nurse when she entered the room.

"For just a few moments," she said. "Take care for his IV."

Bridget sat and held Travis. His vital signs showed less stress within a moment of her cuddling him. Ryder took his turn holding the baby a while later and he was surprised to see he had the same effect on him.

Sometime later, the pediatrician strode into the room. "Lab results are back. Strep," he said. "With antibiotics, he'll be better in no time."

"Are you sure?" Bridget asked. "He seems so listless."

The pediatrician smiled gently. "With the right treatment, these little guys recover so quickly they make me look like a miracle worker. You just need to make sure everyone who's been exposed to him receives preventative treatment, too."

"Tyler," Bridget said to Ryder.

"And Suzanne and the other sitters. Thanks, Carl," he said to the pediatrician. "I know you stayed late for this. I owe you."

"I'm glad it was so easy," he said and glanced at Bridget. "And I don't believe I've met your wife."

Ryder felt a twist of awkwardness, but rushed to correct his colleague for Bridget's sake. "She's not my wife, but we've been damn lucky to have her around. This is Bridget Devereaux."

Carl nodded. "You clearly have a calming effect on the baby. You must be a natural."

Bridget laughed wryly. "I'm not sure I'd call myself a natural, but I'm relieved Travis will be okay. Thank you so very much."

"No problem. We'll have him stay the rest of the night. I wouldn't be surprised if he'll be ready to be released by midday. I'll talk to you later," he said and headed out the door.

Ryder stared at Bridget tenderly holding his nephew, his child, as if Travis were her own child. Something inside him shifted. Stone walls he'd long considered closed cracked open and he felt a burst of sweet oxygen in places that had felt dead. The expansion inside him was almost painful. For a second, he looked away to gather his defenses, to put himself back together the way he needed to be.

When he looked at her again, he saw a tear drop from her eye to Travis's gown. She gave a quick sound of distress and swiped at her cheek.

The sight of her tears shocked him. Bridget was no crybaby. "Are you okay?"

"I apologize," she said, not lifting her head. "I was just so frightened for him. And I felt so helpless."

He couldn't not reach out to her. Pushing her hair from her cheek, he felt the dampness of her tears against the back of his fingers. "Yeah," he said. "Me, too."

She finally met his gaze. "They're so fragile. One minute, he was screaming bloody murder and trying to scoot to get a ball, and the next…this," she said, looking down at Travis as he slept, his energy clearly spent fighting his infection.

Moved more than he'd thought possible, Ryder kissed her cheek. "Thank you for coming."

"There was no other place more important for me to be," she said and met his gaze again.

The powerful emotion he saw in her gaze resonated inside him so strongly that it took his breath. What the hell was going on? Later, he told himself. He would figure it out later. For the moment, his priorities were perfectly clear. Travis and Bridget.

Just as Carl predicted, within hours, Travis began to make a miraculous recovery. He downed a bottle and afterward seemed to be looking for the rest of the meal. "They told us to go slow on the solids," Bridget said as she fed the baby some applesauce.

"But he looks like he's wanting a steak dinner," Ryder said, pleased with Travis's improvement.

Bridget laughed. "I agree, but he won't be getting that from me."

"He won't be getting that from anyone, no matter how cranky he gets," Ryder said protectively.

Moments later, Carl dropped by, examined the baby

and released him. Bridget wanted to ride home with him and the baby. As they walked out of the hospital in the hot summer sun, two men with cameras and microphones suddenly swarmed them.

"Princess Bridget, you've been spending a lot of time with Dr. Ryder McCall and his nephews. Are the two of you serious or is this just a fling?" the reporter asked.

Anger rushed through Ryder, and he stepped in front of her before she could respond. "It's none of your business. Leave her alone. Can't you see we're bringing a recovering baby home from the hospital?"

"But the people want to know," the reporter continued.

"The people don't need to know. It's none of their business," Ryder said.

"You obviously don't understand that royals belong to their people," the man said and tried to shove Ryder aside to get to Bridget.

"Leave her alone," Ryder said and knocked the man to the ground.

A half second later, Bridget's security guard swept her and the baby into a limo.

"But, Ryder," Bridget protested as her guard closed the door of the limo.

The reporter on the ground winced in pain at the same time he shouted to the cameraman, "Did you catch all that? It'll be worth a fortune."

Chapter 10

"You must leave Dr. McCall's house this instant," Stefan said to Bridget over the phone.

Bridget rolled her eyes. "I'm not going to do that. We just brought Travis home. He still needs comfort and Ryder can't do it all."

"Bridget, you're not the mother of these children. You have other duties, and now that the paparazzi has found you, Dr. McCall's house will be stalked day and night. For your safety, let alone your reputation, you can't stay there."

"Oh, to hell with my reputation. If I'm going to be crucified by the press, I can't think of a better reason."

"You're not thinking rationally," Stefan said. "Perhaps I should pull you from this assignment for your own good."

Bridget's heart froze. "You wouldn't dare," she said.

"Of course I would dare," he said. "I must make the calls for everyone's best interest."

"Give me two weeks," she said, determined to keep the desperation out of her voice. "You owe me that."

Silence followed. "It's true that Phillipa will be coming soon, but your doctor friend will need to be prepared for extra security at his house," Stefan said. "I get the impression he doesn't like a lot of intrusion in his private life. He may not like being told what to do."

"Of course he won't," she said. "Would you?"

"That's different," Stefan said.

"He won't what?" Ryder asked from the doorway, his shirt clinging to him in perspiration.

Her heart jumped and she covered the receiver. "It's my brother. He's being impossible."

"I'm not being impossible," Stefan said. "Let me talk to the doctor."

"Let me talk to your brother," Ryder said.

Bridget cringed. "I'd really rather the two of you meet in different circumstances."

"Sorry, sweetheart," Ryder said.

"Now is the time," Stefan said.

Bridget reluctantly handed the phone to Ryder. "Just start out with Your Highness," she whispered.

Ryder took the phone. "Good to meet you, Your Highness," Ryder said. "Your sister has been a godsend to my family."

Silence followed and Ryder tilted his head to one side.

"My position as adviser to the residents at my hospital can't be influenced by my feelings for your sister,"

Ryder said. "I can't send doctors to Chantaine if it's not in their best interest."

Bridget heard Stefan's raised voice and turned her head, wincing.

"I'm sure you understand my responsibility," Ryder said. "Just as you must make the best decisions for your country, I must make the best decisions in advising my residents."

Another quick silence followed, and Ryder met her gaze. "I have no objection to having additional security so that Bridget can come and go here as she pleases. I don't want what happened today to happen again."

A moment later, he said, "We agree on more than you think. Maybe we'll meet in person sometime. Bye for now, Your Highness."

He turned off the phone and handed it to her. "Your brother is a tough negotiator. Not as charming as you," he added with a low laugh. "And I'm sure he's not as hot."

She bit her lip, but couldn't keep from smiling. She closed her eyes for a second, then opened them. "I can be a lot of trouble. My family can be a lot of trouble."

He shrugged. "Everything can be trouble. Depends on whether it's worth it. Come back in the den. Travis is calling for you."

Bridget stayed the day and the day turned to evening. Ryder gave the okay for additional security around the house. He asked Raoul to keep it as invisible as possible. Raoul agreed. Ryder found he couldn't dislike Bridget's guard because he felt the same need to protect her. He was still trying to remember the time he'd punched someone in defense of a woman....

And he would damn well do it again and again for Bridget....

When those reporters had rushed him and Bridget, he'd acted instinctively, with a primitive response. They'd gotten way too close for comfort to Bridget and his baby. His head was still swimming with the reality.

Ryder hadn't realized how important Bridget and the babies had become to him. It was turning him inside out.

That night, against Raoul's advice, she stayed the night. Ryder took her to his bed and stripped off her clothes. He kissed every inch of her, then took her with every beat of his heart and every beat of hers.

His gaze wrapped around hers. At the same time that he took her, Ryder felt taken. In a way he'd never felt before.

Bridget clung to Ryder as he tried to rise from the bed in the morning. He gave a low chuckle that rippled through her.

"Don't want me to leave?"

"I don't," she said, sliding her hands over his muscular chest. "Pippa is coming to Dallas."

"Pippa?" he echoed, scouring her gaze.

"My sister Phillipa," she said. "She's having some problems. I'll have to entertain her a bit. You and I may not have as much time to be together."

"What kind of problems?" he asked, leaning down on his left forearm.

"I'm not sure, but she's stressed enough that my brother sent her here to visit Valentina and me."

He gave a slow nod. "You have a complicated family."

Her heart twisted. "I warned you."

He nodded. "So you did. When do I see you again?"

"I'll have to call you. I'm not sure when she arrives in the States."

"Call me today. I have surgery, but I'll check my messages in between."

Bridget scrambled to make her appointments for the day, then met Ryder at home that night. In between cuddling the twins, they ate sandwiches prepared by Suzanne and Ryder's friend Marshall.

"They seem to be growing very cozy," she said to Ryder as they leaned back against the sofa with the TV playing a ball game about which neither cared.

"Who?" Ryder asked, sliding his hand around hers.

"Suzanne and Marshall," she said.

Ryder groaned. "Don't tell me that. Marshall doesn't have a good history with women. His maximum time is weeks, not months. Days are more likely."

She shrugged. "You never know. Maybe she's the one. Maybe he's ready for the real thing and he's decided she's the real thing."

She felt him study her. "What do you think about the real thing?"

"I think the real thing starts on its own and then you have to keep it going," she said, but when she looked at him, she felt herself spin with emotion. "What about you?"

"I don't know. I always thought it was a figment of everyone's imagination," he said.

"And now?"

He shrugged his muscular shoulders. "Now, I'm not so sure."

* * *

Bridget hit the campaign trail for doctors for Chantaine hard. As one of her last resorts, she even met with the administrator of another medical hospital in Dallas. They were more open to her proposal of sending doctors to her country.

Bridget felt torn at the prospect. She wanted only the best for her country, but she couldn't automatically turn down the hospital's interest. It was more than Ryder could offer. The knowledge stabbed at her. She hated that he couldn't feel her passion for her country the same way she did.

In the meantime, she took deep breaths and decided not to make any impulsive decisions. That night, after rocking the babies, she joined Ryder in his bed. He made love to her with a passion that took her breath away.

Ryder drew her into his arms, flush against his body. She felt his heart beat against her chest. She had never felt closer to another human being in her life.

Travis recovered quickly. It seemed that one moment the baby had been listless and the next he was raring to go, trying to pull up and almost scooting, heaven help them all.

Phillipa arrived at DFW and Bridget greeted her sister with open arms. Bridget was concerned to see that Phillipa had indeed lost weight and there were circles beneath her eyes. "Hello, my darling," Bridget said. "I'm so glad to see you."

Phillipa slumped against her for a moment. "It's so good to see you, too," she murmured, squeezing Bridget tightly.

Bridget's concern deepened, but her instincts told her to mask it. At least for now. "I must prepare you for the Texas humidity," she said. "You can cut the air with a knife. We're headed to Tina's ranch. I'm sure she'll be calling any minute. She's dying to see you." Seconds later, her cell phone rang. "Just as I said." She picked up. "Yes, Tina, she's here and as soon as we get her luggage, we're headed straight for your house."

Bridget nodded and smiled. "Soon, soon. Ciao for now."

She hustled Pippa into the limo, plied her with a couple margaritas, and chattered during the drive to Tina's about Texas and the twins and Ryder. "Of course, Stefan is complaining," she said. "I swear he'd like to put us all in convents."

"So true," Phillipa said. "How did you deal with him?"

Bridget made a mental note of Phillipa's comment. Was Phillipa's problem romance? "Avoidance is the best policy," she said. "Emails. Text messages. Direct conversation is the worst because Stefan is disgustingly intuitive. If he would only get Eve pregnant, maybe he would be a bit distracted."

Phillipa chuckled. "Eve doesn't want to rush another child. She wants to give Stephenia plenty of time to adjust."

"Blast her practicality," Bridget said and took her second sip of her first margarita. "Well, you should know that Tina will arrange for massages and spa treatments. Zach may take us out on his fabulous boat. We also have a social ball to attend in four days."

"Social ball," Phillipa echoed, clearly concerned.

"Oh, it's nothing to worry about," Bridget soothed.

"It's a charity gala in Dallas. Tina and Zach will attend. If you like, we can make an appearance and bug out. You know I'm quick like that when it suits me. Stefan has fussed about it enough. Plus we can go shopping before and you can get a great dress out of it."

Pippa gave a mild smile. "So we don't have to stay all night?"

"Of course not," Bridget said, patting her sister on her knee. "Have the doctoral studies become a pain in the butt? You know, you work entirely too hard."

"My studies are fine, but Stefan insisted I take a break," she said.

"He means well," Bridget said. "But he still needs some work. I'm hopeful Eve can continue his needed transformation."

Phillipa sighed and took another sip of her margarita. "Bridget, you have no idea how much I've needed to see you."

Still concerned, Bridget managed a laugh. "Well, prepare yourself for an overdose."

Pippa smiled and Bridget felt as if she'd scored a small victory. Later, as they arrived at the ranch, Tina rushed down the steps. "Phillipa!" she called stretching out her arms.

Bridget watched her two sisters embrace and her heart squeezed tight with emotion. Tina pulled back. "Look at you. I love your hair. That dress is fabulous. What happened to my sister, the librarian?"

"I'm still here," Phillipa said. "A stylist put together some things for my visit to the States."

"Regardless, you look fabulous, but shorts and no shoes are the summertime uniform here. Come visit your niece. She can't wait to see Aunt Pippa," Tina said, and tossed Bridget a glance of concern before she led them inside the house.

Bridget and Phillipa played with their gorgeous niece until dinnertime when Hildie served a superb, filling meal. Between the margaritas, the food and the security of her sisters, Phillipa grew drowsy early in the evening. Tina ushered her to one of the bedrooms and returned to the den with Bridget and Zach.

"She's different than I expected," Tina said. "Stefan said she was stressed, but—" Tina frowned. "What do you think is behind all this?"

"A man," Bridget said as she sipped a glass of ice water.

Tina's eyebrows rose. "What makes you say that?"

"Something Pippa said on the way here."

"What? Who?" Tina demanded.

"I didn't pry. She just seemed too fragile," Bridget said.

Tina sighed. "How did you get that out of her?"

"It was a sideways comment. I was complaining about Stefan and how he doesn't want any of us to date."

"True," Tina said.

"Too true," Zach said from behind the newspaper he was reading.

Tina glanced at her husband and smiled.

"In this case, I was speaking of Ryder," Bridget said.

"Hmm," Tina said.

"So far, he seems like a good guy," Zach said. "If he was willing to punch out that reporter who was after you, he gets my vote."

"It's all about the violence," Tina said, rolling her eyes.

"Protecting a woman is a primitive response in a man. Protectiveness is an important trait."

"I'm sure Stefan will love hearing that opinion," Bridget said wryly.

"Stefan just needs to be reminded about what he would do to protect Eve," Zach said bluntly, then shook his newspaper and appeared to begin to read again.

"She needs a massage," Tina said. "A ride on the water. And perhaps Hildie's double-strength margaritas."

Three days later, the sisters went to Dallas and shopped for dresses. Bridget was distracted. She was late. Not for an appointment. She was late for her period, and she had been, well, exposed to the possibility of becoming pregnant. Although they had used contraception, Bridget wasn't sure if she had landed in the small percentile of women for whom it had failed.

"What do you think?" Tina asked as Phillipa tried on a gown. "I think the cocoa color is perfect on her."

Bridget blinked, looking at Pippa. "Yes, it's beautiful. It really accentuates all your positive attributes."

"Although, a pastel or dark navy would be fabulous, too, don't you think?" Tina said.

"I completely agree," she said and forced herself to pay attention to the rest of the shopping expedition. She rendered her positive opinion to Tina's choice for a dress, but nixed the idea of getting a new gown for herself.

Tina and Phillipa gasped at once. "Are you ill?" Phillipa asked.

"What is wrong?" Tina demanded. "You never turn down the opportunity to get a new designer gown."

Bridget brushed their concerns aside. "It's nothing," she said. "I have a ton of gowns I brought with me that

I haven't yet worn. We've already spent enough time shopping. It's not necessary to find a gown for me."

"Enough time shopping," Pippa echoed. "You've often said there's no such thing as too much shopping."

Uncomfortable with her sisters' scrutiny, Bridget shrugged her shoulders. "Okay, I'll admit it. I'm hungry and we might end up with rubber chicken tonight."

Tina giggled and rolled her eyes. "Now we have the real answer. I could use a good meal, too. Crab sounds especially good."

The thought of crab turned Bridget's stomach. "Or even a nice sandwich. You know where we can find a good variety of food, Tina. Where should we go?"

Delighted to give the attention back to her sister, Bridget joined her sisters for a late lunch. Her phone rang during their meal and she excused herself to take the call. "Ryder, talk to me. I swear it feels as if it's been three months since I heard your voice."

He laughed. "Same here. Are you having fun with your sisters?"

"For the most part," she said. "We still haven't figured out what's wrong with Phillipa, but I think it's a man. I'm hoping she'll talk with us. It's always more miserable to suffer by yourself. And whatever your problems are, they seem ten times worse if you don't share. Speaking of worries, how are you and the twins?"

"The only way the twins and I could be better would be if you were around," he said.

Her heart went squishy at his words. "Oh, that's so sweet. They've probably already forgotten me."

"No chance."

"You know, the other day, I was wondering, did you ever think you were going to have children? I know becoming a doctor was important, but did you *ever* think you would start a family?"

"It wasn't a priority," he said. "My career was always number one…. Just a moment," he said and she heard him talking with someone else. Then he came back on the line. "Listen, I need to go soon. Are you okay? I'm hearing something in your voice."

"Oh, no," she said, lying because she knew she didn't have time to discuss her real feelings. "It's just family stuff."

He paused a few seconds. "But you mentioned starting a family. What's on your mind?"

"Nothing," she insisted. "I was just thinking about how you'd been thrust into the position of being a father so quickly. I wondered what your original plans were."

She heard him give a quick response to someone on the other end of the line. "Are you pregnant?"

Shocked at the accuracy of his question, she sucked in a quick breath. Something inside her insisted on denial. She would figure that out later. "Oh, my goodness. How could I be pregnant? You and I are so careful."

"Nothing provides perfect protection except abstinence," he said.

"Oh, that's ridiculous. We're fine. We're perfectly fine," she insisted, her heart racing.

"Thanks for the reassurance," he said. "You and I both have enough going on without adding a baby to the mix."

"So true," she said, but her stomach twisted viciously.

"I have to go. I'll call later."

"Ciao," she said and stared blindly at her cell phone. What if she *was* pregnant? It was clear that Ryder didn't want another baby. How would she handle this? Would she have to do it all alone? Panic raced through her. She broke into a cold sweat. She shuddered at the possibility of dealing with her family's disapproval and interference.

"Bridget," her sister Tina said, breaking her out of her reverie. "The food's been here for several minutes. What's wrong with you today? You seem totally distracted."

Bridget took a breath and pulled herself together, forcing a big smile. "Oh, Tina, you know how I am. If I've got more than one and a half things on my mind, I'm distracted. I'm still thinking about the babies and the medical program for Chantaine. I need that sandwich. Thank you for coming to get me," she said and marched back to the table, praying her sister wouldn't ask any more questions.

That night, Bridget and her sisters dressed at her suite at the hotel. She felt as if she were on automatic. A green dress. Green was a good color for her. Mineral powder, subtle eyes, bold, red lips. She didn't feel bold, but she needed to be confident. She needed to be someone bigger than her current self because her current self was feeling confused and vulnerable. Lord, she hoped it was late PMS.

She gave her sister Phillipa a hug. "You look fabulous."

"You overstate," Phillipa said. "You always have."

"Not this time. Look at how gorgeous you look," she said, pointing to the full-length mirror.

Tina stepped into the room from the bathroom. "What are you two arguing about?"

"I told Phillipa she looked fabulous and gorgeous and she said I'm exaggerating and I said I'm not," Bridget said.

Tina walked to Phillipa and put her hands tenderly on her cheeks. "For once, Bridget understated."

Phillipa closed her eyes and squeezed them tight as if she were fighting tears. "You two are being so kind. I know all of this is because you're worried about me."

"Well, it's true we're worried about you," Bridget said.

"Bridget," Tina said with a chiding expression.

"It's true. It's also true that I wouldn't include fabulous and gorgeous in the same sentence if I didn't truly believe it," Bridget said.

Phillipa's lips twitched. "You make a good point. The real you leaks out after a short time."

Bridget lifted her hand. "What did I say?"

Tina sighed. "We just want you to be okay. You're our baby," she said, stroking Phillipa's hair.

"I'm not a baby. I'm a grown-up. I can manage my life. I just need a little recalibration."

"And you can get that here," Tina said.

Phillipa smiled. Tina's cell phone rang and she picked up. "It's Zachary."

Moments later, Zachary arrived in a limo driven by security. The three princesses and Zach rode to the charity ball. As they stepped outside the limo, they were greeted by flashing cameras and reporters.

"Welcome to Dallas's premier Charity Ball, Your Highnesses. To what do we owe the honor of your presence tonight?" a reporter asked.

Just lucky, I guess, Bridget thought, but managed to swallow the comment.

"I live just outside of Fort Worth with my husband and daughter, and I've been so happy to receive visits from both my sisters, Bridget and Phillipa," Tina said.

"Your sister Bridget has been in town for over a month. There have been rumors about her and one of our doctors—"

"We're here tonight to celebrate the charity of the people of Texas, which is so much bigger than rumors, don't you agree?" Tina asked. "It was lovely to meet you."

They moved on to the next reporter, and Tina's responses reminded Bridget why her sister had done such a superlative job representing Chantaine.

"She's so good," Bridget muttered.

"Times two," Phillipa said.

"If only she could be in two places at once," Bridget said with a sigh.

"You're doing pretty well," Pippa said.

"My time is limited," Bridget said. "I don't have Tina's endurance."

"Maybe, this once, you underestimate yourself," her sister said.

"I think not, but I appreciate your kindness. On to our rubber chicken," she whispered and was thrilled she could make Phillipa laugh.

"What are you two talking about?" Tina demanded.

"You don't want to know," Bridget said.

Tina shot her a curt micro-look before she plastered a serene expression on her face. Zach escorted the group inside to their table at the front of the room. They made small talk with the others seated at their table. Soon enough, announcements and presentations began. Bridget was stunned when Nic LaFitte stepped

forward to receive an award of recognition. The Devereaux had a long-standing grudge against the Lafittes.
Nic's father had caused a humiliating scandal for the
royal family.

"What is *he* doing here?" she whispered to Tina.

"Zach says he's a huge contributor here. Everyone
loves him," Tina said distastefully.

"They clearly don't know him," she said and nudged
Phillipa. "Why can't we escape him?" she whispered.
"Maybe it's because he's the devil and that means he
can be everywhere."

When Phillipa didn't respond, Bridget glanced at her
face and saw that her sister had turned white as a sheet.

Chapter 11

"I'm not feeling well," Phillipa said. "Please excuse me."

"Do you want me to go with you?" Bridget asked, her stomach twisting in concern for her sister.

"No, no. I just need a little air," Phillipa said as she slowly rose and lifted her lips in a forced smile. "I'll be back in a little bit."

Bridget watched her sister move through the perimeter of the room as surreptitiously as possible and felt worried.

"Where is she going?" Tina asked in a whisper.

"The powder room," Bridget said. "She says she needs some air."

Tina frowned and glanced at Nic LaFitte as he left the stage. "Do you think this has anything to do with LaFitte?"

"I can't imagine that it would. I mean, none of us would get involved with a LaFitte. Not even the most rebellious of us and Pippa is nowhere near the most rebellious."

Tina nodded and Bridget paid half attention to the speaker, more attention to her watch. "I'm going to check on Pippa," she whispered.

"I'll go with you," Tina said, and stood just after she did.

Bridget tried to be discreet just as Phillipa had been, but she noticed several heads turning in her direction. She immediately searched for the first ladies' room and didn't find Phillipa there. "Where is she?" she muttered to herself.

"I'm starting to get a bad feeling about LaFitte," Tina said as they left the room.

"I can't believe Pippa would be that foolish. She's extremely intelligent and quite practical," Bridget said as she scoured the lobby for her sister.

"I wonder if she went outside," Tina said.

"It's possible. She said she needed some air," Bridget said, then spotted a coat closet and pointed toward it. "You don't think she would be there, do you? It's the last place I would look in this hot, humid weather and the door is closed."

Tina glanced in the same direction and shrugged. "I don't think so, but we may as well check."

Bridget led the way to the door and stopped just outside, pressing her ear closer to listen. Hearing nothing, she cracked the door open.

"This is insanity," Phillipa said. "It will never work."

"Why not?" a male voice demanded. "If I want you and you want me, what is most important?"

"Want is a temporary emotion," Phillipa said. "There are more important things than temporary emotions."

"If that's true, then why are you here with me?" he asked.

Tina gasped and the sound traveled through the door like a thunderclap. Seconds later, Phillipa and Nic LaFitte appeared in the doorway.

"Get away from my sister," Bridget said.

"That's for her to say, not you," LaFitte said.

"You're just using her," Tina said. "You only want her because she can redeem your terrible family name."

"Not everyone finds my family name reprehensible. Some even respect it," he said.

"That's respect you've bought with money," Tina said. "Leave Phillipa alone. You can never be good enough for her. If you have any compassion, you'll at least protect her reputation by leaving now."

LaFitte tightened his jaw. "I'll leave, but Phillipa will make the ultimate decision about the future of our relationship." He glanced behind him and met Phillipa's shocked, pale face. "Ciao, darling. Call me when you get some courage. Some things are meant to be," he said and strode away.

"Oh, darling," Bridget said and immediately went to Phillipa and took her in her arms.

Tina soon followed. "Oh, you poor thing. The LaFittes are so evil. It's clear he intends to trick you."

Phillipa's face crumpled. "He was so kind to me," she whispered.

"Of course he was," Tina said. "He's a snake like the rest of his family. And you're too sweet to know the difference."

"Are you saying he couldn't possibly be attracted

to me just because I'm me?" Phillipa asked, her voice filled with desperation.

Bridget felt her heart shatter at the pain in her sister's voice. "Of course not," she said. "You're an amazing, beautiful and wonderful girl. You're a precious gem and you must be protected from anyone who doesn't deserve you."

"And no LaFitte would *ever* deserve you," Tina said.

Moments later, out of consideration for Phillipa, they left the event. Bridget and Tina fought over where Phillipa should spend the night. Bridget eventually won. "She shouldn't have to ride an extra hour back to the ranch tonight," Bridget said. "I have plenty of room in my suite. Along with the makings of margaritas or any other toddy she may require tonight."

"But Zach and I could protect her from any unwanted advances from LaFitte," Tina said.

"His advances weren't unwanted," Phillipa whispered. "I was attracted to him and wished he would contact me. I finally gave in and sent a message to him. He met me and that was how it all started."

Tina sucked in a sharp breath, then silence fell in the limousine. Zach tipped back a glass of bourbon.

"Well, I'm glad you came to your senses," Tina said.

Bridget gave Phillipa a hug. "We don't need to talk or think about this anymore tonight. You've already had enough stress tonight. You're due some rest. You can come to my room and fall asleep all snug and safe in your bed. You can think about LaFitte tomorrow if necessary. Tonight it's not necessary."

"You sound like that Scarlett O'Hara in the American film *Gone with the Wind*," Tina said.

"In this case, she offered a nice bit of wisdom," Bridget countered.

"Please don't argue," Phillipa said.

"We're not," Bridget said, giving Tina a strong glance. "Tina and I agree, don't we?"

Tina took a quick breath. "Yes, we do. I think we all need some extra rest tonight. In fact, I think Zach and I will stay overnight at your hotel."

"What?" Zach asked.

"Yes," Tina said decisively. "We can stay overnight at Bridget's hotel in a separate suite, of course. I'm sure Hildie won't mind keeping the baby."

"Yes, but—"

"In the morning, we can wake up and all have brunch together," she said brightly.

"And if Phillipa sleeps in, then Mom and Dad can enjoy a night away from their little darling and Phillipa can visit you at the ranch later."

Tina frowned, but nodded.

Moments later, they exited the limo into the hotel and Bridget and Phillipa took the lift to the penthouse. "Thank you," Phillipa said after they entered the elevator.

Bridget took her sister's hand. "We all need a break every now and then. If your sister won't give it to you, then who *will* give it to you?"

"Yes, but Tina clearly hates Nic," Bridget said in a shaky voice.

"All of us hate the LaFitte family. Part of it is not logical. After all, if Father had married the woman who married LaFitte, none of us would exist. Maybe we don't like to lose. Plus there's the matter of the LaFitte who killed one of our great-uncles." Bridget sighed. "And, after all the bad they did to us, they're so bloody wealthy and successful. That's enough of a reason to hate them."

"His mother is dying," Phillipa said.

Bridget glanced at her sister. "Really. How?"

"Cancer. It's been a terribly grueling experience. She's currently near the end."

Bridget took a deep breath. "I don't wish that on anyone."

"Neither do I," Phillipa said as the elevator dinged their arrival to the penthouse.

Bridget clasped her sister's hand. "You must promise me that you won't think about this anymore tonight. You need to take a break from it. It's hurting you. More important, you can't fix it tonight."

Phillipa squeezed her hand in return. "I may not agree with a lot of what you've said, but it's true that I can't fix all of this tonight. I should just go to bed and try to sleep."

Bridget nodded. "And get a massage in the morning. I'll keep Tina away."

"You're usually nagging me to take on more palace duties. When did you become my fairy protector?" Phillipa asked.

"Oh, well, I'll nag again soon enough. Enjoy the respite," Bridget said.

The next morning, Bridget did just as she'd promised and arranged for a soothing massage for her younger sister. Tina would only be put off so long before she was knocking on the door of Bridget's suite. Bridget opened the door. "We're sipping lime water and relaxing on the balcony. Would you like to join us?" she asked. "And whatever you do, don't hound her and don't bring up LaFitte. I've got her nice and relaxed after her massage."

Tina nodded in agreement. "We'll take her out on Zach's new boat."

"But don't try to matchmake," Bridget said.

Tina frowned. "You don't think a male distraction would help?" she whispered.

"No," Bridget said emphatically. "Pippa has fallen hard for LaFitte. She needs to get over him before she moves on to the next."

"You seem to have enormous insight on this matter. Surprising," Tina said, lifting her eyebrow in a suspicious manner.

Bridget feigned an airy sigh. "Underestimated again. When will it end?"

After her sisters left, Bridget returned several calls. As soon as she finished, though, the quiet settled over her like a heavy blanket. She still hadn't started her period yet. Tempted to wear a disguise and buy an early pregnancy test from a drugstore, she put it off. She never knew who was watching and who might discuss her purchase with the paparazzi. Perhaps by tomorrow...

Her cell phone rang and she saw Ryder's return number on her screen. He was the one person to whom she hadn't made a return call. Her heart hammered with nerves as she took the call. "Hello, Ryder," she said.

"Damn good to hear your voice. I was starting to wonder if you'd disappeared or headed to Chantaine or Italy without letting me know," he said.

"I wouldn't do that," she said. "I've just been tied up with my sisters. How are my boys?"

"Your boys are screaming to see you. Even Suzanne says they miss you. Come over for the weekend," he said.

Her heart jumped again and she began to pace. On the one hand, she was desperate to see Ryder again. On the other hand, she was distracted by the possibility that she could be pregnant. Ryder had been much more intuitive about her worries than she would have ever expected.

He made a buzzing sound. "Time's up. Because you didn't say no, that must mean yes. I'll pick you up around five," he said.

"Wait," she said breathlessly. "Let Raoul bring me. That way he can go through his security protocol and I won't be hassled by him or my brother. Hopefully," she added in a low voice.

"Good," Ryder said. "The twins have a trick they want to show you. See you soon," he said.

"Trick?" she echoed, but he'd already disconnected the call.

Anticipation zinged through her and she giggled. Her mood felt as if it had lifted into the stratosphere. Amazing that he had that effect on her so quickly. Frightening, really, if she thought about it too deeply, so she wouldn't.

A few hours later, she tried to ignore the lecture Raoul was giving her about how she was taking risks and how she should stay away from windows.

"Your Highness, do you understand what I'm saying?" Raoul asked.

"Absolutely," she said.

"You haven't been listening to a word I've said," he said.

"That's not true. I've listened to at least every third word you've said. I'm not reckless, but I won't let my position steal my joy. You never know how long you'll have that opportunity. There's so much drudgery you have to grab the joy."

Silence followed. "That's remarkably deep, Your Highness," he said. "But after protecting you for five years, I'm not surprised. You hide your depth well," he said, glancing at her through the rearview mirror.

Bridget felt a twist in her chest at her guard's revelation. "Thank you, Raoul. You deserve sainthood for being my guard."

"You are not as bad as you profess," he said. "But stay away from windows and call me before you walk outside the house."

She laughed as he pulled the car to the curb of Ryder's home. "Way to slide in those instructions," she said and opened her door before he could. "Ciao."

Before she arrived on the porch, the door flung open and Ryder greeted her, sweeping her inside. "Your men are waiting for you," he said and pulled her into his arms.

He felt so strong and wonderful and alive. She felt as if she'd come home. She was safe and more whole than she'd ever dreamed possible. He picked her up and spun her around and she couldn't help laughing.

"You act like you haven't seen me in a year," she said, squeezing his strong shoulders.

"It has been a year," he said and searched her face. "Right?"

A shriek sounded just a few steps away.

Bridget glanced at the floor and saw the twins scooting toward her and Ryder. "Oh, bloody hell," she said, panicked. "They're moving! We have to stop them."

Ryder roared with laughter. "That was my first response, too," he said and squeezed her shoulders. "But crawling is next. After that, standing. Then walking."

Bridget stared, torn between exultation and cold fear, and shook her head. "What are you going to do?"

"Cope," he said. "Manage them, if such a thing is possible. The good news is they get worn out a lot faster," he said.

Tyler stopped at Bridget's feet and gurgled.

Her heart twisted so tightly that she could hardly breathe. "Oh, you darling," she said and bent down to pick up the baby. She groaned. "You've gained weight. Is that possible?"

Ryder picked up Travis and extended him toward Bridget. She gave the baby a kiss and cooed at him. He cooed at her in return and her chest expanded, filling her with an overwhelming sense of love and emotion. "Oh, you darlings. I've missed both of you."

"Both?" Ryder asked.

"All three. Especially you," she said and sank onto the sofa with the baby on her lap. "The last few days have been full of drama. Poor Phillipa has been seduced by one of our family enemies. She's such an innocent. I know he's taken advantage of her, but I'm hoping she'll regain her sense."

"Who's this enemy? I thought you Devereaux were peaceful and moderate," he said, joining her on the sofa.

"We are for the most part," she said. "But the LaFittes have been bad news for our family. One of them murdered my great-uncle. And one seduced my father's bride away from him," she said.

"I can understand the first, but the second, not so much. You wouldn't have been born if your father had married a different woman," he said.

"True," she said. "But the LaFittes are still on our don't list. No discussion," she said.

"What about me?" he asked in a rough voice. "Am I on your don't list?"

Her breath hitched in the back of her throat. "Probably, but that hasn't stopped me, has it?"

His lips lifted in a lazy half grin. "Guess not. I ordered Italian for dinner. Bought red wine on the way home."

"Sounds great, but I'm all about water these days. I'm on a new diet that favors lemon and lime water. It's supposed to cleanse the toxins. Do you have any limes?"

Ryder blinked. "Limes?"

"No problem. Filtered water is good."

"So, red wine is out?" he asked.

"Just during my lime phase," she said with a smile.

They watched the twins scoot around the den until they wore themselves out. Ryder rocked Tyler and she rocked Travis. It took only moments before Travis was drooling on her shoulder. She met Ryder's gaze and he gave a slight nod and they carried the babies up to their cribs.

Seconds later, they walked downstairs and shared a late meal. Although Italian fare didn't appeal to her at the moment, Bridget pushed the food around her plate to make it look as if she'd eaten it. Later, she took her plate into the kitchen and pushed the contents into the trash can.

Did this mean she was pregnant? she wondered. She loved Italian food. If she hated it, now what did it mean? Her stomach twisted into a knot, but she took a deep breath and returned to the den. "Delicious dinner," she said and sat down beside him.

"You didn't eat everything. It must not have been that delicious," he said, sliding his arm over her shoulder.

"I had a late lunch and I'm watching my girlish figure," she said with a smile.

"I'll take care of that second job. I have no problem watching your girlish figure," he said, sliding his lips along her neck.

She laughed, exulting in his caress. Turning toward him, she lifted her mouth to his. "Kiss me," she said.

"Is that an order?"

"Kinda," she said.

He gave a low, dirty chuckle and did as she commanded.

The next morning, Ryder awakened early. Bridget's back was pressed against him. His hand was curled around her bare waist. Her skin was butter soft against his palm. It was a good morning. The best kind of morning. Bridget was with him.

He couldn't remember a time when he'd been more at peace. Something primitive inside him drove him to keep her with him. He started to understand why men kidnapped their women and kept them in luxurious captivity. Which was crazy. When had he ever felt this need for a woman? When had a woman ever filled up all his emptiness and need?

Bridget wiggled against him, then suddenly raced out of bed to the master bath. A couple moments later, she returned, carefully crawling into the bed and inching herself toward him.

Several things clicked through his brain. His gut twisted. "Bridget," he murmured against her ear.

"Yes," she whispered.

"Are you pregnant?"

Silence passed. Way too long. His heart sank. *Another baby?* He couldn't imagine it. How in the world—

"I don't know," she finally said. "I'm late."

A half dozen emotions sliced through him. He couldn't speak.

"How late?" he finally managed.

"A week and a half," she said, still not turning to look at him.

"We should do a test," he said.

"No," she said. "I can't take a test, and you can't do it for me. The press is watching me even more than usual now. I want to know as much as you do, but a few more days may give us the answer without any exposure to the press," she said and finally turned toward him.

"You're late. No red wine. Why didn't you tell me?"

Her eyes clouded with turmoil. "Our relationship is still new. We haven't made any sort of promises to each other."

His heart pounded against his chest. The thought of another baby scared the crap out of him. His brother's babies had become his own. The baby he shared with Bridget would be his to protect as well.

"If you're pregnant, you need to start taking prenatal vitamins as soon as possible. You need to get on a regimen—"

"And if I'm not, I can go back to my red wine–swilling, unhealthy ways," she said.

He bit the inside of his lip to keep from laughing. "I still think you should let me do a test."

She shook her head. "Three more days. I'll live healthy until then."

He searched her face. "I would protect you if you're pregnant with my child, Bridget. I would marry you. I would protect our child."

Her eyes still swam with emotion, some of which he couldn't read. "That's good to know," she said and tucked her head under his chin. "Can we talk about something else until then?"

Ryder spent the weekend secluded in happiness with Bridget. They shared the care of the twins, took the boys for a stroll in the neighborhood despite Raoul's protests and spent their nights together, his body wrapped around hers, her body wrapped around his.

He returned to work Monday wondering if she was pregnant, wishing he could keep her with him. He met with Dr. Hutt.

"Dr. Robinson is still having financial problems due to his family. It's distracting him from his duties," Dr. Hutt said.

Ryder immediately felt defensive. "We need to look for a solution instead of immediately booting him out of the program."

"I agree," Hutt said, surprising Ryder with his response.

"What about your princess friend?" he asked, leaning back in his chair. "Wouldn't this be a perfect solution? She gives him a bonus scholarship, he takes a tour of her country. Win, win."

"Are you serious?" Ryder asked.

"Yes," he said. "You and I must manage residents from all eco-social backgrounds. Not everyone is from your background. Not everyone is from mine."

For the first time in months, he felt a measure of hope. Maybe, just maybe Hutt could see past his privileged upbringing. "Are you sure you shouldn't push him harder?" he asked. "Maybe he just needs to work more."

His colleague frowned. "He's already working hard. Harder than I ever did," he said.

Ryder was stunned. He'd never known Hutt was capable of such insight. "When did this change happen?"

"The last time you and I met, I went home and couldn't sleep. For several nights. Dr. Walters not only kicked my butt, he also *encouraged* you. He wasn't one man to the residents. He stepped into their shoes and gave them what they needed. As advisers, we have to do the same."

Ryder shook his head. "When in hell did you become a reasonable man?"

His colleague laughed. "It's amazing the kind of perspective a wife can offer when you choose to talk to her."

"Your wife did this?" Ryder asked.

Hutt shrugged. "Professionally speaking, of course, she didn't," he said.

Ryder felt a change click through him and extended his hand to Dr. Hutt. "Give my best to your wife," he said.

"And give my best to your princess," Hutt said.

One day later, Bridget called him. He was in surgery, so he checked his messages. "Meet me today. Name the time," she said. "I have good news."

His day was crazy, but he managed to meet her at a quiet cocktail bar after work.

"Rough day?" she asked as she sipped a martini.

He felt a crazy surge of disappointment. The last couple of days, he'd secretly begun to like the idea of having a baby with Bridget. "You're not pregnant."

"I'm not," she said and lifted her glass to his. She smiled in relief. "Cheers."

"Cheers," he said. "And damn."

She blinked. "Damn?"

"Maybe I could have forced you into a shotgun marriage if you were pregnant."

She laughed and took another sip of her martini.

"I wouldn't want a shotgun wedding for you or me," she said.

"I don't know," he said. "I think we could have made the best of it."

She sucked in a deep breath and glanced away. "Perhaps, but now we don't have to," she said with a shaky smile. She bit her lip. "My other news is that another medical center has stepped forward to participate in our program."

Surprised, Ryder searched her gaze. "Really?"

"We finally have doctors willing to come to Chantaine," she said, relief crossing her face. "I followed your advice and found experts willing to visit Chantaine and give training. And this medical center is willing to offer our scholarship and package to their residents. So far, two have signed up for our program. They weren't our first choice, but Stefan is confident this arrangement will be in the best interest of the country."

"Wow," Ryder said. "What a coincidence. Today Dr. Hutt and I agreed to send one of our residents to Chantaine. He's a talented generalist, but he has financial issues you can solve. Still interested?"

"Of course," she said. "I shouldn't say we're desperate, but we're definitely open. We're also going to need a new director for Chantaine's Health Center, but that's clearly a work in progress."

"I guess this means you're headed for Chantaine… or Italy," he said, his gut tightening into a square knot.

"Not right away, but very soon," she said. "I'll go back with Phillipa."

Chapter 12

Ryder returned home well after 9:00 p.m. after meeting Bridget for cocktails and dinner. He had arranged for Suzanne to stay late to watch the twins, but Marshall greeted him.

Marshall handed him a beer. "Hey, big guy. Congratulate me. Suzanne and I got married this weekend in Vegas. I sent her home because she was tired out. I kept her pretty busy this weekend," he added with a wink.

Stunned for the third time today, Ryder stared at Marshall. "What?"

"Suzanne and I got married. Don't worry, she's determined to still be your nanny even though I told her she could be a lady of leisure."

Ryder accepted the beer and took a sip. "Oh, Lord help me."

"That's not quite a congrats, but I'll take it," Marshall said, giving Ryder a fist bump. "You look kinda strange, big guy. What's up?"

Ryder shook his head and sank onto his couch. "Just a crazy day. Are you sure Suzanne is still going to take care of the twins?"

Marshall sat on the other side of the couch. "Yeah. She's determined. You know she can't have babies, right? That's why her husband left her. His stupidity, my good luck."

"Bridget mentioned something about it," Ryder said, his mind falling back a few days to when her pregnancy had still been a possibility. And now she would be leaving soon. He knew the twins would miss her.

"Yeah, I told her there's more than one way to crack that nut. Getting a baby. We'll check out the IVF stuff, then we'll look into our adoption options. She was surprised I would be open to that. She's an amazing woman. I would do anything for her," Marshall said.

"Why didn't you tell me you were going to do this?" Ryder demanded.

"You'd already warned me away from Suzanne, but I wanted to get to know her. It took some work to get her to go out with me, but I knew she was the one for me. She's the first really good woman I've met and I knew I didn't want to let her go."

Ryder felt a twist of envy that Marshall had been able to overcome the obstacles that might have kept him and Suzanne apart. "Congratulations," he said, extending his hand.

Marshall nodded and smiled. "Still can't believe I was able to talk her into eloping. Of course, now is the hard part, but with her, I don't think it's gonna be that hard."

"She's a strong woman. If anyone can keep you in line, she's the one," Ryder said.

"Yeah, speaking of women, what's up with your princess?"

Ryder's gut tightened again. "I think she's headed back to Chantaine soon."

Marshall's eyebrows lifted in surprise. "Whoa. I thought you two—"

"Temporary," Ryder said. "For Pete's sake, she's a princess, and I've got my hands full with the boys and my position at the hospital."

"Hmm," Marshall said. "I could have sworn you two had it going on. Shame you couldn't work it out. Sorry, bud," he said and thumped Ryder on the shoulder. "Hope you don't mind, but my *wife* is waiting for me at home."

"Okay, okay," Ryder said with a faint smile. "Just make sure she gets enough sleep to take care of the boys."

Marshall just gave a dirty laugh and walked out the door.

Ryder stared into the distance and felt more alone than ever. For the most part, he hadn't minded being alone. In the past, it had meant he had to take care of only himself. All that had changed when his brother had died and Ryder had taken on the twins. Now it was just him and the twins.

An image of Bridget floated through his mind and he got an itchy, unsettled feeling inside him. Trying to dismiss it, he went to the kitchen and glanced through the mail for the day, but that itchy feeling didn't go away. Ryder rubbed at his gut, but it didn't do any good. A sense of dread that started in his stomach climbed to the back of his throat.

Ryder swore under his breath. He'd fallen for the woman. Worse yet, he'd begun to rely on her. He, who relied on no one but himself. Shaking his head, he called himself ten kinds of fools. A princess? Putting his trust in anyone was dangerous, but a princess. Talk about impossible situations.

He ground his teeth. She was leaving. He needed to get used to the idea immediately. He needed to cut every thought of her from his mind.

Bridget felt ripped apart at the prospect of leaving Ryder and the boys, but she couldn't stall any longer. She'd completed her assignment and it was time for her to return to Chantaine before she took her long-delayed gap year in Italy. Somehow, she couldn't work up the same kind of excitement she'd felt during the last two years about finally taking a break.

She didn't know which upset her most: leaving Ryder and the twins or the fact that Ryder had ignored all of her calls. Desperate to make arrangements to see him one last time, she took matters into her own hands, went to the hospital and parked herself in his office when his assistant was away from her desk. She wasn't going through any gatekeepers this time.

After forty-five minutes of waiting, she saw Ryder finally open his office door. He looked at her and his expression registered shock, then all emotion seemed to vanish from his face. "Hello, Bridget. Sorry, I don't have time to visit."

His remoteness stabbed her. "I understand. I just didn't want to leave without seeing you and the twins again."

"Why? We won't be a part of your life anymore.

There's no need to pretend we were anything more than a phase."

She dropped her jaw, surprised at his evaluation of the time they'd shared. "A phase?" she repeated in disbelief. "Is that all I was to you? A phase?"

Ryder gave a bitter laugh. "There's no need for drama. Both of us knew this was coming. It just came a little sooner than expected. I appreciate everything you did to help the twins. You provided a needed diversion for all three of us."

"A diversion," she said, feeling herself begin to shake.

"Don't get so upset. We knew from the beginning that there was no future to our relationship. I sure as hell am not the right man to be a princess's husband and you're not the type of woman to put up with a doctor's demanding schedule."

She felt as if he'd slapped her. He made her sound like she was a selfish, high-maintenance shrew. She bit the inside of her lip. "I had no idea you thought so little of me." She swallowed over the lump in her throat. "You really had me fooled. I've spent the last few days searching for ways to continue to see you and be with you. I realize it would be the ultimate long-distance relationship, but I couldn't bear the idea of not being in your life. I fell for both you and the boys." Her voice broke and she looked away, shaking her head. "At least, I fell for who I thought you were. I thought you felt the same way, but clearly I was—"

"No," he said, gripping her shoulders. She looked up and saw in his eyes that he was as tortured as she was. "No, you weren't wrong. I fell for you, too, much more than I intended. I've spent the last days telling myself to forget you. I know that's impossible, but I have to try."

Her eyes filled with tears. "I don't want you to forget me. I don't want you to speak about us in the past tense. You—you've become so important to me."

He winced as if in pain. "But it can't work. Our lives are just too different. We need to make it easy for each other to get used to the facts. The fact is you have to return to your country. You have responsibilities there. I have mine here."

She tried hard to hang on to her composure, but she couldn't. It hurt too much. She dropped her forehead against his chest. "This is so hard," she said, feeling tears streak down her face.

"It is," he said, sliding his hand through her hair and holding her close.

"Promise me you won't forget me," she said and lifted her gaze to look at him. "Give me that much."

"Never," he promised. "Never," he said and lowered his mouth to hers for a kiss. Their last kiss.

Ryder couldn't remember a time when he had felt like his guts had been ripped out and put through a grinder. Every waking moment, he was aware of the breathtaking pain. He tried, but couldn't block the sight of Bridget's tears from his mind. The way she'd felt in his arms. He would never feel that again. He would never feel that sense of unexpected joy just by seeing her smile or hearing her tease him.

Swearing under his breath as he arrived home, he ripped open the top few buttons of his shirt. Not only was he in mental hell, but the hot Dallas weather seemed to be determined to put him in physical hell, too.

"Hey, big guy," Marshall said as he held one of the twins while Suzanne changed the diaper of the other.

"You don't look too good. Did you lose someone on the table today?"

One of the babies squealed at the sight of him. The sound gave Ryder a slight lift. He walked over and gave each baby a hug.

"No, I didn't lose a patient. Just got some things on my mind. Sorry I'm late. Tomorrow should be better."

He saw Marshall lift his eyebrows. "Hey, Suzy Q, how about I help you take the boys upstairs for a while. Ryder and I can drink a beer and watch a couple innings of a ball game. Are you okay with that?"

"Sure," she said. "I'll play some music and read to them."

Marshall gave his wife a firm kiss, then carried both boys upstairs.

A moment later, his friend returned. Ryder had already gotten two beers out of the fridge. "I don't want to talk about it," he muttered as he sank onto the couch.

"Okay," Marshall said and used the remote to turn on the TV. The Dallas team was losing again. Marshall swore. "They just can't pull it together."

"They need a different pitcher," Ryder said.

"They need a different everything," Marshall said.

Silence passed. "Suzanne tells me your princess stopped by today to give the boys some gifts before she returns to Champagne or wherever the hell she lives."

His gut twisted. Tomorrow. "It's Chantaine," he said.

"Whatever," Marshall said. "Suzanne said she held it together with the babies but fell apart on the front porch."

Ryder narrowed his eyes against another stab of emotion and took a quick breath. "It sucks all around."

"Hmm. Seems like a lot of unnecessary torture to me," Marshall said.

Ryder shot his friend a hard glance. "Unnecessary?" he asked.

"Well, yeah, if y'all are that miserable without each other, then stay together."

Impatience rippled through him. "Okay, Mr. Relationship Expert, exactly how would we do that?"

"Ask her to marry you. Ask her to stay," he said and took a sip of his beer. "Nice play," he said, nodding toward the screen.

Ignoring Marshall's comment on the game, Ryder set down his beer. "How in hell can I do that? She's a princess from another country and she works for her country. I work eighteen hours a day and I have twin boys. No woman in her right mind would agree to that kind of life. She deserves better."

"I take it to mean you didn't have the guts to ask her what she would want," he said.

Anger roared through him. "Guts? Who are you talking to about guts? Guts is what it takes to let her go."

"Hmm," Marshall said. "You know, Suzanne and I are gonna have a baby."

"She's pregnant already?" Ryder asked.

"No. We don't know *how* we're going to have a baby. We just know we will. I told you about this the other day, but you probably weren't listening. There are lots of ways to have a baby these days. IVF, surrogacy, adoption in the States, overseas…" He nodded. "Yep, they're putting in the second-string pitcher. Let's see what happens now."

"What's your point?" Ryder demanded.

"There's more than one way to crack a nut," he said.

"There's more than one solution to a problem. You could ask Bridget to move here. You could commute for a while. Just because you commute for a while doesn't mean you'll have to do it forever. Hell, didn't you say her country needed some doctors? If you really wanted to, you could move to Champagne and be a doctor there."

"Chantaine," Ryder corrected, mentally dismissing Marshall's suggestions in one fell swoop.

"Well, my man, you're going to have to make some career changes anyway," Marshall said. "Those babies are little now, but when they get older they're going to need to have their daddy around more than an hour or two every day. You're gonna have to figure out what kind of father you want to be, and I'm guessing it's nothing like the father you had."

Ryder mused over that for a long moment. He'd been fighting change ever since his brother had died. Although he'd done his best with the twins, he'd clung to what was most familiar to him, and that was his career. Outside of the hospital, he'd felt completely out of control. For a time, Bridget had made the new responsibility he'd faced feel a little lighter. She'd even made it fun.

He wondered how she would have responded if he'd asked her to stay. If he'd asked her to marry him. His heart hammered at the ridiculous possibility. The very idea of it was ludicrous. Even more ridiculous was the idea of his quitting his position, uprooting the twins and moving across the world for a completely different life with the woman who had made him fall in love with her. She hadn't asked for that because she hadn't wanted it. Ryder scowled at Marshall. The man was just stirring up a bunch of craziness because he'd found and married the woman of his dreams.

* * *

"At least, we can be miserable together," Bridget said to Phillipa, adjusting her dark, oversized sunglasses as she and her sister strode through the airport. She planned on keeping these sunglasses on her face night and day, inside and outside except when she was in her private quarters. No amount of cosmetics concealed the gutted agony in her eyes.

"It would have been nice to have the private jet," Phillipa said.

"So true, but Stefan always gets first rights to the jet. Plus, it's supposed to be much less expensive to travel commercial on the long-haul flights. At least we'll be together in first class. Hopefully they'll have a distracting movie. Although with my luck, it will be one of those dreadful tales with an unhappy ending from that American author. What's his name?"

"Robert James Waller," Phillipa said. "I've never liked sad movies. I know that some people say crying is cleansing, but I hate it."

"Me, too," Bridget said.

"I don't mean to upset you, but did you ever even ask Dr. McCall if he wanted you to stay?"

Bridget's stomach twisted. "He said our future was impossible. He didn't even want to discuss the possibility of our seeing each other after this trip back to Chantaine." She felt her throat tighten with emotion and took a tiny breath. "No hope," she said.

Pippa reached over to take her hand. "I'm so sorry. You seemed so different once you met him. I'd thought he might be the one."

Her heart stretching and tightening, Bridget squeezed her sister's hand. "I'm lucky to have such a sweet sister."

"Your Highness," Raoul said, stepping to Bridget's

side. "I apologize for the interruption, but Dr. McCall has arrived at the airport. He wishes to speak to you. I must warn you that you don't have much ti—"

Shocked, thrilled, afraid to hope, she felt her breath lodge somewhere between her lungs and throat. "I will speak to him," she managed in a whisper that sounded hoarse to her own ears.

Seconds that felt like eons later, Ryder stood in front of her.

"Hi," he said, meeting her gaze dead-on.

Her heart was hammering so fast that she could hardly breathe. "Hi. What brings you here?"

He took a deep breath and cocked his head to one side. "You mentioned that your country needs a new medical director. I wondered if you thought I could handle the job?"

Stunned and confused, she shook her head. "Excuse me? Are you asking for the position?"

He paused a half beat, then nodded. "Yeah, I guess I am."

Torn between throwing herself in his arms and trying to keep her head from spinning, she bit her lip. "Would you like me to talk to Stefan? I'm sure he would be thrilled."

"That's good. How would you feel about it?" he asked. "How would you feel about the twins and me coming to Chantaine?"

Bridget was so light-headed that she feared she might faint. She grabbed the back of a chair. "I would be beyond thrilled."

"Thrilled enough to marry me?"

She gasped, unable to register his question. "Excuse me?"

He moved toward her and took her hands in his. "I

love you. I want my future with you. I want my children's future with you. I know it's fast, but will you—"

"Yes," she said, her eyes filling with tears of joy. Her heart was overflowing. "Yes, yes and yes."

Ryder took her into his arms and she hugged him tightly. The secret dream of having a man love her just for herself had just come true.

Five months later, Bridget stood in front of Ryder in the chapel of the oldest church in Chantaine and pinched herself. Her sisters dabbed at tears with handkerchiefs. Her brother Stefan beamed his approval. He was so thrilled one of his siblings had finally made a marriage that would benefit Chantaine. With Ryder as the newly appointed medical director of Chantaine, there was no shortage of residents clamoring to come to their country. Her sister-in-law Eve gave her an encouraging nod. The twins ran along the side aisle like the wild rascals they were. Her youngest brother and Raoul chased after them. Bridget had reached a new level of terror when the boys had started pulling up, and worse, walking. Not one day passed, however, when she didn't thank God for Ryder and the boys.

The priest led them in their vows. Ryder's voice was clear and strong. His gaze was resolute. She knew she could count on this man for the rest of her life. Surprisingly enough, she knew he could count on her, too. Ryder's love had triggered something hidden deep inside her, something she'd hoped she possessed, but it had never surfaced. With Ryder in her life, she didn't mind her royal duties, yet she could say no to Stefan when necessary.

Even with all the sacrifices and changes Ryder had made, he seemed happier and more relaxed. At the same time, he saw many opportunities for improvement and expansion in Chantaine's health program. She still couldn't believe how everything had worked out. Every day, she grew closer to Ryder and fell more deeply in love with him. She counted her blessings that she would spend the rest of her life with him and the twins. Despite her best efforts, though, he refused to reveal his honeymoon plans. As long as it didn't involve the desert, and it did involve just the two of them, she would be happy.

With the twins squealing in delight, the priest appeared to smother a chuckle. "I now pronounce you husband and wife. You may kiss your bride," he said.

Ryder took her face in his hands as if it were the most precious thing in the world and lowered his mouth to hers. She threw her hands around his neck and kissed him with all her heart.

Distantly, she heard the sound of laughter and applause. She pulled back and turned to the many witnesses seated in the chapel, glancing toward the twins.

Ryder's mind must have been moving in the same direction. "Tyler," he called. "Travis. Come here right now."

The twins turned suddenly solemn, but made their way to the front of the church. Dressed in pale blue short suits, both boys lifted their arms toward her and Ryder. Heedless of her designer wedding dress, she scooped up Tyler while Ryder picked up Travis.

"Ladies and gentlemen, may God bless this happy union."

As the group in the church applauded again, Ryder leaned toward her and kissed her again. "I'm taking you to Italy, Your Highness. Tomorrow."

* * * * *

Lois Faye Dyer always knew she would be a writer, though the road to her true calling had a few detours and rest stops along the way. Growing up in such picturesque spots as a working ranch in northeastern Montana, the turn-of-the-century coastal town of Mendocino, California, an 1800s home on the shores of Lake Okoboji in Iowa and the Spanish-flavored city of San Buenaventura in Southern California provided Lois with a wealth of inspiration for the fictional tales she would write one day.

After several years spent honing her craft, Lois sold her first contemporary romance in 1990 and retired from her day job shortly after to focus on her writing. Today, when not plotting her next bestseller, Lois enjoys walking her dog, seeing to the needs of her demanding cats and spending time with her family.

Books by Lois Faye Dyer

Harlequin Special Edition

Visit the Author Profile page at Harlequin.com for more titles.

Triple Trouble

LOIS FAYE DYER

For Grant Suh and his proud parents,
Steve and Brenda.

Welcome to America and our family, Grant—
we're so glad you're here.

Chapter 1

Nicholas Fortune closed the financial data file on his computer and stretched. Yawning, he pushed his chair away from his desk and stood. His office was on the top floor of the building housing the Fortune Foundation, and outside the big corner windows, the Texas night was moonless, the sky a black dome spangled with the faint glitter of stars.

"Hell of a lot different from L.A.," he mused aloud, his gaze tracing the moving lights of an airplane far above. The view from the window in his last office in a downtown Los Angeles high rise too often had been blurred with smog that usually blotted out the stars. No, Red Rock, Texas, was more than just a few thousand miles from California—it was a whole world away.

All in all, he thought as he gazed into the darkness, he was glad he'd moved here a month ago. He'd grown tired of his job as a financial analyst for the Kline Corporation in L.A. and needed new challenges—working for the family foundation allowed him time to contemplate his next career move. And a nice side benefit was that he got to spend more time with his brother, Darr.

With the exception of the hum of a janitor's vacuum in the hallway outside, the building around him was as silent as the street below. Nicholas turned away from the window and returned to his desk to slide his laptop into its leather carrying case. He was just shrugging into his jacket when his cell phone rang.

He glanced at his watch. The fluorescent dials read eleven-fifteen. He didn't recognize the number and ordinarily would have let the call go to voice mail, but for some reason he thumbed the On button. "Hello?"

"Mr. Fortune? Nicholas Fortune?"

He didn't recognize the male voice. "Yes."

"Ah, excellent." Relief echoed in the man's voice. "I'm sorry to call so late, but I've been trying to locate you for three days and my assistant just found this number. My name is Andrew Sanchez. I'm an attorney for the estate of Stan Kennedy."

Nicholas froze, his fingers tightening on the slim black cell phone. "The *estate* of Stan Kennedy? Did something happen to Stan?"

"I'm sorry to be the bearer of unfortunate news." The caller's voice held regret. "Mr. Kennedy and his wife were killed in a car accident three days ago."

Shock kept Nicholas mute.

"Mr. Fortune?"

"Yeah." Nicholas managed to force words past the thick emotion clogging his throat. "Yeah, I'm here."

"It's my understanding you and Mr. Kennedy were quite close?"

"We were college roommates. I haven't seen Stan in a year or so, but we keep in touch—*kept* in touch by phone and email." *Like brothers,* Nicholas thought. "We were close as brothers in college."

"I see. Well, Mr. Fortune, that probably explains why he named you guardian of his children. The little girls are currently safe and in the care of a foster mother, but the caseworker is anxious to transfer custody to you. The sooner they're in a stable environment the better."

"Whoa, wait a minute." Nicholas shook his head to clear it, convinced he hadn't heard the attorney correctly. "Stan left *me* in charge of his kids?"

"Yes, that's correct." The attorney paused. "You didn't know?"

Nicholas tried to remember exactly what Stan had told him about his will. They'd both agreed to take care of business for the other if anything happened to them. He'd been Stan's best man at his wedding to Amy and he definitely remembered Stan asking him to look after his bride should anything happen. Even though their conversation had taken place while emptying a magnum of champagne, Nicholas knew his word was important to Stan and he hadn't given it lightly.

But *babies?* And not just one—*three.*

"The triplets weren't born when we made a pact to look after each other's estate, should anything ever happen," he told the attorney. *And neither of us thought he and Amy wouldn't live to raise their daughters.* "But I promised Stan I'd take care of his family if he couldn't."

"Excellent." The attorney's voice was full of relief. "Can I expect you at my office tomorrow, then?"

"Tomorrow?" Nick repeated, his voice rough with shock.

"I know it's extremely short notice," Sanchez said apologetically. "But as I said, the caseworker is very concerned that the babies be settled in a permanent situation as soon as possible."

"Uh, yeah, I suppose that makes sense," Nick said. He thrust his fingers through his hair and tried to focus on the calendar that lay open on his desktop. "I've got a meeting I can't cancel in the morning, but I'll catch the first flight out after lunch." Nicholas jotted down the address in Amarillo and hung up. It was several moments before he realized he was sitting on the edge of his desk, staring at the silent phone, still open in his hand.

Grief washed over him, erasing the cold, numbing shock that had struck with the news. He couldn't believe Stan and Amy were gone. The couple met life with a zest few of their friends could match. It was impossible to get his head around the fact that all their vibrant energy had been snuffed out.

He scrubbed his hand down his face and his fingers came away damp.

He sucked in a deep breath and stood. He didn't have time to mourn Stan and Amy. Their deaths had left their three little girls vulnerable, without the protection of parents. Though how the hell Stan and Amy had ever decided he was the best choice to act as substitute dad for the triplets, Nicholas couldn't begin to guess.

In all his thirty-seven years, he'd never spent any length of time around a baby. He had four brothers but no wife, no fiancée or sister, and his mom had died two years ago. The only permanent female in his immediate family was Barbara, the woman his brother Darr had fallen in love with a month earlier. Barbara was pregnant. Did that mean she knew about babies?

Nick hadn't a clue. And for a guy who spent his life dealing with the predictability of numbers, in his career as a financial analyst, being clueless didn't sit well.

But he had no choice.

Despite being totally unqualified for the job, he was flying to Amarillo tomorrow.

And bringing home three babies.

He didn't know a damn thing about kids. Especially not little girls.

He was going to have to learn fast....

Charlene London walked quickly along the Red Rock Airport concourse, nearly running as she hurried to the gate. The flight to Amarillo was already boarding and only a few stragglers like herself waited to be checked through.

Fortunately, the uniformed airline attendant was efficient, and a moment later, Charlene joined the short queue of passengers waiting to board.

For the first time in the last hour, she drew a deep breath and relaxed. The last three weeks had been hectic and difficult. Breaking up with her fiancé after three years had been hard, but quitting her job, packing her apartment and putting everything in storage had been draining. She'd purposely pared her luggage down to a few bags, since she'd be living with her mother in a condo in Amarillo while she looked for a job and an apartment.

And a new life, she told herself. She was determined to put her failed relationship with Barry behind her and get on with her career.

She sipped her latte, mentally updating her résumé while the line moved slowly forward. They entered the plane and her eyes widened at the packed cabin and aisle, still thronged with passengers finding seats and stowing bags in the overhead compartments.

Thank goodness I used my frequent flyer miles to upgrade to first class. She glanced at her ticket and scanned the numbers above the seats, pausing as she found hers.

"Excuse me."

The man rose and stepped into the aisle to let her move past him to reach the window seat.

He smelled wonderful. Charlene didn't recognize the scent, but it was subtle and clean. Probably incredibly expensive. *And thank goodness he isn't wearing the same cologne as Barry,* she thought with a rush of relief.

She was trying to get away from Barry—and didn't need or want any reminder of her ex-boyfriend. Or fiancé. Or whatever the appropriate term was for the man you'd dated for three whole years, thinking he was the man you'd marry, until you'd discovered that he was… not the man you'd thought he was at all.

Very disheartening.

"Can I put that up for you?"

The deep male voice rumbled, yanking Charlene from her reverie.

"What?" She realized he was holding out his hand, the expression on his very handsome face expectant. He lifted a brow, glanced significantly at her carry-on, then at her. "Oh, yes. Thank you."

He swung the bag up with ease while she slipped into the window seat. She focused on latching her seat belt, stowing her purse under the seat and settling in.

It wasn't until the plane backed away from the gate to taxi toward the runaway that she really looked at the man beside her.

He was staring at the inflight magazine but Charlene had the distinct impression he wasn't reading. In profile, his face was all angles with high cheekbones, chiseled lips and a strong jawline. His dark brown hair was short, just shy of a buzz cut, and from her side view, his eyelashes were amazingly long and thick. She wondered idly what color his eyes were.

She didn't wonder long. He glanced up, his gaze meeting hers.

Brown. His eyes were brown. *The kind of eyes a woman could lose herself in,* she thought hazily.

His eyes darkened, lashes half lowering as he studied her.

Charlene's breath caught at the male interest he didn't bother to hide. Her skin heated, her nipples peaking beneath the soft lace of her bra.

Stunned at the depth of her reaction, she couldn't pull her gaze from his.

Despite his preoccupation with what lay ahead of him in Amarillo, Nicholas couldn't ignore the quick surge of interest when he looked up and saw the woman standing in the aisle.

When he stood to let her reach her seat, she brushed by him and the scent of subtle perfume teased his senses. The sleek fall of auburn hair spilled forward as she sat, leaning forward to slide her purse beneath her seat. She tucked the long strands back behind her ear while she settled in and latched her seat belt.

Finally, she glanced sideways at him and he was able

to catch a glimpse. Her thick-lashed eyes were green as new spring grass. They widened as she stared at him.

She wasn't just pretty. She was beautiful, he realized. And if the faint flush on her cheeks was any indication, she was feeling the same slam of sexual awareness that had hit him like a fist the moment her gaze had met his.

"Everything okay?" he asked when she continued to stare at him without speaking.

She blinked, and just that quickly the faintly unfocused expression was gone, replaced by a sharp awareness.

"Yes." She lifted one slender-fingered hand in a dismissive gesture. "I had to nearly run to catch the plane. I hate being late."

Nicholas nodded and would have said more, but just then the plane engines throttled up, the sound increasingly louder as the jet hurtled down the runaway and left the tarmac. He glanced at the woman beside him and found her gripping the armrests, eyes closed.

Clearly, she didn't like to fly. Air travel didn't bother Nicholas, but he waited until the plane leveled out and her white-knuckled grip relaxed before he spoke.

"I'm Nicholas." He purposely didn't tell her his last name. The Fortune surname was well-known in Red Rock and being part of a rich, powerful family carried its own problems. He'd learned early that many people associated the name with a preconceived set of expectations.

"Charlene London," she responded as she took a bottle of water from her bag. "Are you flying to Amarillo on business?" she asked, sipping her water.

"Not exactly." He paused, frowning.

Charlene tucked an errant strand of hair behind one

ear with an absentminded gesture. *What did that mean?*
"I see," she said.

He laughed—a short, wry chuckle. "I don't mean
to be vague. My trip is both business and personal."

"Oh." Curious though she was, Charlene was reluctant to grill him. Somewhere in the coach section of the
airplane, a baby began to cry.

Nick stiffened and appeared to listen intently until
the cries turned to whimpers. Tension eased from his
body and he looked at her, his gaze turbulent.

"My college roommate and his wife died a few days
ago and I'm guardian of their daughters. I'm going to
Amarillo to take custody of three kids. Triplets." He
sighed. "Twelve-month-old triplets."

Charlene's eyes widened with shock. She was
speechless for a moment. "You're kidding," she finally
managed to get out.

"Nope." His expression was part gloom, part stark
dread. "I'm not kidding."

"Do you and your wife have children of your own?"

"I'm not married. And I don't have any kids," he
added. "The closest I've ever come to having a depen-
dant is my dog, Rufus."

"So you'll be caring for three babies...all by yourself?"

He nodded. "That's about the size of it."

"That's crazy."

"Yeah," he said with conviction. "Insane."

"I'm the oldest of six siblings, two of whom are
twins," Charlene said. "If you'd permit a little advice
from someone who's been there—you should hire a
full-time nanny, and the sooner the better."

Nicholas thought she probably was right—in fact,

the more he considered the idea, the more he was convinced. Before he could ask her more questions, however, the woman walking the crying baby up and down the aisle reached their row.

"Excuse me." Charlene stood.

Nicholas wanted to ask her if she knew anything about hiring nannies, but her abrupt request stopped him. He stepped into the aisle to let her pass him. Her shoulder brushed his chest in the slightest of touches, yet his muscles tensed as if she'd trailed her fingertips over his bare skin.

Nick dragged in a steadying breath, but it only served to flood his senses with the scent of subtle perfume and warm woman.

He nearly groaned aloud. He'd dated a lot of women over the years, but he hadn't reacted to a female with the level of gut-deep, instant lust since he was a teenager. He blinked, frowned and ordered his rebellious body to calm down. He couldn't afford to be distracted just now—he had to focus on dealing with Stan and Amy's little girls.

He dropped back into his seat. He expected Charlene to walk toward the lavatories at the front of the first class section, but instead, she waited until the young mother turned and moved back down the aisle.

"Hi." Charlene smiled at the weary mother. "I bet you're exhausted."

Oh hell. Nick tensed when the woman holding the baby looked like she was going to cry. He hated it when women cried. Fortunately, the woman didn't burst into tears.

"I'm beyond exhausted," the woman murmured, patting the wailing baby on the back soothingly. "And so is she," she added. "I don't think either one of us has slept more than a half hour at a time for days."

"Oh my. My little brother did the same thing," Charlene said, her gaze warm and sympathetic. "He was born several weeks premature and had acid reflux. Poor little guy. It took a while for us to figure out how to handle him so he could fall asleep."

The young mother's eyes widened. "You found a solution? What was it?"

"I'd be glad to show you," Charlene said, holding out her arms.

The woman hesitated, clearly torn about handing her baby to a complete stranger.

"I totally understand if you're not comfortable with having me hold her, after all, we don't know each other," Charlene said reassuringly. "I could try to explain, but it's much easier to demonstrate."

The baby chose that moment to wail even louder than before. The unhappy cry seemed to galvanize the mother, because she eased the tiny little girl off her shoulder and passed her carefully to Charlene.

Nick didn't know much about babies, but every one he'd seen had been cradled or propped against someone's shoulder. Charlene did neither. Instead, she laid the baby facedown on her arm, the little head in the palm of her hand, and gently swayed her back and forth while smoothing her free palm over the tiny back. The baby's arms waved jerkily, slowing in time with her cries that quickly gave way to hiccuping sobs, then blessed silence.

Nick stared at Charlene. *Damn. She's good. Really good.*

He glanced at the baby's mother and found her expression as surprised as he felt.

"How in the world did you do that?" she whispered.

"Experience," Charlene murmured, her fingertips continuing to gently rub in soothing circles over the little girl's back. The pink cotton dress matched the baby's sock-covered feet, now dangling limply on either side of Charlene's arm. "I was twelve when my little brother was born." She glanced down at the baby, fast asleep and seemingly boneless in her arms. "If you tilt her slightly to the right when you hold her, change her diaper or feed her, it helps with acid reflux too. I don't know if your little girl has that problem, but if she does, the pain can make her so uncomfortable that she won't be able to fall asleep or stay asleep."

"Thank you so much." The words carried a wealth of heartfelt appreciation as she carefully took the sleeping baby from Charlene.

"You're welcome," Charlene replied, moving aside to let the mother and child step past her. She watched them move down the aisle and return to their seat in coach.

Nick stood to let Charlene slip into her seat near the window, then dropped into his own.

"Impressive," he told her. "Very impressive."

She shrugged and picked up her water bottle to sip. "Basic stuff, if you've ever helped care for a baby. Unfortunately, most new moms only find out about the little things to make life easier for them and their baby if they talk to someone who's coped hands-on with the problem."

After watching Charlene's easy confidence with the crying baby before she handed the peacefully sleeping child back to her mother, Nicholas knew he'd found the answer to his urgent need for a nanny. "Makes sense.

Experience always counts. I need someone with that level of experience. How about you?" he asked.

"How about me…what?"

"Being the nanny for the triplets. I'll pay you double whatever the going rate is," he went on when she shook her head.

"I'm sorry, I really am. But I'll be looking for a job in Amarillo."

"What if I offered you a substantial signing bonus—say, twenty-five thousand dollars?"

Her eyes widened. "That's a very generous offer—and one that guarantees applicants will be standing in line for the position. You'll have your pick of nannies. You don't need me."

"Yes, I do." Nick was convinced. Charlene didn't appear to share his opinion, however. "In fact, I'm so sure you're the only person for the triplets that I'll add another twenty-five thousand dollar bonus if you stay until their aunt is found and comes to get them."

She stared at him for a loaded moment. "Their aunt is taking them?"

Nick was surprised she didn't ask about the money, but if she wanted information about the babies, he'd give it to her. "I don't have permanent custody of the girls, only temporary care until the estate locates Amy's sister, Lana. She's a teacher, and according to Amy, a career volunteer with various organizations overseas, helping children in third world countries. She's also married." Unlike me, he thought. A confirmed bachelor with no plans to marry anytime soon. "So the girls will have two parents instead of only me."

"I see."

For a brief moment, Nick thought Charlene was going to accept his offer. But then she shook her head.

"I'm sorry, especially since I know how difficult it is to care for more than one baby. But I have plans and I've made promises to people. I can't let them down on such short notice."

"You're sure I can't change your mind?"

"No, I'm afraid not."

"Too bad." He pulled a business card and pen from his inner jacket pocket and wrote on the back of the card. "This is my cell phone number, in case you reconsider the offer. I'll be in Amarillo until tomorrow, when I have reservations to fly the girls back to Red Rock."

"You aren't staying in Amarillo very long," she commented as she took the card, tucking it into her purse without reading it.

"No. I want to take the triplets home as soon as possible and get them settled in. I doubt anything will make this easier for them, but I thought the faster I transfer them, the better." He pointed at her purse where his card had disappeared. "Call me if you change your mind."

"I'll keep your card," she replied. "But I don't think it's likely I'll change my mind."

They parted in the terminal, Nicholas heading for the exit and Charlene moving to baggage pickup.

Saying goodbye felt wrong. Charlene had to force herself not to turn around and give him her phone number, ask him to call…plead until he promised to meet her later.

Her level of conviction that Nick was somehow important to her was profound.

This is crazy. She held her chin up and kept walking, but her thoughts continued to tumble, one over the other, refusing to leave Nick even as she physically moved farther away from him.

She'd never felt anything approaching the instant attraction that had flared between them, her nerves shaking with need during that first long exchange of glances. Lust and sexual attraction were far more powerful forces than she'd imagined. The time spent sitting next to Nick during the flight had given her new insight into just how intensely her body could respond to the right man. Those moments were forcing her to reevaluate whether she'd ever truly been deeply moved before—including with Barry, she realized with sudden shock.

Yet she'd become engaged to Barry, she reminded herself in an effort to regain control of her emotions. Clearly her wisdom in this area wasn't infallible. Besides, a man was the last thing she needed or wanted in her life right now. She definitely didn't need the complication of a man who was about to become an instant father to three little girls.

Still, she'd been impressed with Nicholas's willingness to take on the babies. She couldn't help but compare his heroic, stand-up attitude with her ex's lack of responsibility. She couldn't imagine Barry in Nicholas's situation. She seriously doubted Barry would have agreed to take custody of three children. He was adamantly opposed to becoming a parent. It was one of the issues they couldn't agree on, since she very much wanted children—an issue that, ultimately, had caused her to conclude they were completely mismatched.

Charlene collected her three suitcases and stepped out of the crowd of passengers to pull a jacket from inside the smallest bag. March in chilly Amarillo was a far cry from the warmth of Red Rock, located in southern Texas near San Antonio. Sure enough, when she wheeled her bags outside, she was glad she had the added protection of the coat. She tucked her chin into the shelter of her collar and halted to scan the line of cars crowding the curb.

"Charlene! Over here!" Her mother's voice carried clearly over the hum and chatter of passengers.

Charlene returned Angie's enthusiastic wave and hurried down the walkway.

"Mom, it's so good to see you." Charlene basked in her mother's warm hug, breathing in the familiar scent of Estée Lauder perfume.

"It's been too long," Angie said, scolding with a loving smile as she stepped back, holding Charlene at arm's length. Her eyes narrowed as she swept a swift glance over her daughter, from her toes to the crown of her head. "You're too skinny."

Charlene laughed. "You always say that, Mom. I've lost inches but not pounds—I've been working out at the gym."

"Well, now that you're home, I'm going to feed you," Angie declared firmly.

They loaded Charlene's bags into the trunk. Moments later, Angie expertly negotiated traffic as they left the airport.

"Are you enjoying being in the condo, or do you think you'll miss having a big yard this summer? You spent hours gardening at the old house, and I know you loved the flowers." Charlene's mother had sold the rambler where she and her siblings had grown up after her parents' divorce three years earlier. Following college graduation and Charlene's move to Red Rock, Angie had insisted she should be the one to travel for visits to her six children, especially Charlene, since her job as a Health Unit Coordinator at the hospital E.R. kept her so busy. As a result, Charlene had only seen her mother's condo on two short weekend trips.

"I love condo life," Angie said with a happy smile. "I still garden, but now I'm planting flowers and herbs in terra cotta pots on the lanai. Of course," she added. "I still have to mow the strip of grass in my backyard, but it's tiny compared to the big lawn at the old house."

Angie's voice rang with contentment. Charlene knew what a difficult time her mother had had after the divorce, and was immeasurably relieved that she appeared to have adjusted so well.

"I'm glad you're enjoying it, Mom." She tucked a strand of hair behind her ear and adjusted her Ray-Bans a little higher on her nose to better block the late afternoon sun. "What are you doing with all your free time, now that you're not mowing grass and pulling weeds?"

"I've been busy at work," Angie began before pausing to clear her throat. "And… I've met someone," she blurted.

Surprised, Charlene looked at her mother and was startled to see a hint of color on her cheeks. "That's great, Mom. Who is he?"

"His name is Lloyd Weber and he's an architect for a firm here in Amarillo. We met playing bridge. I joined the group about six months ago."

"So, you're dating?" Charlene could hardly get her mind around the image of her mother dating. Not that she objected—in fact, she'd urged her mom to get out and about. Angie was fifty-two and loved people and social interaction; Charlene truly believed her mom would be happier in a committed relationship.

"Well, yes—we've been dating for a while." Angie pulled up in front of the condo building and parked. Her expression reflected concern and a certain trepidation when she unlatched her seat belt and half-turned to meet Charlene's gaze. "I didn't tell you before, because…well, because I wasn't sure whether Lloyd and I were going to become serious. But two weeks ago he moved in with me."

Charlene stared at her mother, stunned. "You're living together?"

"Yes, dear."

"Here in your condo?"

Angie nodded. "His house is being remodeled before he puts it on the market, and he was staying in a bed-and-breakfast. I told him it was silly to spend all that money when we're together nearly all the time anyway. I convinced him to move in here."

"Well, um," Charlene managed to say. "That's great, Mom. If he makes you happy, I'm delighted."

"You're not upset?"

"Mom, of course I'm not upset." Charlene hugged Angie. "I think it's great." She sat back, laughing at the sheer relief on her mother's face. "If he's a great guy who's being good to you and you're happy, then I'm thrilled for you."

"I'm very happy, and he *is* a great guy," Angie said firmly. "Now come on, let's get your things inside so you can meet him."

Charlene followed Angie up the sidewalk, towing a rolling suitcase behind her.

What am I going to do now? The question made her

feel totally selfish in light of her mother's transparent happiness. But Charlene's practical side told her the situation required a change of plans. She couldn't stay at the condo with her mother and Lloyd during what was surely the honeymoon stage of their relationship.

She needed a new plan. And fast.

What the hell was I thinking?

Nick strode away from Charlene and didn't look back. The airport wasn't crowded and it was a matter of moments before he reached the exit doors and walked outside. He knew it was the worst possible time to meet a woman who interested him. And Charlene London was too pretty to hire as a nanny.

He was going to have enough problems dealing with the sea change about to happen in his life. He didn't need to move a sexy, gorgeous woman into his house to complicate life even more.

He spotted a uniformed driver holding a sign with his name in big block letters, and changed direction to reach the black Lincoln Town Car. During the drive to Andrew Sanchez's office, he scanned a file with information about Stan and Amy's estate the attorney had asked the driver to give him.

Andrew Sanchez was a rotund, balding man in his mid-fifties. Businesslike and efficient, he still exuded an air of concern and sympathy.

"Do you have family or friends available to help with the triplets?" he asked Nick as they concluded their meeting.

"No, but I'm planning to find a nanny. Until then I have a housekeeper, and she's agreed to work longer hours until I can find someone."

"You might want to consider two nannies," Mr. Sanchez commented. "Those three little girls are dynamos." He grinned with wry affection. "I'm glad you're a younger man, because just spending an hour with them at their foster home wore me out. You're going to need all the energy you can muster."

Nick nodded. He didn't tell the older man that he had no clue how much energy one little girl required from a caretaker, let alone three of them at once. "You're continuing to search for Amy's sister?"

The attorney nodded. "I've hired a detective agency to look for her. They told me they can't give us a time frame, since she's out of the country, but at least Amy's email files gave us the name of the mission organization in Africa that employed her. It's a place to start hunting." He sighed. "The email records on Amy's computer indicate her sister stopped communicating a month or so ago. Also that Amy had been trying to contact her but had no success."

"Any idea why?"

"Lana and her husband apparently resigned their positions with the relief agency where they were employed. But we don't know where they went after that. And given that the two are working in a remote area of Africa, well…" Sanchez spread his hands and shrugged. "It's anyone's guess where they've gone or how long before they surface. As I said, the detective agency warned me they can't guarantee a time frame for locating the couple."

"Let's hope they find her soon. I have to believe Amy's sister and her husband will be better at caring for three little girls than I am."

"The important thing is that you're willing to try."

The attorney shook his head. "The interim foster home where the girls are staying is a good situation, but they can't stay there indefinitely. They'll be much better off with you while we're searching for their aunt."

"I hope you're right." Nick wasn't convinced.

It was after 6:00 p.m. before the attorney and Nick finished going over the will and other documents.

"I took the liberty of booking a room for you in a nearby hotel," Sanchez told him as they pushed back chairs and stood. "I understand the triplets are in bed for the night by 7:00 p.m. I thought you might want to wait until morning to see them."

"I appreciate it." Nicholas held out his hand. "Thanks for everything."

"You're welcome." The attorney's clasp was firm. "Let me know if there's anything else I can do for you. And I'll notify you as soon as I receive any information as to the whereabouts of Amy's sister."

Nick walked to the door. "It seems odd to pick up the girls and leave Amarillo without saying goodbye in some way."

"I know." The attorney nodded. "But their wills were very specific. As the closest living relative, Amy's sister will organize a memorial service so friends can pay their respects when she returns."

"I'm damned sure neither of them ever thought they'd die together and leave the kids," Nick muttered, almost to himself.

"No one ever does." Sanchez shook his head. "It's a hell of a situation. We'll just have to do the best we can and search diligently for the children's aunt."

"Right." Nick said goodbye and left the office to climb into the town car once more.

The conversation with Andrew Sanchez had driven home the unbelievable fact that Stan and Amy were gone. Nick barely noticed the streets the limo drove down as they headed toward the hotel.

Despite his conviction that Charlene wasn't the best choice for an employee on a purely personal level, he definitely believed her experience made her the perfect woman to care for Stan's daughters. Before he unpacked his bag in the hotel room, he called his office in Red Rock and asked his assistant to run a preliminary employment check on Charlene London.

Just in case, he told himself, *she called and said yes to the job offer.* He knew the fact that she hadn't given him her contact number made the likelihood a million-to-one shot—but he was a man who believed in luck.

And he was going to need a boatload of luck to get through the next few days, or weeks, or however long it took before the triplets' aunt showed up to claim them.

Chapter 2

The following morning, the same limo driver picked Nick up promptly at 9:00 a.m.

"We're here, sir." The driver's voice broke Nick's absorption in memories and he realized they were parked in front of a white rambler with a fenced yard and worn grass. It looked lived-in and comfortable.

"So we are," he muttered.

"Mr. Sanchez told me to wait and drive you all to the airport when you're ready, sir."

"Good, thanks," Nick said absently, focused on what awaited him within the house.

A round young woman in jeans and green T-shirt answered his knock, a little girl perched on her hip.

"Hello, you must be Nick Fortune. I'm Christie Williams. My husband and I are…were friends of Stan and Amy. We volunteered to be temporary foster parents for the girls. Come in."

She held the door wide and Nick stepped over the threshold into a living room, the green carpet strewn with toys. Two babies sat on the floor in the midst of the confusion of blocks, balls, stuffed animals and brightly colored plastic things that Nick couldn't identify. The girls' black hair and bright blue eyes were carbon copies of the child on Christie's hip, who stared at him with solemn interest.

A woman in a gray business suit rose from the sofa as he entered.

"Mr. Fortune, it's a pleasure to see you." She stepped forward and held out her hand, her grip firm in a brief handshake. "I'm Carol Smith, the caseworker. As you can see, the girls are doing well."

Nick nodded, murmuring an absent acknowledgment, his attention on the two little girls seated on the floor. Both of them eyed him with solemn, big-eyed consideration. They were dressed in tiny little tennis shoes and long pants with attached bibs, one in pale purple, one in pink. He glanced at the baby perched on the foster mother's hip. She wore the same little bibbed pants with tennis shoes, only her outfit was bright yellow.

"They're identical?" He hadn't expected them to look so much alike. If it wasn't for the color of their clothes, he wouldn't be able to tell them apart.

"Yes, they are," Ms. Smith replied. "It's quite rare, actually. In today's world, many multiple births are the result of in vitro procedures and the children are more commonly fraternal twins or triplets. But Jackie, Jenny and Jessie are truly identical."

"I see." *Great. How am I going to tell them apart?*

"Fortunately, Amy had their names engraved on

custom-made bracelets for each of them. She and Stan didn't need to use them, of course, but any time the triplets had a babysitter, the bracelets were immensely helpful," the foster mother added. "This is Jackie." She shifted the little girl off her hip and handed her to Nick.

Taken off guard, he automatically took the child, holding her awkwardly in midair with his hands at her waist.

Jackie stared at him, blue eyes solemn as she studied him, her legs dangling. She wriggled, little legs scissoring, and Nick cradled her against his chest to keep from dropping her.

She responded by chortling and grabbing a fistful of his blue polo shirt in one hand and smacking him in the chin with her other. Startled, Nick eyed the little girl who seemed to find it hilarious that she'd found his chin. She babbled a series of nonsensical sounds, and then paused to look expectantly at him.

He looked at the foster mother in confusion. "What did she say?"

The woman laughed, her eyes twinkling. "I have no idea. She'll be perfectly happy if you just respond in some way."

"Oh." Nick looked down into the little face, still clearly awaiting a response. "Uh, yeah. That sounds good," he said, trying his best to sound as if he was agreeing with an actual question.

Jackie responded with delight, waving her arms enthusiastically and babbling once again.

Five minutes of this back and forth and Nick started to feel as if he were getting the hang of baby chat.

"Do they know any real words?" he asked the two women after he'd taken turns holding each of the little girls and had exchanged similar conversations with Jenny and Jessie.

"Not that I've heard," Christie volunteered. "But at twelve months, I wouldn't expect them to, necessarily."

Nick nodded, watching the three as they sat on the floor, playing with large, plastic, red-and-blue blocks. Jenny threw one and the square red toy bounced off his knee. He grinned when she laughed, waving her hands before she grabbed another block. She tossed with more enthusiasm than accuracy and it flew across the room. Clearly disappointed, she frowned at him when he chuckled.

"They're going to be a handful," he murmured, more to himself than to the two women.

"Oh, they certainly will be—and are," Christie agreed. "Have you hired a nanny to help you care for them?"

"Not yet. I called a Red Rock employment agency this morning, but they didn't have anyone on their books. They promised to keep searching and call the minute they find someone." Nick glanced at his watch. "I have reservations for a noon flight."

"You're going to fly the girls back to Red Rock?"

Nick switched his gaze from the girls to Christie. Her facial expression reflected the concern in her question.

"I'd planned to." He didn't miss the quick exchange of worried looks between the foster mother and social worker. "Is there a problem with taking the girls on an airplane?"

"I'm just wondering how you're going to juggle all three of them, let alone their luggage, stroller and the carry-on bags with their things." Carol Smith pointed at the corner of the living room closest to the outer door.

The area was filled with luggage, a large leather shoulder bag, toys and three ungainly looking children's car seats. A baby stroller for three was parked to one side.

"All of that belongs to the girls?" Nick rapidly considered the logistics, calculating what needed to be moved, stored, checked at the gate before the flight. "I can load their things into the back of the limo and get a redcap at the airport."

"Well, yes, you can," Christie agreed. "But Jessie has an ear infection and is taking antibiotics plus Tylenol for pain, and I'm not at all sure the pediatrician would approve of her flying. And even if he okayed the trip, you'd still have to take care of all three of them on the flight, all by yourself." She eyed him dubiously.

"Is that an insurmountable problem?" he asked.

"For one person, it certainly could be," Carol Smith put in. "Especially when one of them needs a diaper changed or if they all are hungry at once."

"Is that likely to happen?"

"Yes," the two women said in unison.

"I see." Nick really was beginning to see why the women seemed dubious. Maybe they were right to be apprehensive about his ability to care for these kids. Just transporting three babies was going to be much more complicated than he'd anticipated. On the other hand, he'd organized and directed programs for large companies. How hard could it be to handle three little kids?

"You two have a lot more experience at this than me. Do you have any suggestions?"

"If I were you," Christie said firmly, "I'd rent a car and drive back to Red Rock. And I'd hire someone to make the trip with me, because I can't imagine any possible way you can do this without at least one other person to help."

Nick instantly thought of Charlene and wished fervently that he'd gotten her phone number. But he had no way to contact her, *and besides,* he thought, *she'd sounded definite when she'd turned down his offer of employment as the girls' nanny.*

He ran his hand over his hair, rumpling it. "Unless one of you is prepared to volunteer, I'm afraid I'm on my own."

"Is there a family member who could fly here and drive back to Red Rock with you?"

"Maybe." He considered the idea, realizing that he had no other choice. "But it will take time to locate someone, and they probably couldn't get here until tomorrow at the earliest. I'd like to get the girls home and settled in as soon as possible."

The three adults had identical frowns on their faces as they observed the triplets who were happily unaware of the life decisions being considered.

Nick's cell phone rang, breaking the brief silence. He glanced at the unfamiliar number in his Caller ID and nearly ignored it. Instinct, however, had him answering the call.

"Hello." The female voice was familiar. "This is Charlene London."

While eating dinner with her mother and Lloyd, Charlene had felt distinctly like a fifth wheel.

She liked Lloyd and it was clear the man adored Angie. Her mother also clearly felt the same about the charming, gray-haired architect.

Which delighted Charlene. But it left her with a serious problem. Her plan to live with her mother while she searched for a job and an apartment of her own was no longer plausible. But Angie was sure to object if she abruptly changed her plans, and Charlene strongly suspected Lloyd would feel as if his presence had forced her from the condo. *He really is a nice man,* she thought, smiling as she remembered the besotted look on his face when he'd gazed at Angie over dessert.

She knew any one of her sisters or brothers would welcome her into their homes, but they all led crowded, busy lives. She really didn't want to choose that option, either.

What she really needed was an instant job—and a place to live that wouldn't make her mother or Lloyd feel guilty when she left.

"I could take Nicholas's job offer," she murmured to herself. Having retired to her bedroom early, she donned her pajamas. "But that means going back to Red Rock."

She didn't want to return to Red Rock. She wanted a new start, far enough away so there was no possibility she would run into Barry and his friends while shopping, dining out, running errands, or any of the dozens of activities that made up her normal life.

She slipped into bed and spent an hour trying to read, but her concentration was fractured as she continued to mull over her changed situation.

The antique clock in the hallway chimed midnight. Charlene realized she'd spent the last hour lying in the dark, unsuccessfully trying to sleep. She muttered in disgust and sat up to switch on the bedside lamp. It cast a pool of light over the bed as she tossed back the covers and padded barefoot across the carpet to retrieve Nicholas's card from her purse.

The phone number on the back of the card was written in decisive, black slashes. Charlene flipped the square card over to read the front and gasped, feeling her eyes widen.

"Nicholas Fortune?" She stared at the logo on the business card. "He's a member of the Fortune family?" Stunned, she considered the startling information.

Nicholas's status as part of the prominent family eliminated many of her concerns. There was little likelihood she'd run into Barry if she worked as a live-in nanny for one of the Fortunes. The two men moved in far different circles. Which put a whole new slant on the possibility of going back to Red Rock, she realized.

It also explained why he'd offered a two-part employment bonus. Fifty-thousand dollars was probably small change for one of the Fortunes.

She tucked the card carefully into her purse and turned out the light. Working for Nicholas could turn out to be the opportunity she'd been looking for.

On the other hand, how would she deal with her attraction to him? Would she end up sleeping with him if she lived in his house to care for the babies?

She frowned, fingertips massaging the slight ache at her temples.

Surely she could handle living in close quarters with a handsome, sexy man for a few weeks, she told herself. And, given Nick's good looks and probably wealth, he no doubt had beautiful women by the dozens waiting for him to call.

No, it wasn't likely she needed to worry about Nick making a pass at her. The real question was, could she maintain a purely professional attitude toward him?

When she thought about the bonus he'd offered, she

could only conclude she needed to set aside any emotional elements and make a purely practical decision.

The following morning, she waited until she'd showered and broke the news to her mother and Lloyd over breakfast before calling Nicholas.

"Hello."

The deep male tones shivered up her spine, and for a brief second she questioned the wisdom of agreeing to work for a man as attractive as Nicholas Fortune. Then she reminded herself just how badly she needed this job. "If it's not too late, I'd like to take you up on your offer of the nanny position," she said briskly.

"You're hired. How soon can you be ready to leave?"

"Almost immediately—I didn't unpack last night. What time is your flight?"

"Change of plans. I'm not flying the triplets back to Red Rock, we're driving."

"Oh."

"Give me your address and I'll pick you up as soon as I have the car loaded."

Charlotte quickly recited her mother's address and said goodbye. For a moment, she stared at her pink cell phone.

Have I just made a colossal mistake?

At the sound of his deep voice, she'd felt shivers of awareness race up her spine and tingle down her arms to her fingertips.

Then she remembered Barry, and her body instantly calmed as if the reaction to Nicholas had never happened. She wasn't ready to be attracted to another man. All she had to do was remind herself of her poor judgment and disappointment with Barry and she was safe, she realized with relief.

Reassured, she set her nearly full suitcase on top of the bed and tucked her pajamas into it. A quick trip into the bathroom to collect her toiletries, and she was ready to face her mother and Lloyd.

Squaring her shoulders and drawing a deep breath, she slung her purse over her shoulder, picked up her two bags, and headed downstairs.

Across town, Nick wrestled with the complexities of fastening three car seats into the SUV the rental company had delivered. Fortunately, the vehicle was big enough to have a third seat section and had enough room for an adult to sit between two of the triplets, if necessary.

At last, the babies' car seats were securely locked in place and the bags and boxes filled with the triplets' clothes, toys and food were packed into the back of the SUV. The girls were buckled into their seats, each with a treasured blanket and a favorite stuffed toy in her arms, and their foster mother tearfully kissed them good-bye. Nick had a brand-new appreciation for the details of traveling with three babies when he finally pulled away from the curb.

Fortunately for him, the girls all fell asleep within minutes of driving off.

The motion of the car must lull them to sleep. Good to know.

If they had trouble sleeping at his house, he realized, he could always drive them around his neighborhood.

But he knew figuring out this clue about the babies wasn't enough to make him a reliable substitute parent. If he and the triplets were going to survive until the attorney located Amy's sister, he'd need all the help he could get.

Charlene London was his ace in the hole. He was convinced she had the expertise that he knew damn well he lacked.

He hoped to hell he was right, because he was betting everything on her ability to handle the triplets. If he was wrong, this road trip was going to turn into a nightmare.

Nick's relief at the triplets falling peacefully asleep didn't last long. The girls all woke when he reached the address Charlene had given him and the SUV stopped moving. They immediately began to loudly protest being buckled into their car seats. Charlene said good-bye to her mother and friend in the midst of chaos.

Ten minutes after pulling away from the curb, Nick was no longer convinced he'd found the magic bullet to lull the babies asleep. They cried and fussed nonstop, despite the motion of the SUV.

Several hours of driving south and many miles later, Nicholas turned off the highway into a rest stop and parked. The sun shone brightly, but the afternoon air was still chilly. He left the engine running and the heater on to keep the interior as comfortable as possible for Jenny and Jackie while Charlene changed Jessie's diaper. The little girl lay on the leather seat, kicking her bare legs with obvious delight while Charlene stood in the open V of the door. Despite the churning little legs, Charlene deftly removed, replaced and snugly fastened a clean disposable nappy.

"I've done my share of tailgating at football games,

but this is a new experience," Nick commented as Charlene pulled down Jessie's knit pants and snapped the leg openings closed.

"You're in a whole new world, Nick." She lifted the little girl into her arms, tickling her. Jessie chortled and Charlene laughed. They both looked up to grin at him.

Nick shook his head. Crazy as it seemed, he could swear their faces held identical expressions of feminine wisdom and mystery. "I'm not sure I'm ready for a new world," he murmured as he took the diaper bag from Charlene and returned it to the storage area in the back of the SUV. "I'm getting some coffee," he said, louder this time, so Charlene could hear him. "Want some?"

"Yes, please, I'd love a cup."

Nick crossed the patch of grass between the curb where he'd parked the SUV and the concrete apron surrounding the low-roofed building housing the restrooms. Volunteers manned a small kiosk on one side and offered weary travelers coffee and cookies.

By the time he slid behind the steering wheel again, Charlene had Jessie fastened into her car seat and was buckling her own safety belt. She took the foam cup he held out to her and sipped.

"How bad is it?" he asked, unable to look away from the sight of the pink tip of her tongue as she licked a tiny drop of coffee from the corner of her mouth.

"Not too bad."

He lifted an eyebrow but didn't comment.

"Okay, so it's not Starbucks," she conceded with a chuckle. "But it's coffee and I need the caffeine. I was awake late last night and up early this morning. I really, really need the jolt."

Nick glanced at his watch as they drove away from

the rest stop. "The attorney told me the girls are in bed and asleep by seven every night. You're the expert, but I'm guessing it might be a good idea to find a motel earlier rather than later so we can keep them on schedule, if possible."

"I think that's an excellent idea." She glanced over her shoulder at the triplets' drowsy faces. "If we stop earlier, we'll have time to feed them, give them baths, and let them play for a little while before tucking them in for the night."

The motel Nick pulled into was just off the highway. Behind the motel, the tree-lined streets of a small town were laid out in neat blocks, and fairgrounds with an empty grandstand were visible a dozen or so blocks away. Nick was familiar with the motel chain and, as he'd hoped, the staff assured him they could accommodate the needs of three babies.

With quick calculation, he asked for two connecting rooms—one for the girls and Charlene, and one for him. He hoped the babies would sleep through the night.

Not for the first time, he thanked God Charlene had agreed to be the girls' nanny. If he could manage to ignore the fact that she was a beautiful woman, she made the perfect employee.

"If we both carry the girls in first, I can transfer the luggage while you keep an eye on them in the room," he told Charlene when he returned to the SUV. "We're on the ground floor, just inside the lobby and down the hall."

He handed her a key card. "Why don't you carry Jessie, I'll take Jackie and Jenny."

After unhooking the girls and handing Jenny to Nick

while he held Jackie, Charlotte lifted Jessie and followed Nick into the motel.

"Our rooms are through there." He led the way toward the hallway on the far side of the lobby.

Distracted by her view of his back, Charlene forgot to reply. Beneath the battered brown leather jacket, powerful shoulder muscles flexed as Jackie and Jenny squirmed in his hold. The jacket ended at his waist and faded Levis fit snugly over his taut backside and down the long length of his legs.

Get a grip, she told herself firmly. *Stop ogling the man's rear and focus on the job—and the babies.*

"Have you got the key?"

Nick's question startled her and she realized he'd halted outside a room.

Feeling her cheeks heat and hoping he hadn't caught her staring at his backside, she quickly slid the key card through the lock slot and opened the door.

"After you." Nick held the door while she carried Jessie inside.

"Nice. Very nice." She halted at the foot of the queen-size bed and glanced around, taking in a round table with three chairs tucked into one corner near the draped window.

Nick swept the room with a quick, assessing gaze. "Yeah, not bad. The connecting room is ours too." He bent and carefully set Jackie on the carpeted floor, then Jenny. Straightening, he took another key card from his back pocket and crossed the room to open the door to the room on the side. "They're exactly the same," he said after briefly looking. He returned and halted next to Jackie, bending to remove a handful of bedspread from her mouth. "Hey," he said gently. "I'm not sure you should be chewing on that."

"She's probably hungry." Charlene set Jessie on her diaper-padded bottom next to Jackie, and handed both girls a small stuffed bear each. Both beamed up at her and Jackie instantly shoved a furry bear leg into her mouth. "Hmmm, make that she's *definitely* hungry."

"I'll bring up the bag with their food before the rest of the luggage. Anything else you need right away?"

"If you could bring up the diaper bag too, that would be great."

He nodded and left the room.

"Well, girls, let's see what we can do to make you comfortable." Charlene laughed when Jessie blew a raspberry before smiling beatifically. "Are you going to be the class clown?" she teased.

Jessie gurgled and tipped sideways before righting herself and reaching for Jackie's bear.

"Oh no you don't, kiddo." Charlene made sure each little girl had their own stuffed animal before calling the front desk. The clerk assured her he would arrange to have three high chairs from the restaurant sent to the room immediately. He also confirmed that Nick had requested three cribs during check-in and that someone would be delivering and setting them up within a half hour.

Satisfied that arrangements were under way, Charlene barely had time to replace the phone in its cradle before Nick returned with the box containing baby paraphernalia and two bags.

For the next two hours, neither she nor Nick had a moment to draw a deep breath. The high chairs were delivered while he was bringing in the luggage. Later,

Charlene and Nick spooned food into little mouths, wiped chins and sticky fingers and tried to keep strained carrots from staining their own clothes.

Neither of them wanted to tackle eating dinner in the restaurant downstairs while accompanied by the triplets, so they ordered in. Nick insisted Charlene eat first, and she hurried to chew bites of surprisingly good pasta and chicken while he lay on the carpet, rolling rubber balls to the triplets. By the time Charlene's plate was empty, all three babies were yawning and rubbing their eyes.

The two adults switched places—Nick taking Charlene's chair to eat his steak, Jessie perched on his knee while Jackie played on the floor at his feet. Charlene toted Jenny into the bathroom and popped her into the tub to scrub the smears of strained plums and carrots from her face and out of her hair.

By the time she had Jenny dried, freshly diapered and tucked into footed white pajamas patterned with little brown monkeys, Nick had finished eating.

"Hey, look at you," he said to Jenny. "What happened to the purple-and-orange face paint?"

Charlene laughed. "She even had it in her hair."

"I think they all do." Nick rubbed his hand over Jessie's black curls and grimaced. "Definitely sticky."

"I'm guessing that's the strained plums," Charlene said. She handed Jenny to him and lifted Jessie into her arms. "Will you watch her and Jackie while I put Jessie in the tub?"

"Sure—but I can bathe her if you'd like a break. I'm sure I can manage."

"No, I'm fine. Besides—" she perched Jessie on her hip and started unbuttoning and unsnapping the baby's pants and knit shirt "—I'm already wet from being splashed by Jenny. One of us might as well stay dry."

Nicholas wished she hadn't pointed out that she'd been splashed with bathwater. He'd noticed the wet spots on her T-shirt and the way the damp cotton clung to her curves in interesting places. He was trying damned hard to ignore his body's reaction—and he was losing the battle.

"Uh, yeah. Okay, then. I'll keep these two occupied out here." He perched Jenny on his lap and she settled against him, her lashes half-lowered, apparently content to sit quietly. Nick bent his head, breathing in the scent of baby shampoo from her damp curls.

Something about the baby's warm weight resting trustingly in his arms and the smell of clean soap touched off an onslaught of unexpected emotion, followed quickly by a slam of grief that caught him off guard. The sound of splashing and gurgles from the bathroom, accompanied by Charlene's murmured reply, only heightened the pain in Nick's chest.

Stan and Amy must have fed and bathed the girls every night. Stan probably held Jenny just like this.

How was it possible that Stan and Amy were gone—and their children left alone? In what universe did any of this make sense?

It didn't—none of it, he thought. His arms tightened protectively around the baby.

He was the last person on earth who should be responsible for these kids; but since he was, he'd make damn sure they were cared for—and safe. As safe as he could make them.

Which means I have to rearrange my life.

He was a man who'd avoided the responsibilities of

a wife and family until now. He enjoyed the freedom of being single and hadn't planned to change his status anytime soon; but now that surrogate fatherhood had been thrust on him, he would make the most of it.

While Charlene bathed Jessie and Jackie, Nick considered his schedule at work and the logistics of fitting three babies and a nanny into his house and life.

He was still considering the thorny subject when the triplets were asleep in their cribs and he had said good-night to Charlene before disappearing into the far bedroom. He lay awake, staring at the ceiling above his own bed while he formulated a plan.

He'd just drifted off to sleep when one of the babies cried. By the time he staggered into the room next door, all three of them were awake and crying. Charlene stood at one of the cribs, lifting the sobbing little girl into her arms.

"I'll take Jessie into your room to change her diaper and try to get her back to sleep. I think she's running a bit of a fever—probably because of the ear infection. Can you deal with the other two?"

"Sure," Nick mumbled. Charlene disappeared into her room. He patted the nearest baby on the back but she only cried louder. "Damn," he muttered. "Now what do I do?"

He picked her up and she burrowed her face into his shoulder, her wails undiminished. Feeling totally clueless, Nick jiggled her up and down, but the sobbing continued unabated. Willing to try anything, he grabbed her abandoned blanket from the crib mattress and handed it to her. She snatched it and clutched it in one hand, sucking on her thumb. She still cried but the sound diminished because her mouth was closed.

Which left him with the baby still standing in her crib, tears streaming down her face, her cries deafening.

Nick's head began to pound. He leaned over and snagged the abandoned blanket, caught the little girl with one arm and lifted her to a seat on his hip. Then he lowered the two onto the empty bed, his back against the headboard. He managed to juggle both babies until he could cradle each of them against his chest, their security blankets clutched tightly in their hands. The first baby he'd picked up was crying with less volume, but the second one still made enough noise to wake the dead.

Vaguely remembering a comment his mother had made about singing her boys to sleep when they were little, Nick sang the only tune that came to mind. Bob Seger may not have intended his classic, "Rock And Roll Never Forgets" as a lullaby, but the lyrics seemed to strike a chord with the babies.

The loud sobs slowly abated. Nick felt the solid little bodies relax and gradually sink against his own. When the girls were limp and no longer crying, he tilted his head back to peer cautiously at them.

They were sound asleep.

Thank God. He eyed the cribs, trying to figure out how to lower each of the babies into their bed without waking one or both of them.

He drew a blank.

"Aw, hell," he muttered. He managed to shift one of the little girls onto the bed beside him before sliding lower in the bed until he lay flat. Then he grabbed a pillow, shoved it under his head and pulled the spread up over his legs and hips. "If you can't beat 'em, join 'em."

The sheets were still warm from Charlene's body,

and the scent of her perfume clung to the pillow, teasing his nostrils. He gritted his teeth and tried not to think about lying in her bed as he slid into sleep.

Nick woke the following morning with a kink in his neck and the sound of gleeful chortles accompanying thumps on his head from a tiny fist. He slitted his eyes open. He was nose-to-nose with a tiny face whose bright blue eyes sparkled with mischief below a mop of black curls.

He forced his eyes open farther just in time to see a second little girl as she wriggled out of his grasp and crawled toward the edge of the bed with determined speed. He grabbed a handful of her sleeper just in time to keep her from tumbling headfirst onto the floor.

The quick movement corresponded with a hard yank on his hair.

"Ow." He winced, pried little fingers away from his head and sat up. "You little imp." The tiny wrist bracelet told him this triplet was Jackie. "I'm gonna remember this," he told her.

She grinned, babbled nonsensically and began to crawl swiftly toward the end of the bed.

"Oh no you don't. Come back here." He hauled her back, then threw the spread back and stood, a wiggling little girl tucked beneath each arm. He lowered them each into a separate crib and grinned when they stood on tiptoes, reaching for him. "No way. You're trapped now and I'm not letting you out."

"Good morning."

He glanced over his shoulder. Charlene stood in the open doorway to the adjoining room, hair tousled, eyes sleepy. She was dressed in jeans and a pullover knit shirt, Jessie perched on one hip.

Nick was abruptly aware he was wearing only gray boxers.

"Morning." He gestured at the girls in their cribs. "I'll give you a hand with their breakfast as soon as I'm dressed. I'm going to jump in the shower."

She murmured an acknowledgment as he left the room.

Both adults were sleep-deprived and weary, but the triplets seemed little worse for their middle-of-the-night activity. By the time they were fed, dressed and strapped in their car seats, Nick was beginning to wonder if he should hire four or five nannies instead of one or two.

The trip from Amarillo south to Red Rock was just over five hundred and fifty miles. In normal circumstances, pretriplets, Nick could have driven the route in eight or nine hours with good road conditions and mild weather. But traveling with three babies on board drastically changed the time frame. After numerous stops to change diapers and feed the little girls, they finally reached his home in Red Rock in late afternoon of the second day.

Charlene stepped out of the SUV and stretched, easing muscles weary from sitting for too many hours. The SUV was parked in the driveway of a Spanish-style two-story stucco house on a quiet residential street in one of Red Rock's more affluent neighborhoods. She knew very little about this part of town; her previous apartment had been southeast, across the business district and blocks away.

In fact, she thought as she glanced up and down the

broad street, with its large homes and neatly trimmed lawns, she didn't remember ever having been in this part of Red Rock before.

Good, she thought with satisfaction. Her belief that it would be unlikely she might run into Barry or his friends seemed to be accurate.

She turned back to the SUV and leaned inside to unhook Jessie from her seat belt.

"I called my housekeeper this morning," Nick told her as he unbuckled Jackie on the opposite side of the vehicle. "Melissa promised to come by and fill the fridge and pantry with food for the girls. She said she'd wait for the delivery van with the baby furniture too."

Surprised, Charlene's fingers stilled and she stopped unbuckling Jessie's seat belt to look at him across the width of the SUV's interior. "I didn't realize you'd made arrangements—but thank goodness you did."

Nick's gaze met hers and she felt her breath catch, helpless to stop her body's reaction to him.

"We were lucky last night," he said. "The hotel was prepared to accommodate babies. Trust me, there aren't any high chairs or cribs stored in my attic." He lifted Jackie free and grinned. "I'm not sure what we would have done with these three tonight if the store hadn't agreed to deliver and set up their beds today. The only thing I've got that comes close to cribs are a couple of large dog crates in the garage."

Charlene laughed, the sudden mental image of the three little girls sleeping in boxy carriers with gates was too preposterous.

"Exactly," Nick said dryly. He shifted Jackie onto his hip and unhooked Jenny from her seat.

He's much more comfortable with the babies after

only a day. Charlene was impressed at how easily he'd managed to extricate Jenny from her seat while holding Jackie.

She quickly gathered the girls' blankets, stuffed animals and various toys from the floor mats where the girls had tossed them and finished unbuckling Jessie to lift her out of the car. She slung a loaded tote bag over her shoulder and bumped the car door closed with one hip.

"I'll unload the bags after we get the girls inside," Nick told her, gesturing her ahead of him to the walkway that curved across the lawn to the front entry. "Ring the doorbell," he said when they reached the door. "Melissa should be here—that's her car parked at the curb."

Charlene did as he asked and heard muted chimes from inside the house. Almost immediately the door opened.

"Hello—there you are." The woman in the doorway was small, her petite form sturdy in khaki pants, pullover white T-shirt and tennis shoes. Her dark hair was frosted with gray and her deep-brown eyes sparkled, animated behind tortoise-shell-framed glasses. "How was the trip?"

"Exhausting," Nick said bluntly. "Melissa, this is Charlene London. Charlene, this is Melissa Kennedy, my housekeeper. Charlene's going to take care of the girls, Melissa."

"Nice to meet you." Melissa's smile held friendly interest. Charlene's murmured response was lost as Jenny wriggled in Nick's arms, her little face screwing up into a prelude to full-blown tears. Nick stepped inside and handed Jackie to the housekeeper before he cuddled Jenny closer.

"Hey, what's wrong?" He carried the sobbing little girl down the hall.

Charlene followed him into the living room, Melissa bringing up the rear with Jackie.

As often happened with the three little girls, when one of them began crying, the other two soon followed. Charlene rubbed Jessie's back in soothing circles and slowly rocked her back and forth. She only cried harder. Melissa murmured to Jackie and gently patted her back, but Jackie's sobs increased until they matched her sisters' in volume.

"Jessie needs a diaper change." Charlene raised her voice to be heard over the combined cries of the three babies.

"Can you and Melissa handle them while I bring in the bags from the car?" Nick asked, looking faintly frazzled.

"Of course," Charlene responded with easy confidence.

Nick didn't look convinced but he didn't argue with her.

"Did the delivery crew set up the cribs, Melissa?" he asked.

"Yes, and the changing tables and dressers too. I put away the diapers and the other supplies in their room, and I had the men carry the high chairs into the kitchen," she replied.

"Good." Nick gently patted Jenny's back with one hand as he strode across the living room toward the stairway, located just inside the front door. "Let's get them upstairs and I'll bring in the diaper bags."

Charlene followed Nick and Melissa up the open stairway, with its wooden railing. The second-floor hallway branched to the right and left. Nick turned left and soon disappeared into the third room, Melissa and Jackie a step behind.

Charlene brought up the rear with Jessie, slowing to glance briefly into the first two rooms as she passed. One held a white, wrought-iron bed, the floor carpeted in light green Berber. The other was a bathroom, fitted in pale wooden cabinets with green marble tops.

The house was lovely but the sparse furnishings clearly stated that this was a bachelor's home. Downstairs in the living room, she'd noted a large plasma television mounted on one wall, with shelves of electronic equipment beneath. CD cases were piled in stacks on the shelves between stereo speakers. A low, oak coffee table sat in front of a dark-brown-leather sofa and a matching club chair and ottoman, angled next to the hearth of a river rock fireplace and chimney. There was no other furniture in the room, leaving an expanse of pale wooden floor gleaming in the late afternoon sunlight that poured through skylights and windows.

She'd glimpsed a dining room through an archway, but again, saw only the minimum of furniture in a table and chairs. She wondered how long Nick had lived in the house, since it appeared to be furnished with only essentials.

She carried Jessie into the bedroom and paused, feeling her eyes widen as she took in the room. It was large, with plenty of space for three white-painted cribs. Two dressers and changing tables matched the cottage-style cribs, and two rocking chairs with deep-rose seat cushions were tucked into a corner. Despite the number of pieces of furniture, the room didn't feel crowded.

Clearly, Nick hadn't skimped on furnishings here.

"I had the men put the third dresser, changing table and rocker in the empty bedroom down the hall," Melissa said to Nick. "I thought it would be too crowded if all of the furniture was in here."

"We might have to move two of the cribs into other rooms. If one of the girls cries, the other two chime in. Maybe they'd sleep better if we split them up." He looked at Charlene. "What do you think?"

"We could leave them together for tonight and see how they do. You can always move them tomorrow, if sharing a room doesn't work out."

Nick nodded decisively. "We'll try it." Gently, he lowered the now quiet Jenny onto the carpet. "I'll go bring up their bags."

Charlene slipped the canvas tote off her shoulder and lowered it to the floor before kneeling and setting Jessie down next to it. She took a tissue from the bag and wiped the damp tears from Jessie's cheeks before handing the baby her blanket and a stuffed bear.

In Melissa's arms, Jackie's sobs had slowed to the occasional hiccup. She stretched out her arms and babbled imperiously.

Charlene wondered if she could use that combination of regal commands and pleas on Nick. Would he respond with hugs and kisses, as he did with the triplets?

She nearly groaned aloud.

The image of him rising from her bed at the motel, rumpled and sleepy, seemed to have permanently engraved itself on her brain. Try as she might, she couldn't forget how his big, powerful body had looked, clad only in gray boxers, as he'd walked across the room.

Jackie's chattering increased to shriek level and Charlene realized she had no idea how long she'd been standing still, staring unseeingly at the baby. She glanced quickly at Melissa, but the other woman was focused on Jackie, laughing as she jiggled her in her arms.

"I bet the queen of Hollywood divas, whoever she may be this week, doesn't make as much noise as this little girl," Melissa commented as she met Charlene's gaze. The housekeeper's eyes twinkled with amusement.

Mentally sighing with relief that Melissa appeared oblivious to her distraction, Charlene shoved the memory of Nick's powerful thighs and broad chest into the back of her mind. She ordered the image to stay put—and desperately hoped it would obey.

Chapter 3

Jackie shrieked again and Charlene laughed out loud. "Yes, your royal highness," she said teasingly, retrieving the pink blanket with Jackie's name embroidered across one corner and passing it to Melissa.

"Isn't that clever?" Melissa said admiringly, as Jackie hugged the blanket and beamed at Charlene. "I wondered how Nick planned to tell one baby's things from another." She ran a fingertip gently over the bracelet on Jackie's wrist. "But everything has their names on it, including the little girls themselves."

"I thought their parents came up with a brilliant solution," Charlene agreed. "Though I assume they could tell their daughters apart."

Melissa's face sobered. "Such a terrible thing to have happened, isn't it? How awful to lose both parents at such a young age."

"Yes," Charlene agreed, her heart wrenching as she looked at Jessie and Jenny tugging on their stuffed bears. *So innocent—and thankfully, too young to grasp the enormity of their loss just now.*

Nick strode into the room, pulling two large rolling suitcases and carrying a backpack slung over one shoulder, all stuffed to overflowing with the triplets' clothing and toys. "I put your suitcase in the room across the hall," he told Charlene, shrugging the backpack off his shoulder.

"Thank you," she murmured, delighted to know the lovely room with the white wrought-iron bed and green carpet would be hers during her stay.

In the ensuing bustle of changing diapers and tucking away tiny clothing into dresser drawers, Charlene was too busy to dwell on the triplets' orphaned status.

Melissa was a godsend, helping with the girls as Charlene and Nick fed and bathed them, then tucked all three into bed. The adults returned to the living room and collapsed, Nick in the leather club chair, Charlene and Melissa on the comfortable sofa.

"They're wonderful," Melissa told Nick. "But oh, my goodness." She sighed, a gust of air stirring her normally smooth hair, where one of the triplets had rumpled and dampened it while the little girl splashed in her bath. "Talk about energy. What you two need to do is find a way to collect some of that for yourself. You're going to need it." She looked at Charlene. "Do they sleep through the night?"

"They did last night. I've got my fingers crossed, hoping we'll have another quiet ten hours or so."

"I hope they do too." Melissa pushed herself up off

the sofa. "I'd better get home. Ed will be wondering what happened to me."

Nick started to shove up out of the chair but she waved him back. "No, no—don't get up. I can see myself out. You should take advantage of this moment of quiet. Who knows how long it will last?"

"Good point," Nick agreed, settling into the chair, the worn denim of his jeans going taut over muscled thighs as he stretched out his long legs. "We should make the most of this rare minute. It could be the last one of the night."

"Exactly." Melissa grinned at him, eyes twinkling, before she turned to Charlene. "I'll see you in the morning—about eight?"

"Eight works for me. I'm looking forward to it," Charlene replied with heartfelt warmth. After watching Melissa's efficient, comfortable and unflappable handling of the babies over the last couple of hours, Charlene was convinced the housekeeper was going to be an enormous help in caring for the triplets.

"Goodnight, then, you two. I hope you get some sleep. I left my purse and keys in the kitchen. I'll just collect them and let myself out the back," she said. She moved briskly across the living room but stopped in the doorway. "I forgot to tell you, Nick, I left Rufus with Ed today so you could get the girls settled in before they meet him. I'll bring him back with me tomorrow."

"Good thinking," Nick told her. "Dealing with the triplets was chaotic. Adding an excited hundred-and-twenty-five-pound dog into the mix would have made it crazy."

Melissa chuckled and waved a quick good-night as she disappeared.

A moment later, the sound of her car engine reached the two in the living room.

"I take it you have a *big* dog?"

"Oh, yeah," Nick said dryly. "Rufus is a chocolate Lab. Thankfully, he's very mellow and loves kids, so he should be fine with the triplets."

"As long as he likes them, they'll probably think he's wonderful." Charlene yawned, suddenly exhausted. "I think I'll head upstairs." She unfolded her legs and stood, aware of aching muscles from the long car ride. "I could sleep for at least twelve hours straight. I've never understood how sitting in a car and doing nothing can make me tired."

"It was a long trip," Nicholas agreed, getting out of the chair. He rolled his shoulders and stretched. "Did Melissa show you where everything is—towels, coffee for tomorrow morning, et cetera?"

"Yes, thank you."

"If you need anything, just ask. If I don't already have it in the house, I'll get it." He eyed her, his gaze intent. "I'm damned grateful you agreed to take on the triplets, Charlene. I know it's not an easy job. There's no way I could do it by myself."

"You're doing very well for a man who's never had children of his own," she told him. "And I confess, I'm relieved Melissa will be helping. She's good with the girls and nothing seems to faze her."

"She's pretty unshakeable," Nick said. "I normally work long hours, and she keeps the house together and makes sure there are meals in the fridge."

"How long has she worked for you?" Charlene asked, curious.

"Since a few days after I moved to Red Rock. The

employment agency sent over three women and I hired Melissa on the spot."

"Sounds like it was the right decision. Well…" She tugged her white cotton T-shirt into place, suddenly self-conscious. The room was abruptly too intimate in the lamplight and Nick loomed much too large, and much too male. "I'll see you in the morning."

"Sleep well. I have to go to the office for a meeting tomorrow, but I won't leave until Melissa arrives."

She nodded. "Good night."

His answering good-night was a low male rumble. Charlene looked back when she reached the stairway and found him staring after her, his expression brooding. She hurried up the stairs, faintly breathless from the impact of the brief moment her gaze had met his.

He's your employer, she reminded herself as she brushed her teeth in the white-and-green bathroom that opened off her bedroom, *stop lusting after him.*

Apparently, however, the emotional, hormonal part of her was in no mood to listen to the practical, rational command. She fell asleep and dreamed of making love with a man who looked very much like Nick Fortune.

Just as she stretched out her arms, her fingertips mere inches away from the bare chest of her dream lover, a loud wail yanked her awake.

Charlene sat bolt upright, disoriented as she stared in confusion at the dim outlines of bed and dresser in the strange room.

The sound of crying from the triplets' room abruptly scattered the lingering fog of sleep and she tossed back the bedcovers to hurry next door.

"Oh, sweetie," she soothed, lifting Jackie from her

crib. "Sh." She patted the little back while the baby's sobs slowed to hiccups. "What's wrong?"

Jessie rolled over in her crib and sat up. In the third crib, Jenny pulled herself to her feet to clasp the rail. Jackie chose that moment to burst into sobs once more and, as if on cue, Jessie and Jenny's faces crumpled. They burst into tears as well.

The combined sound of their crying was deafening and impossible to ignore. Charlene wasn't surprised when Nick staggered into the room.

"What's wrong?" His voice was gravelly with sleep. He wore navy boxers, his broad chest and long legs bare.

Despite the earsplitting noise of three crying babies, Charlene still noticed that Nick looked as good undressed as he did in faded jeans and T-shirts.

"Jackie woke me, then her crying woke the other two." Charlene crossed to the changing table, gently rocking the still sobbing Jackie while she took a fresh diaper from the drawer. "I think she needs a diaper change. Can you pick up Jenny and Jessie—maybe rock them for a few minutes?"

"Sure." Nick shoved his fingers through his hair, further rumpling it, and lifted Jenny from her crib.

The low rumble of his voice as he murmured to the two babies was barely audible as Charlene quickly changed Jackie's diaper. By the time she snapped the little girl's footed sleeper and tossed the damp disposable nappy into the bin, their crying had subsided into silence. She tucked Jackie against her shoulder and turned, stopping abruptly.

Nick sat in the cushioned rocking chair, a little girl against each bare shoulder, their faces turned into the bend of his neck where shoulder met throat. His broad hands nearly covered each little back, fingers splayed to hold them securely. His hair was rumpled, his eyes sleepy.

Charlene didn't think she'd ever seen anything half as sexy as the big man protectively cradling the two sleeping babies. She felt her heart lurch.

Don't go there, she ordered herself. *Do* not *notice how sexy he is. Remember you swore to avoid men for at least six months after breaking up with Barry.* That was only two weeks ago.

She couldn't remember ever feeling this attracted to her ex-fiancé, but that didn't change the fact that she was determined to never, ever, get involved with her employer.

She moved softly across the room and eased into the empty rocking chair. Jackie stirred, lifting her head from Charlene's shoulder. Charlene quickly smoothed her hand over the baby's silky black curls, gently urging her to lay her head down once more, and set the rocker in motion. Within seconds, Jackie was relaxed, her compact little body feeling boneless where it lay against Charlene.

"Is she asleep?" Nick's murmur rasped, velvet over gravel.

"Yes," Charlene whispered. "What about your two?"

He tipped his head back to peer down at first one, then the other, of the two little girls. "They seem to be." He looked up at her. "Think it's safe to put them back in bed?"

"We can try. Let me put Jackie down and then I'll take one of yours." At his nod, Charlene stood and crossed to Jackie's crib, easing the sleeping baby down onto her back and pulling the light blanket over her before she returned to Nick.

"Which one do you want me to carry?" she whispered.

"Jenny." He leaned forward slightly.

Charlene bent closer to lift the sleeping baby, her hands brushing against his bare skin. He was warm, his skin sleek over the flex of muscles as he shifted to help transfer the little girl to her, and a shiver of awareness shook her. She was aware his head turned abruptly, could feel the intensity of his stare, but she wouldn't, couldn't, allow herself to meet his gaze. Instead, she cradled Jenny in her arms and turned away to carry the little girl to her crib, tucking her in and smoothing the blanket over her sleeping form. Behind her, she heard the soft sounds of Nick tucking Jessie into the third crib.

Nick followed her to the doorway, waiting in the hall as she paused to look back. The room was quiet—no movement visible in any of the three cribs to indicate a restless child.

"I think they're out for the count," Nick murmured behind her.

"Yes, I believe you're right," she whispered, before stepping into the hall and easing the door partially closed. "Let's hope they stay that way for the rest of the night." She gave him a fleeting glance. "Good night."

"Good night."

Once again, she felt his stare as she walked down the hall and into the safety of her room. She closed the door and collapsed against it, the panels cool against her shoulders, left bare by the narrow straps of her camisole pajama top.

There was no way she would ever become involved

with her boss. She'd sworn a solemn oath after she'd learned about her father's affair with his secretary that had ultimately destroyed her parents' marriage. She'd never forgiven him, but for the first time, tonight she had an inkling as to what may have caused her father to stray. If he'd felt anything like the sizzling heat that swamped her every time she got close to Nick Fortune, then maybe, just maybe, she should stop being so angry at him. Maybe he'd literally been unable to help himself.

Or not, she thought, still not completely convinced.

But in any event, she had to find a way to insulate herself against the powerful attraction she felt. Especially since it appeared Nick didn't have to do anything, or even say anything, to make her nerves sizzle and her body heat up.

Apparently, he just needed to breathe in her presence.

Groaning, she climbed back into bed and pulled the sheet and blanket over her head.

The triplets were still fast asleep in their cribs upstairs when Charlene tiptoed down the stairs and into the kitchen just before eight the following morning.

Nick glanced over his shoulder and took down another mug from the open cupboard. "Morning," he said. "Coffee's nearly done."

Charlene breathed in the rich scent filling the kitchen and nearly groaned. "Bless you."

Nick's grin flashed, his eyes lit with amusement. He poured the rich brew into their mugs at the same moment that a knock sounded on the back door.

"That'll be Melissa," Nick told Charlene. He grabbed his computer case and crossed the kitchen to pull open the door.

A huge chocolate Labrador retriever leaped over the threshold and planted his paws on Nick's shoulders, whining with excitement, his tail whipping back and forth.

"Ouch." Melissa stepped inside, moving sideways to avoid getting hit. "That tail of yours is a lethal weapon, Rufus." She waved her hand at the travel coffee mug and leather case in Nick's left hand. "On your way out to work, boss?"

"Yeah." Nick rubbed Rufus's ears. "That's enough. Down, boy." The Lab dropped back onto four paws but continued to wag his tail, pink tongue lolling as he stared adoringly up at Nick. "I'll check with the employment agency today," Nick said, looking over his shoulder at Charlene, "and find out if they've lined up applicants for a second nanny."

"I'll keep my fingers crossed that they have—then maybe we both can start getting more sleep."

Nick grinned, his eyes lit with rueful amusement as his mouth curved upward to reveal a flash of white teeth. Charlene suspected she was staring at him like a hopelessly lovestruck teenager, but she couldn't bring herself to look away.

No man should be that gorgeous.

"I'll tell them we're staggering from sleep deprivation. Maybe they'll take pity on us," he said.

"We can only hope," Charlene said, tearing her gaze away from his smile. Unfortunately, she was immediately snagged by his glossy black hair, thick-lashed brown eyes, tanned skin with a faint beard shadow despite the early hour, handsome features... Were all the Fortune men this blessed by nature? she wondered. If so, heaven help the women who caught their attention—

because females didn't stand a chance against all that powerful, charming, handsome male virility. Perhaps she was fortunate that he was her boss and thus off-limits, not to mention he was also clearly far more sophisticated than she. Never mind the fact that he was also not interested in her. Because if he ever turned that undeniable charm on her, she'd give in without a whimper.

It's a pitiful thing when a woman has *no* resistance to a man, she realized with wry acknowledgment.

"So long, boss," Melissa's voice yanked Charlene out of her thoughts. "Have a good day."

"Good luck with the triplets." Nick bent to give Rufus's silky ears one last rub before disappearing through the door.

Charlene echoed Melissa's goodbye before pouring herself another mug of coffee. "The coffee's fresh," she told Melissa. "Want some?"

"Sure, why not." Melissa slid onto a stool at the counter.

Charlene handed her a steaming cup and took a seat opposite her.

"Are the babies still asleep?" Melissa asked.

"Yes." Charlene glanced at the digital clock on the microwave. "They're sleeping in, probably because they were awake several times last night."

"I was telling my Ed about the triplets just this morning—" Melissa began.

Whatever she was about to say was lost as someone rapped sharply on the back door.

Charlene looked inquiringly at Melissa.

"That's probably LouAnn," Melissa said as she left the counter and crossed the room.

Charlene barely had time to wonder who LouAnn

was before Melissa pulled open the door. She felt her eyes widen.

"Good morning, Melissa." The throaty rasp seemed incongruous, coming as it did from a woman who Charlene guessed weighed at best a hundred pounds, maybe a hundred and ten at the most.

"Hi, LouAnn." Melissa gestured her inside. "We're just having coffee. Want some?"

"Of course." LouAnn followed Melissa to the counter, her bright blue gaze full of curiosity and fixed on Charlene. "And who are you, dearie?"

"I'm Charlene, the nanny." Charlene tried not to stare, but the silver-haired woman's attire was eye-popping. She wore a turquoise T-shirt with a bucking horse and rider picked out in silver rhinestones. The black leggings below the T-shirt clung to her nonexistent curves and hot-pink, high-top tennis shoes covered her feet. Skinny arms poked out of the loose short sleeves of the shirt, and both hands boasted jewelry that dazzled. Charlene was pretty sure the huge diamond on her left hand was real, and more than likely, so was the sapphire on her right. Not to mention the large diamond studs that glittered in her earlobes. She was tan, toned and exuded energy that fairly vibrated the air around her pixie frame.

"Nanny?" LouAnn's penciled eyebrows shot toward the permed silver curls of her immaculate, short hairdo. "Why does Nick need a nanny?"

"Have a seat, LouAnn, and we'll fill you in." Melissa pulled out a chair next to hers and across the island's countertop from Charlene. "Charlene, this is Nick's neighbor, LouAnn Harris."

"Pleased to meetcha." LouAnn hopped onto the tall

chair, crossed her legs and beamed at Charlene. "You might as well know you're likely to see a lot of me. I'm a widow. I live alone and my son and daughter live too far away to visit me often, so I tend to get bored. I was delighted when Nick moved in here and hired Melissa—we've known each other for at least twenty years. My, you're young, aren't you?"

"Uh, well…" Charlene looked at Melissa for guidance. The housekeeper grinned, her eyes twinkling. Clearly, she wasn't bothered by the neighbor's bluntness. "I suppose I am, sort of," Charlene replied, taking her cue from Melissa.

LouAnn snorted. "No 'sort of' about it, honey. Compared to me, you're a child. But then, I'm seventy-six, so most everyone *is* younger." She sipped her coffee. "I have to get me a coffeemaker like Nick's. Your coffee is always better than mine, Melissa."

"That might be because I grind the beans. Nick has them sent from the coffee shop he used to go to in L.A.," Melissa explained to Charlene.

"I thought it was the coffeemaker." LouAnn leaned forward and lowered her voice to a raspy whisper. "It looks like it belongs on a space ship."

Charlene laughed, charmed by LouAnn's warm camaraderie.

LouAnn grinned at her, winked, and turned back to Melissa. "Now, tell me why Nick needs a nanny. I thought he was a confirmed bachelor with no interest in kids."

"He is—and he doesn't, or didn't, pay attention to children," Melissa agreed. "At least, he had no interest in children until recently. It's a sad story, really."

When she finished relaying a condensed version of

the situation, LouAnn clucked in sympathy. "How terrible for those poor little girls. And how lucky for them—and Nick—that you were willing to step in and help," she added, reaching across the marble countertop to pat Charlene's hand.

"It was fate," Melissa said firmly. "That's what I think."

"Three little ones—all the same age." LouAnn shook her head. "How are you all coping?"

"Except for a serious lack of sleep, fairly well, I think." Charlene looked at Melissa. "Sometimes it's chaos, of course, but the girls seem to be doing okay. Jessie has an ear infection at the moment, so she's a little cranky. But by and large, they're very sweet little girls."

"I can't wait to see them. How old are they?"

"They're a year—uh-oh." The sound of one of the girls, chattering away upstairs floated down the stairway and into the kitchen. "I think you're about to meet the dynamic trio." Charlene slipped off her chair and headed for the door.

"I'm coming up with you," LouAnn announced, joining Charlene.

Melissa brought up the rear as the three women left the kitchen.

Nick had a long list of priorities for the day, but as he backed his Porsche out of the garage and drove away, he wasn't focusing on the work waiting for him at the Fortune Foundation. Instead, he was distracted by the memory of Charlene coping with the babies in the middle of the night.

The picture of her in the bedroom, lit only by the glow of a night-light, was seared in his memory. Her auburn hair had been rumpled from sleep, her long legs covered in soft-looking, blue-and-white pajama bottoms. Jackie had clutched the neckline of the brief little white tank top Charlene wore, pulling it down to reveal the upper curve of her breasts.

Even half-asleep, he'd been damn sure she wasn't wearing anything under that top. He felt like a dog for looking, and hoped she hadn't noticed.

He'd known having the beautiful redhead living in his house was bound to cause difficult moments, but he hadn't been prepared to be blindsided by a half-naked woman when he was barely awake.

Which was stupid of me, he thought with disgust. *She's living in my house. I knew she'd be getting out of bed if one of the triplets woke during the night.*

And as long as he was being brutally honest, he had to admit the pajamas she wore hadn't come close to being blatantly suggestive. Nevertheless, Charlene's simple pajama bottoms and tank top would stop traffic on an L.A. freeway.

Maybe he wouldn't have felt as if he'd been hit by lightning when he saw her in those pajamas if she were a woman with fewer curves.

Or maybe, he thought with self-derision, *if she'd been wearing a sack I'd still have been interested.*

He knew he was completely out of line. He just didn't know how to turn off his body's response to her. Not only was she his employee, she was too damned young for him. His office assistant had telephoned with results of a preemployment background check before he'd left his hotel to drive to the triplets' foster home. The report not only confirmed Charlene had a spotless employment record, it also told him she'd graduated from college only three years earlier.

A brief mental calculation told him that if she'd gone to college immediately after high school, then graduated after four or five years before working for three more years, she most likely was twenty-five or twenty-six years old.

And he was thirty-seven. Too old for her.

Unfortunately, his libido didn't appear to be paying attention to the math.

He'd reached the office while he'd been preoccupied with the situation at home, and swung the Porsche into a parking slot. He left the car and headed for his office, determined to put thoughts of the curvy redhead at home, busy with his new instant family, out of his mind.

He quickly scanned the pink message slips the receptionist had handed him and tossed the stack on his desktop. He rang his brother Darr while he plugged in his laptop and arranged to meet him for lunch at their favorite diner, SusieMae's. Then he closed his office door and tackled an inbox filled with documents and files.

Nick gave the waitress his and Darr's usual lunch order and she bustled off. SusieMae's Café was crowded, but he had a clear view of the door, and saw his brother enter.

Darr swept the comfortable interior with a quick glance, nodding at acquaintances as he crossed the room and slid into the booth across from Nick.

"Where have you been?" he demanded without preamble. "I left two messages on your machine. You never called back."

"You didn't say it was an emergency." Nick shrugged

out of his jacket and eyed his brother across the width of the scarred tabletop. "Was it?"

"Not exactly. I wanted to know if you'd talked to Dad or J.R. lately."

"I haven't." Nick took a drink of water. "Why?"

"Because I called and neither one answered. Come to think of it—" Darr frowned at Nick "—none of you called me back."

Nick grinned. "Probably because we all assumed you were too busy with Bethany to care if we called you or not."

"Huh," Darr grumbled.

Nick noticed his younger brother didn't deny the charge.

"How's Bethany doing?" he asked. He felt distinctly protective toward the petite, pregnant blonde, especially since Darr was in love with her. When the two married, she'd become Nick's sister-in-law. As far as he was concerned, Bethany Burdett was a welcome addition to their all-male family.

"Good." Darr leaned back to let their waitress set plates and coffee mugs on the tabletop in front of them. "She's good."

Nick didn't miss the softening of his brother's face. He was glad Darr had found a good woman. Bethany made him happy, and he seemed content in a way Nick hadn't seen before.

"You didn't answer my question, where have you been?"

Nick waited until the waitress left before he spoke. "I made a trip to Amarillo. I've been pretty busy since I got back."

"Yeah? What were you doing in Amarillo?" Darr

took a bite of his sandwich, eyeing Nick over the top of a double-decker bacon-and-tomato on wheat.

"I picked up Stan's kids." Nick saw Darr's eyes widen. "Three of them," he added, smiling slightly at the shock on his brother's face. "They're all girls—only a year old. Triplets."

Darr choked, set down his sandwich, grabbed his coffee and washed down the bite in record time. "What the hell? Why? What happened?"

Nick lost any amusement he'd felt at his brother's dumfounded expression. "He and Amy were in a car accident—neither one of them made it out alive." Saying the words aloud didn't make the truth any less surreal.

The shock on Darr's face made it clear he was just as stunned as Nick had been at first hearing the news.

"Both of them?" He shook his head in disbelief when Nick nodded. "They were so young. You and Stan are the same age, right?"

Again, Nick nodded. "And Amy was a year younger."

"And you have custody of their babies?" Darr queried.

"Yeah."

"Why?"

"Because Stan's will named me guardian if Amy's sister Lana couldn't take them." Nick took a drink of coffee, hoping to erase the lump of emotion in his throat. He still hadn't come to terms with the abruptness with which Stan and Amy had disappeared from the world. "So they're with me until the attorney locates Lana."

"Where is she?"

"No one knows." Nick stared broodingly at his plate, holding a sandwich and chips. "She and her husband work in Africa and Amy seems to have lost track of them a few months ago."

"Damn." Darr eyed him. "Who's taking care of the kids while you work?"

"I hired a nanny," Nick replied. "And Melissa's working longer hours while I'm at the Foundation during the day."

Darr stared at him. Nick took a bite of his sandwich.

"And?" Darr prompted when Nick didn't elaborate.

"And what?"

"Don't give me that. You're stalling. What else aren't you telling me?"

"The nanny I hired works full-time. Her name is Charlene. She's a redhead and she's great with the triplets."

Darr lowered his coffee mug to the table without taking his gaze from Nick's face. "She's a babe, isn't she."

It wasn't a question. Darr knew him too well to be fooled.

"Yeah. She is." Nick shoved another bite of sandwich into his mouth.

"Full-time," Darr said consideringly. "What hours does she work?"

"She's pretty much on call twenty-four hours a day."

"So...she's living at your house?"

"Yeah."

"Sleeping down the hall from you?"

Nick nodded, saw the glint appear in Darr's eyes and bristled. "Yes, *down the hall*. She has her own bedroom. What the hell did you think, that she was sharing mine?"

Darr shrugged. "It did cross my mind. Face it, Nick, you've never been slow with the ladies. You said she's pretty—and she's living in your house...." He spread his hands. "Sounds like a no-brainer to me."

"Well, it's not," Nick snarled, restraining an urge to wrap his hands around his brother's neck and choke that grin off his face. "She works for me. Have you heard of sexual harassment? She's off-limits."

"Too bad." Darr lifted his coffee mug and drank. "So," he said, setting the mug down and picking up his sandwich, "just how good-looking is Charlene?"

Too beautiful. Nick bit back the words and shrugged. "Beautiful."

"On a scale of one to ten?"

"She's a fifteen."

Darr's eyes widened. "Damn."

"And she's too young," Nick continued.

"How young?"

"She's twenty-five."

"Thank God." Darr pretended to wipe sweat off his brow in relief. "I thought you were going to tell me she's underage and jailbait."

"Might as well be," Nick growled. "She's twelve years younger than me. That's too damned young."

Darr pursed his lips. "Let me see if I've got this straight. You're cranky because you've got a nanny you can't make a move on because you're her boss and she's younger than you."

"Yeah, pretty much," Nick conceded.

Darr grinned. "Maybe you should fire her. Then you can date her."

"I can't fire her—and I don't want to," Nick ground out. "She's good at her job. If she wasn't helping me take care of the girls, I'd be screwed."

"So hire someone else—and then fire her."

"Yeah, like she's likely to go out with me after I've fired her." Nick rubbed his eyes. They felt as if there was a pound of sand in each of them. If he didn't get some sleep soon, he'd need more than the saline eye-drops he'd been using in a vain attempt to solve the problem. "There's no solution that's workable. Believe me, I've considered all the angles."

"Where there's a will, there's a way."

"Stop being so damned cheerful," Nick growled.

"Aren't you the one who told me there's always another girl just around the corner? Wait a week and there'll be another corner, another girl. If things don't work out with the redhead, why do you care?"

Because I've never met anyone quite like her.

Nick didn't want to tell Darr that Charlene was unique. He was having a hard enough time accepting that he'd met a woman who broke all the rules he'd spent thirty-seven years setting.

"Maybe you're right," he said with a slight shrug, neither agreeing nor disagreeing. "Have you heard anything new about the note Patrick got at the New Year's Eve party? Or about the ones Dad and Cindy received?"

"No." Darr didn't appear thrown by Nick's abrupt change of subject. "That's one of the reasons I wanted to talk to Dad and J.R.—to ask if they've learned anything more."

The Fortune family had gone through a series of mysterious events over the last few months, starting with the cryptic note left in Patrick Fortune's jacket pocket during a New Year's Eve party. The strange message—"One of the Fortunes is not who you think"—baffled the family, even more so when they learned the same message had been left anonymously with Cindy Fortune and William, Nick and Darr's father.

Patrick had called a family conference at Lily Fortune's home on the Double Crown Ranch in February, on the very day Red Rock had been hit with a freak snowstorm.

Darr hadn't been present at the gathering, since he'd been snowed-in with Bethany in her little house. But Nick had brought him up to speed on everything that happened, including the family's assumption the notes were the precursor to a blackmail demand. So far, however, no such demand had been made. But two subsequent fires—one that burned down the local Red Restaurant, and a second that destroyed a barn at the Double Crown—were suspicious. And potentially connected to the mysterious and vaguely threatening notes.

"Let me know if you reach Dad and J.R.," Nick said. "Meanwhile, I had a message from Ross Fortune when I got back to the office today. We set up a meeting to discuss the notes and fires. Has he contacted you?" Nick and Darr's cousin was a private investigator with an agency in San Antonio. His mother, Cindy, had convinced the family they should hire him to check into the cryptic threats.

"Not yet," Darr said, "but I heard he's in town. The Chief said he called and asked for copies of the department's report on the fire at Red." Darr pushed his empty plate aside and leaned his elbows on the tabletop, his voice lowering. "This isn't for public knowledge, but I'm sure my boss agrees with us—he has serious reservations as to whether the fire was accidental."

"What about the barn that burned at the Double Crown?"

"He didn't want to talk about that one—I suspect he believes I'm too close to the subject, since it happened on Lily's ranch."

"Do you have a gut feeling as to his opinion?"

"Yeah. I'm convinced he believes the Double Crown fire wasn't an accident, either."

"I hope to hell Ross's investigation gets some answers," Nick said grimly. "You or someone else could have died in those fires."

"Bethany damn near did," Darr said darkly, his features hardening. "She was barely conscious when I found her on the bathroom floor at the restaurant. She could have died of smoke inhalation."

"We have to find out who's behind these threats to the family before someone loses their life," Nick said. "I hope Ross is good at his job."

"When are you talking to him?"

"Tomorrow afternoon at one." Nick glanced at his watch. "I have a meeting in a half hour. Gotta get back to the office."

Darr nodded and both men dropped money on top of the check.

"Thanks, guys," their waitress called after them as they left the booth and headed for the exit.

Nick shrugged into his jacket as he stepped outside, a brisk breeze cooling the air, although the sun beamed down, warm against his face.

"Let me know what Ross has to say tomorrow," Darr said, pausing on the sidewalk. "I have the day off, but I'm not sure what Bethany's plans are or if I'll be home, so call my cell phone."

"Sure." Nick stepped off the curb. "Tell Bethany hello from me."

"Will do." Darr headed down the block to his vehicle.

Nick climbed into his Porsche, the powerful engine turning over with a throaty, muted roar when he twisted the key. The low-slung car had only two seats—room for the driver and one passenger.

"Too small," Nick murmured as he backed out of the slot. "I need to get an SUV." Or a minivan. He shuddered. He didn't think he could bring himself to drive a minivan—even for the triplets. Minivans were mommy cars. For a guy who loved fast cars and powerful engines, a minivan was a step too far, vehicle-wise.

He made a mental note to go SUV shopping on his lunch hour tomorrow. Charlene could use it to drive the babies during the week and he'd use it on the weekends if he needed to take the little girls anywhere.

If anyone had told him two weeks ago that he'd be contemplating buying a vehicle to transport babies, he would have laughed at the sheer insanity of the idea.

He didn't do kids. Never had. And kids hadn't been part of his plans for the future.

There was some kind of cosmic karma at work here. Nick couldn't help but wonder what fate planned to hit him with next.

Chapter 4

Nick returned to the office, where he forced himself to concentrate on meetings. By the time he reached home that evening, he'd almost convinced himself he'd over-reacted that morning.

Surely he'd overestimated the power of his attraction to Charlene.

The neighborhood was quiet, the street lamps casting pools of light in the early darkness when he slotted the car into the garage and got out, tapping the panel next to the inner door to close the garage door smoothly behind him. He unlocked the door leading from the garage into the utility room and passed through, stopping abruptly in the open doorway to the kitchen when he saw Charlene. She stood at the stove across the room, her back to him as she poured steaming water from the stainless steel teakettle into a mug. A box of tea sat on the counter next to the cup. Her hair was caught up in a ponytail, leaving her nape bare above a short-sleeved green T-shirt tucked into the waistband of faded jeans. She wore thick black socks and she looked comfortable and relaxed, as if the kitchen were her own.

Coming home after a long day at work and finding a pretty woman in my kitchen is kind of nice.

The thought surprised him. He'd never really understood married friends when they insisted that walking into a house that wasn't empty was one of the great things about being married. He liked his privacy and didn't mind living alone. In fact, he thoroughly appreciated the solitude of his quiet house after a day spent in meetings.

But finding Charlene in his kitchen, clearly comfortable and making herself at home, felt good.

Of course, he thought wryly, *maybe I'd feel differently if she was a girlfriend with marriage on her mind and not the nanny.* Maybe her employee status erased the natural wariness of a bachelor when confronted with an unmarried, attractive woman puttering in his kitchen.

Whatever's going on here, Nick thought, *I'm definitely glad to see her.*

Before he could say hello, Rufus bounded in from the living room, his nails clicking against the tile floor. Woofing happily, he charged. Nick quickly lowered his leather computer bag to the tile and braced himself. The big dog skidded to a halt, reared onto his back legs, planted his front paws on Nick's shoulders and tried to lick his face.

"Hey, stop that." Nick caught Rufus's head in his palms and rubbed his ears.

"Hi." Charlene looked over her shoulder at him. She set the kettle on the range and carried her mug to the island where a notebook lay open beside her laptop computer. "I thought I heard your car pull into the garage. How was your day?"

"Busy," he said, releasing Rufus and bending to pick up his computer bag. The big dog followed Nick to the island and flopped down next to Charlene's chair. "How was yours?"

"Busy."

He laughed at her dry, one-word response. "Yeah, I bet it was. How did it go with the girls?"

"Fine." Charlene spooned sugar into her tea and stirred. "Jackie bonked her chin on a chair rung and has a new little bruise. Jessie smeared oatmeal in her hair and had to have a second bath this morning barely an hour after her first one. And Jenny..." She paused, her eyes narrowing in thought. "Come to think of it, Jenny had a fairly quiet day."

"That doesn't sound possible."

"I know," she laughed. "But she doesn't seem ill, so I'm happy—but surprised—to report that although I've only known them for three days, there's a possibility that maybe one of them has an uneventful day on occasion."

"Well, that's a relief."

"Did you talk to the employment agency today?"

"Yeah, they might have three candidates for me to interview soon. They're running background checks and verifying references for each of the women." Nick turned on the tap and washed his hands, turning to lean against the counter as he dried them. "What did Melissa make for dinner?"

"Lasagne, french bread and salad—she left a plate for you in the fridge and the bread is in the pantry." Charlene set down her mug and shifted to stand.

Nick waved her back. "Stay where you are, I'll get it." The stainless steel, double-door refrigerator was only a step away. He located the plate and salad bowl, took a bottle of dressing from the inner-door shelf and let the door swing closed behind him as he walked back to the counter. He peeled the plastic wrap off the lasagne and slid it into the microwave to heat, tapping the timer before closing the door.

"What do you want to drink?"

He glanced around to see Charlene at the fridge, glass in hand.

"Ice water sounds good, thanks."

He heard the clink of ice and the splash of water behind him as he walked to the island and pulled out one of the low-backed stools. The microwave pinged just as he finished pouring vinegar and oil dressing on his salad and he returned to the counter, grabbing a knife and fork from the cutlery drawer. Charlene set his glass of water down next to his salad bowl and returned to her seat as he carried his steaming plate back to the island. He sat across from Charlene and folded his shirt cuffs back, loosening and tugging off his tie.

"Tell me about the triplets," he said. "How did Melissa survive the day?"

"She said she's going to cancel her gym membership. Evidently, lifting and carrying three babies for eight hours is more fun than weight lifting with her trainer." Charlene laughed. "Seriously, she's great with them, and they seem to like her as much as she likes them."

"I thought they would," Nick commented. "She's

good with Rufus, and dealing with him seems to be a lot like having a toddler in the house—he makes messes, demands food regularly, requires massive amounts of attention and sometimes wakes me up in the middle of the night."

"So, what you're saying," Charlene said dryly, arching one eyebrow as she eyed him, "is that three little girls can cause as much havoc as a hundred-and-twenty-five-pound dog?"

"Pretty much," Nick agreed, grinning as she shook her head and frowned at him. The effect was ruined by the small smile that tugged her lips upward at the corners. "As a matter of fact, I can pick him up. I doubt I could juggle all three of the girls at the same time."

"You could, if you had a baby carrier," she said promptly.

"What's a baby carrier?"

"It's sort of a canvas backpack that an adult wears over their shoulders. The child is buckled into it so you can carry them on your chest or your back. Some are made for younger babies, but you can also get one to use for toddlers."

"Ah!" he said, nodding. "Remind me to get one of those. Then, if either of us ever has to take all three of the girls somewhere alone, we won't risk dropping one of them."

"That sounds like an excellent plan," Charlene agreed. "I met your neighbor LouAnn today."

"Did you?" Nick grinned and lifted an eyebrow. "What did you think of her?"

"She's a very interesting woman."

He laughed outright. "Got that right. She's a character. I hope I have that much energy when I'm seventy-something."

"Me too," Charlene agreed, smiling as she remembered LouAnn playing on the floor with the triplets. "She's wonderful with the babies. I'm not sure who had more fun playing peekaboo, her or the girls."

Nick chuckled, the sound sending shivers of awareness through Charlene's midsection. As he ate, they discussed the wisdom of keeping all three girls in the same bedroom.

Charlene sipped her tea, staring with fascination as Nick tipped his head back slightly and drank from the water glass. He'd unbuttoned the top two buttons of his shirt when he removed his tie earlier, and the strong, tanned muscles of his throat moved rhythmically as he swallowed. There was something oddly intimate about sitting in the cozy kitchen with him as he ate and they discussed his children.

"…What do you think?"

"Hmm?" She realized with a start that he'd been speaking while she'd stared at him, mesmerized, and felt embarrassed heat flood her cheeks. "I'm sorry, I didn't catch that. What do I think about…?"

His expression was quizzical. She suspected he noticed her pink cheeks, but she was determined not to become flustered. So she met his gaze with what she hoped was a serene look.

"I asked if you thought it was a good idea to give the girls a week or so together before we decide if they need to sleep in separate bedrooms."

"I think it makes sense to see whether they continue to wake each other, as they did last night." Charlene didn't want to remember the intimacy of the babies' darkened bedroom and the mental image of Nick wearing navy boxers and nothing else. Resolutely, she focused on the other bedrooms she'd seen during the tour of the house Melissa had given her that afternoon. "There's certainly plenty of room if you decide to have them sleep apart. Do you know if their parents had their cribs in separate bedrooms or if they all slept in the same room?"

Nick paused, his expression arrested. "The foster mother had the beds in two small bedrooms but I never thought to ask what the arrangements were at Stan and Amy's." He put down his fork with a thunk. "I should have asked," he said with disgust. "It never even occurred to me."

"If you have a phone number, I can try to reach her tomorrow," Charlene offered, touched by the sheer frustration on his face as he thrust his fingers through his hair and raked it back off his forehead.

"I'd appreciate that. I have her contact information in my desk in the den. Remind me to look it up before I leave for the office in the morning, will you?"

"Of course." Charlene sipped her tea and considered what she knew about the triplets' situation while Nick ate the last few bites of his lasagne. "Did the attorney have any estimate as to how long it might take to locate the babies' aunt?"

"No." Nick rose to carry his empty china and dirty cutlery to the sink. He turned on the tap. "He asked me to let him know if I remembered anything Stan or Amy may have said that would help find her. So far, all I've come up with is going through the photographs."

"Photographs? Does the investigator need a picture?"

"No, he has one." Nick slotted his rinsed dishes and

utensils into the rack of the dishwasher and closed the door. "But Amy loved taking photographs— so did Stan—and Amy almost always jotted little notes on the back of the pictures. I'm sure some of the holiday photos they sent included her sister. I'm hoping there might be something in one of Amy's notes that will help locate Lana."

"That's a great idea," Charlene said, encouraged at the possibility of finding a clue.

"I hope it's a productive one, but who knows whether I'll learn anything new." He shrugged. "Still, it's one place we haven't looked yet, and given how little information the investigator has, any small piece might make a difference. When I moved in, I shoved the photo boxes into the back of a closet upstairs. I thought I'd bring one downstairs tomorrow night and start looking."

"I'd be glad to help you search through them," she offered.

"Thanks, but I should warn you, I've never organized the pictures. All the photos I have are tossed in a couple of boxes, and the ones from Stan and Amy are mixed in with all the rest. There might be hundreds of pictures to look at. My mom divided family photos a few years ago and gave me a carton full."

"I'll still volunteer," she said. "Did the attorney search the triplets' house for an address book? I keep a notebook with family and friends' addresses and phone numbers in a drawer by the phone. And in a computer file too," she added as an afterthought.

"Sanchez and the investigator both checked Amy's home computer but didn't find anything helpful. They also looked for an address book at the house," Nick said. "They didn't find one. Whether she carried one with her is unknown because they didn't find her purse at the accident scene. They're assuming it was probably lost or destroyed, if she even had it with her."

"What about old letters from her sister? Didn't Amy keep correspondence?"

"Yes, but the last letter Amy received from Lana was several months ago—just after Thanksgiving. The investigator tried contacting her using the phone number at that residence, but she's no longer living there. The landlord didn't have any forwarding information."

"So, what will he do now? Surely she just didn't disappear?"

"I'm guessing the agency will send someone to Africa to interview the landlord in person, talk to her former employer, et cetera. It's hard to investigate someone's whereabouts from halfway around the world—on another continent," Nick said grimly.

"Yes, I'm sure it is. Who knew it could be so difficult to locate someone?" she murmured. "This is a real wake-up call for me. I should think about what personal files and paperwork to organize in the remote chance I might suddenly disappear. I've never given any thought to the subject before now."

"Most people don't," Nick said, a slightly gravelly edge to his deep voice.

"Of course," she agreed, her tone softening. "It must have been a shock to get that phone call. Had you known each other a long time?"

"Since college." Nick's expression shuttered.

Charlene sensed his withdrawal. His expression didn't invite further questions. Without further comment, she logged off her computer and closed it before picking up her mug and walking to the sink.

"It's late. I think I'll try to get some rest while the triplets are all asleep."

"Not a bad idea." Nick yawned. "I need to let Rufus outside before I come up."

"Good night."

He murmured a response and Charlene left the room. She heard the click of a latch behind her and paused, glancing back. Nick was turned away from her as he held the door open for Rufus. The big dog trotted through and Nick followed, his tall frame silhouetted against the darkness by the kitchen light spilling through the open door.

She was struck by how very alone he looked, standing in the shaft of golden light, facing the black night, before she turned away and climbed the stairs.

He's your boss, she reminded herself firmly. *He's also older, more experienced. There is absolutely no reason for you to assume he's lonely. He's charming and probably wealthy, given his family ties, and no doubt has a little black book filled with the phone numbers of numerous women who'd be happy to keep him company.*

Fortunately, she didn't lie awake thinking about Nick. Being wakened by the triplets several times the night before, combined with her long day, made her tired enough to fall asleep almost the moment her head hit the pillow.

Unfortunately, Charlene wasn't allowed to remain asleep for long.

The first cry woke her just after 1:00 a.m. She tossed back the covers and fumbled for her slippers with her bare toes but couldn't find them. Giving up the search, she hurried across the hall to the triplets' room.

Jessie was standing up in her crib, holding on to the railing with one hand, the other clasping her beloved blanket. Although the room was lit by only the dim glow from the plug-in Winnie The Pooh night-light, Charlene could see the tears overflow and trickle down Jessie's flushed cheeks.

"Sh, sweetie," Charlene murmured, crossing the room and lifting the little girl into her arms. "What's wrong?"

Jessie burrowed her face against Charlene's neck. The heat coming from the little body was palpable.

"You're running a temperature," Charlene murmured, realizing the ear infection was no doubt responsible for the rise in body heat. Jackie and Jenny appeared to be sound asleep. Charlene sent up a quick prayer that they would remain so as she quickly carried Jessie out of the bedroom and into the room next door. Her sobs were quieter now, muffled as her damp face pressed Charlene's bare throat. Charlene rubbed her hand soothingly over the small back.

Earlier that day, Melissa had helped Charlene move a changing table and rocking chair into the empty bedroom next to the triplets' room. The babies still refused to fall asleep unless they were all in the same room— they fretted and worked themselves into a state if the adults tried to separate them. Nevertheless, Charlene was determined to find a solution to their waking each other in the night. If one of them cried, the other two inevitably woke, and the loss of sleep for everyone was a problem that desperately needed solving.

Charlene managed to ease Jessie back, putting an inch or so between them, just enough to unzip her footed pajamas. The pink cotton was damp, as was the diaper beneath.

"Let's change your clothes before we get your medicine," she said, lowering Jessie to the changing table.

The little girl whimpered in complaint and when Charlene stripped off the damp pajamas, Jessie's little mouth opened and she wailed.

In the bedroom next door, one of the other triplets protested and then began to sob. Charlene groaned aloud. The sound was bound to wake Nick.

She took Jessie's temperature with a digital ear thermometer, relieved when it registered only a degree above normal. As she quickly replaced Jessie's wet diaper with a dry one and tucked her into clean pajamas, Charlene fervently wished the employment agency would find a suitable nanny applicant soon. If the triplets had two nannies—herself and another—then maybe Nick wouldn't feel required to get up at night when the babies woke.

And she wouldn't be confronted with seeing him in the pajama bottoms he'd started sleeping in after that first night when he'd staggered into the triplets' bedroom in navy boxers. He might believe he'd found a modest alternative to underwear, but as far as she was concerned, the low-slung flannel pants only made him look sexier.

The low rumble of Nick's voice as he talked to the babies carried through the wall separating the rooms and Charlene was certain both Jackie and Jenny were awake.

"Come on, sweetie," she murmured to Jessie, lifting her.

She left the room and paused in the doorway of the triplets' bedroom. Nick had Jackie in one arm and Jenny in the other. Both babies were sobbing, blankets clutched in tiny fists.

"Jessie's temperature is up again. I'm taking her

downstairs to get her medicine out of the fridge." Charlene had to raise her voice to make sure Nick could hear her over the crying babies. His brief nod told her he'd understood, and she headed downstairs, leaving him to cope with the two fractious little girls.

As she pulled open the refrigerator door and took out the prescription bottle, she heard Nick come down the stairs and go into the living room. Jackie and Jenny were still crying, although the volume wasn't quite as loud as before.

Jessie's sobbing had slowed to hiccups and intermittent outbursts. Charlene managed to unscrew the lid from the bottle and fill the eyedropper with the proper dose of pink medicine while balancing the little girl on her hip.

"Open up, sweetie." Fortunately, the medication was strawberry flavored and Jessie's mouth immediately formed an O. Just like a little bird, Charlene thought. Jessie's lips closed around the dispenser and Charlene emptied the pink liquid into her mouth. "Good girl, you like that don't…"

A sudden blast of music from the living room startled Charlene and she jumped, nearly dropping the bottle. Jessie's eyes grew round, her little body stiffening in Charlene's grasp.

"What in the world?"

The volume lowered as quickly as it had blared. The music didn't cease, though, and Charlene wondered why Nick felt a concert by Bob Seger was a good 1:00 a.m. choice for year-old babies.

Jessie, however, seemed to wholly approve of Nick's selection. She kicked her feet and gave Charlene a toothless grin.

"You like that?" Charlene replaced the lid on the bottle and returned it to the refrigerator. Then she took a baby wipe from the container next to the sink and smoothed the cool, damp towelette over tearstained downy cheeks, closed eyes and brow. When she wiped Jessie's mouth and chin, the little girl stuck out her tongue and left a faint pink streak across the baby wipe.

"Feel better?"

Jessie babbled a reply and Charlene nodded gravely. "Excellent. Let's go see how Uncle Nick is doing with your sisters. And let's ask him why he decided to have you all listen to rock 'n' roll before dawn."

She and Jessie reached the archway to the living room. Nick sat on the sofa, Jackie lying across his chest and Jenny sprawled on the soft leather cushion with her head on his thigh. Neither little girl was asleep but they'd stopped crying and appeared to be content. Rufus lay on the floor at Nick's feet, his head on his outstretched paws. He looked up at Charlene and wagged his tail, but didn't get up.

Charlene crossed the room and dropped into the big armchair. Jessie laid her head on Charlene's shoulder, popped her thumb in her mouth, and was blissfully quiet.

"What did you do to them?" Charlene said, just loud enough to be heard over the music. Bob Seger had finished and she was fairly certain the current song was Tom Cochrane's "Life Is a Highway."

"They love music," Nick said simply. "I should have thought of this earlier."

"But this isn't exactly a lullaby," she said. "Great song, I love it. But not what a year-old baby usually likes."

"Not normal babies, maybe. But Stan and Amy loved music—all kinds of music. We never discussed it, but

I'd be willing to bet the triplets have been listening to everything from Seger and Cochrane to Sinatra and Ella Fitzgerald since the day they were born. Probably before they were born," he added with a tired grin. Gently, he lifted Jenny and laid her facedown on her tummy on the sofa cushion beside him. She murmured, stirred, then went still.

"How did you figure it out?" Charlene lowered her voice to a whisper as the state-of-the-art sound system randomly selected tracks from CDs and segued smoothly from Cochrane to Ella Fitzgerald. The chanteuse's mellow tones, smooth as butter, alternately crooned and belted out the lyrics of "A Tisket, A Tasket."

"I remembered my mother telling me she used to sing us to sleep. When the girls woke up at the motel the other night, I sang to them—would have tried a lullaby but I didn't know one, and the only song that came to mind was a Bob Seger favorite." He shrugged and glanced down at Jackie, whose eyes were closed. One tiny fist clutched her blanket while the other held fast to a handful of the cotton pajamas covering his thigh. "I don't have the greatest voice, but it worked—so I thought I'd try the real thing."

"I think you've discovered the magic bullet," Charlene said, smiling at him. "They're sound asleep."

He smiled back, laugh lines crinkling at the corners of his eyes. His hair was rumpled from sleep, his jaw shadowed with beard stubble and his big body sprawled on the sofa with a baby asleep on each side of him. The warm light from the lamp on the end table illuminated half of his face, brushing the arch of his cheekbones and the line of nose and jaw with gold, and threw shadows across the other.

"Sugar," he drawled, his eyes twinkling, "it's a good thing something finally worked. Because after days of little to no sleep, if we were married and these were our kids, I'd seriously consider divorcing you and giving you custody—just so I could have eight hours of uninterrupted sleep."

Charlene burst out laughing.

Jessie stirred, her eyelids lifting. Charlene immediately muffled her laughter, smoothing her palm in circles over the baby's back, and she drifted asleep once more.

When Charlene looked up at Nick, he was watching her through half-closed eyes. Her heartbeat accelerated, her lungs seized as she stared at him. Then his features shifted, erasing whatever she thought she'd glimpsed on his face, and his big body shifted restlessly against the cushions. She could no longer read his expression— was no longer sure the moment had even happened, or if she'd imagined the sudden blaze of sexual awareness she'd felt between them.

"I think it's safe to take them back to their cribs," he said, stroking one big palm over Jackie's back. The little girl didn't stir.

"At least Jackie," Charlene agreed. She glanced down at Jessie, who seemed as deeply asleep as her sister. "And Jessie. What about Jenny?"

"She's out like a light." Nick gently picked up Jackie and stood. "If you'll keep an eye on Jenny, I'll take Jackie up and come back."

Charlene nodded and he headed for the stairs, Jackie cradled in his arms. She turned to watch him go just as Ella reached the end of her song. A heartbeat later, the opening lyrics of Prince's "Little Red Corvette" thumped from the speakers and filled the room.

"I've got to stop watching Nick walk away from me," she muttered to herself. *We have a professional relationship, employer-employee, and ogling the boss's very fine backside is probably taboo. Not to mention embarrassing should he turn around and catch me staring.*

Rufus's tail thumped against the wood floor. Charlene looked down at him and found him eyeing her, pink tongue lolling, ears alert.

She could swear he was laughing.

The following morning, Charlene wanted nothing more than to hit her alarm clock's Snooze button and roll over for another hour of sleep. But she knew if she didn't shower and have her coffee before the triplets awoke, she wasn't likely to do so until their afternoon nap.

She barely had time to pour a cup of coffee and say good-morning to Nick when he entered the kitchen to fill his travel mug before Melissa arrived. Nick left for the office moments later and the purr of the Porsche's engine had barely trailed away to silence outside when LouAnn knocked on the back door. The triplets awakened soon after, and the day's chaos began. When the babies napped after lunch, Charlene fell into bed and slept dreamlessly.

Just about the time that Charlene was catching her much-needed nap, Ross Fortune arrived in Nick's office for their meeting.

"Ross. Good to see you." Nick shoved his chair back and stood, leaning across the desk to shake his cousin's hand. He hadn't seen Ross since the New Year's Eve party at Red Restaurant. His brown hair was longer, brushing his shoulders. On a less rugged man it might have looked effeminate. On Ross, the long hair had the opposite effect. "Have a seat."

Ross sat in one of the two chrome-and-leather chairs facing Nick's desk and took a small notebook and pen from the inner pocket of his jacket. "I appreciate your cooperation in agreeing to see me today. I know it was short notice."

"No problem." Nick dropped back into his chair, leaning back and linking his fingers across his midriff. "I'm happy to do anything that might help you find out what's going on with the family."

"Good." Ross's brown eyes were shrewd, his gaze direct. "Give me the highlights."

Nick's eyes narrowed. "Someone slipped a note into Patrick's pocket at Red Restaurant during the New Year's party. He called us all together at the Double Crown last month to tell us about it."

"What did the note say?"

"'One of the Fortunes is not who you think,'" Nick quoted, shaking his head. "Makes no sense, at least as far as I can tell. We all thought it was the first contact in a blackmail attempt, but everyone at the meeting insisted they had no idea what it could mean, nor who the blackmailer might be."

"Hmm." Ross glanced at his notes, flipped a couple of pages, and looked back at Nick. "And there have been three more notes?"

Nick nodded. "My dad received one—so did Cindy. That's when your mom suggested we contact you and begin an official investigation." Nick saw Ross's eyes shutter, his face unreadable. He knew Ross and his mother had problems—in fact, as the eldest of Cindy's four children, Ross had pretty much taken over the role of caretaker for his younger siblings. It looked like there were issues between the two that went deeper than a mother-son disagreement. "All three of the original notes said exactly the same thing," he continued. He didn't know Ross well enough to comment or question him about what, if anything, his response to Nick's naming his mother meant. "But then Aunt Lily received a fourth that was more threatening."

"And what did it say?"

"'This one wasn't an accident, either,'" Nick quoted, his voice deepening as anger rose. "She got that after the second fire—the one at the Double Crown."

"The first was the restaurant that burned down?"

"Yeah." Nick said grimly. "Darr's fiancée, Bethany, could have easily died in the restaurant fire. And Darr could have died when the barn burned at the Double Crown." He leaned forward, his forearms resting on his desk, and pinned Ross with a level stare. "Whoever the hell is doing this has to be stopped before someone gets hurt."

Ross nodded, his keen gaze fixed on Nick. "There haven't been any other accidents or threats to anyone in the family?"

"Not that I'm aware of," Nick confirmed.

Ross tapped his pen against his notebook, a faint frown veeing his brows downward. "And no one in the family has any idea who might have sent the notes?"

"None."

"Are you aware of any skeletons that might be rattling in someone's closet? Any gossip about a family member having an affair? Anybody gambling? Anyone with a drug or alcohol habit?"

"No." Nick shook his head. "But I've lived in Red Rock for less than two months. Before that I was in L.A. and off the grid on up-to-date family gossip—you might want to ask Aunt Lily. She seems to have her finger on the pulse of what's happening with the Fortunes."

Ross nodded and jotted a note on his pad. "What about the Foundation?" he asked when he finished and looked up at Nick. "Any controversial deals or activity?"

"Not that I know of, although I've only been working here for about six weeks, give or take."

"I understand the Red Restaurant is owned by the Mendozas, and they have a long-standing connection to the Fortunes. Do you have any reason to believe the notes and the fire at the Double Crown might be connected in some way to the Mendozas rather than the Fortunes?"

Nick shook his head. "I'm the wrong person to ask, I'm afraid. My dad might have better information, or Uncle Patrick, or the Mendozas themselves."

Ross nodded and made another note. "I'll be honest with you," he said when he looked back at Nick. "It's time to call in the cops. This has gone beyond possible blackmail. Lives have been endangered and that last note seems to threaten the family with more arson fires."

"I agree," Nick said, nodding abruptly. "But Aunt Lily is dead set against calling in the police. She's adamant about keeping this inside the family."

"The cops can spread a wider net, use forensics on the notes…" Ross stopped, glancing down at his pad before continuing. "If the fire department is investigating the two fires for possible arson, they'll eventually turn their report over to the police."

"I sure as hell hope so," Nick said with feeling. "Nobody in the family wants to upset Lily. It would be good news if the fire chief suspected arson and the department investigators could tie the two fires together, then refer both cases to the police."

"In the meantime, I'll keep digging." Ross stood and so did Nick. "Thanks for your cooperation, Nick."

Nick shook Ross's outstretched hand and walked him to the door. "Anything I can do to help, just ask. I know Darr feels the same."

"Good. I need to talk to him too." Ross took a business card from his pocket. "Would you ask him to give me a call? On my cell phone, not my office number."

"Be glad to."

After Ross disappeared down the hall, Nick placed a call to Darr but got his answering machine. After leaving a brief message to phone him, Nick hung up and walked down the hall to the coffee machine before returning to his desk and the cost analysis file he'd been working on earlier.

It occurred to him that he had more than the Fortunes to worry about now. Charlene and the triplets were living in his house, under his protection.

The possibility that their proximity to him and the rest of the Fortunes might have placed them in danger sent a surge of fierce anger through him.

Ross better solve this mystery—and fast.

But why didn't Lily want the cops brought in? Not for the first time, Nick wondered if she was trying to protect someone.

Could she be afraid of what the police might uncover?

Much as he cared for Lily, he thought grimly, Charlene and the babies had to be protected. If Ross didn't find answers, and soon, he'd go to the cops himself.

Chapter 5

Later that evening, with dinner over and the little girls tucked into their cribs for the night, Charlene made a pot of decaf coffee and carried a tray with the carafe, two mugs and a plate of Melissa's chocolate-chip cookies into the living room. She set the tray on the coffee table just as Nick's boots sounded on the stairs.

"Here's the first box," he said as he entered the room and dropped the carton on the floor in front of the sofa.

"The *first* one?" Charlene said dubiously, eyeing the box. She wasn't great at estimating size, but the cardboard box looked at least twelve inches deep and two feet square.

"There's another one just like it upstairs." Nick glanced at her, half-smiled and shrugged. "You don't have to do this, Charlene. Much as I appreciate your help, it's going to be boring. I'm sure the official nanny job description doesn't include shuffling through the boss's old photo-graphs."

"I'm sure it doesn't," Charlene said dryly. "But I promised to help and I will." She dropped onto the leather sofa cushion and took a stack of photos from the box.

"I brought down this picture of Stan's family," Nick said, handing her a five-by-eleven photo. A wedding party was frozen in time, smiling and happy. "This is Lana."

He tapped the photo with his forefinger.

Charlene studied the young bridesmaid's facial features, noting the dark hair and athletic build until she was sure she'd recognize the triplets' aunt. Then she gathered a handful of photos and began to skim them.

On the sofa beside her, Nick settled back with a lapful of pictures. He thumbed through a stack of snapshots, paused to squint more closely at one, then tossed them into the reject pile atop the coffee table. Pretty soon the stack teetered and began to slide, glossy photos slithering across the oak table.

"Damn." He grabbed the pile and stood. Rufus lifted his head from his paws and eyed him expectantly. "I'll get an empty box to hold these. Otherwise they'll be all over the floor."

The big dog padded after him as he left the room.

Charlene continued to sort through the jumbled photos on her lap until she reached a colored snapshot of three teenage boys taken on a beach. Behind them, the ocean was bright blue. A younger Nick had an arm slung around the shoulder of one of the other boys, a surfboard lying on the sand beside him. His hair was shaggy, much longer than his current spiky cut, and his lean body was bronzed, white surf shorts hanging low on his hips.

Charlene studied the picture, her lips curving in a smile.

I bet you broke hearts in high school.

Reluctantly, she shuffled the photo to the bottom of her stack and continued to search for Amy's sister. Several photos later, she stopped abruptly. In what was clearly a professional studio portrait, a baby smiled out of the simple frame. A thatch of black hair and dark eyes, combined with the wide grin were inescapably Nick's features.

She trailed her fingertips over the photo, tracing the curve of his smile. Nick had been a darling baby and she couldn't help but wonder what his own children would look like. Would they inherit his charming smile and thick-lashed dark eyes?

What if she and Nick had children—would they be born with her thick auburn mane or with his black hair? And which gene would dominate to create their eye color, his dark brown or her own green?

With a start, Charlene realized she needed to get a grip. *Nick Fortune isn't interested in having babies with you,* she told herself, determinedly slipping the baby photo to the back of the stack. She continued to methodically scan the pictures, searching for Amy's sister while consciously refusing to allow herself to linger over the snapshots of Nick.

By the time he returned and held out a nearly empty carton, she'd finished searching through her stack of pictures and gathered them up, dropping them into the box. With Nick's entries, they made a formidable pile.

"So, how did you happen to buy a house this big?" Charlene asked, desperate to get her mind off her fantasies. "It seems huge for only one person."

"It's a lot of space," Nick admitted, glancing around

the big living room as he dropped onto the sofa once more and picked up another handful of photos. "But the previous owners had already bought another house in Dallas and were anxious to move, so I got a great deal. I needed a place to stay in Red Rock, didn't want to rent, and this is a good investment." He scanned the sparsely furnished room once again and frowned. "I keep thinking I should buy some more furniture. I guess I'll get around to it sooner or later, if I decide to stay in Red Rock."

Surprised, Charlene looked at him. "Are you thinking of moving?"

"At some point, probably, but I don't have any definite plans." He thumbed through a small sheaf of photos and tossed them into the reject carton. "I moved here from Los Angeles a month ago to spend time with my brother, Darr."

"But I thought the Fortunes had settled in Red Rock for generations. In fact, I thought the family was a local institution." Charlene tried to remember where she'd heard that, but couldn't recall if someone had told her when she'd first arrived, or if she'd assumed it because the Fortunes were often referred to as a prominent local family. As it turned out, the three years she'd lived in Red Rock meant she'd been a resident for much longer than Nick.

"Not my branch of the family. I was born in California—grew up in a beachhouse in Malibu. My brother, Darr, moved to Red Rock a while back—then he talked me into moving here to work at the Foundation." Nick gathered a handful of photos from the slowly diminishing pile in the storage box. "How about you? Were you born in Red Rock?"

She shook her head, her hair brushing her shoulders. "No, I lived in Amarillo all my life until college."

"What brought you here?"

"A job offer after I graduated." Charlene didn't want to tell him the move hadn't been her decision. She would have preferred to begin her postcollegiate life in Amarillo. Barry had been the one who chose to accept a job offer in Red Rock, and she'd reluctantly agreed when he'd asked her to move here too.

"When we met on the plane, were you moving back to Amarillo to be closer to your mother?" Nick said.

"Something like that," Charlene replied, not wanting to go into an explanation of her breakup with Barry. "But then she told me she'd met Lloyd and he'd moved in with her—I knew I needed a change of plans."

"And thank God you did." Nick eyed her across the width of leather sofa cushion that separated them. "I'm sorry your original plan didn't work out, but if it had, you wouldn't be here. And I don't know what I'd do with the triplets without you."

Sincerity rang in his words and a warm glow of satisfaction filled Charlene. "Thanks, Nick. It's always nice to be appreciated."

"Are you planning to go back to Amarillo after I turn the triplets over to Lana and her husband?"

Nick's question wiped the smile from her face.

"I hadn't thought that far ahead. I suppose so." She realized she truly hadn't given a thought to what she'd do after the triplets no longer needed her. Once their aunt took custody, Nick would return to being a bachelor. He certainly wouldn't employ a nanny. She wouldn't have a reason to see him again.

She frowned at the photos in her hand. Why did the prospect of not seeing Nick on a regular basis bother her so much? She barely knew him. In fact… She mentally counted the days since they'd shared an airline flight. Was it really less than a week?

How could she have become so attached to Nick and the triplets in such a short time?

Granted, it had been an intensive few days, but still…

She looked sideways through her lashes at Nick. He was frowning down at a photo with fierce concentration.

"Did you find something?" she asked.

"Maybe." He leaned across the sofa toward her, his forefinger pointing out a woman in the snapshot. "Amy sent this in a card at Thanksgiving last year. See the girl standing with Lana?"

Charlene bent over the picture, eyes narrowing as she focused. The tangle of jungle was a backdrop for several rough huts surrounding a white wooden building. A woman easily recognizable as Lana stood on the porch steps, her arm around a pregnant young native girl. They both smiled happily into the camera.

"Who is she?"

Nick flipped the photo over but there was only a date—November 15th—scribbled on the back. "Damn. Amy didn't write details." He turned the photo faceup. "I remember talking to Stan and Amy around Thanksgiving, though. Lana had called from Africa and told them she and her husband were thinking of leaving their jobs to take over a privately owned center. Lana wanted to establish a clinic for women and provide prenatal care. Amy asked me if I'd volunteer accounting and financial services for the clinic if Lana could make arrangements with the local government to back the plan. This photo was taken at the center—Amy wanted me to see an example of how young the mothers are that Lana would be helping." He frowned and ran his hand over his hair, rumpling it, as he tried to remember. "I never heard whether Lana and her husband went through with the plan, but since they've dropped out of sight, maybe they did."

"But why wouldn't they have told Amy and Stan where they were going?"

"Stan said Amy hoped her sister wouldn't follow through with the idea because the center was in an isolated area. Maybe there isn't Internet service there—or phones." He looked grim. "Or maybe something happened to them."

"Don't even think it." Charlene fervently hoped nothing had happened to Lana and her husband. The possibility that the triplets might have lost their only remaining blood relative was too awful to even consider. "Is there anything in the photo that might tell you where the private clinic is located?"

They both bent over the snapshot.

"The sign above the porch overhang... I can't read it, can you?" Charlene asked, trying to decipher the faded lettering painted on the rough siding.

"Only a couple of letters. Not enough to know what the word is." Nick studied the photo intently before he gave up. "I'll take it to the office with me tomorrow and ask a friend in the Foundation's publicity department to take a look at it. He has a computer program that scans and enlarges without losing detail. Maybe he can identify the rest of the letters."

"And maybe that will give you the name of the place Lana and her husband have relocated to." Charlene mentally crossed her fingers that the results would be good.

"With any luck, they're one and the same. Although

there's no way of knowing until the investigator checks it out." Nick glanced at his watch before he stood, tucking the photo into his shirt pocket. "It's getting late, we'd better call it a night. At least it's Saturday tomorrow and I don't have to go to work. Although," he added dryly, "I doubt the triplets understand the concept of sleeping in on the weekend."

Charlene rose too, dropping the handful of photos she hadn't yet looked at into the first box. "Do you want to go through the rest of these?" she asked, waving at the box, its pile of photos much smaller. "Or will you wait until the investigator gets back to you about the clinic photo?"

"Might as well keep looking," Nick replied as he stacked the boxes and carried them into the hall.

Charlene followed, snapping off the lamp as she went. Rufus padded after her, leaning his head against her thigh when she stopped at the foot of the stairs. She rubbed his ears and he closed his eyes with a low rumble, leaning more heavily against her.

The muted cry of a baby sounded from upstairs, the whimper carrying easily to the three in the hallway.

Rufus's ears lifted and he swung his head toward the stairway.

Charlene's fingers stilled on Rufus's silky fur and she froze, listening intently. Almost immediately on the heels of the outcry, Willie Nelson's gravelly voice rasped out the opening bars of "Pancho And Lefty."

When she didn't hear another sound from the triplets, Charlene looked across the foyer. Nick stood at the open hall closet door, just as frozen as she. The silence stretched, broken only by the lyrics from Willie. Nick's taut body relaxed. He winked at her and his mouth curved in a heart-stopping grin.

"Looks like it worked." He shut the closet door and strolled toward her.

"Wiring the sound system into the girls room was a brilliant idea. And making it sound-activated was even better. Do you think it will keep them asleep all night?" she asked.

"I have no idea." Nick shrugged. "But it's a good sign the system came on and the girls fell back to sleep just now." He yawned and scrubbed his hand down his face. "I sure as hell hope it works every time they wake up. I could use the sleep—and I'm sure you could too."

"Absolutely," Charlene said with heartfelt conviction.

Rufus nudged her hand, his tail wagging as he rumbled.

"He needs to go out," Nick said. "I'll take him." He snapped his fingers and Rufus left Charlene's side.

"See you in the morning," she called after him as Nick and the big dog headed toward the kitchen.

He looked over his shoulder at her, his eyes darker, unreadable. "Sleep well."

Charlene waited until they disappeared down the hall before she climbed the stairs.

I'm getting way too attached to that man.

Admitting it didn't make the knowledge any less palatable, she realized with annoyance.

The following morning, Nick and Charlene had the girls to themselves, since Melissa didn't work on weekends.

"Let's walk down to the coffee shop," Nick suggested as he lifted Jenny out of her high chair. Elbows stiff and arms straight, he dangled her in front of him while he walked to the sink.

Charlene automatically grabbed a baby wipe from

the container on the counter and handed it to him. He set Jenny on the edge of the counter, holding her firmly with one hand while he applied the towelette to the oatmeal smeared over her cheeks and chin.

"I'm sure the girls would love it, but are you sure you're up for it?" Charlene asked, eyeing him dubiously.

"Sure, why not?" he replied, concentrating on washing sticky spots off Jenny's face as she wiggled and squirmed, protesting. Finally, he tossed the towelette in the trash, perched the now clean Jenny on his hip and looked at Charlene. "What? You don't think I can survive taking them on a twenty-minute walk?"

Clearly, he'd read her expression and knew she had reservations about his ability to endure an outing with the three babies. "Have you got earplugs and tranquilizer pills in your pocket?"

"Very funny," he said with amusement, the corners of his mouth curving upward. "You obviously have no faith in me. I survived the drive from Amarillo here to Red Rock, didn't I? I've won my stripes. I can handle a walk to the coffee shop."

Charlene rolled her eyes but couldn't stop the answering smile that tugged at her lips. "All right. But remember, this was your idea."

"We'll take Rufus too."

Charlene didn't comment. A half hour later, after a search for Jackie's blanket and a last-minute change of diaper for Jenny, they finally left the house.

"We're a parade," Nick commented.

He pushed the girls' stroller and Charlene walked beside him, holding Rufus's leash. The dog trotted beside the girls, his wagging tail whacking the stroller's sunshield with each stride. Seated closest to him, Jessie laughed and grabbed for Rufus's tail but missed.

Tongue lolling, he veered closer and licked her face. She grimaced and chortled, pounding the stroller tray with delight.

"Rufus, stop that!" Charlene commanded.

"It's just a little dog spit," Nick told her. "It won't hurt her."

"That's such a guy thing to say," she said, frowning at him. "Who knows what he's been eating in the backyard this morning."

"Probably dirt from the rocks he chews on. A little dirt won't hurt Jessie. In fact—" he looked sideways at her "—I read an article on the internet the other day that said kids today are too clean. Too many parents use antibacterial soap to keep kids from catching germs and they don't develop antibodies when they're little. Makes them susceptible later in life."

Charlene was stunned. She didn't know which was more surprising, that Nick was reading child-rearing articles online, or that he thought the girls should eat dirt.

"So you're advocating adding dirt to the girls' diet?"

"No, but I am saying that being licked by Rufus isn't likely to harm Jessie. And she likes it." He pointed at the little girl, squealing with delight when the big dog trotted close enough to enable her to grab a fistful of fur.

Rufus veered away from the stroller, leaving a handful of hair in Jessie's closed fingers.

"Jessie, don't eat that!" Charlene reached down and pried strands of dog fur from the baby's fist just as Jessie was about to shove her hand into her open mouth.

Nick stopped pushing the stroller, waiting while Charlene bent over Jessie and brushed away the remaining strands of brown fur that clung to her fingers.

"Okay, so I can see why we wouldn't want her to eat

dog fur," he conceded when Charlene eyed him with exasperation. "Think she'd get fur balls?"

Charlene burst out laughing.

"I think you're getting punch-drunk from lack of sleep," she told him. "I know I am."

"I noticed the girls don't seem to be bothered," he said as they resumed walking.

"That's because they catnap during the day. Probably building up their strength to keep us awake at night," Charlene added darkly. Even though she'd only gotten up once with Jessie, all of the girls had stirred several times during the night and set off the audio system. While she was thankful she hadn't had to go into their room more than once, being wakened by the music still broke her sleep.

"Did your siblings do this when you took care of them?" he asked.

"Sometimes, but certainly not every night, and not on a regular basis," she said. "Usually there was a reason—like they were teething, or they had a cold, or something. But the triplets seem to wake when nothing's wrong. Often, the one that cries first and wakes the others doesn't even have a wet diaper."

"Maybe all the changes they've gone through in the last two weeks have disturbed them to the point that they can't get back to a normal routine."

"Possibly." Charlene glanced sideways at Nick. She couldn't read his eyes, hidden behind aviator sunglasses, but his lips were set in a straight line with no hint of humor. His expression had lost its earlier amusement. "But if that's what's going on, they'll find their balance," she said with quiet reassurance. "Children are resilient."

Rufus chose that moment to bark loudly and bound

forward, dragging Charlene with him. Startled, she held on, pulling on his leash in an effort to stop him. He out-muscled her, determined to reach a cat sitting on a lawn several yards ahead. Surprised, the cat leaped into defense mode and raced to a nearby tree, clawing its way up the trunk and out onto a limb before stopping to glare down at Rufus and Charlene.

"Look at the cat's tail," Nick said, grinning as he stopped the stroller on the sidewalk next to Charlene, Rufus and the tree with the cat.

The tabby seemed twice its former size, the fur all over its body standing on end, including its tail, which looked like a bottle brush. It stuck straight up in the air and seemed to quiver with outrage. Rufus barked again, his ears alert with interest. The cat narrowed its eyes and spat, hissing in fury. "Rufus, I don't think the cat wants to play," Nick said dryly.

The big dog whined, paws dancing against the grass beneath the tree.

"Maybe the cat isn't feeling sociable, but Rufus clearly thinks he's found a friend," Charlene observed.

"Good thing the cat's up there and he's down here," Nick said. "Or Rufus might learn a lesson about unfriendly cats."

Rufus barked and the triplets pounded on the stroller tray, their excited shrieks adding to the noise.

Nick winced and grabbed Rufus's collar, towing him away from the tree while pushing the stroller ahead of them and several feet down the sidewalk.

Still holding the big dog's leash, Charlene gave one quick glance at the tree behind them, where the cat continued to hiss and glower.

"I'm not sure who's more disappointed that the cat wouldn't come down," she said with a laugh when the dog and the triplets had subsided into relative quiet, "Rufus or the girls."

"If sheer noise could tell us, I'd say it's a toss-up." Nick released Rufus's collar and the big Lab ambled along, apparently having given up on the cat.

"Rufus is loud," Charlene agreed. "But I think the triplets outweigh him when it comes to the length of time they can sustain decibels at an earsplitting level."

"That's because there are three of them and they can pace themselves. Two can keep yelling while the third one breathes," Nick argued. "Rufus has to stop barking to drag in air, and he doesn't have a backup buddy to keep the sound going."

"Who knew chaos could have such a logical analysis?" Charlene said, amused.

"I'm an analyst. It's what I do."

"And you apply the basics of your work to humans? And dogs," she added belatedly when Rufus tugged on her leash.

"Sometimes," Nick acknowledged.

She couldn't see his eyes behind the sunglasses, but she knew there were laugh lines crinkling at the corners.

When they reached the corner coffee shop, Nick tied Rufus's leash to a metal ring set into the wall. Charlene dropped into a chair at one of the little bistro tables, facing the triplets in their stroller.

"Are you okay here?" Nick asked, adjusting the sunshade atop the stroller seat to shade the triplets.

"Absolutely," Charlene replied, laughing at Jessie as she tried unsuccessfully to grab a handful of Rufus's tail.

"What do you want with your coffee?" he asked, grinning as Rufus managed to lick Jackie's face.

"Surprise me." Charlene eased the stroller out of the

big dog's reach. Nick disappeared into the shop just as both dog and babies grumbled their disapproval of their forced separation. "Here, you three, have some water."

She handed each little girl a small sippy cup and they went silent, each sucking industriously on the opening in the lids.

"This is a healthy habit to develop, girls," Charlene told them. "Drink lots of water—it's good for you. And don't forget to eat lots of fruits and vegetables."

Three pairs of bright blue eyes watched her, apparently entranced, totally absorbed in what she was saying.

This is the thing about babies, she thought as she smiled at them. *They're fascinated by adults. They pay attention. Too bad they outgrow it later on.*

A small blue sports car zipped past on the street, slowing to wedge into a parking space halfway down the block. A couple got out, doors slamming, and walked toward Charlene.

The sun was at their backs, making it difficult for her to see them clearly, but there was something very familiar about the man. He walked with his arm slung over the woman's shoulders as they strolled nearer, apparently absorbed in each other and their conversation.

It wasn't until they drew nearer that Charlene realized the man was Barry.

Too late to run—and nowhere to hide. She knew precisely the moment when Barry recognized her, because he stopped abruptly, his jaw dropping in surprise.

"Charlene?"

"Hello, Barry," she said coolly, laying a restraining hand on Rufus's collar as he rose to his feet. A low growl rumbled in the dog's throat, his stance protective. "It's all right, Rufus," she soothed.

Barry looked from the dog to the three little girls in the stroller, and then back at Charlene, clearly puzzled.

"I thought you were in Amarillo."

"I was—for a day."

"And now you're back in Red Rock?"

"Obviously."

"With a dog and three kids?" The disbelief coloring his tones was palpable.

Since confirmation seemed unnecessary, Charlene looked at his companion and smiled. "Good morning."

The blonde eyed Charlene with a distinctly antagonistic narrowing of her eyes before she looked back at Barry. He was still staring as if dumbfounded at the girls in their stroller. "Good morning," the blonde said finally, her tone cool but polite.

"Where did you get the kids?" Barry demanded.

"In Amarillo."

He glared at her, clearly annoyed by the brevity of her response.

She smiled back at him but didn't elaborate.

"I think I deserve an explanation." His voice held controlled impatience.

"Really?" she said coolly, lifting an eyebrow consideringly. "I can't imagine why."

Barry's face turned a deeper shade of red. Before he could say anything further, the door to the coffee shop opened and Nick stepped out.

He set down two takeout cups of coffee and a bag on the tabletop. His eyes were still hidden behind the designer shades, but she knew with certainty that he'd swiftly assessed the situation. The two men couldn't have provided a stronger contrast—Nick with his dark hair and eyes, black T-shirt stretched across broad shoulders and chest, faded jeans outlining the powerful muscles of thighs and long legs. Barry's more slender frame seemed almost effeminate compared to Nick's well-toned body, while his blond hair seemed washed out in the bright sunshine, his skin pale next to Nick's California-sun-tanned features.

"I hope you like chocolate doughnuts," Nick said, shifting so he stood on her left and slightly in front of her, effectively placing himself between her and Barry.

The move was subtle but Barry clearly got the message. His face turned even ruddier and he fairly bristled at Nick.

"Who are you?" he demanded.

"Nick Fortune," he said with easy confidence, smiling at the woman with Barry.

Charlene had no trouble understanding why the blonde nearly melted into her hot-pink flip-flops.

"Hello," the woman breathed, clearly dazzled. "I'm Gwen."

"Pleased to meet you, Gwen." Nick smiled at her again and she batted her eyelashes, her smile widening.

Barry stiffened. The blonde met his angry stare with cool aplomb before she looked back at Nick, ran her fingers through her hair and swept it back over her shoulders.

Well, well, Charlene thought. Instantly annoyed at the flirtatious gesture, she glanced at Nick. She couldn't see his eyes behind the sunglasses, but he seemed to have missed the blonde's invitation. He was turned toward Barry and his big body seemed to radiate menace.

Barry looked at Nick, his frown deepening.

"Fortune?" he said, unable to hide his disbelief. "Not one of the Fortune Foundation family?"

"Guilty, I'm afraid," Nick said.

Gwen seemed to suddenly become aware of the tension in the air. She glanced uneasily at Charlene. Charlene shrugged to indicate she was staying out of what appeared to be a brewing storm.

The blonde frowned and clasped her hands around Barry's arm, just above the elbow. "I'm dying for an ice cream, Barry." Gwen tugged determinedly. "Let's go in."

"I don't…" Barry began, resisting her urging as if he wanted to say more.

The triplets had been surprisingly quiet during the exchange. Jessie chose that moment to bang her sippy cup on the stroller tray, interrupting Barry as she babbled imperiously. Charlene turned to the girls, and out of the corner of her eye saw Gwen draw Barry away. A moment later, she heard the bell on the shop door jingle.

"Well, that was interesting." Nick dropped into the chair next to her and took the lid off one of the cups. He slid the other coffee across the small tabletop to her and opened the bag. He took out a doughnut and bit into it, waiting until Charlene finished calming Jenny and turned back to pick up her cup before he continued. "So, who was he?"

"My ex-fiancé," she said calmly.

He paused, the doughnut halfway to his mouth, and stared at her. "You're kidding."

"No, I'm not." She frowned at him. "Why would you think I'm kidding about having an ex-fiancé? Do you find it impossible to believe that someone would want to marry me?"

"Hell, no." He frowned back at her. "I'm just surprised you said yes—he looks like a jerk."

"He's not," she denied. Then she considered her response and shrugged. "Okay, maybe he *is* kind of a jerk."

She had the distinct impression that Nick was rolling his eyes behind his sunglasses.

"No kidding." He finished his doughnut in one bite. "How long were you engaged?"

"We weren't actually officially engaged. He never gave me a ring. But we were together for three years."

"Three years, huh?" He took a drink of coffee and studied her over the cup rim. "Where did you two meet?"

"In college." She picked a doughnut from the bag and broke off a bite, popping it into her mouth.

"Let me guess—I bet he was in a drama class with you. Or was it a poetry class?"

She narrowed her eyes at him consideringly. "It was poetry. How did you know that's where we met?"

"Just a wild guess. He looks like the kind of guy who'd pick up girls in poetry class."

"He does?" Charlene considered Barry's blond hair, classically handsome features, a frame that might be called lanky but never muscled, and narrow, scholarly hands, without a callus to be found on the smooth, soft skin. "Hmm, I think I see what you mean."

"You said he was your *ex*-fiancé. What happened?"

"I suppose you could say we drifted apart in the years since college and grew to have different goals for our lives," Charlene said slowly, thinking about his question. The breakup with Barry had been coming for months. Their final argument had followed weeks of escalating bickering over a variety of issues, including whether they should pool their money and buy a house. It had ended with her walking out, their relationship over.

She could hardly believe only a few weeks had passed since they'd officially parted ways. So much had been packed into the last week with Nick and the triplets that it seemed much longer.

She'd dreaded running into Barry. She'd been sure it would be an awkward, emotionally painful encounter. But in fact, she realized, she'd felt very little beyond mild regret and annoyance.

What did that say about the depth of their attachment? Had she really loved him—or had they drifted into a relationship through sheer convenience and habit?

"When did you break up?"

"A few weeks ago."

"So that's why you were leaving Red Rock and flying to Amarillo?"

Charlene nodded. "I was going to stay with my mother while I found a new job and an apartment."

She rubbed her temples with her fingertips, feeling a headache coming on.

"You okay?" Nick asked.

His words interrupted her reverie, yanking her back to the present. She immediately ceased rubbing her temples and picked up her coffee.

"Of course. I'm fine. What was I saying?" She paused to sip her coffee, gaining a moment to recall his earlier question. "Oh, yes—being engaged. Actually, becoming un-engaged." She shrugged. "It's not uncommon for couples to discover they're not well-suited during a long engagement."

"If you say so." Nick looked at her over the rims of his sunglasses, his eyes intent. "Three years is a long time to be engaged."

"We wanted to establish our careers, save money for a house and so on."

"Couldn't you have done that after you were married?" His deep voice held a touch of derision.

"I suppose so, but it seemed wiser to wait until we

were more settled." She frowned at him. "I suppose you would have leaped straight into marriage?"

"Damned straight," he said with emphasis. "If I cared enough about a woman to ask her to marry me, I wouldn't be willing to put off the wedding for three years."

"And if *she* wanted to wait, I'm suppose you'd toss her over your shoulder and haul her off to your cave?"

His mouth quirked and he laughed. "No, I'm not that much of a caveman—although I'd be tempted." He stared at her for a moment. "Charlene," he said bluntly, "your ex-fiancé is a fool. He should have hustled you off to the altar the day you said yes. I'd never make that mistake."

Charlene felt her eyes widen. Her heart threatened to pound its way out of her rib cage. There was something about the intensity of his stare beneath lowered eyelids and the curve of his mouth that was more sensual than amused.

"I don't…" she began. She had to pause and clear her throat, her voice husky with the effort to speak. She lost track of what she'd been going to say when his gaze shifted from her eyes to focus on her mouth, lingering there for a long moment.

His lashes lifted and his gaze met hers. Charlene caught her breath. Focused male desire blazed in his eyes. She felt caught, unable to look away.

Behind him, the door to the coffee shop burst open and a crowd of teenagers poured out onto the sidewalk. Their laughter and raised voices was boisterous and loud, but it wasn't enough to break the web that Charlene felt spun out between her and Nick.

But then one of the boys bumped the back of Nick's chair and he looked away from her, over his shoulder at the kid.

"Sorry." The teenager raised his hands in apology. "Didn't mean to do that."

"No problem." Nick's voice was clipped.

When he turned back, his face was blank and Charlene could no longer read his eyes.

"Ready to go?" he asked, rising to take his cup and the empty doughnut bag to the trash can.

"Yes, of course." Charlene followed suit.

Despite the distraction of the three babies and an energetic dog on the walk home, Charlene couldn't forget the heat in Nick's eyes. Nor could she ignore her reaction to the sexual tension that still sizzled in the air between them.

She pretended to be unaware, busying herself with Rufus's lead as they entered the house. The dog raced away, disappearing into the kitchen, and she turned to help Nick with the girls.

He bent to unhook Jessie just as Charlene moved. The resultant bumping of shoulders knocked her off balance, and Nick grabbed her, his big hands closing over her biceps to keep her from falling.

"Damn, I'm sorry—are you okay?"

"Yes… I, um…" She couldn't finish the sentence. He stood so close she could see the fine lines fanning at the corners of his eyes and the faint shadow of dark beard along his jawline. Bare inches separated their bodies, and his heat, combined with the subtle scent of aftershave and soap, urged her to close the distance and wrap her arms around him. The need to feel him pressed against her, breast to thigh, was overpowering.

His gaze searched hers, his frown of concern replaced with sensual awareness. His eyes narrowed; his hands tightened on her shoulders and he lowered his head. She waited, breathless, unable to tear her gaze from his.

Rufus bounded back into the room, barking as the babies greeted him with shrieks of delight.

For one brief moment, the two adults remained frozen.

Charlene thought she caught a flicker of frustration in Nick's eyes before he stepped back, releasing her.

"Rufus, down." His voice was deeper, gravelly.

She bent to unlatch Jessie from the stroller.

"Time for the girls' morning snack." Charlene knew she was blatantly using the babies as an excuse, but she needed to put space between herself and Nick.

If this morning was any example of how successfully she could handle her attraction to Nick, she was in big trouble.

Chapter 6

The following day was Sunday and the hours flew by. Caring for the triplets left little time for more personal discussions. Charlene was relieved when Nick seemed more than willing to keep conversation in neutral territory and far away from any deeply personal or potentially intimate subjects.

After Nick left for the office on Monday, Charlene felt tension drain out of her body like air from a punctured balloon. She had an entire day ahead of her to shore up her defenses and come to terms with the desire she'd read in Nick's eyes on Saturday. She wasn't sure it would be long enough.

Not that she hadn't been *trying* to do so every hour since it happened. She just wasn't having a lot of success.

Improbable as it seemed, Nick was attracted to her. She couldn't mistake or deny what she'd seen in his eyes. What she didn't know was whether he'd feel the same for any female he'd been thrown into daily contact with. Their situation—sharing a house, sharing the care of the triplets—was tailor-made to promote intimacy.

As she and Melissa cared for the triplets, Charlene pondered the question. By noon, she'd decided that Nick was only reacting as any male would in their situation.

It's not me, she decided. Living in each other's pockets for a week had created a false attraction. Probably like survivors of a shipwreck who are stuck in the same lifeboat together.

Unwelcome though it was, she had to conclude that if she wanted to keep her heart intact, she had to ignore any shivers of longing she might feel for Nick.

The triplets were tucked into their high chairs in the big kitchen while she and Melissa monitored them as they tried to eat lunch. They missed their mouths more often than not, and it was a toss-up as to whether there was more food on the girls' faces, hair and clothes than in their stomachs. The women laughed as much as Jessie and Jenny when Jackie bent over and slurped applesauce directly from her bowl.

When she lifted her head, her mouth, chin, cheeks and the tip of her nose were covered with applesauce.

Jessie and Jenny shrieked and instantly copied Jackie, making smacking noises.

Charlene rolled her eyes and collected the dispenser of wipes from next to the sink and carried them back to the counter, holding the box out for Melissa to extract several before she removed three herself and set the box down within reach.

The phone rang as she and Melissa were removing

sticky applesauce and peas from the squirming little girls.

"I'll get that." Melissa tossed stained towelettes in the trash and lifted the phone to her ear. "Fortune residence." She paused, listening. "Yes, she is, just a moment." She handed the phone to Charlene. "It's for you."

Surprised, she mouthed, "Who is it?" but Melissa only shrugged.

"Hello?"

"Charlene? This is Kate."

Hearing her friend and former coworker's voice instantly had Charlene smiling with surprise and delight. The swift exchange of hellos and how are yous made her realize how insulated she'd been over the last week. She hadn't even taken time to let Kate know she was back in town.

"How did you know I was here?" she asked, curious.

"I called your mom and she gave me this number. Meet me for coffee," Kate demanded. "You've got to tell me why you're in Red Rock!"

"I can't—I'm working." She listened as Kate protested. Melissa looked up from wiping Jackie's fingers and lifted an inquiring brow. "No, really, I can't."

"If you want to go out, I can handle things here after the girls go down for their nap," Melissa said.

"Hold on a second, Kate." Charlene covered the mouthpiece with one hand. "Are you sure, Melissa?"

"Absolutely," the housekeeper said firmly. "You haven't been away from the babies since you got here. You should get out of the house. Go meet your friend."

"All right." She confirmed a time with Kate and rang off. "Thanks so much, Melissa. Kate and I used to work together. It'll be so nice to chat and catch up."

"No problem," Melissa assured her.

An hour later, Charlene and Kate sat at a table in the back of the neighborhood coffee shop. The café was nearly empty, the lunch rush over.

"I can't believe you didn't call me. When did you come back to Red Rock?" Kate asked.

"About a week ago, maybe a bit more. Days and nights are just a blur. I've been seriously sleep deprived up until a couple of days ago and I haven't caught up yet."

Kate's dark brows zoomed upward. "Why? What are you doing—or shouldn't I ask?"

"I'm working as a nanny."

Kate stared at her blankly. "A nanny? You left a perfectly good job at the hospital to babysit?"

Charlene chuckled and sipped her iced tea. "Hearing you put it in those terms, it does sound pretty illogical, doesn't it?"

"You think?" Kate rolled her eyes. "Why did you do it?"

Charlene spent the next few moments reciting the sequence of events leading to her accepting Nick's job offer. When she was done, Kate was speechless.

"So, here I am." Charlene waved her hand, indicating the café's interior and the greater world of Red Rock beyond the glass windows. "Back in Red Rock. And working as a nanny."

"I'm not sure where to start," Kate told her. "I've got a dozen questions. Let's get right to the big item on my list." She glanced around the sparsely populated café then leaned forward, elbows on the table, and whispered. "Is Nicholas Fortune as drop-dead gorgeous as rumor says he is?"

Charlene almost choked on her coffee. She leaned toward her friend and whispered back, "Yes. Definitely."

"Ah." Kate's dark eyes twinkled. "I knew there was more to this story than your needing to find a job superquick."

Charlene told her about the bonus offer, grinning as her friend's eyes widened and she gasped.

"Geez, why didn't I meet him first?" Kate groaned. "I'd work as a nanny for that kind of money. That's amazing."

"That's what I thought. I couldn't afford *not* to take the job. And given how desperate I was to get out of my mom and Lloyd's way, the bonus was just icing on an already great cake."

"What are you going to do with all that money—stash it in a 401K?"

"Part of it, probably. I might go back to school for my master's."

"Great idea," Kate said, nodding with enthusiasm. "So nice to have options. Have I mentioned that I'm green with envy?" She added. "Daily contact with the gorgeous Nick Fortune, *and* you're making incredible money for this gig. Life surely couldn't get any better."

Unless Nick is interested in me for more than my babysitting skills. Charlene didn't voice the thought aloud. She didn't want anyone, even Kate, speculating about her feelings for Nick. She didn't doubt they'd remain unspoken by her and unacknowledged by him.

"We should celebrate," Kate went on, obviously unaware of Charlene's lack of comment.

"We are celebrating." Charlene lifted her tea and saluted her friend.

"No, no—we need to celebrate with champagne and a night on the town."

"I'd love to—but I don't have any nights off."

"What? That's not right."

"I'm the triplets' primary caretaker during evenings and overnight. I can take a little time off during the day when Melissa is at the house, but not at night."

"That's got to be illegal. Aren't employers required to give an employee set times for coffee breaks, lunch, dinner, et cetera?"

"I'm sure they do, but this isn't a normal work situation. In fact, the job is only temporary. Once the girls' aunt is found and she arrives to take custody of them, my job will be finished. And I don't mind working long hours."

As she said the words, Charlene realized that when Lana arrived to collect the triplets, she would have to say goodbye—to both the girls and to Nick.

And no amount of bonus money was going to make it easier to walk away.

At the very moment Charlene was joining Kate for coffee at the café, Nick's cell phone rang across town just as he returned to his office after lunch. A quick glance at Caller ID had him grinning.

"Hey, J.R., what's up?" Nick greeted his older brother enthusiastically. The rest of the world might use his given name of William, but to his close friends and family he was always J.R.

"Not much. How's it going in Texasville? Are you wearing a ten-gallon hat yet?"

Nick laughed at his older brother's teasing. "I told you when I left L.A.—I don't think I'm the John Wayne type."

"Too bad," J. R. Fortune drawled. "Women love cowboys."

"Yeah," Nick said wryly. "So I've heard."

"How's the new job?"

"I'm still settling in, but it's going well."

"And what about life in a small town? How's that working for you?"

"A few challenges, but that only makes life more interesting, right?" Nick said, carefully noncommittal.

"What kind of challenges?" J.R.'s tone told Nick that his attempt at evading his brother's question hadn't worked. J.R. knew him too well.

"Hasn't Darr told you?"

"I haven't talked to Darr. He called and left a message—I returned the call and got his machine. We keep missing each other."

"Then you haven't heard I've become a father."

The statement was met with dead silence.

"Uh, you want to explain that?" J.R. said finally, his voice carefully neutral.

"I'm the guardian of three baby girls—one-year-old triplets."

J.R.'s swift, drawn-out expletive was a testament to his shock. It wasn't often J.R. was caught off guard.

"First of all, they're not mine," Nick said, taking pity on his brother. "Not by blood, anyway—they're Stan and Amy's little girls. I have temporary custody until the estate's attorney locates Amy's sister, then she'll take them."

"Damn."

For the next few moments, Nick and J.R. had a nearly word-for-word repeat of his conversation with Darr.

"You're the last person I'd expect someone to leave their kids to," J.R. said finally. "Especially little girls.

And especially three of them at a time. How the hell are you taking care of them, anyway? I can't see you changing diapers. Did you hire staff?"

"My housekeeper went from part-time to full-time, and I hired a nanny."

Something in his voice must have given him away, because J.R. pounced on the comment.

"Yeah? What's she like?"

Irritated, Nick swung around in his chair and glared at the window in front of him. "That's the same question Darr asked me. She's female. She takes care of the kids. What else is there?"

"Yeah, right." J.R.'s drawl held a wealth of disbelief. "If there wasn't something else, you wouldn't care if I asked."

"She's female," Nick repeated. "She has red hair. She's around twenty-five, maybe twenty-six. And she's beautiful." He bit off the words.

"And she's living in your house?"

"Yeah, she lives in the house."

"Okay, okay. Don't be so touchy. Did I ask you if you were sleeping with her?"

"No," Nick growled. "But you were thinking it."

"Well, maybe," J.R. conceded, amusement coloring his tone. "But if our roles were reversed, you'd be wondering the same thing about me."

"I'm her boss," Nick said wearily. "She's a…very nice, very *young* woman."

"Well, that's good. If she's going to take care of your best friend's kids, then she needs to be an upstanding citizen. How does Rufus feel about her?"

"He's crazy about her." Nick half-grinned, remembering the goofy, adoring expression on the big Lab's face when Charlene rubbed his ears and said goodnight. "The feeling seems to be mutual."

"She sounds like Mom."

His brother's voice held a deep note of affection. Nick considered the comment. "Yeah, she's a lot like Mom."

Molly Fortune had been a tomboy, and her easygoing, fun-loving nature made her a much-loved member of the sprawling Fortune family. Her death two years earlier had left her husband and sons grief-stricken.

"Then you'd better marry her," J.R. said.

"Marry her?" Nick sat upright. "I said she's beautiful. I didn't say I wanted to marry her. Where'd *that* come from?"

"Any woman that reminds you of Mom has to be serious marriage material."

"Yeah, but I'm not serious about marriage."

"Not in the past." J.R.'s voice held amusement. "That was before you met the beautiful red-haired nanny."

"Doesn't matter. Even if I was the type to consider marriage, Charlene is too young for me—and way too smart."

"I get the age difference thing, although I don't agree with it. But what do you mean, she's too smart?"

"I don't know. I haven't asked her how many college degrees she has, but it wouldn't matter. What she's got doesn't come with a degree."

"What are you talking about?"

"She's very intuitive—she knows a lot about people. I haven't seen anyone yet that doesn't love her at first sight, including my dog." *And that idiot ex-fiancé of hers,* Nick thought. Despite Barry's hostile attitude, Nick was sure he hadn't misread the possessive vibes from Charlene's ex-boyfriend.

"All the more reason to marry her."

"I'm not getting married. I'm not serious about the nanny. Besides," he continued, "I'm her boss. She's strictly off-limits as long as she's working for me." Nick refused to consider the possibility of keeping Charlene in his life permanently. But thinking about how much he wanted her only drove him crazy with frustration.

"Sounds to me like you're blowing smoke," J.R. said. "Who are you trying to convince? Me? Or you?"

"Let's change the subject. What's new with you?"

"I'm actually planning a trip to Red Rock—not sure when, but fairly soon. I'm thinking of making a few changes in my life, and since you and Darr like Texas so much, I thought I'd check it out."

"Damn, that's great news. Have you told Darr?"

"No, I haven't been able to reach him, remember?"

"Well, keep trying. If I see him, I'll tell him to call you. It would be great to have you living here."

"No promises," J.R. said. "I'll let you know when I have a firm date to visit. I want to meet your nanny— see if she really *is* anything like Mom. If you're really not interested, maybe I will be."

Nick ground his teeth but let the comment pass. Arguing with J.R. would only convince him that Nick was serious about Charlene.

And I'm not. Not even close.

Some small portion of his brain whispered that he was suffering from serious denial, but Nick refused to listen.

With both Charlene and Nick determined to keep their relationship strictly platonic and each other at arm's length, the next few days went by uneventfully.

They focused on the girls while they were awake and retreated to their own rooms when the babies napped or went to sleep in the evening. Since the triplets were now consistently sleeping through the night, there were no more middle-of-the-night encounters in the babies' room.

On Thursday morning, Charlene woke early. It was still dark outside her window, the eastern sky only faintly beginning to brighten with dawn. Unable to fall back to sleep, she tossed and turned for another half hour before throwing back the covers and rising to take a quick shower, dress and apply light makeup. Moving quietly into the hall, she eased open the door to the triplets' room and peeked inside to find the three sleeping soundly. Certain she had an hour or two of uninterrupted quiet before the girls woke and her day began in earnest, she tiptoed down the stairs and into the kitchen.

She halted abruptly just inside the doorway.

The rich smell of brewing coffee filled the room, lit only by the small light over the stove. Nick stood next to the coffeemaker, his hips leaning against the countertop, arms crossed over his bare chest. Faded Levis covered his long legs, his feet bare on the tile floor. The muscled width of his chest was smooth, with only a narrow strip of black hair that started at his belly button and arrowed downward, disappearing beneath the low-slung waistband of his jeans. His shoulders and biceps, chest and abs were California tanned, padded with toned muscles that shifted and flexed when he moved.

He looked up and saw her. His eyelids lowered, shielding his eyes behind the thick screen of black lashes and making it impossible for her to read his expression.

"Morning." His voice was rusty, gravelly with sleep. His dark hair was tousled and damp, as if he'd rubbed it dry with a towel after his morning shower, then ran his fingers through it before heading for the kitchen and caffeine.

"Good morning." Charlene forced her feet to move. She crossed to the island and turned on her laptop. "You're up early."

"I have a meeting in San Antonio this morning." He yawned, dragging his hand over his eyes. "Thought I'd get an early start." He nodded at the coffeemaker. "Coffee should be done soon."

"Great." Charlene walked to the counter and opened an upper cabinet. She took down two pottery mugs and paused, glancing over her shoulder at Nick. "Do you want your travel mug?"

"Sure."

The metal mug with the UCLA logo Nick carried to work each morning was on the top shelf. She stretched, going up on tiptoe, but the mug was just beyond her fingertips. "I need a ladder," she murmured, trying to stretch another half inch.

"Here, I'll get it."

Before Charlene could step back and out of his way, Nick was behind her, bracketing her between his body and the countertop when he reached above her.

She was surrounded by him. The scent of clean soap and the faint tang of his aftershave enveloped her while the warmth of his body narrowed the brief distance between them even more. He leaned forward slightly as he picked up the mug and his bare chest brushed her shoulderblades.

Her breath caught in a faint, audible gasp, and she froze, immobilized as she struggled to deal with an overload of emotions.

Nick heard the quick intake of breath, felt the swift, slight press of her shoulders against his chest as she inhaled. He fought the fierce urge to claim and possess, his muscles locking with the effort. But then her rigidly held body eased slightly against his and his control slipped a notch.

He set the mug down and planted his palms on the countertop, bracketing her between his arms. The faint scent of flowers teased his nostrils and he bent his head until his lips nearly touched her hair, closing his eyes as he breathed in the smell of shampoo and warm woman.

She turned, her shoulder brushing against his chest, faced him, her back to the counter. Her green eyes were dark with awareness when her gaze met his, the curve of her mouth vulnerable. A spray of small freckles dusted the bridge of her nose and the arch of her cheekbones, golden against her fair skin.

Nick clenched his fists against the counter, muscles bunching in his biceps as he fought to keep from touching her. A lock of hair slipped out of the narrow clip holding it away from her face. Tempted beyond reason, Nick lost his battle and gently brushed the strand away from her cheek, tucking it behind her ear.

Her skin was as soft and silky as the bright threads of hair. Lured by the warmth under his hand, he traced his fingertips over the tiny freckles on her cheekbones then followed the smooth curve of her jawline. Her pulse fluttered at the base of her throat and he tested the fast beat with the pad of his thumb, his fingers and palm cupping the curve where shoulder met throat.

His gaze flicked up, met hers. Her green eyes were nearly black, a faint flush heating her throat and coloring her cheeks. Her lips were fuller, slightly parted, her breathing quicker.

The moment spun out, tension thickening the air between them.

"Tell me to step away," he rasped, his voice rougher, deeper than normal.

"I can't," she murmured.

"Why?"

"I don't want to."

"We shouldn't do this." His thumb stroked slowly, compulsively over the fast pound of her pulse point.

She lifted her hands and laid them, palms down, on his chest. Her fingers flexed and he groaned, his fingers tightening reflexively on her shoulder. Her gaze fastened on his mouth and she slid her arms higher around his neck, going up on tiptoe, her body lying flush against his.

Nick lost the struggle. He bent his head, meeting her halfway as her lips sought his.

Determined not to lose control, he pressed his fists against the countertop, resisting the urge to wrap his arms around her and press her close.

Equally determined not to give in to the raging need to devour her mouth, he brushed her lips with his, refusing to deepen the contact when she opened her mouth under his and licked his lower lip.

"You taste like honey and mint," he muttered against her mouth, changing the angle to taste the corner of her mouth. Primal satisfaction seared through him when she gasped and pressed closer.

"Stop teasing and kiss me," she demanded, frustration in her voice. She cupped the back of his head in her palms and refused to let him move away as she crushed her lips against his with pent-up desire.

Nick lost the ability to reason. He wrapped his arms around her and pinned her between his body and the counter behind her. Their mouths fused in a heated exchange.

On some distant level, he knew he had to stop this—stop *them*—before he lifted her onto the counter and slipped off her clothes. He reached for control, struggled to bring them back from the precipice, until at last their breathing slowed.

He took his mouth from hers, her lips clinging in protest, and rested his forehead against hers while his heartbeat continued to slam inside his chest and thunder in his ears. "You're killing me," he murmured.

She eased away from him, just far enough to look up and search his face. "What do you mean?"

"I've wanted this since I looked up and saw you walking down the plane aisle," he told her.

"Really?" Her face glowed. "Me too."

"Don't tell me that." He groaned when his body leaped in response. "I'm having enough trouble keeping my hands off you. And you're off-limits. You work for me. I don't kiss employees."

"Then maybe I should quit." The bemused smile she gave him held a hint of mischief.

"I wouldn't blame you if you did," he said grimly. "But for God's sake, don't. The girls need you."

Her smile disappeared. Her thick lashes lowered, screening her eyes.

"Of course," she said, her voice cooler, more distant. "For a moment I forgot the circumstances."

She eased back, separating their bodies and putting a bare inch of space between them.

Somehow, Nick felt as if she'd moved across the room.

"I think I'll take my coffee upstairs. I have a few things to do before the girls wake up."

He wanted to drag her back into his arms and kiss her until the cool remoteness dissolved under heat and she was once again pliant and eager. But he knew it was far better that she'd put distance between them. He'd reached the limits of his control. If he spent much longer with her in his arms, he doubted whether he could make himself let her go.

"Right." He shifted away from her, leaning his hips against the counter, arms crossed, while he waited for her to pour her coffee and leave the room.

She didn't look back, her murmured goodbye and "have a good day" spoken over her shoulder, her face half-turned from him.

Then she was gone and he was alone in the kitchen.

He couldn't be sorry he'd kissed her. But now that he knew what she felt like in his arms, what her mouth tasted like under his, he knew keeping their connection strictly employer-employee was going to be damned near impossible.

Frowning blackly, his temper on edge, he filled his coffee mug and headed upstairs to finish dressing before heading for San Antonio.

* * *

Once safely in her bedroom, Charlene slumped against the wood panels and closed her eyes to blank out the light.

Stupid. That was so stupid, Charlene.

She never should have given in to the need to discover what it would be like to kiss Nick.

And it was mortifying to admit he would have walked away if she hadn't turned to face him, hadn't been the one to wrap her arms around his neck and instigate that kiss.

She nearly groaned with embarrassment. He was her boss. He'd said he didn't kiss his employees.

And it's against every principle I believe in to have an affair with my boss, she told herself. *So why didn't I stop?*

She'd never been tempted to break her own rules before. What was it about Nick Fortune that blew all her good intentions to dust?

She pushed away from the door and crossed to the bathroom. Running cold water, she pressed a dampened washcloth to her still-flushed cheeks, lowering it after a moment to stare at herself in the mirror.

"Nick is off-limits," she said to her reflection. "From now on, act as if this morning's kiss never happened."

Just how she was going to do that, she had no idea.

She hoped she was a better actress than she suspected, otherwise, Nick would know with one look that she was playing the role of disinterested woman.

And nothing on earth could be further from the truth.

On Saturday evening, two days after their fateful encounter in the kitchen, Andrew Sanchez telephoned.

Nick and Charlene were in the upstairs bathroom, taking turns bathing the triplets before tucking them into their pajamas.

Nick left Jackie and Jenny chortling, happily sitting naked atop their damp towels on the bathroom floor, and stepped into the hall just outside the bathroom, covering one ear with his palm as he talked.

When he hung up, Charlene knew by his solemn, faintly grim expression that something had happened. Despite her vow to keep their conversations to business issues only, concern compelled her into speech. "Is something wrong?"

"The attorney in Amarillo found Lana and her husband."

"Oh." Charlene stared at him, torn between relief and dread. "Are they all right?"

"Yes."

"Where were they?"

"At the privately run clinic. The investigator used the information we found in the photo, flew to Africa and tracked her down. She's been out of touch because a river flooded and cut off the clinic from contact with the outside world."

"Are they on their way home?"

"Yes."

"How long before they arrive?"

"Sanchez wasn't sure—probably a few days, maybe a week, at most."

Which meant their time with the triplets was growing short, Charlene realized. Her arms tightened unconsciously, protectively around Jessie's chubby little body.

"I'm going to miss them," she said, her voice husky with emotion.

"Yeah. Me too." Nick's eyes roiled with emotion.

Playing on the floor at his feet, Jackie grabbed a fist-ful of Nick's jeans just below the knee and pulled herself to her knees. Nick broke eye contact with Charlene and went down on his haunches next to her. Jenny imme-diately crawled toward him too, babbling imperiously.

"Hey, you two. What are you doing? Are you trying to stand up, Jackie?"

The gentle affection in his voice brought tears to Charlene's eyes. She turned away, Jessie perched on her hip, and leaned over to fiddle with the tub, twisting the release to let the water drain. By the time she turned back, she had her emotions under control once more.

"I'll get Jessie ready for bed. Would you like me to take Jackie or Jenny too?"

"No, I'll bring them." Nick slipped an arm around each baby and lifted them as he stood. The babies gur-gled and shrieked as they rose.

"You're a brave man," Charlene said in an effort to lighten the moment. "Neither of them are wearing di-apers."

"I like to live dangerously," he replied with a half grin.

Later, when the girls were tucked into bed, Nick and Charlene stood in the hall outside their room.

"I think I'll read for a while before I go to sleep," she murmured.

"Wait." Nick caught her arm as she turned away, stopping her.

The feel of his warm fingers and palm on the skin of her bare arm sent heat shivering through her veins, making her heart beat faster. But the moment she stopped and turned back, he released her.

"Yes?"

"I meant to talk to you about this earlier, but after I spoke with Sanchez, I forgot...." He paused, thrusting a hand through his hair. "I want to take the girls to a party celebrating the reopening of Red. The Mendozas are longtime friends, and most of my family will be there. And I'd like you to come with me."

Charlene's brain stopped functioning. Had Nick just asked her out on a date? Then she realized he'd said he wanted to take the girls. He needed her help.

"Of course," she replied. "When is it?" She calculated swiftly when he told her the date. The opening would be before Amy's sister arrived to take custody.

They said good-night and Charlene headed down the hall to her room. She wanted time to come to terms with the sadness she felt, knowing that her time with the triplets would soon end.

She suspected Nick would miss the babies as much as she would.

Charlene knew the dinner at Red Restaurant wasn't a real date. It was a family affair, a chance for Nick to introduce the triplets to his extended family and friends. Despite sternly lecturing herself that she was accompanying them as an employee only, the evening of the grand reopening found her standing in front of her open closet, torn between choosing a sexy black cocktail dress or a less glamorous gown.

"Oh, get over yourself," she muttered impatiently. She scanned the contents of the closet and took a dress from a hanger. The black-and-white print was less likely to show food stains if one of the triplets tossed dinner at her, and the modest, scooped neckline wouldn't expose too much skin if one of the girls tugged it lower.

She stepped into the dress and pulled it on, zipping the side before standing back to look in the mirror. The dress was comfortable, the fitted waist and full skirt with its just-above-the-knee hem pretty but less figure-revealing than the body-hugging, midthigh hem of her favorite little black dress.

But the one I'm wearing is far more practical for an evening spent with three one-year-olds, she told herself.

She consoled herself by choosing frivolous, black, strappy sandals with three-inch heels before she slipped black pearl studs into her earlobes. Experience told her to skip a necklace, since the triplets delighted in playing and tugging on her jewelry. Instead, she settled for the matching black-and-white pearl ring.

Then she caught up a black clutch evening bag, tucked a few essentials into it, and left the room.

She heard LouAnn's distinctive raspy voice, followed by Nick's quick laugh, and followed the sound to the living room, pausing on the threshold.

LouAnn sat on the ottoman, her skinny frame bent at the waist as she supported Jenny. The little girl was on her toes, wobbling back and forth with a delighted grin.

Jackie and Jessie sat on the carpet, watching Jenny with fascination. All three of the little girls were dressed in matching blue jumpers with white knit blouses beneath, the neat Peter Pan collars edged in blue embroidery. They wore cute little patent-leather Mary Jane shoes with lace trimmed, pristine white socks. Each of them had a white satin bow in their black hair. They looked adorable.

Charlene purposely saved the best part for last. Her

gaze found Nick, standing next to the stereo system. He wore black slacks that she was sure must have been tailored for him, a black leather belt and a white dress shirt with the cuffs folded back to reveal the gold Rolex on his wrist.

He looked over his shoulder at LouAnn, smiling as he watched her encourage Jenny. Then he looked past her and saw Charlene. His smile disappeared. His gaze ran from her face to her toes, then back again and something hot flared in his dark eyes.

"There you are," LouAnn said, breaking the spell that held Charlene. "Don't you look nice." She beamed and stood, picking Jenny up.

Charlene forced her gaze away from Nick and smiled at LouAnn. "Thank you."

"And you're right on time," LouAnn continued, waving a hand in the direction of the mantle clock. "You all better scoot or you'll be late."

"She's right." Nick walked toward them, pausing to pick up Jackie and Jessie. "The car's out front." He stopped in front of Charlene. "If you'll take Jackie, I'll collect the girls' diaper bag from the kitchen."

"Of course. Come here, sweetie," Charlene murmured, holding out her arms.

"I'll meet you at the car," Nick said, his face reflecting no emotion beyond casual friendliness.

"I'll carry Jenny out and buckle her in," LouAnn said, leading the way. "I would have been happy to babysit the girls for you and Nick tonight," she continued as they followed the sidewalk around the front of the house and reached the SUV, parked on the drive in front of the garage. "But Nick said he wanted his family to meet them."

"Mmm hmm," Charlene murmured.

"I must say, I'm impressed by our Nick," LouAnn chattered on as the two women tucked the girls in their car seats and fastened buckles. "He's really stepped up to the plate to take care of these three. Not many confirmed bachelors would have changed their whole life to accommodate babies at the drop of a hat."

Before Charlene could agree with her, Nick joined them. Moments later, the diaper bag was stored away, Jessie was buckled into her car seat, and the SUV was reversing out of the drive to the street.

LouAnn stood in the drive, waving good-bye as they pulled away.

She's right, Charlene thought as the house disappeared in the rearview mirror. *Nick really has reacted in an exceptional way. If I were in desperate need of help, he's the person I'd want on my side.*

And as a woman, he's the man I want in my bed.

The unbidden thought brought a flush of heat to her cheeks. She glanced sideways at Nick. Fortunately, he was looking at the street as he drove, otherwise she was sure he would have known she was picturing him naked.

Chapter 7

Nick ushered the girls and Charlene into the courtyard of Red and her eyes widened in surprise. Holding Jessie in her arms, she turned in a slow half circle.

"They've restored it just as it was," she exclaimed with delight. The square patio was tucked into the center of the building, edged on all sides with the dark walls of the restaurant. A fountain dominated the middle of the area. Its trickling water splashed against blue-and-white Mexican tiles, greeting diners with soft music. Several fan trees dotted the space, their green ribs draped with strings of tiny white lights. Tables were scattered around the courtyard, the underside of their colored umbrellas sporting more of the small white lights. Before the fire, the courtyard had boasted masses of old bougainvillea; these new plants were smaller, younger, but still colorful with bursts of vivid fuchsia, purple and gold.

"This has always been one of my favorite restaurants in Red Rock, and I was hoping the new version would have the same feel."

"They wanted to rebuild as close to the original restaurant as possible," Nick confirmed. "The basic structure is an accurate replica, but some of the furnishings were irreplaceable. A few of the antiques dated as far back as 1845, when President Polk welcomed Texas into the Union." He nodded at the fan trees. "The trees and bougainvillea will need a few years to reach the size of the originals."

"But they will—in time," Charlene said.

"Nicholas!"

Charlene and Nick both turned to find Maria Mendoza moving quickly toward them, her husband, José following more slowly.

Nick's face eased into a broad grin.

"How's my best girl?" he teased, bending to kiss the older woman's cheek.

She laughed and shook her head at him, the silver streaks in her black hair gleaming when the strands shifted against her shoulders. "Always the charmer." She beamed at Jackie and Jenny. Perched on Nick's arms, they each clutched a handful of his shirt in a tiny fist as they eyed her with open curiosity. Her gaze moved to Charlene and she lifted an eyebrow, a gleam of speculation in her dark eyes. "And who is this, Nicholas?"

"Charlene London, I'd like you to meet Maria and José Mendoza, the owners of Red and our hosts for the evening."

The adults exchanged pleasantries before Maria nodded at the triplets. "And are these adorable little girls your daughters, Charlene?"

"They're mine." Nick laughed when Maria's eyes widened with surprise. "Temporarily. I'm caring for them until their aunt arrives. Charlene took pity on me and agreed to help."

"They're beautiful," Maria enthused. "Aren't they, José?"

"Yes," the older man agreed, exchanging a very male look with Nick. Over six feet, José towered over his diminutive wife.

"What about your girls? Are they here?" Nick asked, glancing over the crowd.

"All three of our daughters and their husbands are here. Plus Jorge and Jane, of course—and even Roberto," Maria added with a proud smile.

Before Nick could comment, a waitress rushed up and whispered to José. He frowned and touched Maria's arm.

"I'm afraid we're needed in the kitchen—small emergency." He clapped Nick on the shoulder and smiled at Charlene. "Have fun, you two, enjoy your meal. I'm sure we'll see you later."

He ushered Maria away, following in the wake of the harried-looking waitress.

"I hope everything's okay," Charlene commented.

"I'm sure it's nothing José and Maria can't handle," Nick said. "Let's go inside and find a table—and some food."

They wound their way through the growing crowd on the patio, but it took them several moments to enter the restaurant. Nick seemed to know everyone present, and all of them wanted to say hello and ask about the triplets.

At last, they crossed the threshold and stepped inside the main dining room. Charlene was happy to see that here too, every effort had apparently been made to replicate the original ambiance and decor. Bright Southwestern blankets were displayed on the walls, together with paintings depicting battles between Mexican General Santa Anna and the Texans. A portrait of Sam Houston dominated one wall, next to a collection of period guns and a tattered flag in a glass case.

Guests sat or moved from table to table, visiting and eating beneath the glow of colorful lanterns hung from the ceiling.

"What a beautiful room," Charlene said. "Filled with beautiful people," she added with a smile.

Nick grinned back. "That's my family—the Fortunes are a handsome lot, aren't we?"

Charlene rolled her eyes. "And modest too."

He laughed out loud and shifted Jenny higher against his shoulder. "Yes, ma'am." He nodded toward an empty table just left of the center of the big room. "Let's grab a seat over there."

No sooner had Nick and Charlene settled the three girls into wooden high chairs and given their order to a waitress than Patrick Fortune and his wife, Lacey, stopped to say hello.

"It's a blessing you were available to help Nick with the babies, Charlene," Lacey said when introductions had been made all around. "We raised triplets too—three little boys. My goodness, what an experience that was!"

"Oh, yes." Patrick's eyes twinkled and he winked at

Charlene. "I remember those days well—looking back, I'm amazed we survived it. Very little sleep, nonstop changing diapers and bottle-feeding—not to mention that the boys had an uncanny ability to synchronize catching colds and earaches." He shook his head. "Taking care of three babies is above and beyond the call of parenting duty."

"But they're worth every moment," his wife said fondly, slipping her arm through the crook of his elbow and laying her head on his shoulder.

"We realized that quite quickly," Charlene assured her. The two women exchanged a look filled with understanding. If all Nick's relatives were as genuinely likeable as the Mendozas and this couple, Charlene thought, she could easily understand why the Fortunes held such a powerful and respected position in the community of Red Rock.

Across the room, Maria Mendoza chatted with her cousin, Isabella, having left José to finish dealing with a minor menu mix-up in the kitchen.

"Nick seems very happy with his new family, doesn't he?" she said, smiling fondly at the gathering of Fortune family members at the table where the three little identical girls held court.

"Yes, he does," Isabella agreed, her gaze following Maria's. "I never would have imagined Nick being comfortable with children, but he's clearly enjoying them."

Just then, one of the little girls tugged the white satin bow from her hair and tossed it at Nick. It bounced off his sleeve and landed in his water glass. The adults at the table burst into laughter.

Maria and Isabella chuckled.

"They're darling little girls," Maria said. She sipped from her champagne glass and eyed Isabella over the rim. "I'm so glad you could be here tonight—I've been meaning to get in touch with you. I'd love to have you sell some of your blankets and tapestries at my knitting shop."

Isabella's eyes widened. "What a lovely compliment, Maria. Especially since I know how carefully you plan your displays at the Stocking Stitch. But are you sure my work will be a good fit?"

"Without a doubt," Maria said promptly. "Your tapestries will be an inspiration for my customers."

Isabella flushed, pleased beyond measure. "I would love to have my work in your shop," she said with heartfelt warmth. "But I can't help but wonder if you're hoping our connection through the Stocking Stitch will bring Roberto and me together."

"Much as I'd love to see that happen, Isabella, I've given up hoping matchmaking efforts might succeed with Roberto," Maria said, her expressive face serious. "I suspect he gave his heart away at some point in the past. I'm afraid he's never gotten over whoever the woman was, and may never do so."

"I'm so sorry, Maria." Isabella instinctively reached out, her hand closing in swift sympathy over Maria's where it clutched her purse.

"No need to apologize, my dear," Maria said, her smile wistful. "If I thought matchmaking for Roberto would work, I'd try. But as it is…" Her voice trailed off and she sighed. "Be that as it may," she said determinedly after a brief moment. "I'm delighted you're agreeable to my proposal. When can you drop by the shop and discuss the details?"

The two women spent several moments arranging a date before Maria was called away by Lily Fortune.

"I need to speak to you in private," Lily murmured. She glanced about the crowded room before catching Maria's arm and walking with her to the relative quiet of a corner.

Intrigued, Maria went willingly.

"What is it?" she asked when they had a small degree of privacy.

"I wanted to ask if you've learned anything new from the investigators about the fire that burned down the restaurant," Lily said softly.

"Not that I'm aware of," Maria said, just as quietly. "But José stays in touch with the fire department and asked the chief to contact us if there are any new developments. I'm assuming he'll be in touch when he has any information. Why? Have you heard something?"

Lily sighed. "I can't help feeling the fires at Red and the Double Crown are related. I received a second anonymous note that said, 'This one wasn't an accident, either.'"

"You didn't tell me about the notes." Maria caught her breath. "What did the first one say?"

Lily glanced around, assuring there was no one near enough to hear their whispered conversation. "'One of the Fortunes is not who you think,'" she quoted.

Maria frowned. "That's terribly vague. What do you suppose it means?"

"I have no idea." Lily's face was strained. "At first I thought someone was planning to blackmail the family. But then the fires happened—and the second note arrived." She bit her lip. "I'm afraid someone is going to be seriously hurt."

"We can't let that happen," Maria said with emphasis. "It's a miracle someone wasn't injured already in one of the two fires."

"My family has hired Cindy's son, Ross, to investigate. He wants me to call in the police, but I dread the publicity that would surely follow."

"I can't say I blame you," Maria agreed. "But you mustn't take chances, Lily. You live alone out on the Double Crown. I think you should hire protection."

"You mean an armed guard of some sort?" Lily asked, clearly startled by the suggestion.

"Absolutely," Maria said stoutly. "What if this anonymous person decides to set fire to someone's house next? And with you living alone...well, it's just too dangerous."

Lily shook her head. "No, I refuse to give in to intimidation. I have staff at the ranch and I'll warn them to be more alert for anything that seems unusual. But I'm not going to let this person, whomever it is, terrorize me."

"Then promise me you'll be careful, very careful," Maria admonished.

"I will." Lily smiled at her friend. "And if I'm afraid for any reason to stay alone, I promise I'll show up on your doorstep, bags in hand, and ask to use your guest room."

"José and I will be delighted to have you," Maria said promptly, and enfolded Lily in a warm hug.

As Maria and Lily made plans, Nick and Charlene were scraping tomato and guacamole off Jessie's blue jumper.

"I'll take her to the restroom and sluice the rest of it

off her face and hands," Nick said. "Are you okay here with these two?"

Charlene glanced at Jenny and Jackie. They were chortling, waving their white linen napkins and stretching to reach a bowl of guacamole and chips just out of reach.

"We're fine." She laughed and moved the green guacamole across the table, out of Jenny's reach. "If they try to eat the table, I'll call 9-1-1."

Nick grinned, laugh lines crinkling at the corners of his eyes. "You might want to put that on speed dial."

He headed for the bathroom, glancing over his shoulder just before he left the room. Two of Maria's daughters and their husbands were standing next to Charlene, talking animatedly.

There was a lot to be said on occasion for a large family, he thought.

When he left the rest room, Jessie's face and hands scrubbed clean and dried, he'd barely entered the dining room when his cousin, Frannie, stopped him.

"Nick!" She caught him in a warm hug. He returned the affectionate embrace one-armed, keeping Jessie from being sandwiched between them by tucking her higher against his shoulder.

"Hey, Frannie." He smiled down at her. "Are you solo tonight or is Lloyd here?"

"Not only Lloyd, but also Josh and his girlfriend, Lyndsey," she said. "You look better than ever, Nick. What have you been doing with yourself?"

Given that sexual frustration rode him hard nearly every hour of the day, Nick was taken aback at Frannie's comment. "Must be my girls," he said, retrieving his balance with quick aplomb. He chucked Jessie under the chin and she grinned at him. "Is that true, Jessie?"

"Your girls?" Frannie repeated, clearly stunned. "I didn't know you had children, Nick. When did this happen?"

"I'm their temporary guardian. This is Jessie and those…" he pointed across the room "…are Jessie's identical sisters, Jackie and Jenny."

Frannie stared at him, eyes wide. "Tell me how this happened."

By the time Nick repeated his story, Frannie was tickling Jessie's fingers, trying to get her to accept a hug. But Jessie clung to Nick, although she giggled when Frannie made a comical face.

"…And that's the short version of the whole story," Nick concluded. "You've done the parenting thing, Frannie, do you have any expert advice for me?"

Frannie's smile faded. "I'm afraid I'm the last person you'd want advice from, Nick. Neither Lloyd nor I approve of Lyndsey, our son's latest girlfriend. I think Josh is too young to be so involved. I wish they would both date other people and gain more experience before they get serious. But they're so intense about each other."

"If I remember correctly," Nick said gently, "I think you were around Josh's age when you married Lloyd, weren't you?"

"Exactly," Frannie said grimly. "I don't want Josh to make the same mistakes I did." Her gaze swept the big room, stopping abruptly.

Nick half-turned to see what had caught her attention and located Josh, deep in conversation with a pretty young blonde girl. She was petite and looked almost fragile.

"I take it that's Lyndsey?"

"Yes." Frannie sighed. She looked at Nick. "Be glad you're only the temporary guardian of the triplets, Nick, and won't be spending their teenage years sleepless and worried about the choices they make."

Someone called her name and she excused herself to hurry off before Nick could respond. He watched her go, wondering what, exactly, she thought Josh was up to with Lyndsey.

He hoped to God there wasn't a pregnancy involved. After caring for the triplets, he was convinced no teenager should have babies.

Maybe not even twenty-year-olds should have kids.

He looked at Jessie, bent to kiss the top of her silky curls, and shifted her higher against his shoulder.

"No dating for you until you're forty," he told her sternly. "And maybe not even then. Remember, celibacy is a good concept."

She laughed, burbled nonsensically, and bopped him on the chin with a little fist.

Pleased she seemed to understand his lecture, Nick wove his way around diners toward the table where Charlene waited with Jackie and Jenny.

As Nick moved to join Charlene, José Mendoza was deep in conversation with Ross Fortune in one of the smaller, table-filled rooms just off the big main dining room.

"I'm convinced the fire here at the restaurant wasn't an accident," José said forcefully. He glanced around, lowering his voice as he continued. "We installed a state-of-the-art sprinkler system not four months before the fire and the smoke alarms are checked each week.

There's no way a fire could have burned out of control and destroyed the building unless someone tampered with the protection systems."

"And used a powerful accelerant," Ross commented, eyes narrowing in thought.

"Probably." José nodded decisively. "Although I can't figure out why anyone would want to burn down the restaurant."

"I'm working on the theory that the two fires might be connected—the one here at Red and the barn out at the Double Crown," Ross said, lowering his voice to keep from being overheard.

José looked taken aback. "What makes you think they're connected?"

Ross scanned the clusters of people, chatting and laughing. "I'd like to show you something." He took a note from his pocket and handed it over.

The older man unfolded the paper, read the single line and frowned. He looked up at Ross. "'This one wasn't an accident, either,'" he quoted. "Where did you get this? What does it mean?"

"It's a copy of a note that was slipped into Lily's pocket after the fire at the Double Crown. She doesn't have a clue who put it there, nor who wrote it. But it certainly suggests the two fires are connected." Ross took the note from José and tucked it back into his jacket pocket. "I was hoping you might shed some light as to who might have a grudge against your family and the Fortunes."

José frowned, his eyes narrowing as he considered the question.

"The Mendoza and Fortune families have been close

for a long time," he said after a moment. "But I can't imagine anyone would want to hurt my family this way, nor how it could be connected to the Fortunes."

"The two families are more than friends—your daughter, Gloria, married Jack Fortune. Do you know of any disgruntled boyfriends who might want to get back at you because of the marriage?"

"No." José's reply was swift and certain. "I can't think of anyone angry enough about their wedding, nor about any other situation with our families, to plan this sort of revenge."

"No disgruntled employees or business deals gone bad?" Ross prodded.

Once again, José shook his head. "The only mutual ties between our families are our long-standing friendship and the marriage between Gloria and Jack. I don't see how either of those could drive someone to blackmail or arson."

"Which makes me wonder if there might be some other link between your two families. Something we're not seeing," Ross mused.

"What's this about blackmail and arson?" Roberto Mendoza interrupted, joining them. He listened as his father quickly filled him in.

"This is a hell of a situation," he said when José finished his narrative.

"Yeah," Ross agreed.

"How close are you to finding out who did this?" Roberto asked grimly.

"No way of telling." Ross shrugged. "I still have people to interview and leads to follow."

Ross continued to speak but Roberto didn't hear him.

Distracted, his gaze was focused through the archway and across the dining room, his dark face solemn and intent.

Across the busy main room of Red Restaurant, hidden in the shadows, two figures watched the chattering, laughing groups of celebrants. Frowns of dislike twisted each face into matching expressions of irritation.

"Despite all this celebrating, I have it on good authority the Fortunes are concerned and taking the threats seriously."

"They seem to have changed their attitude since the second fire—which was a brilliant move, if I say so myself. If this were a chess game, I'd say we're very close to declaring checkmate." The voice held satisfaction.

"Yes." The response was smug, with a hint of gloating. "The Fortunes think they're so smart and powerful. Well, we'll see who wins in the end."

"I don't doubt the Fortunes will lose this game. Perhaps we should step up the plan? Raise the stakes—rattle the Fortunes even more. We have to make sure our position is secure."

"Are you saying the measures we've taken up to this point haven't been sufficiently threatening?" The words were laced with hostility.

"No, of course not." The response was instant and faintly irritated. "The Fortune family's sense of well-being has clearly been damaged. I'm merely suggesting it might be wise to push them even harder."

"I see your point."

"Excellent." The word oozed satisfaction. "I'm sure

if we decide to plan another…incident, we can execute it every bit as well as the prior ones."

"Absolutely." Conviction and a bone-chilling malice underscored the word.

Nick and Charlene left the party early, but even so, the hour was late for the triplets and past their bedtime. The three nodded off in their car seats on the drive home.

By the time Charlene and Nick carried the girls into the house, changed diapers and tucked the babies into their pajamas, the fractious girls were overtired and too awake to fall back to sleep.

"Why don't I take Jessie and Jenny downstairs," Nick said. "I'll turn on the music and walk the floor with them while you rock Jenny up here. When she falls asleep, you can put her in her crib. With luck, one of my two will be asleep by then and we can each deal with one."

"Good plan," Charlene agreed. She was settling into the rocking chair as Nick left the room. A few moments later, Norah Jones's husky voice floated up the stairwell. Charlene contemplated switching on the audio sensor in the bedroom to activate the nearest speaker. But the music was loud enough without the added sound, so she rejected the idea and cuddled Jenny, singing along with Norah Jones.

Jenny squirmed and fussed, unhappy, frustrated, and much too tired to settle. Finally, her eyelashes drifted lower and her breathing slowed. Five minutes later, Jenny's sturdy little body had gone boneless in Charlene's arms.

Rising from the rocker, Charlene carried her across the room and laid her in her crib, tucking her blanket over her. Jenny sighed and curled onto her side, dragging her blanket with her to cuddle the satin binding against her cheek.

Charlene stood over the crib for a moment, struck by the deep sense of contentment the moment held. Then she headed downstairs.

In the living room, Nick walked back and forth with a baby against each shoulder. Jackie and Jessie were still awake, their cheeks stained with tears, but their eyes were half-closed and their blankets hugged close.

"How's it going?" Charlene said softly.

"Another few minutes and they'll be out for the count." Nick tipped his head to look at Jackie, whose face was nearly hidden behind her blanket in the curve of his shoulder. "If you'll take her, I'll walk Jessie for a little longer."

They managed the handoff without rousing either child, and barely a half hour later they had tucked the two sleeping little girls into their cribs, then tiptoed quietly out of the room.

"Well…" Charlene tucked her hair behind one ear and gestured vaguely. "It's been a long day."

"Yeah, it has." Nick shoved his hands in his slacks pockets. "Thanks for helping out with the girls. I really appreciate it."

She couldn't read his face, although instinct told her there was suppressed emotion behind his polite remote expression.

"I was glad to do it. And it was a pleasure meeting your family—and the Mendozas and all their friends." She smiled, willing him to let whatever he was feeling break through the impassive facade. "I enjoyed myself—and I think the girls did too."

A faint smile curved his mouth, lightening his expression and easing the hard lines of his face. "They would have enjoyed themselves more if we'd let them climb on top of the table and play in the guacamole bowls."

"I'm sure they would," she said wryly. "Fortunately for the rest of the guests, we managed to restrain them."

His smile faded, his eyes hooded as he looked at her with an intensity she felt as surely as if he'd stroked his hand over her skin.

"Well…" she said, suddenly strung with nerves. "I'll see you in the morning, then. Good night."

She reached her bedroom door before he responded. "Good night."

The simple words held dark undertones that shivered up her spine like a caress. She didn't look back, only slipped quickly inside and closed the door with the distinct impression that she'd just avoided danger.

Living in the same house with Nick Fortune was fraught with temptation. And she was a woman who had little resistance when it came to the undeniably handsome bachelor.

As she'd learned such a short time ago. During that mind-numbing kiss in the kitchen.

Nick hadn't spent his bachelor years avoiding women, she knew. The man could kiss. Just the memory of his mouth on hers made her toes curl and her heart pound.

Since she had very few defenses against Nick, she could only hope his commitment to keep them at arm's length while they worked together held fast.

Because she wasn't at all sure she could withstand him if he crooked his finger and smiled at her to lure her closer.

Chapter 8

Both Nick and Charlene were hyperaware that their time with the triplets was running out. Much too quickly the days flew by, and all too soon the much-awaited telephone call was received. The babies' aunt and uncle had arrived, checked into a local hotel and wanted to arrange a time to come to the house.

Fortunately, it was Sunday morning and the timing was right. Nick was home, stretched out on the living-room floor while he stacked blocks with the triplets. The girls happily knocked them over as soon as he built a tower, then crawled after the rolling blocks to toss them back at him. Charlene sat on the sofa, smiling at their antics. She jumped nervously when the doorbell rang, her gaze flying to meet Nick's.

"You stay here with the girls. I'll get the door."

Wordlessly, she nodded and Nick left the room. She

heard the door open and the quick murmur of voices. A moment later, Nick ushered a man and woman into the living room.

"Charlene, this is Lana Berland and her husband, John," Nick said as they approached. He bent and lifted Jackie into his arms. "This is Jackie. Charlene's holding Jenny—and Jessie is trying to chew the remote control for the stereo system. Jessie, give me that." He bent his knees and scooped the little girl up to perch on his arm. She instantly patted his face and burbled a stream of unintelligible chatter. "Yes, I know, honey, but you can't chew the remote. If you ate it, you'd wind up with plastic rash somewhere."

The three adults, watching him, burst into laughter at the same time, breaking the awkwardness of the moment.

"They're such beautiful babies," Lana said, her eyes welling as she looked at them. "They look so much like their parents. They have Amy's eyes and Stan's black hair."

"Would you like to hold Jessie?" Charlene asked.

"Oh, yes, please." Lana eagerly held out her arms but the little girl clung to Charlene, burying her face against Charlene's neck.

"Perhaps she needs a bit more time to get used to you," Charlene suggested, seeing Lana's stricken expression. "Won't you have a seat?" She gestured at the sofa and perched on the chair with Jessie when Lana sat on the nearby end of the leather couch.

"They're shy with new people," Nick comented, taking a seat on the far end of the sofa with Jackie and Jenny.

"They couldn't remember us," Lana said, glancing at John. "We were back in the States shortly after they were born, but then we left for Africa. We'd planned to return in December to spend Christmas with Stan and Amy this year…" Her voice broke and she faltered.

John sat beside her and took her hand, threading her fingers through his.

"It was a huge shock to hear about Stan and Amy, as I'm sure you understand," he said quietly. "Lana hasn't had time to come to terms with it."

"I understand," Nick said, the bones of his face suddenly more prominent, his jaw tight. "I'm not sure how long it's supposed to take, but a week certainly isn't enough time."

"No," Lana said softly, her eyes filled with compassion and empathy.

"I understand you two were stranded by flooding," Nick said, abruptly changing the conversation. "How long were you cut off?"

Lana and John seemed relieved at Nick's steering the conversation away from the tragedy that had brought them all together. For the next half hour, they chatted companionably about the flooding and the political situation in the area of southern Africa where Lana and John had lived and worked. They also discussed the triplets as Nick and Charlene related episodes that had all four adults laughing.

When Nick told them about the girls' difficulty sleeping through the night and using music to quiet them, Lana clapped her hands with appreciation.

"What a brilliant solution," she said with admiration. "I wouldn't be surprised if Amy and Stan used some of the same music."

"I don't know if they've always been little night owls or if they were upset by the drastic changes in their lives," Nick said. "The court temporarily placed them with a foster mother in Amarillo for several days after the accident before I picked them up and brought them here. It has to be confusing for them—so I guess we shouldn't complain about their not sleeping at first."

"That brings up something John and I wanted to talk to you about," Lana said. She looked at her husband, then back at Nick. "We spent most of the plane ride home discussing how to make the transition with the least impact on the girls."

Charlene saw Nick's body go taut. She doubted Lana or John noticed, but she recognized the telltale signs. She too braced herself.

"As you said, their lives have been terribly disrupted already and by switching their home and caretakers, yet again, we're going to upset their schedules. We thought perhaps the best way might be to ease them into the transition—by having them remain with you for several days, perhaps a week, while John and I visit daily. That would give the girls time to grow accustomed to our being around and allow us to ease into their lives. If the change isn't quite as abrupt, hopefully the stress of transition for the girls will be less when they come to live with us full-time."

Some of the tenseness eased out of Nick's body. "Sounds like a reasonable plan." His gaze met Charlene's for a moment. "I've wondered whether they'll be okay with another sudden shift in their living arrangements. I'm sure Charlene has too."

"Yes, I have," Charlene acknowledged, swept with relief that Lana and John's first concern was for the triplets' welfare. Something cold and scared inside her chest eased and she drew a deep breath. "Will you be taking them back to Amarillo?"

"We haven't had time to make definite plans, but that seems the most reasonable choice. We're temporarily without jobs, or a home—my sister's estate is left to the girls under our guardianship and their house in Amarillo is available, of course." She glanced at her husband and once again, he squeezed her hand comfortingly. "John and I don't have any personal ties there, now that Amy and Stan are gone." She blinked back tears.

"We don't have to decide all the details right this minute, sweetheart," John murmured, slipping an arm around his wife's shoulders.

Jessie chattered, squirming. Charlene shifted her grip on the little girl.

"What is it?" she asked before she realized Jackie and Jenny were also fussing. She glanced at her watch. "It's nearly twelve—time for the girls' lunch." Her gaze met Nick's. "Would you like me to feed them while you discuss arrangements with Lana and John?"

"I think we'll have time to work out details over the next few days. Why don't we all go into the kitchen and make lunch." Nick surged to his feet, bringing Jackie and Jenny with him. "Might as well start getting the girls more comfortable with their aunt and uncle." His lips quirked in a grin. "There's nothing like dodging strained carrots to bring a one-year-old closer to an adult—especially when one of the triplets starts and the other two join in because they think it's hilariously funny. It's a real bonding experience." He lifted an eyebrow at John. "Have any objections to getting applesauce in your hair?"

"None," John said promptly, his eyes twinkling.

"Good." Nick waved the three adults ahead of him. "We need to find something to cover you with, Lana, or the dress you're wearing is going to have food all over it by the time the girls are done eating."

Lana laughed. "Looks like I need an apron."

"Melissa has one in the kitchen—I'll get it for you," Charlene said as they all trooped out of the living room and down the hall.

During the following days, Nick and Charlene had time to get to know Lana and John. Observing their interaction with the triplets put to rest any lingering fears as to how well the couple would cope as parents.

On the last night the triplets would spend at Nick's home, Charlene couldn't fall asleep. She tried reading a new novel, but was too restless to sink into the story. Giving up, she put the book aside and booted up her laptop. Her efforts to focus on updating her resume and making job-search lists were no more successful than her earlier attempts to read.

She found herself staring blankly at the screen. *This is probably the last night I'll spend here,* she thought, her gaze leaving the laptop to move around the comfortable room.

And the last night I'll sleep in Nick's house.

Would she see him again after the triplets left with Lana and John?

Probably not, she acknowledged, her heart twisting with regret and pain. Her job would end when Nick no longer needed her help with the babies.

No more shared laughter with Nick over the babies' antics. No more shared outings, like their walk to the coffee shop or the evening at Red.

And no more unexpected hot kisses with early-morning coffee.

Tears clogged the back of her throat. She'd never know what those kisses might have led to—Nick was clearly determined not to get involved with her. She had to focus on saying goodbye to the triplets—and then move on.

She closed her files, shut down the laptop and moved it to the bedside table before she switched off the lamp. She fluffed her pillow, tugged the sheet higher, and determinedly closed her eyes.

A half hour later, she checked the digital clock for the third time and groaned aloud. The luminescent dial told her the time was twelve-thirty in the a.m.

Frustrated, she stared at the ceiling and tried counting sheep. Their woolly shapes quickly morphed into babies with black curls and sparkling blue eyes. All of them looked exactly like Jackie, Jenny and Jessie.

Muttering, she pulled her pillow over her head and tried not to picture adorable laughing triplets.

The muffled sound of music penetrated the soft down-filled pillow. Clearly, the audio system had activated in the triplets' room.

Perhaps she shouldn't be glad she would have this one last chance to check on them in the dark hours of night, she thought as she left her bedroom and crossed the hall. But somehow, she couldn't regret that one of them had wakened.

The door to their bedroom was ajar and she slipped inside noiselessly, only to halt abruptly.

Nick stood next to Jenny's crib, the little girl cradled against his chest. His head was bent, lips touching the crown of her silky curls as he gently rocked her in his arms.

Charlene's heart caught and tears welled. Clearly, she wasn't the only one having a hard time letting the girls go.

Unwilling to intrude on Nick's privacy, she turned to leave.

His head lifted and he glanced over his shoulder.

She stopped, held by the intensity in his dark eyes, shadowed further by the dim night-light.

"I didn't know you were here," she said softly, whispering so as not to wake the babies. "I heard the music and thought I'd make sure the girls were okay."

Nick nodded and carefully lowered Jenny into her crib. She stirred, curling on her side on the white sheet with its pattern of pink bunnies in flowered hats.

He tucked her blanket closer. She clutched it tightly and sighed, her eyes closed, her limbs sprawling as she fell more deeply asleep.

Nick joined Charlene at the door and motioned her outside, pausing to pull the door nearly closed.

"If I'd known you were here, I wouldn't have interrupted," she whispered.

"Don't worry about it." He ran his hand over his hair, further rumpling it. "I didn't mind checking on Jenny."

"The music didn't put her back to sleep?" Charlene asked, wondering if the little girl was coming down with something.

Nick shrugged, his expression wry. "It might have, but she saw me when I looked in. I thought she might wake the others, so I picked her up."

"Ah." Charlene nodded. She suspected Nick may have had the same reaction she'd had to hearing the music click on and used it as an excuse for a quiet moment with Jenny. "It's hard to believe they'll be gone tomorrow."

"Yeah." His eyes turned somber. "It is."

"I'm going to miss them."

He nodded. "When all this started, I never thought I'd wish I could keep them, but somehow I do."

Charlene fought the onslaught of tears and lost. Despite her best efforts, her eyes filled, then overflowed with tears. They spilled down her cheeks.

"Hey," he said softly, moving closer, narrowing the space between them to mere inches. He cupped her face, brushing the pads of his thumbs over the tears dampening her cheeks. "Don't cry."

"I can't help it," she managed to get out past a throat clogged with emotion. "I know I shouldn't have grown so attached, but I couldn't help myself. I didn't plan to," she shrugged helplessly. "It just happened."

Nick cupped her shoulders and gently urged her forward, tucking her against his chest and wrapping his arms around her. "I know," he said soothingly, his chin resting against the crown of her head. "If it's any comfort, I feel the same way. God knows I never thought I'd get used to having three babies around. They cause total chaos—there's food in crazy places I can't reach in my kitchen because they threw it there. I hate changing dirty diapers. And staggering through ten-hour workdays after a couple hours of sleep in the beginning sure as hell wasn't fun. Despite all that, they somehow sneaked under my radar when I wasn't looking. They've grown on me. I actually like the little tyrants."

Charlene accepted the comfort of his embrace without questioning, giving in to the need to be held. His hands moved in soothing circles on her back, the solid warmth of his body supporting her, and her sobs gradually slowed.

She calmed. And was instantly too aware of Nick.

The hall was nearly dark, only faintly lit by cool, silvery moonlight, filtered through the leafy tree outside the window at the far end.

The arms that held her were warm and bare—so was the muscled chest she lay against. Her thighs were pressed against his hair-roughened ones.

She realized with a sudden rush of heat that Nick wasn't wearing the pajama bottoms he'd pulled on in the earlier days when the triplets often got him out of bed in the middle of the night. He was wearing boxers.

Her clothing was just as minimal. The thin tank top she wore over cotton sleep shorts may as well have been made of air for all the barrier it provided between her skin and his.

Her breath hitched. Her heart beat faster, driven by the slow excitement that coiled in her abdomen and spread outward to her fingers and toes. Every inch of her was much too aware that this was Nick who held her—and she wanted him.

She heard his breathing change, felt the subtle tension in the muscled body surrounding her.

"Charlene," his voice rasped, deeper, huskier.

"Yes?" She tilted her head back and looked up at him. His mouth had a sensuous fullness, his eyes slumberous between half-lowered lids.

"You're fired," he said roughly.

"What?" She blinked, disoriented.

"I'm fresh out of self-control. And we can't make love if you're working for me. When we wake up in the morning, you're hired again. But for tonight—" he brushed the pad of his thumb over her bottom lip. "It's just us."

"Are you sure about this?" She didn't want a repeat of their moment in the kitchen when she'd been swept away, only to crash, bruised and hurt, when he told her he regretted kissing her.

"I'm sure," he muttered. "The question is, sugar, are you? 'Cause if you aren't, you're fast running out of time to tell me."

Knowing this may very well be the last night she'd spend in his house and perhaps the last time she'd have a chance to be with him, Charlene didn't hesitate. With swift decision, she met his gaze and gave the only answer possible.

"I'm sure."

Instantly he crushed her mouth under his for one fierce kiss, then bent and swung her into his arms.

Like the hallway, his bedroom was lit by silvery moonlight. He set her on her feet, her legs slowly sliding against his, and threaded his hands through her hair, tilting her face up to kiss her again. The kiss scorched her nerve endings, the slow, thorough exploration of her mouth sending shivers of excitement through her. When he finally lifted his lips, her knees were weak. She clutched his biceps for support when he eased back, his hands settling at her waist, thumbs stroking beneath the hem of her tank top.

"You're wearing too many clothes," he rasped, his voice thick with arousal.

She licked her lips. "So are you," she murmured, her gaze fastened on the sensual twist of his mouth as he smiled briefly.

"I can fix that." His hands moved, carrying her top upward and baring her torso. He pulled the cotton shirt free of her hair and tossed it behind him.

The moonlight fell across his face, highlighting his intent expression as he stared at her, his eyes half-lidded. Charlene's breasts swelled under his gaze, heavy and sensitive. Her knees nearly buckled when he palmed her, stroking his thumbs over the sensitive tips.

She clung tighter, gasping when he bent his head and took her nipple in his mouth. Her head spun as he licked her, the warm, wet cavern of his mouth soothing the tender flesh.

He slipped his hands beneath the waistband of her shorts and pushed them down and off before his arms wrapped around her to pull her flush against him.

"Please. Please, Nick," she murmured, nearly frantic with the need to have him closer.

He muttered what sounded like a curse and, one-handed, shoved his boxers to the floor.

The covers were tossed to the foot of the king-size bed and Nick lowered her to the sheet, following her down.

His weight blanketed her from shoulders to thighs, his big body crowding hers. He levered himself up on his forearms, the hard angles of his hips tight against the softer cove of hers, and bent his head to take her mouth. She shuddered, her hands clutching his shoulders as she welcomed the urgent thrust of his tongue. Taut with excitement, she lifted to press her breasts against his chest, shifting against him, the drag of bare skin against his hard, sleek muscles ratcheting up the tension that gripped her. He kissed her mouth, chin, then trailed his lips down the curve of her throat. The warm weight of his hand settled at her waist. His thumb grazed the small hollow of her belly button. Then his fingers moved higher, over her midriff, until the backs of his fingers brushed the underside of her breast.

The harsh intake of his breath was audible, his hard body going taut.

Impatient, Charlene hooked one leg over his, her

calf sliding over the hair-roughened back of his thigh, urging him closer.

His mouth took hers at the same moment his hand closed over her breast and his hips rocked against hers. Heated moments later, Charlene was frantic with need.

He shifted away from her to don protection, then nudged against her center and she wrapped her arms and legs around him, opening herself as he groaned and thrust home.

Charlene came awake slowly, drifting upward through layers of sleep. Heat branded her back, thighs and calves. Something heavy lay across her waist. She shifted, stretching lazily, her toes brushing hair-roughened muscles.

Her eyes popped open and she stared blankly at the bar of early morning light that lay across the end of the bed. For one baffled moment, she tried to understand why her bedspread was now a deep cobalt blue when it had been white and green last night.

Memory washed over her and her eyes widened.

This wasn't her bed—or her bedroom.

It was Nick's. Carefully, she turned her head on the pillow to look over her shoulder at the man sharing the bed.

Nick's body—his bare, naked body—was curled against hers, branding her from shoulderblades to toes. And it was his arm that lay like a possessive bar over her waist, his fingers curled loosely over her ribcage, just below her breast.

A soft smile curved her mouth. There was such an overwhelming sense of rightness—waking with Nick wrapped around her. For several long moments she lay still, basking in the sheer pleasure and the memories of the night they'd spent making love.

Nick was an amazing lover. She should have known he would be by that sizzling first kiss in the kitchen, she thought.

Her gaze drifted lazily past Nick's broad shoulder and landed on the alarm clock.

Her eyes widened.

Good Lord, was that the right time?

The triplets would be awake before long and Lana and John were picking them up today. There were a million and one things to accomplish before they arrived.

With a last lingering look at Nick's sprawled body, Charlene slipped out of his bed. Catching up her top and sleep shorts from where they lay in a heap on the floor, she stole silently out of his room to take a shower in her own bathroom.

"They're here," Nick announced, his voice carrying up the stairs.

Charlene drew a deep breath.

"You okay, honey?" LouAnn's raspy voice held warm concern.

"Yes." Charlene glanced sideways and found the older woman's face soft with compassion.

"It's not easy saying goodbye when you've become attached to little ones," LouAnn said. "I've had to do it a time or two myself." She picked up Jessie, balancing her on one bony hip. "I've never been sorry I had the experience, though, once I had a few weeks to cry my eyes out and get used to them being gone."

Charlene laughed. Granted, it was more of a half laugh, half sob, but LouAnn's blunt and thoroughly practical observation was enough to get her past the emotional moment.

"Thanks, LouAnn."

The older woman winked at her. "Don't worry. I expect you'll be having babies of your own one of these days, soon enough. I've seen Nick look at you, and if ever a man is head-over-heels, it's Nick. I'd bet my last dollar on it."

Charlene didn't reply, busying herself with picking up Jackie and Jenny. She didn't want to think about what Nick did or didn't feel—she'd spent too many hours over the last days agonizing over him. And making love last night had sent her emotions cartwheeling out of control. She simply couldn't think about Nick now—not if she was going to say goodbye to the triplets with any semblance of dignity.

"There you are." Nick met them halfway up the stairs and lifted Jenny out of her arms. "You should have waited—I'd have carried one of them downstairs."

"Not to worry, we managed." She avoided his gaze and looked over his shoulder at the couple standing in the foyer. "Hello, Lana, John."

"Good morning," they responded.

A mountain of luggage, three diaper bags stuffed to overflowing and boxes with toys poking out of the top filled one corner of the foyer.

Lana held out her arms and Jackie went happily, chattering away as her aunt listened intently and nodded.

The interaction between the two was bittersweet for Charlene—comforting because Jackie clearly felt at home with her aunt, but saddening because she left Charlene's arms so willingly.

"We have some good news," John said.

"What's that?" Nick asked, sitting Jenny on the floor with a stuffed green dragon.

"Do you want to tell them, Lana?" John grinned at his wife.

For the first time since descending the stairs, Charlene noticed Lana wore an air of suppressed excitement.

"Yes, let me." Lana nodded emphatically, beaming at Nick, then Charlene. "We have fabulous news. John has been offered a job at the Fortune Foundation and we're not going back to Amarillo—we're going to stay right here in Red Rock. And we found the loveliest house not more than a mile or so from here. So the babies won't be going far," she ended with a lilting laugh. "Isn't that wonderful? I was feeling so badly, knowing we were taking them so far away from you both and you wouldn't be able to see them regularly. But now we'll practically be neighbors, so anytime you want to drop in and visit the girls, you can."

Nick looked as stunned as Charlene felt. Then he smiled, a broad grin that lit his face.

"That's great news."

"Yes, absolutely wonderful," Charlene added.

"This deserves a celebration," Nick declared. "Come into the kitchen—there's a bottle of champagne in the fridge. I promise I won't give either of you more than a swallow or two, since you'll be dealing with the triplets today."

They trooped into the kitchen, babies and all, and while Nick took out champagne and Charlene found flutes in the cupboard, Lana and John filled in the details.

"I'll be managing a project to establish an afterschool enrichment program for underprivileged kids in San

Antonio," John said as Nick handed around flutes with the bubbling gold liquid.

"I'm familiar with it," Nick said. "I worked up projection figures for the costs. The proposal for services was impressive."

"The work is tailor-made for John," Lana put in, clearly elated. "His primary interest has always been in programs that enhance the lives of children."

Nick winked at her and lifted his glass. "With the triplets in your house and heading up the Foundation's new project, I'd say he's hit the jackpot."

Laughter filled the kitchen, glasses were raised, and it was an hour later before Lana glanced at her watch.

"Look at the time, John. I didn't realize it was so late." She stood, balancing Jessie on her hip. "By the time we get the girls' things loaded, drive to the house and unload, it will be nearly time for the girls' naps." She tapped a forefinger on the tip of Jessie's upturned nose. "We don't want to start off on the wrong foot."

"Agreed."

Since the new house was so close, Nick insisted he help transport and unload the triplets' belongings.

Much too soon, Charlene found herself standing at the curb, waving good-bye as the two vehicles drove away down the street.

She went inside, the silence seeming to close about her when she shut the door. She walked into the kitchen to wash the crystal flutes and return them to their shelf. After wiping down the marble countertop, she glanced once more around the kitchen and then headed upstairs.

It was time to pack—and leave.

Chapter 9

"What are you doing?"

Charlene stiffened, steeling herself before she turned. Nick stood in the open doorway, frowning at her.

"I'm packing." She walked to the closet and slipped the little black cocktail dress off its hanger, folding it as she returned to the bed and the open suitcase.

"I can see that," he said impatiently. "Why?"

She tucked the dress into the bag before she looked at him. "Because it's easier to carry clothes in suitcases, of course."

"Where are you going?"

"I'm not sure yet." She opened a dresser drawer, removed several T-shirts and laid them on top of the black dress. "Now that the girls are with Lana and John, my job here is finished."

"Yeah, I suppose it is."

Charlene felt her heart drop and realized she'd been

holding her breath, hoping he'd tell her to stay. The scowl on his face, however, was convincing evidence that he had no interest in prolonging her time. She forced a smile. "I'll be out of your way in another half hour and you'll have your house to yourself again. I'm sure you'll be glad you can return to peace and quiet," she said as she crossed the room to fetch her toiletries from the bathroom.

"Not likely," he muttered.

"I beg your pardon?" She paused, sure she must have misheard him.

"I hope you've been comfortable here," he gestured at the room, not directly answering her question.

"Oh, yes." She looked about her, knowing she would miss the way the early-morning sun shone through her window each morning, throwing a leafy pattern across the bed from the tree just outside. And she'd miss the well-planned cozy kitchen downstairs, and Nick's state-of-the-art coffeemaker. She drew in a deep breath and managed another vague, polite smile in his direction. She didn't look at him for fear the tears pressing behind her eyes would escape her rigid control and spill over. "You have a lovely home, Nick. Anyone would enjoy spending time here."

"The hell with this," he ground out.

Startled, Charlene switched her gaze from the suit-case to Nick and found him stalking toward her.

"You can't leave." His face was taut. He caught her shoulders in his big hands and held her. "I don't want you to leave."

"You don't?" Charlene was stunned, too afraid to hope, even more afraid that she might leap to conclusions. She needed him to spell out exactly what he meant. "Why?"

"Because I want you to marry me, live with me, have babies with me."

"But…" Charlene's brain spun, trying to absorb this sudden switch. "But you said you never planned to marry. Or have children. You said you couldn't imagine having a family—that you thought Stan and Amy were crazy to pick you to take care of their girls."

"I said a lot of stupid things," Nick said with disgust. "The only reason I was a confirmed bachelor is because I hadn't met you."

"Really?" Charlene's eyes misted. "That's a lovely thing to say."

"I should have said it before." His hands tightened. "I wanted you the day I met you but I told myself all I felt was lust. And you worked for me. I've never crossed the line and slept with an employee." His eyes darkened, his hands stroking down her back to settle at her waist and tug her forward to rest against him. "I couldn't stop myself last night."

"Neither could I," she admitted.

"Darr and J.R. knew I was in love with you. I've known for a while, but it took seeing you packing your suitcase to make me say the words out loud."

"I don't mind." Charlene cupped his face in her palms. "As long as you said it." Her words eased the tension from his face.

He bent his head and brushed his mouth over hers. "Now it's your turn."

Charlene slipped her arms around his neck and went up on tiptoe. "I love you too," she murmured, her lips barely touching his before he leaned back, preventing her from reaching him. Her mouth skimmed his chin.

He bent his head and nuzzled her neck. "That's the best news I heard all day."

"Mmm." Distracted by the movement of his warm mouth against her skin, she was having difficulty following their conversation. She tilted her chin as he nudged aside her shirt. Dazed, she realized she hadn't even felt him unbutton the blue cotton.

He smiled, his mouth branding an amused curve on her skin, and then he lifted his head to look down at her.

"Just remember when we talk about this later—you agreed."

He caught the edges of her shirt. Buttons popped as he ripped it open and stripped it off her shoulders. He shoved the suitcase off the bed and it hit the floor. Charlene barely noticed that the contents spilled out in a fan of color against the pale-green carpet.

His eyes flared with heat as he traced the curve of her breasts in the lacy white bra before he forced his gaze downward and began unsnapping her jeans. His head was bent, his black hair inches from her face, his eyelashes dark fans against his tanned skin as he slid the zipper downward.

"Nick," Charlene breathed.

He glanced up, his fingers going still on her waistband.

"You're wearing more clothes than I am."

He smiled slowly, closing the distance between them to slick his tongue over her bottom lip. "So take them off," he murmured.

She fumbled with the shirt buttons, breathing rapidly while her heartbeat pounded faster. She reached the button at his waistband and he let go of her jeans to grab his shirt and pull it free.

She reached behind her and unhooked her bra, shrugging her shoulders to let it fall free.

Nick reached for her, pulling her against him, skin-to-skin, and kissed her.

"I feel as if the world is still spinning," Charlene confided an hour later as they sat on her bed, a tray of food between them.

"Why is that?" Nick held out a bite of scone, dripping with butter and jam.

"Mmm." Charlene opened her mouth, chewed and swallowed. "These are heavenly. What did you say the name of the bakery is?"

"Mary Mac's. Hold still." Nick leaned over and licked the corner of her mouth. She tasted raspberry jam when he kissed her.

"Can we have these scones every Sunday?" she asked, caught by the intimacy of the moment.

"Absolutely." Nick grinned at her. "Marry me, babe, and I'll open an account there. You can have scones every day of the week if you want."

She laughed. "You don't have to bribe me. I already said I'd marry you—but the scones are definitely an added inducement," she added.

"Good to know what works," he said. "In case I need to bribe you in the future."

"You won't need bribes," she said softly. "Just ask."

His eyes heated. "You may regret that. I've built up a lot of hunger over the last few weeks."

Charlene's heart skipped, heat moving through her

veins. "We've just spent hours in this bed. Aren't you exhausted?"

"Babe, I'm just catching my breath." He waggled his eyebrows at her suggestively and she laughed out loud. He grinned, clearly pleased he'd amused her. "I want to buy you something. What do you want for a wedding present? Diamonds? Rubies?"

"What?" Startled, Charlene searched his face and realized he was serious. "You don't have to buy me expensive things." She wanted to make it clear to Nick that his wealth wasn't why she loved him. But he clearly felt strongly about giving her a gift and she didn't want to disappoint him. She beamed, certain she had the perfect idea.

"There is something I'd love to have," she told him.

"You've got it," he said instantly. "What is it?"

"I would absolutely love it if we could set up a college fund for the triplets," she said earnestly.

He stared at her. "You want me to give the girls money for college?" he said slowly, eyeing her.

"Yes." She nodded emphatically. "Please," she added.

A slow smile curved his mouth. "You're something else, darlin'." He pressed a passionate kiss against her lips. "Any suggestions as to how big the fund should be?"

"No, you're the financial expert." She was still reeling from that kiss. "Oh, wait." She sat bolt upright, excited. "What if we ask the wedding guests to contribute to the girls' college fund in lieu of gifts for us?" She waved her hand at the comfortable, expensive furnishings in his big bedroom. "You have a whole houseful of stuff. What could we possibly need that you don't already have?"

He smiled, his expression tender. "There's nothing I need that I don't already have—now that I have you." He kissed her, wrapping his arms around her and rolling with her on the big bed until she was beneath him. "I think it's a great idea. Let's do it. We'll tell Lana and John this week."

"Good," she managed to say.

She felt surrounded by him—safe, loved, cherished and infinitely desired.

"I love you," she murmured, seeing the instant blaze of heat and fierce emotion in his eyes, just before he covered her mouth with his and the whole world fell away.

* * * * *

SPECIAL EXCERPT FROM

(H) HARLEQUIN
SPECIAL EDITION

*Raising a family was always Adam Mills' dream,
although solo parenting and moving back to tiny
Garnet Run certainly were not. Adam is doing his best
to give his daughter the life she deserves—including
accepting help from their new, reclusive neighbor
Wes Mobray to fulfill her Christmas wish…*

*Read on for a sneak peek at
The Lights on Knockbridge Lane,
the next book in the Garnet Run series and
Roan Parrish's Harlequin Special Edition debut!*

Adam and Wes looked at each other and Adam felt like
Wes could see right through him.

"You don't have to," Adam said. "I just… I accidentally
promised Gus the biggest Christmas light display in the
world and, uh…"

Every time he said it out loud, it sounded more
unrealistic than the last.

Wes raised an eyebrow but said nothing. He kept
looking at Adam like there was a mystery he was trying
to solve.

"Wes!" Gus' voice sounded more distant. "Can I touch
this snake?"

"Oh god, I'm sorry," Adam said. Then the words
registered, and panic ripped through him. "Wait, snake?"

"She's not poisonous. Don't worry."

HSEEXP0921

That was actually not what Adam's reaction had been in response to, but he made himself nod calmly.

"Good, good."

"Are you coming in, or…?"

"Oh, nah, I'll just wait here," Adam said extremely casually. "Don't mind me. Yep. Fresh air. I'll just… Uh-huh, here's great."

Wes smiled for the first time and it was like nothing Adam had ever seen.

His face lit with tender humor, eyes crinkling at the corners and full lips parting to reveal charmingly crooked teeth. Damn, he was beautiful.

"Wes, Wes!" Gus ran up behind him and skidded to a halt inches before she would've slammed into him. "Can I?"

"You can touch her while I get the ladder," Wes said.

Gus turned to Adam.

"Daddy, do you wanna touch the snake? She's so cool."

Adam's skin crawled.

"Nope, you go ahead."

Don't miss
The Lights on Knockbridge Lane
by Roan Parrish, available October 2021 wherever Harlequin Special Edition books and ebooks are sold.

Harlequin.com

Love Harlequin romance?

DISCOVER.

Be the first to find out about promotions,
news and exclusive content!

f Facebook.com/HarlequinBooks

y Twitter.com/HarlequinBooks

◉ Instagram.com/HarlequinBooks

◉ Pinterest.com/HarlequinBooks

You Tube YouTube.com/HarlequinBooks

ReaderService.com

EXPLORE.

Sign up for the Harlequin e-newsletter and
download a free book from any series at
TryHarlequin.com

CONNECT.

Join our Harlequin community to
share your thoughts and connect
with other romance readers!
Facebook.com/groups/HarlequinConnection

HARLEQUIN

HSOCIAL2021

HARLEQUIN

Heartfelt or thrilling, passionate or uplifting—Harlequin is more than just happily-ever-after.

With twelve different series to choose from and new books available every month, you are sure to find stories that will move you, uplift you, inspire and delight you.

HNEWS2021